"STUPENDOUS... AN EXHILARATING THRILLER."
—*Midwest Book Review*

"WITHOUT A DOUBT, ROSE IS IN THE TOP ECHELON OF SUSPENSE MASTERS!"
—*Romantic Times BOOKreviews Magazine*

She's run out of time.
Now there is
no place to hide...

more . . .

"Takes off like a house afire . . . There's action and chills galore in this nonstop thriller."
— **TESS GERRITSEN**, *New York Times* **bestselling author**

"Rose cranks up the heat in more ways than one . . . another winning mystery thriller . . . Emotional subplots, engaging characters, and a string of red herrings will keep readers hooked."
— *Publishers Weekly*

YOU CAN'T HIDE

"This novel is, in a word, riveting."
— *Romantic Times BOOKreviews Magazine*

"An immensely enjoyable read . . . that will have the reader glued to the pages from beginning to end."
— *Romance Reviews Today*

"[Karen Rose] is the queen of murder and suspense . . . just terrific!"
— **RomanceReviewsMag.com**

NOTHING TO FEAR

"A pulse-pounding tale that has it all: suspense, action, and a very hunky private investigator."
— *Cosmopolitan*

"4½ Stars! Top pick! . . . Filled with heart-stopping suspense and graphic terror . . . In the pantheon of horrific killers, [this one] surely ranks near the top."
— *Romantic Times BOOKreviews Magazine*

"Readers can always count on Rose to deliver an action-packed book, and this one is no exception."
—*Southern Pines Pilot* (NC)

"A tense, chilling suspense that readers will appreciate from start to finish."
—*Midwest Book Review*

"Rose's well-crafted story sets pulses pounding and pages turning."
—*BookPage*

"A caring women's advocate heroine, a determined, gritty hero, and a diabolical villain drive the plot of Rose's riveting story."
—*Library Journal*

I'M WATCHING YOU

"TOP PICK! Terrifying and gritty."
—*Romantic Times BOOKreviews Magazine*

"The suspense unfolds right up to the last page."
—*Southern Pines Pilot* (NC)

"A sensual, riveting book that kept me on the edge of my seat."
—*Rendezvous*

"Action-packed . . . a thrilling police procedural romance . . . fans will enjoy this tense thriller."
—*Midwest Book Review*

more . . .

"It's perfect . . . Love the characters, loved the side stories. It doesn't get any better than this!"
                                    —*Romantic Review*

HAVE YOU SEEN HER?

"Heart-racing thrills . . . showcases her growing talent . . . readers will . . . rush to the novel's thrilling conclusion."
                                    —*Publishers Weekly*

"Terrifying and gripping."
                        —*Romantic Times BOOKreviews Magazine*

DON'T TELL

"Rose delivers the kind of high-wire suspense that keeps you riveted to the edge of your seat."
            —**LISA GARDNER,** *New York Times* **bestselling author**

"As gripping as a cold hand on the back of one's neck . . . and tempered by lovable characters and a moving romance."
                                    —*Publishers Weekly*

"A well-written thriller—a definite page-turner that never lets up until the last page."
                                    —**RomRevToday.com**

"Action-packed [with a] story line [that] is character driven."
                                    —*Midwest Book Review*

KILL FOR ME

KAREN ROSE

KILL FOR ME

GRAND CENTRAL
PUBLISHING

NEW YORK   BOSTON

Copyright © 2009 by Karen Rose Hafer
Excerpt from *I Can See You* copyright © 2009 by Karen Rose Hafer
All rights reserved. Except as permitted under the U.S. Copyright Act of 1976, no part of this publication may be reproduced, distributed, or transmitted in any form or by any means, or stored in a database or retrieval system, without the prior written permission of the publisher.

Cover design by Diane Luger
Cover photograph by Herman Estevez

Grand Central Publishing
Hachette Book Group
237 Park Avenue
New York, NY 10017
Visit our Web site at www.HachetteBookGroup.com

Grand Central Publishing is a division of Hachette Book Group, Inc. The Grand Central Publishing name and logo is a trademark of Hachette Book Group, Inc.

Printed in the United States of America

Originally published in hardcover by Hachette Book Group
First mass market edition: July 2009

10 9 8 7 6 5 4 3 2 1

*To Martin, for always believing in me
even when I don't. I love you.*

*To Sarah, for achieving your dreams despite all the
obstacles. You inspire me. Life, Prosperity, Health.*

Acknowledgments

Danny Agan for answering all my questions about police procedure.

Shannon Aviles for all her support and wonderful ideas.

Doug Byron for his help in DNA procedure.

Kay Conterato for going above and beyond the call of duty when she researched radio ID badges while hospitalized!

Marc Conterato for all of his medical expertise — my drugged, shot, stabbed, and poisoned characters thank you, too.

Angela Maples for her guidance in the tracking of pharmaceuticals.

Shirley McCarroll, Tommy Gianides, Suzanne Verikios, and Jan Sarver for all their priceless information on Greek families and customs.

Frank Ouellette for answering my questions on the Chattahoochee River.

Nate VanNess for his help on tracking ISPs.

Terri Bolyard, Kay Conterato, and Sonie Lasker for helping me get unstuck. You all are awesome.

Karen Kosztolnyik, Vicki Mellor, and Robin Rue for all you do to make my dreams come true.

As always, all mistakes are my own.

KILL FOR ME

Prologue

Monica Cassidy felt a flutter in her stomach. *Today would be the day.* She'd waited for sixteen long years, but today the wait would be over. Today she'd be a woman. Finally. And wasn't it about time?

She realized she was twisting her fingers together and forced herself to stop. *Calm down, Monica. There's nothing to be nervous about. This is, like, natural.* And *all* her friends had done it. Some of them a lot more than once.

Today, it's my turn.

Monica sat on the hotel bed and brushed the dirt off the keycard, which had been hidden exactly where Jason said it would be. She shivered, her lips curving in a small smile. She'd met him in a chat room and they'd clicked right way. She'd meet him in person soon. *In the flesh.* He'd teach her things. He'd promised. He was a college guy, so he'd be a lot better at it than the gross boys that tried to cop a feel every time there was a crush in the hallway between classes.

Finally she'd be treated like an adult. Not like her mom did. Monica rolled her eyes. She'd be a forty-year-old virgin if her mother had her way. *Good thing I'm smarter.*

She grinned to herself, thinking of all the steps she'd taken to cover her tracks that morning. No one friend knew where she was, so they couldn't blab if they wanted to. She'd be back home, well and truly fucked, before her mother made it home from work.

How was your day, honey? Mom would ask. *Same old, same old*, Monica would answer. And as soon as she was able, she'd come back. Because she was sixteen years old for God's sake and nobody was going to tell her what to do ever again. Bells trilled and Monica dug furiously in her purse for her cell. She drew a breath. It was him.

RU there? she read.

Her thumbs were actually trembling. *W8ing 4 U. WAU.* "I'm waiting for you. Where are you?" she murmured as she entered her reply.

POS. PITA. SYS. ILY, he answered. His parents were watching him over his shoulder, she thought, rolling her eyes again. His folks were as big a pain in the ass as hers. But he'd see her soon. She smiled. *He loves me.* This would be so worth it.

ILY2, she typed and snapped her phone shut. It was an old phone. It didn't even have a camera. She was the only one in her crowd without a damn camera on her phone. Her mom had one. But did Monica? *No.* Mom was such a control freak. *You'll get a phone when you bring up your grades.* Monica sneered. *If you only knew where I am. You'd shut up.* She stood up, suddenly restless. "Treat *me* like a fucking kid," she muttered, taking her purse to the dresser and staring in the mirror. She looked fine, every hair in place. She looked pretty, even. She wanted to be pretty for him.

No, she wanted to be *hot* for him. Monica rummaged in her purse, pulling out the condoms she'd pilfered from her mother's ancient, never-used supply. But they hadn't hit their ex-date, yet, so they'd still be good. She looked at her watch.

Where was he? She was going to be late getting home if he didn't get here soon.

The door creaked open and she turned, the feline smile she'd practiced firmly in place. "Hello there." Then she froze. "You're not Jason."

It was a cop and he was shaking his head. "No, I'm not. Are you Monica?"

Monica lifted her chin, her heart pounding. "What's it to you?"

"You don't know how lucky you are. I'm Deputy Mansfield. We've been tracking your 'boyfriend' Jason for weeks. Your 'boyfriend' is really a fifty-nine-year-old pervert."

Monica shook her head. "No way. I don't believe you." She rushed for the door. "Jason! Run, it's a trap! They're *cops!*"

He caught her shoulder. "We arrested him already."

Monica shook her head again, slower this time. "But he just IM'd me."

"That was me using his phone. I wanted to be sure you were in here and that you were unhurt." His face gentled. "Monica, you really are a lucky girl. So many predators out there are trolling for girls just like you, pretending to be boys your age."

"He said he was nineteen. A college boy."

The deputy shrugged. "He lied. Come on, get your things. I'll take you home."

She closed her eyes. She'd seen stories like this on TV and every time her mom would wag her finger. *See?* she'd say. *Perverts out there everywhere.* Monica sighed. *This can't be happening to me.* "My mom is going to kill me."

"Better your mom than that perv," he said evenly. "He's killed before."

Monica felt the blood drain from her face. "He has?"

"At least twice. Come on. Moms never really kill you."

"Shows what you know," she muttered. She grabbed her purse, furiously. *I am so dead.* She'd thought her mother was crazy protective before. *She'll lock me up and throw away the key.* "Oh God," she moaned. "I can't believe this is happening."

She followed the deputy to an unmarked car. She could see the light on the dash when he opened the passenger door. "Get in and buckle up," he said.

Grimly she obeyed. "You can just take me back to the bus station," she said. "You don't have to tell my mom."

He just gave her an amused look before slamming her door shut. He got behind the wheel and reached behind the seat, grabbing a bottle of water. "Here. Try to relax. What's the worst your mom can do?"

"Kill me," Monica muttered, twisting the top off the bottle. She drank a third of it in great gulps. She hadn't realized she was so thirsty. Her stomach growled. And hungry. "Can you stop at MickeyD's at the exit? I haven't eaten today. I have my own money."

"Sure." He started the car and pulled onto the stretch of highway that went back to the interstate. In a few minutes he'd covered what had taken her an hour to walk that morning after the last ride she'd hitched let her off at a gas station at the exit.

Monica frowned when the world went spinning. "Whoa. I must be hungrier than I thought. There's a . . ." She watched the golden arches disappear behind them as he got back on the interstate. "I need to eat."

"You'll eat later," he said coldly. "For now, just shut up."

Monica stared at him. "Stop. Let me out."

He laughed. "I'll stop when I get to where you're going."

Monica tried to grab the door handle, but her hand didn't move. Her body didn't move. *She couldn't move.*

"You can't move," he said. "Don't worry. The drug's only temporary."

She couldn't see him anymore. She'd closed her eyes and now couldn't open them. *Oh God. Oh God. What's happening?* She tried to scream, but couldn't. *Mom.*

"Hey, it's me," he said. He'd made a call on his phone. "I have her." He laughed softly. "Oh, she's very pretty. And she just might be a virgin like she claimed all along. I'm bringing her in. Have my money ready. Cash, like always."

She heard a sound, a terrified keening, and knew it came from her own throat.

"You shoulda listened to your mama," he said mockingly. "Now you're mine."

Chapter One

The ringing of Bobby's cell phone brought an abrupt halt to their chess game.

Charles paused, his forefinger hovering over his queen. "Do you need to get that?"

Bobby checked the caller ID and frowned. It was Rocky, calling from her private phone. "Yes, I do. Excuse me, please."

Charles gestured his assent. "By all means. Should I leave the room?"

"Don't be ridiculous," Bobby said, then into the phone asked, "Why are you calling?"

"Because Granville called *me*," Rocky said tensely, road noise in the background. She was in her car. "Mansfield's with him at the river place. Mansfield got a text from Granville saying Daniel Vartanian knew about the product, that he's coming with the state police. Granville says he didn't send the message. I don't think he's lying."

Bobby said nothing. This was far worse an outcome than expected.

After a moment of silence, Rocky hesitantly added, "Vartanian wouldn't have warned them. He would have just shown up with a SWAT team. I . . . I think we were too late."

"*We* were too late?" Bobby asked scathingly and there was silence.

"All right," Rocky said quietly. "I was too late. But it's done now. We have to assume the river place has been compromised."

"Fuck," Bobby muttered, then winced when Charles lifted his brows admonishingly. "Clear out by the river, not the road. The last thing you want is to meet the cops coming in as you're driving out. Call Jersey. He's moved shipments for me before."

"Granville called him and he's on his way. Trouble is, we can only fit six in the boat."

Bobby scowled. "Jersey's boat is big enough to fit twelve in the cargo hold, easily."

"That boat's elsewhere. This is the only vehicle he had available."

Dammit. Bobby glanced at Charles, who listened avidly. "Eliminate what you can't carry. Make sure you leave nothing behind. Understand? *Nothing can remain.* Use the river if you don't have time to make other arrangements. There are some sandbags behind the generator. Bring them here. I'll meet you at the dock."

"Will do. I'm on my way down there to make sure those two don't fuck it up."

"Good. And watch Granville. He's . . ." Bobby glanced at Charles again, saw he now appeared amused. "He's not stable."

"I know. One more thing. I hear Daniel Vartanian went to the bank today."

This was far better news. "And? What did you hear that he came out with?"

"Nothing. The safe-deposit box was empty."

Of course it was. Because I emptied it myself years ago. "That's interesting. We'll discuss it later. Now move. Call me when the job is done." Bobby hung up and met Charles's curious gaze. "You know, you could have told me Toby Granville was unraveling before I took him on as a business partner. Freaking crazy SOB."

Charles's mouth curled up in a self-satisfied smile. "And miss all the fun? I don't think so. How is your new assistant working out?"

"Smart. Still gets a little green around the gills when she has to process orders, but never lets the men see it. And it's never stopped her from getting the job done."

"Excellent. Glad to hear it." He tilted his head. "So is everything else all right?"

Bobby sat back, brows lifted. "Your business is fine. Nothing else is your business."

"As long as my investment continues to pay dividends, you may have your secrets."

"Oh, you'll get your dividends. This has been a very good year. Base business profits are up forty percent and the new premium line is just flying out the door."

"But you're about to 'eliminate' stock."

"That stock was at the end of its useful life anyway. Now, where were we?"

Charles moved his queen. "Checkmate, I believe."

Bobby swore lightly, then sighed. "So it is. I should have seen that coming, but I never do. You've always been the master of the chessboard."

"I've always been the master," Charles corrected, and pure reflex had Bobby sitting up a little straighter. Charles nodded, and Bobby swallowed back the annoyance that rose every time Charles tugged the reins. "Of course, I didn't drop by simply to beat you at chess," he said. "I have some news. A plane landed in Atlanta this morning."

An uneasy shiver skittered up Bobby's spine. "So? Hundreds of planes land in Atlanta every day. Thousands even."

"True." Charles began putting the chess pieces in the ivory case he carried with him everywhere. "But this plane carried a traveler in whom you have a vested interest."

"Who?"

Charles met Bobby's narrowed eyes with another satisfied smile. "Susannah Vartanian is back in town," he said, holding up the white ivory queen. "Again."

Bobby took the queen from Charles's hand, trying to appear blasé, when inside a geyser exploded. "Well, well."

"Well, well, indeed. You missed last time."

"I didn't try last time," Bobby snapped defensively. "She was only here a day when the judge and his wife were buried last week." Susannah had stood at her brother's side at their parents' grave, her face expressionless even though turbulence had churned in her gray eyes. Just seeing her again after all this time. . . . The turbulence in Susannah's eyes was nothing compared to the seething rage Bobby had been forced to swallow.

"Don't you snap the head off my queen, Bobby," Charles drawled. "She was hand-carved by a master craftsman outside Saigon. She's worth more than you are."

Bobby placed the queen on Charles's palm, ignoring that last jab. *Calm down. You make mistakes when you're riled.* "She went back to New York too quickly last week. I didn't have time to adequately prepare." It sounded whiny, which made Bobby angrier.

"Planes fly both ways, Bobby. You didn't have to wait

for her to return." Charles snuggled the queen into her velvet slot within his ivory case. "But, it would appear you now have a second chance. I hope you plan more effectively this time."

"On that you can depend."

Charles's smile was cagey. "Just promise me a ringside seat when the fireworks begin. I'm partial to the red fireworks myself."

Bobby's smile was grim. "I can guarantee lots of red. Now if you'll excuse me, I have some pressing business to attend to."

Charles stood. "I have to be going anyway. I have a funeral to attend."

"Who's getting buried today?"

"Lisa Woolf."

"Well, Jim and Marianne Woolf better enjoy it. At least they won't have to fight the other reporters. They'll have a ringside seat, right on the family pew."

"Bobby." Charles shook his head in mock outrage. "Such a thing to say."

"You know I'm right. Jim Woolf would sell his own sister for a byline."

Charles settled his hat on his head and picked up his walking stick, his ivory box tucked under his arm. "And someday, you may be able to say the same."

No, Bobby thought, watching Charles drive away, *not for something as insignificant as a byline.* Now for a birthright . . . that was an entirely different matter. But there would be time for dreams later. Now there was work to be done.

"Tanner! Come here. I need you."

The old man appeared, seemingly from nowhere, as was his way. "Yes?"

"Unexpected guests are on the way. Please prepare accommodations for six more."

Tanner gave a single nod. "Of course. While you were in with Mr. Charles, Mr. Haynes called. He'll be coming by tonight to secure a companion for the weekend."

Bobby smiled. Haynes was a premium client, a rich man with depraved tastes. And he paid cash. "Excellent. We'll be ready."

Charles stopped his car at the end of the street. From here the turrets of Ridgefield House were still visible. The house had stood in that place for nearly a hundred years. It was a strong house, built the way they used to be. Charles had an appreciation for good architecture, having lived in many places a rat wouldn't call home.

Bobby used Ridgefield to house "inventory," and the location was ideal for this purpose. Situated far off the main road, most people didn't even know the house still stood. It was close enough to the river for convenience, but far enough away that it was safe if the river swelled. It wasn't large enough or beautiful enough or even old enough to be on any conservator's list, which made it simply perfect.

For years Bobby had spurned this house as old and ugly and beneath consideration, until maturity had revealed what Charles had learned long ago. *Flashy packages draw attention. The mark of true success is invisibility.* Being able to hide in plain sight had enabled him to pull the strings of the flashy, the pompous. *Now, they are nothing but my puppets. They dance to my tune.*

It made them angry, powerless, but they didn't know the true meaning of powerlessness. They lived in fear of losing the possessions they'd accumulated, so they surrendered their pride, their decency. Their *morality*, which was merely a religious man's farce. Some surrendered with barely a nudge. Those people Charles viewed with contempt. They had no idea what it meant to lose everything. *Everything.* To be stripped bare of physical pleasure, to be deprived of the most basic of human needs.

The weak feared losing their stuff. But Charles did not. Once a man was stripped to the bone of his humanity . . . then he had no fear. Charles had no fear.

But he did have plans, plans that included Bobby and Susannah Vartanian.

Bobby was a level higher than all the others. Charles had molded Bobby's quick mind when it was young and molten and full of fury. Full of questions and hate. He'd convinced Bobby the time would come for revenge, for claiming the birthright that circumstances—and certain people—had denied. But Bobby still danced to Charles's tune. Charles simply allowed Bobby to believe the tune was original.

He opened the top of his ivory box, lifted the queen from her slot, and pressed the hidden spring that had a lower drawer sliding out. His journal was on top of the belongings he never left home without. Thoughtfully he thumbed to the first blank page and began to write. *Now is the time for my protégé's revenge, because I wish it to be. I planted the seed years ago. I've only watered it today. When Bobby sits down at the computer to work, the photograph of Susannah Vartanian will be waiting.*

Bobby hates Susannah, because I wish it. But Bobby was indeed correct on one score: Toby Granville is becoming more unstable every year. Sometimes absolute power—or the illusion thereof—does corrupt absolutely. When Toby becomes too big a danger, I'll have him killed, just like I had Toby Granville kill others.

Taking a life is a powerful thing. Sticking your knife into a man's gut and watching the life seep from his eyes . . . a powerful thing indeed. But forcing another to kill . . . that is the ultimate power. Kill for me. It's playing God. Charles smiled. *It's fun.*

Yes, Toby would soon need to be killed. But there would be another Toby Granville. In time, there would be another Bobby. *And I will go on.* He closed his journal, replaced it and the queen in their proper places as he'd done countless times before.

Dutton, Georgia, Friday, February 2, 2:00 p.m.

She hurt. All over. They'd beaten her head this time, and kicked her ribs. Monica firmed her lips in grim satisfaction. But it had been worth it. She'd get away or die trying. She'd force them to kill her before she let them use her anymore.

Then they'd lose a *depreciable asset.* That's what they'd called her. She'd heard them, talking on the other side of the wall. *They can kiss my depreciable asset.* Anything, even death, was better than the life she had lived for . . . how long had it been?

She'd lost track of how many months had passed. Five, maybe six. Monica had never truly believed in a hell before. She sure as hell did now.

For a while she'd lost her will to live, but thanks to Becky, she'd gotten it back. It was Becky who'd tried to escape so many times. They'd tried to stop her, to break her. They'd broken Becky's body, but not her spirit. In the short time they'd whispered through the wall that separated them, Monica had drawn strength from the girl she'd never seen. The girl whose death had rekindled her own desire to live. *Or die trying.*

She drew what she'd wanted to be a deep breath, wincing before her lungs fully inflated. Her rib was probably broken. Maybe more than one. She wondered where they'd taken Becky's body after they'd beaten her to death. She could still hear the crunching blows, because they'd meant for her to. They'd opened all their doors so they could hear every punch, every kick, and every one of Becky's moans. They'd meant for them all to hear. To be afraid. To learn a lesson.

Every girl in the place. There were at least ten of them, in varying degrees of *depreciation.* Some were newly initiated, others old hands at the oldest profession in the world. *Like me. I just want to go home.*

Monica gave her arm a weak shake and heard the resulting clink of the chain that held her to the wall. Just like every girl in the place. *I'm never going to escape. I'm going to die. Please, God, just let it be soon.*

"Hurry, you idiots. We don't have time to fuck around."

Someone was out there, in the hall outside her cell. *The woman.* Monica's jaw clenched. She hated the woman.

"Hurry," the woman said. "Move. Mansfield, put these boxes on the boat."

Monica didn't know the woman's name, but she was bad. Worse than the men—the deputy and the doctor. Mansfield was the deputy, the one who'd kidnapped her and brought her here. For a long time she hadn't believed he was a real deputy, had thought that his uniform was just a costume, but he was for real. It was when she'd realized he was a real cop that she'd given up hope.

As mean as Mansfield was, the doctor was worse. He

was cruel, because he enjoyed seeing them in pain. The look in his eyes when he was doing his worst . . . Monica shivered. The doctor wasn't sane, of that she was certain.

But the woman . . . she was evil. To her, this horror, this so-called *life* . . . it was "just business." To the woman, every girl in the place was a depreciable, renewable *asset*. Renewable because there were always more teenaged girls stupid enough to be lured away from the safety of their families. Lured here. To hell.

Monica could hear the grunts as they moved the boxes onto . . . what? She heard squeaking and immediately recognized the sound. It was the gurney with the rusty wheels. It was where the doctor "fixed them up," got them ready to go "back in the game" after a "client" had beaten the ever-living shit out of them. Of course sometimes the doctor did the beating, then all he had to do was lift them from the floor to the gurney, making his job that much easier. She *hated* him. But she feared him more.

"Take the girls in ten, nine, six, five, four and . . . one," the woman said.

Monica's eyes flew open. She was in cell number one. She squinted, willing her eyes to get used to the darkness. *Something's wrong.* Her heart started to beat faster. Someone was coming to help them. *Hurry. Please hurry.*

"Cuff their hands behind them and take them out one at a time," the woman snapped. "Keep your gun on them at all times and do not let them get away."

"What do we do with the others?" It was a deep voice. The doctor's guard.

"Kill them," the woman said flatly, without hesitation.

I'm in cell one. She's going to put me on a boat and take me away. Away from the help that was coming. *I'll fight. By God, I'll get away or die trying.*

"I'll take care of them." It was the doctor, whose eyes were so eager. So cruel.

"Fine," the woman said. "Just don't leave their bodies here. Dump them in the river. Use the sandbags behind the generator. Mansfield, don't just stand there. Get those boxes and girls on the damn boat before we have cops crawling up our asses. Then bring the gurney back for the good doctor. He'll need it to get the bodies to the river."

"Yes, sir," Deputy Mansfield sneered.

"Don't get smart," the woman said, her voice fading as she moved away. "*Move.*"

Silence hung in the air, then the doctor said quietly, "Take care of the other two."

"You mean Bailey and the reverend?" the guard asked in a normal voice.

"Sshh," the doctor hissed. "Yes. Do it quietly. *She* doesn't know they're here."

The other two. Monica had heard them, through the wall. The doctor's office was next to her cell, so she heard a lot. The doctor had beaten the woman he'd called Bailey for days, demanding a key. *A key to what?* He'd beaten the man, too, demanding a confession. What did he want the reverend to confess?

In a few seconds Monica forgot about Bailey and the reverend. Shrieks and sobs filled the air, louder even than the blood pounding in her ears. The screams scraped at the inside of her mind as one girl was dragged away, then another, then another. *Stay calm.* She had to stay focused. *They're coming for me.*

Yes, but they have to unlock the chain before they cuff you. For a few seconds, your hands will be free. You'll run, scratch, claw their goddamn eyes out if you have to.

But even as she tried to bolster her courage, she knew it was useless. Before the last beating she might have had a chance. And once she got out, then what? They were miles from anywhere. She'd be dead before she got to the hallway.

A sob rose in her throat. *I'm sixteen and I'm going to die. I'm sorry, Mom. I should have listened to you.*

Crack. She flinched at the gunshot. More screams, terrified, hysterical screams. But Monica was too tired to scream. She was almost too tired to be afraid. Almost.

Another shot. And another. And another. Four shots so far. She could hear his voice, the doctor. He was taunting the girl in the next cell.

"Say your prayers, Angel," he said, laughter in his voice. Monica hated him. She wanted to kill him. She wanted to see him suffer and bleed and die.

Crack. Angel was dead. And four others.

The door flew open and Deputy Mansfield stood in the opening, his face hard and hateful. He was on her in two strides, unlocking the chain that held her to the wall, none too gently. Monica squinted at the light as Mansfield yanked the shackle from her wrist.

She was free. *So fucking what?* She was trapped, just the same.

"Come on," Mansfield grunted, dragging her to her feet.

"I can't," she whispered, her knees giving out.

"Shut up." Mansfield jerked her to her feet as if she weighed no more than a doll. At this point, that wasn't too far from the truth.

"Wait." The woman was in the hallway, right outside Monica's door. She stood in the shadow, as she always did. Monica had never seen her face, but still she dreamed of the day she could claw the woman's eyes out.

"The boat's full," the woman said.

"How can it be?" the doctor asked, from out in the hall. "It holds six. You took five."

"The boxes took up a lot of the space," the woman answered, her tone short. "Vartanian will be here any minute with the state cops. We need to be downstream before he gets here. Kill her and get the bodies out of here."

So it'll be now. No need to run or fight. Monica wondered if she'd hear the gun fire or if she'd be dead instantly. *I won't beg. I won't give him the satisfaction.*

"This one's not that bad off," the doctor said. "She can still work for months, maybe a year. Toss some of the boxes overboard or burn them. But make room for her. Once I break her, she'll make the best asset we've ever had. Come on, Rocky."

Rocky. The woman's name was Rocky. Monica committed it to memory. Rocky moved closer to the doctor, so that she emerged from the shadows and Monica had her first look at the woman's face. Monica squinted, trying to block out the spinning room as she memorized every feature. If there was a life after death, Monica would come back and haunt her until the woman was a drooling lump of insanity.

"The boxes stay on the boat," Rocky said impatiently.

The doctor's mouth twisted in contempt. "Says you?"

"Says Bobby. So unless you want to tell Bobby why you left incriminating records behind that would ruin us all, you'll shut your mouth and kill this bitch so we can get out of here. Mansfield, come with me. Granville, just do it and hurry. And for God's sake, make sure they're all dead. I don't want them screaming as we chuck them in the river. If any cops are close, they'll come running."

Mansfield released Monica and her leg buckled. She dropped to her knees holding on to the dirty cot for support as Mansfield and Rocky left the room, leaving her staring at the end of the doctor's gun.

"Just do it," Monica hissed. "You heard the lady. Hurry up and do it."

The doctor's mouth turned up in that cobra smile that turned her gut to water. "You think it's going to be fast. You think it's going to be painless."

Crack. Monica screamed as the pain in her head was drowned out by the burning in her side. He'd shot her, but she wasn't dead. *Why am I not dead?*

He smiled at her as she twisted, trying to make the pain stop. "You've been a thorn in my side since the day you got here. If I had time, I'd slice you to ribbons. But I don't. So say good-bye, Monica." He lifted the gun, then jerked his head to one side, his face darkening in rage at the same moment another shot rang in her ears. Monica screamed again as fire burned across the side of her head. Squeezing her eyes shut, she waited for the next shot. But it never came. Blinking back tears, she opened her eyes.

He was gone and she was alone. And not dead.

He missed. Goddamn him to hell, *he missed.* He was gone. *He'll be back.*

But she saw no one. *Vartanian will be here any minute with the state cops.* The woman had said this. Monica didn't know anybody named Vartanian, but whoever he was, he was her only chance at survival. *Get to the door.* Monica pushed to her knees and crawled. A foot. Another foot. *Get to the hall and you can get away.*

She heard footsteps. A woman, beaten and bloody, her clothes torn, was staggering toward her. *The other two*, the doctor had said. This was Bailey. She'd gotten away. *There was still hope.* Monica lifted her hand. "Help me. Please."

Bailey hesitated, then yanked her to her feet. "Move."

"Are you Bailey?" Monica managed to whisper.

"Yes. Now, move or die." Together they staggered down the hall. Finally they came to a door and stumbled into daylight, so bright it hurt.

Bailey came to an abrupt stop and Monica's heart dropped to her stomach. In front of them stood a man with a gun pointed straight at them. He wore the same uniform as Mansfield. The badge on his shirt said "Sheriff Frank Loomis." This wasn't Vartanian with the state police. This was Mansfield's boss and he wouldn't let them get away.

So this is how it would end. Tears seeped down her face, burning her raw skin as Monica waited for the next crack of gunfire.

To her shock Sheriff Loomis put his finger to his lips. "Follow the trees," he whispered. "You'll find the road." He pointed to Monica. "How many more in there?"

"None," Bailey whispered harshly. "He killed them all. All except her."

Loomis swallowed. "Then go. I'll go get my car and meet you by the road."

Bailey tightened her hold. "Come on," she whispered. "Just a little bit longer."

Monica stared at her feet, willing them to move. One step, then another. Freedom. She'd get to freedom. Then she'd make them all pay. Or die trying.

Dutton, Georgia, Friday, February 2, 3:05 p.m.

Susannah Vartanian stared at the passenger side mirror as the house in which she'd grown up grew smaller as each second passed. *I have to get out of here.* As long as she remained here, at this house, *in this town*, she was no longer the woman she'd become. She was no longer a successful New York City assistant district attorney who commanded respect. As long as she was here, she was a child, alone and afraid, hiding in a closet. A victim. Susannah was damn tired of being a victim.

"Are you all right?" The question came from the man behind the wheel. Special Agent Luke Papadopoulos. Her brother's partner and best friend. Luke had driven her here an hour before and then the growing dread in the pit of her gut had made her wish he'd slow down. Now that it was over, she wished he'd drive faster.

Get me away from here. Please. "I'm fine." She didn't need to look at Papadopoulos to know he watched her. She'd felt the weight of his gaze from the moment they'd met the week before. She'd been standing next to her brother at their parents' funeral and Luke had come to pay his respects. He watched her then. He watched her now.

But Susannah's gaze was fixed on the passenger side mirror. She wanted to look away from the rapidly shrinking house of her youth, but her eyes would not obey. The lone figure standing in the front yard compelled her to keep watching. Even from a distance she could feel the sadness that weighed down his broad shoulders.

Her brother Daniel was a big man, as their father had been. The women in their family were small, but the men were hulking and large. Some larger than others. Susannah swallowed back the panic that had lurked at the base of her throat for the past two weeks. *Simon's dead, for real this time. He can't hurt you anymore.* But he could, and he would. That he could torment her from beyond the grave was an irony Simon would find hilarious. Her older brother Simon had been one son of a bitch.

Now he was a dead son of a bitch and Susannah hadn't shed a single tear. Her parents were dead as well, because Simon had killed them. Now, only the two of them remained. *Just me and Daniel*, she thought bitterly. *Just one big happy family.*

Just she and her oldest brother, Special Agent Daniel J. Vartanian, Georgia Bureau of Investigation. One of the good guys. Daniel had built a career trying to make up for the fact that he was Judge Arthur Vartanian's spawn. *Just like I have.*

She thought of the devastation in his eyes when she'd walked away, leaving him standing in the front yard of the old house. After thirteen years, Daniel finally knew what he'd done, and more importantly, what he had not.

Now Daniel wanted forgiveness, Susannah thought bitterly. He wanted atonement. After more than ten years of total silence, her brother Daniel wanted a relationship.

Her brother Daniel wanted too damn much. He'd have to live with what he had done, and what he had not. *Just like I have.*

She knew why he'd left, so long ago. Daniel hated the house almost as much as she did. *Almost.* She'd managed to avoid the house the week before, when they'd buried their parents. After the funeral Susannah walked away, vowing never to return.

But a phone call from Daniel the day before had brought her back. *Here.* To Dutton. *To this house.* To face what she had done, and importantly, what she had not.

An hour ago she'd stood on that front porch for the first time in years. It had taken every ounce of her strength to walk in that door, up those stairs, into her brother Simon's old bedroom. Susannah did not believe in ghosts, but she did believe in evil.

Evil lived in that house, in that bedroom, long after Simon died. *Both times.*

The evil had settled around her as soon as she'd entered Simon's room, sending panic clawing up her throat along with a scream she kept silenced. She'd drawn on her last reserves, keeping the illusion of serenity and control intact as she'd forced herself into the closet, dreading what she feared lay behind its walls.

Her worst nightmare. Her greatest shame. For thirteen years it had remained hidden in a box in a hidey-hole behind Simon's bedroom wall, unbeknownst to anyone. *Even me. Especially me.* After thirteen years, the box was out of the closet. *Ta-da.*

Now, the box resided in the trunk of the car belonging to Special Agent Luke Papadopoulos, GBI. Daniel's partner and friend. Papadopoulos was taking the box back to GBI headquarters in Atlanta where it would be entered into evidence. Where CSI techs and detectives and the legal team would sort through the contents. Hundreds of pictures, hideous and obscene and very, very real. *They'll see. They'll know.*

The car went around a bend and the house disappeared. The spell broken, Susannah eased back against the seat and drew a quiet breath. It was finally over.

No, it was only beginning for Susannah, and nowhere near the end for Daniel and his partner. Daniel and Luke were chasing a killer, a man who'd murdered five Dutton women in the last week. A man who'd turned his murder victims into clues to lead authorities to what was left of a band of rich-boy thugs who'd wreaked their own evil on Dutton's teenaged girls thirteen years before. A man who, for his own reasons, wanted the rich boys' crimes made public. A man who hated the band of rich-boy bastards almost as much as Susannah did. Almost. No one hated them more than Susannah. Unless it was one of their twelve other surviving victims.

Soon they'll know, the other victims. Soon everyone will know, she thought.

Including Daniel's partner and friend. He still watched her, his eyes dark and brooding. She sensed Luke Papadopoulos saw more than she wanted anyone to see.

He'd certainly gotten an eyeful today. Soon, everyone would. Soon . . . Her stomach pitched and she concentrated on not throwing up. Soon her greatest shame would be the chatter around water coolers and coffee pots all over the country.

She'd overheard enough water cooler chatter to know exactly how it would go. *Did you hear?* they'd whisper, pretending to look horrified. *Did you hear about those rich boys down in Dutton, Georgia, who drugged and raped those girls thirteen years ago? One of them even murdered one of the girls. They took pictures. Can you imagine?*

And they'd all shake their heads, imagining it and secretly wishing those pictures would get leaked to the Web where they might "accidentally" stumble upon them.

Dutton, another would muse, unwilling to be left out. *Isn't that the town where all those women were murdered and left in drainage ditches? Just in the last week?*

Yes, another would confirm. *It's also that Simon Vartanian's hometown. He was one of the rich-kid rapists—he took the pictures thirteen years ago. He's also the one who killed all those people up in Philadelphia. Some detective up in Philly killed him.*

Seventeen people dead, including her own parents. Countless lives destroyed. *I could have stopped it all, but I didn't. Oh my God. What have I done?* She kept her expression cool and her body stationary, but in her mind she rocked like a scared child.

"That was difficult," Papadopoulos murmured.

His rumble of a voice brought her back and she blinked hard, remembering who she was now. An adult. A respected attorney. One of the good guys. *Yeah. Right.*

She turned away from him, fixing her gaze once again on the side mirror. *Difficult* was far too sanitized a word for what she'd just done. "Yes," she replied. "Difficult."

"Are you all right?" he asked again.

No, I am not all right, she wanted to snap, but kept her voice cool. "I'm fine." And outwardly, she was. Susannah was skilled at maintaining the illusion, as she should be. She was Judge Arthur Vartanian's daughter, after all, and what she hadn't inherited through blood she'd learned by watching her father live a lie every day of their lives.

"You did the right thing, Susannah," Papadopoulos said quietly.

Yeah, right. Thirteen years too late. "I know."

"We'll be able to put away three rapists with the evidence you helped us find today."

There should have been seven men going to prison. *Seven.* Unfortunately, four of them were already dead, including Simon. *I hope you're all burning in hell.*

"And thirteen women will be able to face their attackers and get justice," he added.

There should have been sixteen women facing their attackers, but two had been murdered and the other had taken her own life. *No, Susannah, there should have only been one victim. It should have stopped with you.*

But she'd said nothing then, and she'd have to live with that for the rest of her life.

"Facing one's attacker is an important part of dealing with an assault," Susannah said levelly. At least that's what she'd always told the rape victims who were uncertain about testifying in court. In the past she'd believed it. Today she wasn't so sure.

"I guess you've prepared your share of rape victims to testify." His voice was incredibly gentle, but underneath she heard the tremble of a barely leashed fury. "I imagine it will be more difficult when you're the one in the witness box."

There was that word again . . . *difficult*. It wouldn't be *difficult* to testify. It would be the most terrifying experience of her life. "I told you and Daniel that I'd stand with the other victims, Agent Papadopoulos," she said sharply, "and I meant it."

"I never thought anything different," he said, but she didn't believe him.

"My flight to New York is at six. I need to be at the Atlanta airport by four. Can you drop me off on your way back to your headquarters?"

He shot her a frown. "You're going back tonight?"

"I missed a lot of work with my parents' funeral last week. I need to get back."

"Daniel had hoped to spend some time with you."

Annoyance flared and her voice hardened. "I think Daniel has his hands full with picking up the three surviving . . ." She faltered. "Members of Simon's club." But the word she used daily on the job would not roll off her tongue. "Not to mention catching whoever's killed five Dutton women in the last week."

"We know who the killer is." His own annoyance came through. "We will find him. It's just a matter of time. And we've got one of the rapists in custody already."

"Ah, yes. Mayor Davis. That one surprised me." Thirteen years ago Garth Davis had been a dumb jock, not the type to lead a gang of his peers to assault his classmates. But he'd certainly followed along. The pictures didn't lie. "But Deputy Mansfield escaped, killing his tail." Randy Mansfield had always been a weasel. Now he wore a badge and carried a gun, a terrifying prospect considering he was still roaming free.

A muscle twitched in Luke's jaw. "Mansfield's *tail* was a damn good agent named Oscar Johnson," he said tightly. "He left behind three kids and a pregnant wife."

He was grieving. He was also Daniel's friend, and obviously loyal. "I'm sorry," she said more gently. "But you have to admit you and Daniel do not have the situation under control. You don't even know who the third . . ." *Say it. Now.* She cleared her throat. "Who the third rapist is."

"We'll find him," Papadopoulos repeated stubbornly.

"I'm sure you will, but I still can't stay. Besides, Daniel has a new lady friend to hold his hand," she added, hearing that edge in her voice she despised. That Daniel had found happiness out of all this mess seemed . . . unfair. Of course that was childish. Life wasn't fair. Susannah had learned that long ago. "I wouldn't dream of intruding."

"You'd like Alex Fallon," he said, "if you'd just give her a chance."

"I'm sure I would. But Miss Fallon's had a hard day, too, seeing her sister's picture in that box with all the others." *Including mine. Don't think about it.* Instead, she focused on Alex Fallon.

Daniel's new girlfriend was connected to their lives in a very real way. Alex's twin sister had been murdered thirteen years ago by one of the boys who'd assaulted so many. Susannah might be childish enough to resent Daniel's happiness, but she could not wish anything bad on Alex Fallon. The woman had suffered a great deal in her life.

Luke grunted in reluctant agreement. "True. And her stepsister's still missing."

"Bailey Crighton," Susannah said. One of the four dead rapists was Bailey's brother. On the way out to the house, Luke had told her that Bailey's brother Wade had written a confession letter of sorts and shortly after its receipt, Bailey had been abducted. They believed one of the rapists had gotten nervous about what Bailey knew.

"Bailey's been gone a week now," Luke said.

"It doesn't look good for her then," Susannah murmured.

"No. It doesn't."

"So, like I said before, Daniel has his hands full. As do you. So . . ." She blew out a quiet sigh. "Back to my original question, Agent Papadopoulos. Can you drop me off at the airport on your way back to your headquarters? I need to go home."

His own sigh was weary. "It'll be tight, but yeah. I can."

Chapter Two

Luke stole a look at Susannah before fixing his eyes on the curving road ahead. The first time he'd seen her she'd stood next to Daniel at their parents' funeral wearing a conservative black suit, her face so pale he'd wondered if she'd remain standing. But she had, exhibiting a calm strength that impressed him and a delicate beauty that had him looking twice. But under her calm façade was a darkness that drew him like a lodestone. *She's like me*, he'd thought, unable to rip his eyes away. *She'd understand.*

Today she sat in his passenger seat, dressed in another black suit, this one a bit trendier. Once again her face was pale and once again he sensed the darkness that vibrated within her. She was angry. She had every right to be.

I'm fine, she'd said, but of course she was not. How could she be? She'd just come face to face with her worst nightmare in a brutally graphic way. An hour ago she'd marched into Simon's bedroom and pulled the box from the hidey-hole behind his closet, as calmly as if it had been filled with baseball cards instead of vile photos of rape. *Her own rape.* Luke had wanted to punch a wall, but he'd maintained his control. He'd done his job. And so had she, with a composure that would put any cop to shame.

Still, Susannah Vartanian was definitely not "fine."

And neither am I. Then again, Luke had not been "fine" in a very long time. He could feel his own fury, way too close to the surface. It had been a very bad week. It had been a very bad year. Too many faces stared at him from the depths of his mind. All taunting him. Haunting him. *You were our only hope, and you were too late.*

They'd been too late once again, thirteen years too late this time. A shiver slithered down his back. Luke was by no means a superstitious man, but he'd been his mother's son too long not to have a healthy respect for the number thirteen. Thirteen surviving rape victims, the crime perpetrated thirteen years before.

One of the thirteen survivors sat in his passenger seat, her eyes haunted.

She blamed herself. It was clear. If only she'd said something . . . the other victims would have been spared. There would have been no band of rapists on which a present-day murderer could seek revenge and five Dutton women might still be alive. If she'd said something back then, Simon Vartanian would have been arrested with the other rapists and never would have gone on to kill so many himself.

Of course she was wrong. Life just didn't work that way. Luke wished it did.

He wished that her coming forward thirteen years ago would have erased the box of photos he carried in the trunk of his car. But he knew if she'd said anything, Arthur Vartanian would have bailed Simon out and brought his son home, as he had every other time. Simon would have killed her, of this Luke was certain. There had been no way out for Susannah then, and no way of knowing Simon had orchestrated the rape of others.

Now that she knew, she'd come forward in a way that

inspired his profound respect. She'd been hurt and angry and scared. But she'd done the right thing.

"You know you're not to blame," he said quietly.

Her jaw tightened. "Thank you, Agent Papadopoulos, but I don't need the pep talk."

"You're thinking I don't understand," he said mildly even though he wanted to snarl.

"I'm sure you *think* you do. You mean well, but—"

Dammit, he didn't *think* he did. He *did*. The lid on his temper rattled. "Four days ago I found three kids dead," he interrupted, the words out of his mouth before he knew he planned to say them. "Nine, ten, and twelve. I was less than a day too late."

She drew a deep breath and let it out quietly. Her body seemed to settle. Her fury seemed to rise. "How did they die?" she asked, her voice ominously quiet.

"Shot in the head." And he could still see their small faces every time he closed his eyes. "But before they were murdered, they'd been molested in front of a Webcam. For *years*," he spat. "For *money*. For perverts all over the world to see."

"Bastards." Her voice trembled. "That must have been horrible for you."

"More horrible for them," he muttered and she made a small sound of agreement.

"I guess I'm supposed to say you're not to blame. Obviously you think you are."

His hands gripped the wheel so hard his knuckles ached. "Obviously."

A few moments passed, then she said, "So you're one of those."

He could feel her studying him and it made him feel unsettled. "One of what?"

"One of those guys who works Internet sex crimes against kids. I've worked with a few, through the DA's office. I don't know how you guys do it."

His jaw tightened. "Some days, I don't do it."

"But most days, you do what you have to do. And a little more of you dies each day."

She'd articulated the state of his life very well. "Yeah." His voice was rough, unsteady. "Something like that."

"Then you're one of the good guys. And you're not to blame."

He cleared his throat. "Thanks."

From the corner of his eye he saw she still watched him. Some of the color had returned to her face and he knew he'd given her something else to think about. He didn't want to talk about this, wished he hadn't mentioned it, but it was distracting her from her shock and to accomplish that, he'd talk about anything she wanted.

"I'm confused," she said. "I thought you and Daniel were Homicide, not Internet."

"Daniel's Homicide. I'm not. I've been on the Internet task force for over a year."

"That's a long time to have to live with such filth. I know guys who've worked Vice for ten years that didn't last a month on the child porn task forces."

"Like you said, we do what we have to do. I'm not normally Daniel's partner. This is a special assignment. After Tuesday, when I found the kids, I asked for a temporary reassignment. Daniel was chasing this guy that's been killing Dutton women and everywhere he turned he kept running into Simon. Simon was everywhere in this case. This killer wanted us to find Simon's club. Simon's pictures. Simon's key."

"The key to the empty safe-deposit box where you thought you'd find the pictures."

He'd told her that much on the way out to the Vartanian house. "Yeah. This killer ties keys to the toes of his
victims, so we knew the key was important. The Philly
detective found a safe-deposit box key among Simon's
things, but when Daniel took it to the bank today, the box
was empty. If the pictures had ever been stored there,
somebody took them." He looked over at her. "But you
knew where to find Simon's stash."

"I didn't know about the box. I only knew Simon had a
hiding place."

Because she'd had a similar hidey-hole behind her
own bedroom closet, he thought bitterly. Simon had left
her there, drugged unconscious, after his friends had assaulted her. He couldn't even imagine waking up in that
dark little space, afraid, in pain. That she hated the house
had been apparent. That she hated this town was also apparent, which was why he wasn't sure if he had the right to
ask her to stay, even for Daniel.

"The bastard is really dead this time," he said bitterly,
"but he won't stay buried."

"Even dead, Simon's a pain in the ass."

His lips curved, her wry observation venting some of
his steam. She'd approached her fear with humor, and he
respected that. "Well put. Anyway, Daniel was tracking
this killer and needed a data analyst. That's what I do, so
I joined the team. Yesterday we got a tip, leading us to the
O'Brien family. Their oldest son was part of Simon's club."

"Jared," she murmured. "I remember him. He thought
he was God's gift to women in high school. I had no idea
he was one of the ones who . . ." She let the thought trail.

Who'd raped her. Luke shoved his anger aside. She
was coping. So would he. "Jared went missing a few years
ago. We think the others in the club got rid of him be-

cause they were afraid he'd talk, give them up. I was up all night gathering all the information I could find on Jared O'Brien and his family. This morning everything looked good. I found out his younger brother Mack was just released from prison. Mack had grudges against all the dead women. He's our primary suspect. We were ready to roll. We had tails on the two rapists we'd ID'd and a BOLO out on Mack O'Brien."

"Why didn't you just pick up the mayor and the deputy?"

"Two reasons. One, we still don't know the identity of the third man."

"If you arrested the mayor and the deputy, they'd likely roll on the third man."

"Maybe. And maybe he'd go under and we'd never find him. Mostly we didn't bring them in because Mack O'Brien has been using his victims to draw out the surviving club members. They killed his brother. He wanted revenge."

"And once you'd arrested them all, he'd figure he was finished and go away."

"Basically. We'd planned a simultaneous sweep, once we'd located O'Brien, but Mansfield changed that. Sonofabitch."

"He killed his tail. Agent Johnson. I am sorry."

Me, too. "We'll find Mansfield and we've got teams out searching for O'Brien. I just hope when we find Mansfield, he leads us to Bailey." *And if not, I'll make the toad tell us where she is.*

"You told Alex Fallon not to give up hope, but do you really think Bailey is still alive?"

He shrugged. "She's been gone a week. Like you said before, it doesn't look good."

A cell phone trilled and Susannah leaned forward to get her purse.

"It's my phone," Luke said and frowned at the display. "It's Daniel." He listened, his frown deepening, then hung up, turning to Susannah. "You'll have to take a later flight."

She grabbed the armrest as he did a fast U-turn. "Why? Where are we going?"

"Back to Dutton. Daniel said he got a call from Sheriff Loomis."

"And?" Susannah said, clearly irked.

"Loomis says he knows where Bailey Crighton is being held."

"The same Sheriff Loomis who's being investigated by your state attorney's office for tampering with evidence in the murder of Alex Fallon's sister thirteen years ago?" she asked sarcastically. "I saw it on the front page of the newspaper on your desk."

Luke punched his accelerator. "The same Sheriff Loomis who's blocked every attempt to find Bailey? Yes, that's the sheriff I'm talking about."

"For God's sake. And you *believe* him?"

"No, but we can't ignore this lead. Bailey's life could very well depend on it. Daniel's supposed to meet Loomis at the mill site. He said you'd know where that was."

"The O'Brien mill? That would certainly be ironic."

"Wouldn't it? But we've had teams combing the current mill looking for Mack O'Brien all day. Daniel said out past the *old* mill. Do you know where that is?"

She bit at her lip. "Yes, but I haven't been out there since I was in fourth grade and we went on a field trip. Nobody goes there anymore—it's a pile of rubble and too dangerous. Plus, there's a sulfur spring nearby and the whole area smells like rotten eggs. I don't think even kids go there to smoke or make out anymore."

"But can you find the road?"

"Yes."

"That's all I wanted to know. Hold on, it could get bumpy."

Dutton, Friday, February 2, 3:30 p.m.

Too much time had passed. Rocky checked the restraints on each of the five girls, careful not to meet their eyes. They were looking at her. A few with defiance, but mostly with desperation and despair. But she didn't look back. Instead she climbed to the deck and frowned at Jersey Jameson, the old man who owned this boat. He'd been fishing this river his whole life, quietly smuggling whatever contraband was in vogue at the time. The river patrol never gave Jersey a second glance, so he was good cover.

"Why are we still here?" she hissed.

Jersey pointed to the retreating form of Deputy Mansfield. "He said to wait for him to bring the doctor back. I told him he had five minutes, then I was moving this cargo." He slanted her a disgusted look. "I've hauled a helluva lot of shit for you, Rocky, but nothin' like this. Tell your boss I ain't doin' this again."

"Tell Bobby yourself." Jersey's jaw tightened and she laughed. "I thought not." Bobby didn't take kindly to being told no by anyone. "Where are those guys? I'm about ready to go in after them. They're supposed to be hauling out what we couldn't pack."

"I don't want to know any more," Jersey said.

They waited another two minutes and there was no

sign of Mansfield. "I'm going after them." She'd stepped onto the dock when a gunshot cracked the air.

"That came from the road out front," Jersey said.

Rocky hopped back on the deck. "Let's move. Now."

Jersey was already pulling back the throttle. "What about the doc and the deputy?"

"They're on their own." Bobby wouldn't be happy that she'd left bodies behind, and the thought of facing Bobby's rage made Rocky nauseous. "I'll be below."

Dutton, Friday, February 2, 3:35 p.m.

Susannah watched as Luke's speedometer climbed. This was likely a wild goose chase, she thought darkly as they hit a pothole and went momentarily airborne. Then she remembered the agonized fear in Alex Fallon's eyes. The woman's stepsister had been missing a week, her disappearance all wrapped up in this mess Daniel and his partner had been dragged into. They owed it to Bailey to check every lead.

I can catch a flight first thing in the morning. She'd just need to call the kennel and ask them to keep her dog a little longer. Nobody else was depending on her return. Nobody would be waiting for her. It was a dismal truth.

"Daniel called Sheriff Corchran in Arcadia," Luke said tersely, his eyes focused on the road. "Arcadia's only twenty miles from here, so Corchran should get there soon. Daniel trusts him, so you and Alex will go with him, to where it's safe. Understood?"

Susannah nodded. "Understood."

He lifted his brows. "You're not going to argue?"

"Why would I?" she asked evenly. "I don't have a gun and I'm not a cop. I'm quite content to let you guys do what you do and take the baton hand-off in court."

"Fine. Do you drive?"

"Excuse me?"

"Can you drive?" he repeated, enunciating each word. "You live in New York. I know New Yorkers that never get a license."

"I have a license. I don't drive often, but I can." In fact, she only drove once a year, always to the same place, north of the city. On those rare days she rented a car.

"Good. If something goes wrong, you get in the car with Alex and drive. Got it?"

"Got it. But what—?" Susannah blinked, her brain not initially accepting what her eyes saw on the road ahead. "Oh my God. Luke, watch—"

Her shout was lost in the squeal of tires as he threw on his brakes. The car fishtailed and swerved, coming to a stop inches from where a body lay in the road.

"Shit." Luke was out of the car before she caught her breath and hopped out after him.

It was a woman, crumpled and bloody. Susannah thought she was young, but her face was too battered to be certain. "Did you hit her? My God, did *we* do this?"

"We didn't hit her," he said, hunkering down beside the woman. "She's been beaten." From his pocket he pulled two pairs of latex gloves. "Here, put these on." He yanked on his, then ran his hands down the woman's legs, his touch gentle. When he got to her ankle, he stopped. Susannah leaned forward to see a tattoo of a sheep, barely visible beneath the blood. He lifted the woman's chin. "Are you Bailey?"

"Yes," she said, her voice rough and raspy. "My baby, Hope. Is she alive?"

He smoothed Bailey's tangled hair from her face. "Yes, she's alive and she's safe." He handed Susannah his cell phone. "Call 911 for an ambulance, then call Chase. Tell him we found Bailey. Then call Daniel and tell him to come back."

Luke ran to his trunk for a first aid kit and Susannah dialed 911, then Special Agent in Charge Chase Wharton, her hands fumbling the keypad in Luke's oversized gloves.

Bailey grabbed Luke's arm when he began to bandage the gash on her head that was still bleeding profusely. "Alex?" When Luke looked up the road the way Daniel had gone, Bailey's eyes filled with new panic. "She was in that car that just went by?"

His eyes narrowed. "Why?"

"He'll kill her. He has no reason not to. He killed them all. He killed them all."

He killed them all. Susannah's heart stumbled as she found Daniel's number on Luke's speed dial. Daniel's phone rang as Luke tried to get Bailey to say more.

Luke squeezed Bailey's chin. "Who? Bailey, listen to me. Who did this to you?" But the woman didn't speak. She only rocked in a way that was terrifying to behold. "Bailey. Who did this to you?"

Daniel's voicemail picked up and Susannah left a terse message. "Daniel, we found Bailey. Fall back and call us." She turned back to Luke. "I called for an ambulance, and Chase says he's sending Agent Haywood for backup, but Daniel doesn't answer."

Luke stood, a muscle twitching in his cheek. "I can't leave you here. It'll be another ten minutes before Corchran gets here. Stay here with her," he commanded. "I'm going to have him send as much local backup as he can muster."

Susannah knelt by Bailey and smoothed her gloved hand over the woman's matted hair. "Bailey, my name is Susannah. Please tell us who did this to you."

Bailey's eyes fluttered open. "They have Alex."

"Daniel's with her," Susannah soothed. "He won't let them harm her." Whatever her issue with Daniel, Susannah believed that. "Did Deputy Mansfield hurt you?"

Bailey's nod was faint. "And Toby Granville." Her lips twisted. "*Dr.* Granville."

Toby Granville. The missing part of the surviving trio. Susannah started to rise, to get Luke's attention, but Bailey grabbed her arm. "There's a girl. Down there." Weakly she pointed. "She's hurt. Help her. Please."

Susannah stood and peered down the embankment but saw nothing. *Wait.* She squinted at a light patch just inside the tree line. "*Luke.* There's someone down there."

Susannah heard him shout her name, but she was already scrambling down the embankment, stumbling in her high heels and narrow skirt. It was a person, she could see. She started running. A girl. *Oh my God. Oh my God.*

The girl lay still as death. Susannah dropped to her knees and pressed her fingers to the girl's neck, feeling for a pulse, and drew a breath, relieved. She was still alive. Her pulse was thready, but there. She was a teenager, petite and so thin her arms were like sticks. She was so covered in blood it was hard to see where she was wounded.

Susannah started to stand so she could wave Luke down, when the girl's bloody hand shot up and gripped her forearm. The girl's eyes flew open and in them Susannah saw fear and intense pain.

"Who . . . are you?" the girl choked out.

"My name is Susannah Vartanian. I'm here to help you. Please don't be afraid."

The girl fell back, gasping. "Vartanian. You came." Then Susannah's heart stopped in her chest. The girl was staring up at her like . . . like she was God. "You finally came."

Susannah gingerly pulled at the girl's tattered T-shirt until she saw the bullet hole. Panicked, she let the shirt fall. *Oh, God.* She'd been shot in the side. *Now what?*

Think, Vartanian. You remember what to do. Pressure. She needed to put pressure on the wound. Quickly she stripped off her jacket, then her blouse, shivering when the cold air hit her skin. "What's your name, honey?" she asked as she worked, but the girl said nothing, her eyes again closed.

Susannah lifted the girl's eyelids. No response, but she still found a pulse. Rapidly she wound her blouse into a tight ball and gently pressed it to the wound. "Luke!"

She heard the footsteps behind her a second before his snarled curse. A look over her shoulder had her eyes widening at the gun in his hand.

"I told you to stay—Holy Mother of God." His eyes flicked briefly to her lacy bra, then focused on the girl. "Do you know who she is?"

She dropped her eyes back to her hands, pressed to the girl's side. "No. Bailey told me to help her while you were on the phone. She also said Granville and Mansfield were the ones holding her."

"Granville." He nodded. "The town doctor. I met him this week at one of the crime scenes. So he's the third rapist."

"I think so."

"Did the girl say anything to you?"

Susannah frowned. "She said my last name, then 'You came. You finally came.' Like she was expecting me." *Then she looked at me like I was God.* It made her uneasy. "She's been shot and she's lost a lot of blood. Give me your belt. I need to wrap it around her to put pressure on this wound."

She heard the whistle of his belt being drawn through his belt loops. "Put on your jacket," he said, "and go wait with Bailey."

"But—"

He dropped to one knee, briefly met her eyes. "I'll take care of her. Whoever did this might still be around. I don't want Bailey alone." He hesitated. "Can you handle a gun?"

"Yes," Susannah answered without hesitation.

"Good." He drew a pistol from an ankle holster. "Now run. I'll carry her."

Susannah grabbed her jacket and shoved her arms in the sleeves. "Luke, she's just a kid. She's going to die if we don't get her help soon."

"I know," he said grimly, slipping his belt around the girl's body. "Now go. I'll follow."

Chapter Three

Luke was tightening the straps on his Kevlar vest when two Arcadia squad cars pulled up. A man got out, taking in the scene. "I'm Corchran. Where's Vartanian?"

"Right here." Susannah looked up from where she knelt between Bailey and the girl. The jacket she'd buttoned up to her throat was covered in blood, as was her skirt. The pair of plastic gloves Luke had given her dwarfed her small hands, which continued to put pressure on the hole in the girl's side. "Where's the damn ambulance?"

Corchran frowned. "En route. Who are you?"

"This is Susannah Vartanian, Daniel's sister," Luke said. "I'm Papadopoulos."

"So where is *Daniel* Vartanian?" Corchran asked.

Luke pointed. "He went that way and he's not answering his cell or his radio."

Corchran's brows bunched in obvious concern. "Who are these two?"

"The woman is Bailey Crighton," Luke said. "The girl's a Jane Doe. Both are unconscious. I have a chopper coming to airlift them to Atlanta. It's possible whoever did this is still holed up wherever these two women escaped from." He drew an uneasy breath. "And I think Daniel's in trouble. Now that you're here, I'm going after him."

Corchran pointed to the two officers from the second squad car. "Officers Larkin and DeWitt. I have six more officers plus another ambulance on the way and reinforcements standing by. Larkin and DeWitt can stay and direct the incoming vehicles. I'm with you."

"Agent Pete Haywood will be here soon. When he gets here, send him after us." He nodded to Corchran. "Let's do this."

"Agent Papadopoulos, wait." Susannah handed him his backup pistol. "I don't need it anymore and you might." She went back to putting pressure on the girl's wound.

She'd been calm and courageous and level-headed. When he had a chance to breathe, Luke knew he'd be impressed as hell, once again. And he knew he'd be mentally replaying how she looked kneeling in the forest in her bra. But now he needed to focus. Daniel's life could depend on it.

"If Bailey comes to, get her to tell any details she can. Number of men inside, doors, weapons she saw. Have Larkin radio us with anything, no matter how small."

She didn't look up. "All right."

"Then let's roll."

They approached silently, Luke in his own car and Corchran following behind. He rounded a bend, and Luke's heart simply froze. "Oh my God," he whispered. *Ambush.* Frank Loomis had set Daniel up.

Luke was looking at a concrete bunker, at least a hundred feet long. Behind the bunker he could see the river. In front of the bunker were parked three cars. Two were Dutton squad cars. The third was Daniel's sedan, its rear crashed up against one of the Dutton squad cars, which was parked across the road, blocking Daniel's escape.

Both front doors of Daniel's car stood open and Luke

could see Daniel's driver side window was streaked with blood. Quietly Luke approached, gun drawn, his heart thundering in his ears. He silently motioned Corchran to the passenger side.

Luke silently exhaled the breath he'd held. Daniel's car was empty. Corchran leaned in the passenger side. "Blood," he murmured, pointing to the dash. "Not a lot. And hair." He picked up a few strands from the floorboard. It was long and brown.

"It's Alex's," Luke said quietly, then saw the male body on the ground, about forty feet away. Running, he dropped to one knee next to the body. "It's Frank Loomis."

"Dutton's sheriff." Corchran looked pained. "He's involved in all this, too?"

Luke pressed his fingers to Loomis's throat. "He's been blocking Daniel's murder investigation all week. He's dead. How long before your six guys get here?"

Corchran looked back to the three squad cars pulling around the bend. "Now."

"Position them around the structure. Weapons on ready and secure cover. I'm going to check for available entrances and exits." Luke started walking. The bunker was bigger than it looked from the front, an L-shaped offshoot pointing toward the river. There was a window at one end and a door at the other. The small window was too high for even a tall man to see through.

Then he heard the shot from the other side of the wall. He could hear voices, muffled and indistinct. "Corchran," he hissed into his radio.

"I heard it," Corchran said. "The second ambulance just pulled up in case we have casualties. I'm coming around the other side."

Luke heard another shot from inside and started running. He met Corchran at the door. "I'll take the top, you take the bottom." He began to move, then jerked back. "Someone's coming."

Corchran backed around the corner, waiting. Luke crept away, keeping his eyes on the door. Then it opened and a woman emerged, covered in blood.

Ridgefield, Georgia, Friday, February 2, 4:00 p.m.

"Hurry." Rocky shoved the last of the girls off the boat. "We don't have all day."

She ran her gaze over the five she'd gotten out, assessing their worth. Two were on the scrawny side. One was tall, blond, an athlete. She'd command top price. The other two were reliable performers when they were healthy. If she'd had to pick, at least she'd chosen well. The five girls were kneeling on the ground, pale. One of them had gotten sick all over herself in the hold and the others had turned their faces from her.

That was good. Camaraderie among the assets was bad. They'd had a few girls develop relationships and Rocky had nipped that in the bud. She'd had to sacrifice a top performer to do so, but having Becky beaten to death in view of the others had done the job. Becky had gotten a few of the girls to talk, and talking invariably led to escape planning and that would not be tolerated.

A horse trailer pulled up, white and nondescript, Bobby at the wheel. Rocky braced herself for the storm of temper she knew would erupt once Bobby did a head count.

Bobby got out of the van, eyes narrowed. "I thought you were bringing six. And where are Granville and Mansfield?"

She looked up, meeting Bobby's cold blue eyes, her heart thundering in her ears. Still, the girls were listening and how she responded would impact how she'd be perceived in the future. Ninety percent of handling these kids was fear and psychological intimidation. They stayed because they were too terrified to leave.

So Rocky held her ground. "Let's get the cargo loaded and then we'll talk."

Bobby stepped back. "Fine. Do it fast."

Rocky herded the girls into the horse trailer quickly, ensuring their cuffs were fastened to the wall. She slapped a strip of duct tape over their mouths, just in case any of them got the bright idea to yell for help while they were stopped at a traffic light.

Jersey made no eye contact as he stacked the boxes on the hay. When he was finished, he turned to Bobby. "I'll move whatever else you please. But no more kids."

"Of course, Jersey," Bobby said silkily. "I wouldn't dream of making you feel uncomfortable in any way." Which Rocky knew meant Bobby would now ask Jersey to move all their human cargo, blackmailing him with what he'd already done.

From the look on his face, Jersey knew it, too. "I mean it, Bobby." He swallowed hard. "I've got granddaughters their age."

"Then I recommend you keep them out of chat rooms," Bobby said dryly. "You do of course realize all the other 'stuff' you move winds up in kids way younger than these?"

Jersey shook his head. "That's voluntary. Anybody who pays for smack does it because they want it. This ain't voluntary."

Bobby's smile was sarcastically indulgent. "You have a

strange and faulty moral code, Jersey Jameson. You'll be paid in the usual fashion. Now go."

Bobby closed the trailer doors and Rocky knew her time was at hand. "Granville and Mansfield are still back there," she said before Bobby could ask again. She braced herself, closing her eyes. "Along with the bodies of the girls Granville killed."

There was silence for what seemed like an eternity. Finally Rocky opened her eyes and every ounce of her blood went cold. Bobby's eyes were sharp and furious.

"I told you to make sure nothing remained." The words were quietly uttered.

"I know, but—"

"But nothing," Bobby snapped, then walked away, pacing back and forth. "Why did you leave them behind?"

"Granville was still in the bunker and Mansfield had gone in to get him, to help him bring the bodies out. Jersey and I heard shots from the road. We figured it was better not to be caught with live cargo on our hands."

Bobby stopped pacing and abruptly turned to rake her with an icy glare. "It would have been *better* to do your *job* and leave *nothing* behind. What else?"

Rocky met Bobby's glare head-on. "On the way here, I was listening to Jersey's scanner. The police found Frank Loomis's body outside."

Bobby's brows bunched. "Loomis? What the hell was he doing there?"

"I don't know."

"How many?"

Rocky shook her head. "How many what?"

Bobby grabbed her, lifting her to her toes. "How many bodies did you leave behind?"

Rocky struggled to stay calm. "Six."

"Are you sure they're dead? Did you see their bodies?"

She hadn't, and she should have. She should have watched Granville kill each one and dump the body in the river. Truth was, Rocky had found she had a weak stomach for murder when the rubber hit the road. But Granville was a sick bastard and if he'd done nothing else, he'd killed them all. "Yes, I'm sure."

Bobby's grip loosened and Rocky's feet hit the ground. "All right."

She swallowed hard, still feeling the pinch of Bobby's knuckles against her windpipe. "The girls we left behind can't be identified. We're safe, unless Granville or Mansfield decide to talk. That is, if they got caught."

Bobby let go, pushing her away. "I'll deal with them."

Rocky stumbled, quickly catching herself. "But what if they did get caught?"

"I will deal with them. Mansfield's not the only cop I have on my payroll. What else?"

"I made sure we left no documents. Granville hadn't shredded them."

Bobby scowled. "Sonofabitch. I should have killed him years ago."

"Probably."

Bobby leaned in close and murmured, "I could kill you now. With my bare hands. I could snap your neck in two. And you'd deserve it. You totally fucked up, Rocky."

Again Rocky's blood went cold. "But you won't." She forced her voice to be steady.

"And why won't I?"

"Because without me, you wouldn't have access to the chat rooms and all the 'pretties' we have in the pipeline would be lost. Your supply would dry up faster than spit on a fryin' pan." She leaned up on her toes until they were chin to chin. "And that's bad business. So you won't kill me."

Bobby stared at her, then laughed bitterly. "You're right. And you're lucky. Right now, I need you more than I hate you. But it's a real close call, kid. One more fuckup and I'll take the chat room hit. I can find someone to replace you, and the base business will keep me flush enough to stay afloat until I build a new pipeline. When we get to Ridgefield, you get these girls cleaned up. I have a client coming over tonight. Now get in." Bobby got behind the wheel, cell phone in hand. "Hey, Chili, it's me. Gotta a coupla jobs for you, but they have to be done fast. Like, in the next hour."

Rocky could hear Chili's rather boisterous protests when Bobby held the cell phone at arm's length with a wince.

"Look, Chili, if you don't want the job, that's fine. I'll find someone else . . ." Bobby smirked. "I thought so. I need you to torch two houses for me. Usual pay, usual way . . ." Bobby's smirk flattened. "All right. Double. But I want them both burned to the ground, nothing saved. Nothing should remain."

Dutton, Friday, February 2, 4:15 p.m.

"*Alex.*" Luke rushed the door when Alex Fallon stumbled out of the bunker into the sunlight, covered in blood. "She's hit. Corchran, get the medics."

Alex pushed Luke's hands away. "Not me. Daniel's been hit. He's critical. He needs to be airlifted to a level one trauma center. I'll show you where he is."

Luke caught her arm as she went back through the door. "He's alive?"

"Barely," Alex snapped. "We're wasting time. Come on."

"I'll radio Larkin to have the chopper coming for the girl wait for Vartanian," Corchran said, motioning for the paramedics. "You go."

Alex was already running back through the bunker. Luke and two paramedics with a squeaky gurney followed. "Bailey escaped," Alex said when he caught up with her.

"I know," Luke said. "I found her. She's alive. In pretty bad shape, but she's alive."

"Thank God. Beardsley's in here, too."

"Beardsley? You mean the army chaplain?" Captain Beardsley had been missing since Monday—since he'd gone looking for Bailey in her Dutton home.

"Yeah. He's alive. He may be able to walk out on his own, but he's bad, too."

They got to the room at the end of the long hall and Luke stopped dead in his tracks. Two paramedics pushed around him to get to Daniel, who lay in the corner on his side, a makeshift bandage covering his chest, probably Alex's handiwork. His face was gray. But he was breathing.

That was more than Luke could say for the three dead bodies littering the floor. Deputy Mansfield lay on his back, two shots to his chest. Mack O'Brien was crumpled in a heap, a neat bullet hole in the middle of his forehead. A third man also lay on his back, five gunshots to his chest and one to his hand. His bloody wrists were cuffed behind his back. His face was gone, blown away by a high-caliber weapon.

A fourth man sat against the wall, breathing hard. His face was covered in blood and grime and his eyes were closed. Luke assumed this was the missing army chaplain, although he looked more like Rambo at the moment.

"Holy Mother of God," Luke breathed, then looked

over at the slim woman who was the only participant in the action still standing. "Alex, did you do all this?"

Alex looked around as if seeing the destruction for the first time. "Most of it. Mansfield shot Daniel, then I killed Mansfield. Then Granville came in." Grimly she looked over at the man with no face. "Dr. Granville was the third rapist."

"I know," Luke said. "Bailey told us. So you killed Granville, too?"

"No, I just wounded him. O'Brien killed Granville. It was O'Brien's revenge."

Luke nudged O'Brien with his shoe. "And this one?"

"Well, after O'Brien killed Granville, he put his gun to my head. And then Reverend Beardsley took O'Brien's gun and Daniel made the head shot." A sudden grin lit up her face. "I think we did good."

Her silly grin had Luke smiling back, despite the sick clenching of his stomach at the sound of Daniel's groan as the medics moved him. Daniel was groaning, which meant he was alive. "I think you did good, too. You took care of all the bad guys, kid."

But the army chaplain shook his head. "You were too late," Beardsley said wearily.

Alex instantly sobered. "What are you talking about?"

He killed them all, Bailey had said. Dread swept away any momentary satisfaction Luke had felt. "You stay here with Daniel," he told Alex. "I'll go see."

Alex looked over at the medics. "His vitals are steady?"

"Steady, but weak," one of the men said. "Who sealed this sucking chest wound?"

"I did," Alex said. "I'm an ER nurse."

The medic gave her a nod of approval. "Nice job. He's breathing on his own."

Alex's nod was unsteady. "Good. Let's go," she said to Luke. "I need to know."

Luke supposed she would. Her stepsister, Bailey, had been held in this place for a week and though everyone had told her that Bailey was a junkie who had probably just disappeared, Alex had never given up hope.

Beardsley pushed himself against the wall until he stood. "Then come with me." He pulled on the first door to their left. It was unlocked, but not empty.

Luke drew a breath, dread becoming horror. A young girl lay on a thin cot, her arm chained to the wall. She was gaunt, her bones clearly visible. Her eyes were wide open and there was a small round hole in her forehead. She looked about fifteen.

He killed them all.

Luke slowly walked to the cot. *Dear God,* was all he could think. Then the shock of recognition punched his gut. *I know her.* Dammit, he'd seen this girl before. Pictures scrolled through his mind, vile, obscene pictures that he could never forget. Faces he could never forget.

This face, he knew. *Angel.* Her abusers, the subhumans who'd paraded her across their Web site, who'd committed acts so depraved . . . They'd called her Angel.

Bile rose in his throat as he stood, staring down at her. Angel was dead. Emaciated, tortured. *You were too late.* The shock began to fade as the fury that simmered inside him boiled over and he clenched his fists, trying to keep it inside. Controlled. He couldn't let the fury keep him from doing his job.

To protect and serve, his mind mocked.

But you didn't protect her. You failed. You were too late.

Alex dropped to her knees next to the cot, pressing her

fingers to the girl's thin neck. "She's dead. Maybe an hour ago."

"They're all dead," Beardsley said harshly. "Every one that was left behind."

"How many?" Luke asked, his voice hard. "How many are dead?"

"Bailey and I were locked up at the other end," Beardsley said. "I couldn't see anything. But I counted seven shots."

Seven shots. The girl Susannah had saved had been shot twice, once in the side. The other bullet had grazed her head. So five other shots. Five dead. *Dear God.*

"What is this place?" Alex whispered.

"Human trafficking," Luke said succinctly and Alex stared at him, open-mouthed.

"You mean all these girls . . . ? But why kill them? *Why?*"

"They didn't have time to get them all out," Beardsley said tonelessly. "They didn't want the ones left behind to talk."

"Who's responsible for this?" Alex hissed.

"The man you called Granville." Beardsley leaned against the wall and closed his eyes and Luke noticed the dark stain on his shirt. It was spreading.

"You got shot, too," Alex said. "For God's sake sit down." She pushed him down and knelt next to him, peeling his shirt away from the wound.

Luke flagged one of the paramedics, a serious-faced kid whose badge said Eric Clark. "Captain Beardsley was hit. We need another gurney." He visually assessed Daniel from the doorway. His friend was still deathly pale, his chest barely moving. But it was moving. "How is he?"

"As stable as we can get him in here," Clark replied.

"Then radio for another crew," Luke said, "and come with me. We have one dead teenager. There may be four more." Rapidly Luke and the young medic checked every small cell. There were an even dozen, each dark, dirty. Fetid. Each had a filthy, rancid mattress on a rusted cot frame. The one right next to the office was empty, but a sweep of Luke's flashlight revealed a trail of blood leading from the door. The steady drips of blood continued down the hall. "This is the one that escaped," he said. "Next cell."

The next cell held another body, as emaciated as Angel. Luke heard Eric Clark suck in a horrified breath. "Oh my God." Clark started to rush in, but Luke held him back.

"Careful. For now just see if she's alive, but don't touch anything else."

Clark tried to find a pulse. "She's dead. What the hell happened here?"

Luke didn't answer, methodically leading Clark from cell to cell. Out of twelve cells they had five dead. The other seven were empty, but a few of the mattresses were damp, the smell of bodily fluids still heavy in the unventilated room. These rooms had been recently occupied. Now they were not. One cell had belonged to the girl Susannah had saved. That meant up to six had been taken. *Six.*

There were no leads, no way of knowing how many or who the girls were. No descriptions. Nothing, except the girl Susannah had saved. She might be their only hope.

Like Angel, the other four victims were shackled to the wall of their cells, each staring vacantly at the ceiling, a bullet hole in the center of each forehead. Careful not to disturb the scene, Clark checked each girl. Each time he shook his head.

At the end of the hall, Luke drew a breath, but his insides didn't calm. It was just as Beardsley had said. *No survivors.* None except the girl Susannah had discovered in the woods. What had she seen? What did she know?

Clark was breathing hard, visibly shaken. "I've never . . . Oh my God." He looked up at Luke, his eyes horrified and suddenly very old. "They're kids. They're just kids."

It was a scene that would have turned the stomachs of most seasoned cops. Eric Clark would be forever changed. "Come on. Let's check this back hall."

There were only two cells in the back, older and more fetid, if that was possible. One of the doors was open and a body lay across the threshold. Another sweep of Luke's flashlight had him fighting the urge to gag. The man was dead, gutted like a pig.

The cell was otherwise empty, but Luke could see a hole had been dug under the wall to the next cell and realized that Beardsley had pulled Bailey from the other cell through the hole and together they'd escaped.

"Do we break down the door?" Clark asked unsteadily.

"No, it's empty. Go back to Vartanian. I'll call the ME for the dead men." Luke swallowed. "And the girls."

The innocents. Young girls the same age as his nieces. They should be going to school dances and giggling about boys. Instead they'd been tortured, starved, and God only knew what else. And now they were dead. They'd been too late.

I can't do this anymore. I can't look at this kind of depravity anymore.

Yes, you can. You will. You have to. He tightened his jaw and straightened his spine. *Then you'll find who did this. It's the way you'll stay sane.*

The medic went back to Daniel and Luke returned to

the first cell where Alex knelt next to Beardsley, her hands pressing fresh gauze pads to his side.

"How many girls did they get out?" Luke asked quietly.

Beardsley's eyes were weary. "Five or six. I heard them talking about a boat."

"I'll notify the local police and the water patrol," Luke said. "And the Coast Guard."

Out in the hall, Daniel was being wheeled out on one gurney as a second gurney was brought in for Beardsley. Alex thanked him for saving her life, then left the small cell to join Daniel. Luke took her place, crouching next to Beardsley, careful not to get in the way of the paramedics. "I need to know exactly what you saw and heard."

Beardsley grimaced as he was lifted to the gurney. "I wasn't that close to the office, so I didn't hear much. They kept Bailey and me in the cells at the other end of the bunker. Kept us separated. Every day-they took us to the office. For questioning."

"You mean the room where Mansfield and the others died?"

"Yeah. They wanted Bailey's key. They beat her and . . ." His raspy voice broke. "Oh, God. Granville *tortured* her." He gritted his teeth fiercely, anguish in his eyes. "All because of a *key.* You have no idea how much I wanted to kill him."

Luke looked over at Angel, dead on the cot, then thought of Susannah Vartanian and all the other innocents victimized by Dr. Granville and his club. "Yeah, I think I do."

He needed to call his boss. They needed to regroup. They needed a plan.

They needed Susannah's girl to survive.

Luke followed Daniel's gurney out into the sunshine. He was met by Agent Pete Haywood, one of Chase's team. "What happened in there?" Pete demanded.

Luke gave Pete the short version, Pete's eyes growing larger with each detail. "Now I've got to talk to that girl. She might be the only one who knows who took the others."

"You go," Pete said. "I'll stay. Call me with news on Daniel."

"Secure the scene. Nobody in and radio silence until we inform Chase and the Bureau." He started running toward his car, dialing Chase Wharton as the medics loaded Daniel into the waiting ambulance.

"Goddammit," Chase snarled before Luke could speak. "I've been trying to get you for twenty minutes. What the hell's going on down there?"

The ambulance pulled away. "Daniel's alive, but critical. Alex is unhurt. O'Brien, Mansfield, Granville, and Loomis are dead." Luke filled his lungs with fresh air, but the taste of death remained on his tongue. "And we have one hell of a situation."

Chapter Four

Susannah watched the medics load the girl into the helicopter. "Can I ride with her?"

The older of the two medics shook his head. "Against regs. Plus there's no room."

Susannah frowned. "An ambulance took Bailey. The girl's the only one in there."

The medics shared a look. "We're waiting for another patient, ma'am."

Susannah had opened her mouth to ask *who* when another ambulance appeared, Luke's car behind it. Luke jumped out of his car at the same time Alex Fallon climbed out of the ambulance. She was covered in blood, but she appeared unhurt.

"What happened?" Susannah demanded. Then she could see for herself. *Daniel.*

Her brother was strapped to the stretcher, an oxygen mask covering his face. She watched, frozen, as they wheeled him past and loaded him into the waiting helicopter.

He'd always seemed strong, invincible. Now, strapped to a stretcher, he seemed frail. And in that moment, all she had left in the world. *Don't die. Please don't die.*

Luke put his arm around her shoulders, lifting her, and

she realized her knees had gone weak. "He's alive," Luke said into her ear. "He's in bad shape, but he is alive."

Thank God. "Good," she said. She started to move away from Luke, whose support suddenly seemed too important, but he grabbed her arms, looking her in the eyes.

"The girl. Did she say anything else?"

"She regained consciousness only a minute or two. She kept saying, 'He killed them all,' then asked for her mother. What did she mean? What *happened* back there?"

Luke's eyes were intense. "Did she say anything else? *Anything. Think.*"

"No, nothing else. I'm sure. She started gasping for air and then the medics intubated her. Dammit, Luke, *what happened*? What happened to Daniel?"

"I'll tell you on the way." He guided her to the front seat, then helped Alex into the back. "Maybe Jane Doe will be awake by the time she gets to the ER." He gave Susannah a sharp glance as he drove away. "Do you have any open cuts?"

"No." The dread in her stomach twisted like a snake. "Why?"

"There were five others back there, other teenage girls. All dead. Looks like some kind of human-trafficking operation. Somebody moved some live girls away from here. But we don't know who. Maybe Jane Doe is the only one who does."

"Oh my God." That her girl had been so victimized ... Then Luke's query hit home. "We're covered in her blood," she said quietly. They'd worn gloves, but Susannah's jacket was blood-soaked, as was Luke's shirt. "If she's got anything, we're exposed."

"They'll test us for everything when we get to the ER,"

Alex said. "They'll be more worried about hepatitis than HIV. We'll get gamma globulin shots for the hepatitis."

"How long for HIV test results these days?" Susannah asked levelly.

"Twenty-four hours," Alex answered.

"Okay." Susannah settled in her seat, willing her stomach to settle. Twenty-four hours wasn't too bad. *Faster turnaround than the week it took last time I got tested.*

"Luke," Alex said suddenly, "Granville said something, right before he died."

Excuse me? Susannah twisted around to look at her again. "Granville's *dead*?"

"Mack O'Brien killed him." Alex studied Susannah's face, then her eyes flickered in sympathy. "I'm sorry. You never got to confront him."

Daniel's new lady friend was perceptive. "Well, that still leaves two."

Alex shook her head. "No. Mansfield's dead. I killed him after he shot Daniel."

Gratification warred with frustration. "Did they at least suffer?"

"Not enough," Luke said grimly. "Alex, what did you mean? What did he say?"

"He said, 'You think you know everything, but you don't. There were others.'"

Luke nodded. "That makes sense. Somebody kidnapped the remaining girls. There had to have been others working with him."

Alex shook her head slowly. "No, it wasn't like that. He said, 'Simon was mine. But I was another's.'" She grimaced. "Like it was some kind of . . . cult or something. Creepy."

I was another's. A nasty shiver raced down Susannah's

spine as a memory nagged, an overheard conversation, so long ago.

"Did he say who the others might be?" Luke was asking.

"He might have, but that's when O'Brien came in and shot his head off," Alex replied.

"*Tick*," Susannah murmured and Luke turned to her with a puzzled frown.

"What did you say?"

"*Tick*," she repeated, remembering now. Now it made sense. "I heard them."

"Who, Susannah?"

"Simon and someone else. A boy. I didn't see his face. They were in Simon's room, talking. Arguing. The other boy had apparently bested Simon at some game and Simon accused him of cheating. But the boy said he'd been taught how to win by another." Mentally she put herself back to that day. "Something to the effect that he knew how to anticipate his opponent's moves, manipulate his opponent's response. Simon was still going to beat him up. But the boy convinced him to play another game."

Alex leaned forward. "And then?"

"Simon lost again. Simon was a bully, but he was also very smart. He wanted to learn how the other boy had done it. I think he was already trying to figure out how to use the skill. He demanded to be taken to the person who'd taught the boy. The boy said it was his *tick*. His master. I thought at first he was joking, and Simon did, too, but the other boy was very serious. He spoke so . . . reverentially. Simon was intrigued."

"So what happened?" Luke asked.

"The boy said if Simon went with him, he'd be forever changed. That he'd 'belong to another.' Those were his exact words. I remember because it made my skin cold and I shivered even though it had to have been a hundred degrees in . . . where I was. Then Simon laughed and said something like, 'Yeah, yeah. Let's go.' "

"How did you overhear them?" Luke asked.

"I was hiding." Her wince was involuntary.

"In your hidey-hole?" His voice was gentle, but his jaw was taut.

"Yeah." She drew a breath. "In my hidey-hole. When I was hiding behind the closet I could hear every word that was said in Simon's room."

"Why were you hiding that day, Susannah?" Luke asked.

"Because earlier in the day Simon had told me to be home. He said he had a friend coming who wanted to 'meet' me. I was only eleven, but even then I understood what that meant. It was a good thing I'd hid. The boy said he'd take Simon to his *tick*, but he wanted to visit my room first. He was very angry when I wasn't there."

"Who?" Luke asked. "The boy or Simon?"

"Both."

"Simon didn't know about the hidey-hole at that point?"

"I guess not, but I'm not sure. He might have known, but let me think he didn't so I'd think I was safe. Simon was big on mind games like that. Being able to manipulate his opponent's responses would have been very attractive to him."

Luke frowned. "What the hell is a *tick* anyway? Like an insect?"

"I don't know. I tried looking it up in the library the next day, but couldn't find it. And I couldn't risk asking anyone."

"Why not?" Alex asked warily.

She hesitated, then shrugged. "Because my father would have found out."

"Your father wouldn't let you talk to librarians?" Luke asked, very carefully.

"My father wouldn't let me talk to anyone."

Luke opened his mouth, then closed it again, opting against saying whatever was on his mind. "Okay. So is it possible the boy that day was Toby Granville?"

"Highly possible. Toby and Simon were friends back then. Simon had just lost his leg and most of the kids were spooked by his prosthesis, but Toby thought it was cool."

"So let's assume it was Toby. He had a mentor, a teacher. Someone who instructed him in the art of manipulation. The other he belonged to. His *tick*. It's something."

"That was years ago," Susannah said doubtfully. "That person may not even be alive. And if he is, he might not be Granville's partner."

"True," Luke said. "But until our warrant for Granville's house is signed or Jane Doe wakes up, it's all we've got." He took out his cell phone. "Susannah, call Chase and tell him what you told us. Ask him to start researching 'tick.'"

Susannah obeyed, taking her laptop from her briefcase. Chase had gone to meet Daniel's helicopter. By the time she'd explained to his clerk, her laptop was awake.

"Any word on Daniel?" Alex asked expectantly.

Susannah shook her head, quelling the pitch of her stomach. *He's strong. He'll be fine.* The girl's status should worry her more. "Not yet. Chase's clerk said the helicopter is expected to land in about fifteen minutes. Until then, we can keep busy."

Luke glanced at her laptop. "What are you doing?"

"Your research. I have a wireless card."

He looked impressed. "Cool. So google '*tick*'—with a *k, c,* and *ck*—and 'master.'"

"I already did." She waited impatiently, then frowned at the result. "Well, 'tik' is crystal meth in South Africa. And it means 'land and sky' in Cambodian. But nothing else pops. Unless . . ." *Cambodian* jogged another memory to the front of her mind, a page from a college textbook.

"Unless?" Luke prompted.

"Unless it's just pronounced 'tick,'" Susannah said, revising her search. *Pronounced tick master*, she typed and nodded at the result. "It's a Vietnamese word, spelled *t-h-í-c-h*. A respectful title for a Buddhist monk." She looked at Luke, dubious. "But Buddhism is all about peace and harmony. That would have to be one hell of a twisted monk."

"True, but one twisted monk is a hell of a lot more than we had a half hour ago." His brows lifted. "Well done, grasshopper."

She pushed back the sudden flutter of pride. "Thank you."

Dutton, Friday, February 2, 6:00 p.m.

Charles turned off his police scanner and sank against the cushions of the sofa in his upstairs parlor. He'd known this day was coming. Still, the news was hard to bear.

Toby Granville was dead. *Dead*. His jaw hardened. Dead at the hands of an amateur like Mack O'Brien. Mack had shown imagination and cruelty, but no finesse. Which was why Mack was dead, by a bullet from Daniel Vartanian's gun. At least Toby had not died at Daniel's hands. That would have been impossible to bear.

Toby. He'd been such a brilliant boy. Always seeking, searching. Always experimenting. Philosophy, mathematics, religion, human anatomy. Toby had been first in his class at med school. Why wouldn't he be, when he'd done his own dissections right in Charles's own basement? No cadavers for Charles's protégé. No, sir. Charles had provided his pupil with live subjects and Toby had derived such joy from their use.

Charles thought of the subject strapped to the table in his basement at this very moment. Toby hadn't finished with him. The subject still had secrets to spill. *I guess I'll have to finish him myself.* Anticipation shivered down his spine despite his sadness.

Because Toby was dead, and under the most dire of circumstances. There would be no proud funeral procession, no well-attended service in the church, no tears in Dutton's cemetery. Toby Granville had died in shame and would receive no honors after death.

Charles stood. *So I'll see you off, my young friend.* From his closet he pulled the robe that had first caught Toby's attention. Donning it, he lit the candles around the room, sat in the special chair he'd had made just for his sessions with Toby. The boy had been so easy to lure, yet so hard to keep. But Toby had served his master well.

Charles began the intonations that meant less than nothing to him, but that had opened the world of the occult to a thirteen-year-old with a thirst for knowledge and for blood. Charles believed none of it, but Toby had and it had made him sharper, crueler. Perhaps, ultimately, it had fed his mental instability. *Farewell, Toby. I will miss you.*

"Now," he murmured aloud. "Who can I find to take your place?" There were always others, waiting, anxious to serve. Charles smiled. *To serve me*, of course.

He rose, blew out the candles, and put the robes away. He'd use them again very soon. His clients who wished to see signs and portents liked him to dress the part.

Atlanta, Friday, February 2, 6:45 p.m.

Luke stood at the glass, staring into the interview room where two men sat at the table in silence. One was Dutton's mayor, Garth Davis, the other, his attorney. Garth's unsmiling face was bruised and the right sleeve of his coat was dusty with red Georgia clay.

Luke glanced over at Hank Germanio, the agent who'd arrested Davis earlier that day. "Did he resist arrest?"

Germanio shrugged. "Not too much."

Luke thought of Susannah and Alex's twin sister and all the other women Garth Davis had violated thirteen years before and was relieved he hadn't been the one to arrest the man. One little bruise wasn't nearly enough. "Too bad."

"I know. I kinda wished he had."

"Has he said anything?"

"Only to ask for his lawyer. Slimy little SOB. The lawyer, too."

Luke checked his watch. "Chloe said she'd meet me here."

"And she has." State's Attorney Chloe Hathaway closed the outer door. She was a tall, curvy blond with an eye for style, but anyone who believed that's all she was, was mistaken. A shrewd mind ticked behind her pretty face, and Luke was happy she was on this case. "Sorry I'm late. I've been drafting your warrants for Granville's, Mansfield's, and Davis's houses and businesses."

"Are they signed?" Luke asked.

"Not yet. I wanted my boss to check them over. I don't want anything being excluded when you all finally search. The fact that you have a doctor, a deputy, and a lawyer-turned-mayor presents all kinds of confidentiality issues depending on how you search and what you find. I don't want any evidence slipping through our fingers."

"I don't want five kidnapped girls to slip through our fingers, either, Chloe," Luke said, trying to control his impatience. "The longer it takes to search Granville's house, the farther away his partner could be."

"I understand," Chloe said. "I really do. But once you find the partner, you don't want to lose him on an illegal search, do you?"

Luke gritted his teeth. She was right, but so was he. "How long?"

"An hour. Two tops."

"Two hours? *Chloe.*"

"*Luke.* Let's focus on Davis for now. Out of seven original rape club members, he's the only one left alive. What do we have to tie him to these five murdered girls, besides the photos you found in Daniel's old house?"

"Only his social connection to Granville and Mansfield. They were all community leaders. We haven't had an opportunity to question any of his constituents, neighbors, coworkers, anything."

"How about his family?"

"His wife left town with their two kids yesterday when one of Garth's cousins was murdered by Mack O'Brien. She was afraid for their safety and said Garth wouldn't come to the police. We don't know where she is, exactly. Her sister-in-law, Kate Davis, told us Garth's wife was going 'somewhere out west.'"

"Well, once this hits the airwaves, she'll know it's safe and she'll probably come back," Chloe said. "What about Davis's parents, siblings?"

"Parents are both dead, one sister's living—Kate Davis. We'll talk to her again."

Chloe sighed. "So we don't have anything."

"Not yet," Luke admitted.

"Garth Davis might not know anything about Granville's side business. If he does, I'm expecting that his attorney will want to cut some kind of deal on the thirteen-year-old rapes."

Luke had thought the same thing. "And will you?" he asked, mildly.

She shook her head. "I sure don't want to. And I won't even consider a deal without knowing what information he has and if it's genuine. I've got a dozen victims to consider here. They deserve their day in court. But . . ." She let the thought trail.

Thirteen, Luke thought, but didn't correct her. Susannah's name hadn't been on Daniel's original list because he hadn't known at the time. Luke decided to let Susannah contact Chloe on her own. One more victim would not make Garth Davis any less guilty. "But you might have to cut him a deal." The thought made him sick. "We can search his house, his office. Find out if he had any dealings with Granville."

"That's the kicker, Luke," she said. "And that's why I've worded these warrants so carefully. I can only include on the warrant evidence you find relevant to the rapes unless I have probable cause to link Davis to the trafficking. If you find anything in your search that implicates him, I can't use it otherwise."

"At least we'd be a step closer to finding the girls."

"That's true, *if* he has something incriminating in his home or office. You'd have to find it first. And I know I don't have to tell you this, Luke," she added gently, "but the clock is ticking. We're in a damned if we do, damned if we don't position."

"I don't want this bastard to walk, Chloe. I don't care what he knows."

"You won't know what he knows until you ask him," Germanio inserted reasonably.

Chloe adjusted her briefcase strap on her shoulder. "Also true. So let's ask, Papa."

Garth Davis waited until Luke and Chloe sat at the table before opening his mouth. "This is a ludicrous charge," he said. "I raped no one. Not now, not thirteen years ago."

Luke said nothing, simply sliding a folder across the table. It contained only four of the photos graphically implicating a teenaged Davis. Davis took one look at the pictures, drew a breath, and closed the folder, stone-faced and pale.

His attorney scowled. "Where did you get these? They're doctored. Obviously."

"They're genuine," Luke said. "These were the first I came across while sorting through the several hundred we have in our possession." He picked up one of the pictures and studied it. "You've aged well, Mayor Davis. Some men might have developed a gut in thirteen years. You're in as fine a shape now as you were then."

Davis's stare was hate-filled. "What do you want?"

"Garth," his attorney cautioned.

Davis ignored him. "I said, what do you want?"

Luke leaned forward. "To see you rot in jail for the rest of your miserable life."

"Agent Papadopoulos," Chloe murmured and Luke sat

back in his chair, still staring Davis down. "We have fifteen victims here. Fifteen counts of your client engaged in nonconsensual sexual relations with minor females, drugged and helpless. At a mandatory ten a pop, that does equate to the remainder of your natural life, Mayor Davis."

"I said," Davis said through his teeth, "what do you want?"

"Tell him what you want, Agent Papadopoulos," she said.

Luke watched Davis's face. "Tell me about Toby Granville," he said, and for an instant saw a flicker of fear. Then it was gone, replaced with contempt.

"He's dead." His smile was smug. "Kind of bad for you."

Luke's smile was congenial even though he wanted to knock the smirk off Davis's face. "One could say that. One could also say that Granville's death concentrates the venom of your surviving victims. More hate to focus on you. You're the only one left of the seven. You'll be taking the fall for the other six bastards, Mayor Davis. And I guarantee, your surviving victims will be pissed, and totally out for their pound of your flesh. Yours and yours only. Because you're not dead. Kind of bad for you."

Davis's attorney whispered something in his ear. Davis's jaw went taut, then his expression smoothed, almost as if he'd slipped into his politician skin. "Granville was the town doctor. Coughs, colds, skinned knees. That's all I know."

"Come on, Mayor Davis," Chloe said. "You know better than that."

Davis and his attorney whispered again. "We want a deal."

She shook her head. "Not till I hear what you've got."

Davis's attorney sat back. "Then he'll have no leverage."

Luke spread the four photos across the table. "I have dozens of these, with Mayor Davis smiling in every one as he rapes another girl." He met Davis's eye once more. "You have no leverage. You have only the mercy we opt to give you. And right now, the quality of my mercy is very strained indeed. So stop wasting my time."

Davis glanced at his attorney and the attorney nodded. "The club was Toby and Simon's idea. It started out as a game, but then took on a life of its own."

"Did you ever meet or talk to or see anyone other than the club members?"

"No."

"Where did these rapes occur?"

"Depended on the weather. When it was warm, outside. When it got cold, indoors."

"Where?" Luke asked again, more harshly. "I want a location."

"Different houses, depended on whose parents weren't home at the time."

"Was there ever a time when you used a house or other structure not belonging to one of the club members?" Luke pushed.

"Once. We'd had it all planned to go to Toby's house, but Jared O'Brien's mother came down with something and canceled the party she was throwing that night. That meant all our parents would be home, so we needed another spot. Toby found us one."

Luke pushed out a breath. "Where and to whom did it belong?"

"I don't know and I don't know. Toby had us all get in

the back of a van he'd borrowed from his mother's gardener. No windows and he hung a sheet up, so we couldn't see out the front. Simon sat in the back, making sure nobody peeked. And with Simon on guard, nobody peeked. He was a crazy SOB, even then."

"How long did you drive?"

Something cagey moved in Davis's eyes. "I don't remember."

Chloe's annoyed huff let Luke know she'd seen it, too. "I think you do, Mr. Davis."

"I'm ready to go back to holding." Garth turned to his attorney. "Keep looking."

Keep looking for what? *Or who.* "Must be rough, having your wife desert you that way," Luke said mildly. "Not knowing where your kids are, or if they're okay. Two boys, right? Seven and four. Awfully little to be on the run. So many dangers out there."

A muscle in Davis's unbruised cheek twitched. "You know where she is."

Luke lifted a shoulder. "I don't remember."

Davis sat down. "I want to see my wife and my children."

"I may be able to arrange that," Luke said quietly. "How far did you drive that night?"

Davis's cheeks hollowed as his eyes grew ice cold. "Less than an hour. It was a cabin. Up in the mountains."

"That's all?" Luke asked. "That's not nearly enough."

"It was a goddamned cabin, all right?" Davis snarled, eyes blazing. "It had a fireplace and a kitchen. Like every other goddamn cabin up there."

"Any knickknacks, anything to tell you whose it might have been?"

Garth's eyes grew cold once more. "Yeah. And you'll

get it when I see my kids. And not before. I don't know why that cabin's so important to you, Agent Papadopoulos, but it is and that's all the leverage I've got right now." He stood up. "I'm done."

Chloe waited until they were back in the viewing anteroom. "You mind telling me what that was all about?"

Luke sighed. "Granville's last words were 'Simon was mine. But I was another's.' Someone was mentoring him. Guiding him. Maybe even pulling his strings."

"Could be his trafficking partner," Chloe said. "Or not. Could have been the owner of that cabin. Or not." Then she smiled. "But that was a good Hail Mary, Luke. You got us some leverage without dicking around with a plea. I may still deal, but I'd rather hold that card as long as I can."

Over my dead body that asshole gets a deal, Luke thought. "Thanks. I only hope we can get Mrs. Davis back here before those missing girls are so far gone we never find them." He turned to Agent Germanio, who'd been watching the entire interview. "What was Garth doing when you picked him up?"

"He was on the phone with the airport." Germanio looked at Chloe. "Just don't ask."

Chloe rolled her eyes. "Hank, how many times do I have to tell you the phone is off limits until I get a damn warrant?"

Hank was unapologetic. "I told you not to ask."

"So who was he talking to? When you hit redial," she added in a mutter.

"A lady named Kira Laneer. She works check-in at one of the smaller airlines."

"Sounds like a stripper's name," Chloe groused. "I'll find out if Mrs. Davis and her boys boarded a flight, either yesterday or today. You keep away from Kira Laneer until I get a warrant for Davis's phone records."

"Did you get enough to beef up the warrant to cover anything we find in Davis's house linking him to trafficking?" Luke asked, unsurprised when she shook her head.

"No. But look anyway."

"I will. Pete Haywood is waiting with his search team at Granville's house for your call. As soon as that judge signs his name, call Pete and let him know he can go in. It's been almost three hours since we discovered the girls were missing."

"If they're headed out of the country, they've got a good head start," Germanio said.

"I know," Luke said grimly. "We've posted advisories with the Coast Guard and border patrol, but until we get a description, either on the partner or the girls, we got nothin'. I'm going back to the bunker and see what Ed and the crime lab have found."

Atlanta, Friday, February 2, 6:45 p.m.

Susannah stood at the hospital waiting room window, trying to block out the constant stream of activity behind her. It seemed every cop in Atlanta had heard about Daniel and had come to sit with the family. Her lips lifted, but bitterly. She was the family. *I'm it. For all the good that does either of us.*

Everyone who came wanted to tell her how wonderful her brother was, how brave. How honorable. Susannah's face hurt from the smile she'd forced while thanking each cop for their kind words. Alex had arrived a half hour ago, after visiting her stepsister, Bailey, so Susannah was letting her greet the well-wishers and retell the story of how Daniel had yet again vanquished the evil foe.

And Susannah had escaped to this window. From here she could see city lights, the movement of cars as rush hour subsided. If she pretended hard enough, she could believe she was home in New York and not here in Atlanta caught up in this nightmare.

Because after the initial adrenaline of the drive from Dutton, of the search for *thích*, reality had intruded. She'd been poked with needles, fore and aft. They'd taken her blood and shot her in the behind, just as Alex had said they would. Some kind nurse had given her scrubs to wear as her clothes had been ruined.

Luke's boss, Chase Wharton, had questioned her about the events of the afternoon. The girl was in surgery, never having regained consciousness in the helicopter.

Susannah thought that was just as well. Her heart quailed thinking of the horrors the girl had seen, endured. Her heart froze thinking of the girls Granville's partner had spirited away. What they'd be subjected to if they weren't found quickly.

She didn't need imagination to know what they'd do to those girls. She'd seen the aftermath of prostitution and rape. *Up close and very personal.* The hum of activity around her faded as her mind brought back one very personal victim. There had been blood that day, too. And a body battered beyond saving.

Darcy, I'm sorry. I was afraid. I failed you. But Susannah knew her apologies were worthless. Darcy would never hear them. Darcy would never hear anything ever again.

"Excuse me."

The soft voice yanked her back from an old nightmare

to this new one. She straightened, ready to greet yet another well-wisher. This one was a petite blonde.

"I'm Felicity Berg," she said. "I'm with the medical examiner's office."

Susannah's mouth dropped open and the woman quickly patted her arm.

"Nobody's dead," Dr. Berg said, then winced. "Well, that's not true. Lots of people are dead, actually. But not Daniel." She leaned closer. "And not the girl you saved."

"How did you know?" Susannah asked. Chase and Luke were keeping the girl's existence as closely guarded a secret as possible.

"Luke called me, told me what happened this afternoon at the bunker. We've had a busy week, with Mack O'Brien's victims, and now these. They'll start arriving soon and I won't have a chance to see you after that. I just wanted to tell you that your brother is a kind man. I'm praying for him. And for you."

Kind. No matter what Daniel had done, and what he had not, that he was a kind person was a fact Susannah could never deny. Her throat tightened and she had to swallow before the words could escape her throat. "Thank you."

Dr. Berg glanced at the noisy cops. "My mother was here for surgery last year, and the waiting room was one big party with her friends from bingo night and her clogging class." She made a face. "Let's not even discuss the friends from Chippendale night."

Susannah smiled and Dr. Berg smiled back, shyly pleased. "I escaped to the chapel," Berg confided. "It's always quiet there."

Suddenly, that seemed the natural place to be. "Thank you."

Dr. Berg squeezed her arm. "Take care. And all those loud guys? They'd go to the wall for you, just because you're Daniel's sister. If you need anything, don't hesitate to ask them. I'd say you could ask me, but . . ." She sobered. "I have a job to do."

So do I. It was why she'd boarded a plane that morning. She still needed to give her statement regarding the rapes thirteen years before. Everyone had been so focused on the events of the bunker, there hadn't been time to discuss events of the past. But before she spoke with the state's attorney, she needed to call her boss in New York. Her involvement would likely make the news. He deserved to hear about it from her and not CNN. "Your job may be the hardest of all, Dr. Berg."

"No. Luke's will be. Once we identify all the victims, he'll have to tell their families that their daughters are never coming home. The chapel's on the third floor."

Friday, February 2, 7:00 p.m.

I have to get out of here. Ashley Csorka clutched the towel around her body. She was no longer in the concrete hellhole, but this was no better. It was a house, but it was a prison just the same. There were no windows in this room. There weren't even any air vents, even if she'd been small enough to fit into one, which she wasn't. The house had to be a hundred years old. The bathtub was old and cracked, but surprisingly clean.

She was clean now, dammit. The woman had forced her to bathe. Ashley's dad had always told her if she was attacked to throw up on herself—it was one way to deter a would-be rapist. When they'd been shoved into the boat she hadn't needed to force her stomach to spew—she'd never been able to tolerate boats. Her father had always found that strange, seeing as how she was such a strong swimmer.

Dad. Ashley struggled not to cry. Her dad would be looking for her. But he'd never find her here. *I'm sorry, Daddy. I should have listened to you.* All his restrictions and rules now seemed so right. But now it was too late.

They'll whore me. I'll die here. No. Don't give up. She made herself think of her dad and little brother. They needed her. Her team needed her. A sob rose in her throat. *I'm not supposed to be here. I'm supposed to go to the Olympics.*

So find a way out. Any way out.

Someone was looking for them. She'd heard the woman talking to the crazy doctor. Someone named Vartanian had been coming with the state cops. *Please find us.*

She had first wakened from that drugged sleep chained to the wall like an animal. But she'd managed to leave something behind, scratched into the metal cot frame at some personal cost. She ran her tongue over her teeth, felt the raw edge of her broken incisor. *Please find my name. Tell my dad I'm still alive. And find me. Find all of us, before it's too late.*

Chapter Five

Luke stood at the door to the bunker, ignoring the reporters' shouts for a comment. TV news vans parked along the road and a helicopter made sweeps of the area.

Chase Wharton would be giving a press conference in less than an hour in which he'd relate all the events of the day, including the murders of the five dead teenagers and the abductions of the unidentified others. Until then, they'd maintained radio silence on everything but the capture and death of O'Brien, Granville, Mansfield, and Loomis, as well as the unidentified guard Luke had found at the far end of the bunker.

Five dead, guilty men. Five dead innocent girls. His mama would say the numbers were an omen. He wasn't entirely sure she'd be wrong.

But they'd had some luck, managing to get the helicopter bearing Daniel and the girl off to Atlanta before the first reporter arrived. They hoped to keep the surviving Jane Doe's existence under wraps until she woke and told them exactly what had happened.

After the press conference, they'd move the bodies of the five teens to the morgue and the media would be like rabid dogs. Luckily Chase was handling the media. Luke always came too close to telling them all to fuck off, and that wouldn't do.

"You can go in, Agent Papadopoulos," the officer guarding the door said. He was a state trooper, one of many called in to maintain security.

"Thanks. I'm trying to work up the energy." *More like the nerve*. They were still in there, waiting. Five dead girls. *You have to face them*. But he didn't want to.

The trooper's face creased in sympathy. "Any news on Agent Vartanian?"

"He's okay." Alex had called him with the news. *So get in there and get this done*. It had been three hours since he'd first entered the bunker. In that time they'd moved the dead men to the morgue. They'd fielded questions from reporters who still thought the capture and killing of Mack O'Brien was the day's big story. How little they knew.

Hell. Mack O'Brien was old news by now. But in a twisted way, it was O'Brien who had blown the lid off Granville and his depravity, both now and thirteen years before.

He still stood at the bunker door. *Stop procrastinating, Papa*.

Which of course he was. Every time he closed his eyes he could see Angel's dead eyes staring. He didn't want to see her again. But rarely did Luke get what he wanted. He'd opened the bunker door when his cell rang. "Papadopoulos," he said.

"I know," the familiar voice said dryly. "You said you would call. You never called."

Luke thought of his mother sitting by the phone, waiting for word on Daniel, who she considered her adopted son. "I'm sorry, Mama. I've been a little busy. Daniel's fine."

"Well, that I now know, no thanks to you," she said mildly, and he knew she wasn't angry. "Demi finally came to get the children and I drove myself to the hospital."

"You did? On the highway?" His mother was terrified of I-75 during rush hour.

"I did. On the highway," she affirmed, sounding pleased with herself. "I am sitting in the ICU waiting room with Daniel's Alex. She's strong, no? She'll be good for Daniel."

"I think so, too. So what did the doctor tell you, exactly?"

"He said Daniel is in the ICU, but stable, and you can visit him tomorrow."

"That's good. How will you get home, Mama?" She didn't drive well at night.

"Your brother will come get me when he closes up his store for the night. You do what you need to do, Luka, and do not worry about your mama. Bye-bye."

You do what you need to do. "Wait. Have you seen Daniel's sister yet?"

"Of course. I met her at her parents' funeral last week."

"No, I mean she's there, right now, in the hospital."

"She is hurt, too?" his mother asked, alarmed.

"No, Mama. She may be waiting with another patient who was also hurt today."

"But Daniel is her *brother*," she said, her ire clearly up now. "She should be *here*."

Luke thought of the expression on Susannah's face when they'd loaded Daniel into the helicopter. She'd looked stricken and conflicted. And so incredibly alone.

"It's a little more complicated than that, Mama."

"Complicated! There's nothing compli— Oh, wait." Her voice abruptly slid from outraged to approving. "Alex has told me Daniel's sister is in the chapel. That is good."

Luke's brows lifted. Somehow the thought of Susannah Vartanian in a chapel didn't quite click. "Make sure she knows about Daniel, please."

"Of course, Lukamou," she said quietly, and the endearment soothed his soul.

"Thanks, Mama." Luke straightened his shoulders and entered the bunker. A heavy quiet hung over the place, broken only by an occasional hushed voice. Shadows filled the hallways, but the rooms in which the crime lab teams worked were brighter than day, lit by CSU's big lights. Ed Randall's people knew their jobs and did them expertly.

Luke slowly reexamined each cell as he passed, the horror of looking at the five dead teenagers freezing his gut all over again. Their hands and feet had been bagged by the ME, and a body bag sat neatly folded beside each body, waiting to be used.

Look away. But he wouldn't allow himself to. He hadn't arrived in time to save them, but the dead still needed him. *Who were they? How did they get here?* Had they been abducted, or like Angel, had they been victims long before arriving in this place?

Luke found the ME tech bagging one of the girls' hands, his head bent low. In the quiet Luke heard a single muted sob that tore at his own heart.

"Malcolm?" Luke said.

Malcolm Zuckerman stilled, then placed the girl's hand carefully at her side. When he looked up, the man had tears in his eyes. "I've seen a lot of shit on this job,

Papa, but this . . . never anything like this. She can't weigh more than eighty pounds. Her hair came out in my hand," he whispered harshly. "What kind of animal could do this?"

"I don't know." Luke had seen victims just like this, way too many times, and had asked that same question, way too many times. "Have you printed them?"

"Yeah. Trey took the prints up to the lab. He's driving the five dead guys to the morgue." Malcolm's smile was twisted. "He won the toss."

"Lucky bastard. We'll run the girls' prints through NCMEC and cross our fingers that they're in the system." The National Center for Missing and Exploited Children kept the prints of missing kids in a database—when prints were available. So many parents meant to get their kids printed, but for various reasons never did. Luke had made sure his sister Demi's six kids were printed. It was the least he could do to protect his own.

"Fingers crossed. When can we take these victims out of this place?"

"Forty-five minutes. Maybe an hour. After Chase's press conference."

Malcolm snorted, back to his old demeanor. "Chase's gettin' to be a regular celebrity. This is what . . . his third press conference this week?"

"With all the press conferences on the O'Brien case, this one will be his fourth."

Malcolm shook his head. "Goddamn crazy week."

"For all of us. I'll let you know when it's okay to take the bodies."

"Luke?" It was Ed Randall, his voice muffled. "Come here, quick."

Luke found the head of the crime lab crouched next

to an empty cot frame. The mattress sat on the floor on a plastic sheet. "What is it?" Luke asked.

Ed looked up, his eyes sparkling. "A name, part of one anyway. Come see."

"A name?" Luke crouched next to where Ed was shining his flashlight. The name had been scratched into the metal, barely breaking the rusted surface. "Ashley," Luke murmured. "Ashley Os—that's all she wrote. Osborne, Oswald? It's a start."

"I think Ashley wanted to hide that she'd done it. The etching was covered with a paste of dirt mixed with something else."

"Something else?" Luke asked, his brows raised. "What else?"

"I'll know when I test it," Ed said, "but probably urine. There were definitely at least three other victims held here, Luke. Their mattresses are soaked with fresh urine."

Luke's nose had supplied him with the same information. "Can we get DNA from any of the mattresses or from this dirt paste you scraped off Ashley's name?"

"Chances are fair. That they're all postpubescent girls will make it easier."

"Why?"

"Because the DNA from urine comes from epithelial cells shed by the skin in passing, not from the urine itself. I've already sent samples back to the lab for testing." Ed rocked back on his heels. "Before you ask another question, how is Daniel?"

"He's okay. We can visit him tomorrow."

"Thank God. Did Daniel see anything this afternoon, before he was shot?"

"We'll ask him when he wakes up. What else have you

found here? Chase is going into a press conference in thirty minutes and needs an update."

"A box of prefilled IV bags, a box of syringes, an old gurney, and an IV pole."

Luke frowned. "This was some kind of hospital? That doesn't make sense. These girls were held in filth and look like they didn't have proper nutrition for weeks."

"Just telling you what I found," Ed said. "We have eight guns, seven cell phones, two homemade knives, one switchblade, and a kit of wicked-looking scalpels."

"What about the cell phones?"

"Excepting the phones belonging to Daniel, Alex, and Loomis, all the rest are throwaways. I noted all the calls on the logs, in and out."

Luke scanned Ed's notes. "Mansfield and Loomis both got texts from Mack O'Brien." He looked up. "Luring them here."

"The only call that stood out was from Granville to a number that doesn't match any of the others. He made it about a half hour after Mansfield's text from Mack O'Brien."

Luke's eyes narrowed. "He called his partner."

Ed nodded. "That's what I thought."

"This is more than I thought we'd have. I'll call Chase with the update. After that, I'm going to Granville's. Pete Haywood's doing the search of his house as soon as Chloe gets us a signed warrant. Let's meet in Chase's conference room at ten tonight."

"Agent Papadopoulos!" The urgent shout came from the door, echoing in the hall.

Both Luke and Ed ran to the entrance where the state trooper beckoned. "Urgent call from an Agent Haywood. Toby Granville's house is on fire."

Atlanta, Friday, February 2, 8:00 p.m.

Sitting alone in the quiet of the chapel, Susannah had finally sorted through her thoughts and knew what she had to do. She'd known since that morning when she'd boarded the flight in New York. She was going to testify, lend her voice to the outcry of the others. She was going to see justice done, no matter how high the cost.

The cost would be very high indeed, but the return had dropped substantially. This morning she'd been prepared to see several men sitting at the defendant's table. Now, after the dust had settled, there would be only one. Mayor Garth Davis was the sole survivor of Simon's club. Only one man would face those whose lives he'd ruined.

Only one. But the cost had not dwindled an iota. Her life, her job . . . all would be forever changed. Still, she would testify, for the fifteen other rape victims whose lives might have been spared such pain had she spoken sooner. For the five girls Luke had found dead in that bunker, and for the ones who were still missing. For the Jane Doe who'd looked up at her like she was God. *And for you, too, Susannah?*

"Yes," she murmured. "For me, too." *For my self-respect. I want my self-respect.*

"Excuse me. May I sit here?"

Susannah looked up at a tall woman with dark hair and intense eyes, carrying a purse the size of Susannah's briefcase. The chapel was empty except for the two of them. There were many other seats. Susannah opened her mouth to say no, but something about the woman's eyes stopped her. *Perhaps she needs company,* Susannah thought, and silently nodded her assent.

The scent of peaches tickled Susannah's nose as the woman sat and settled her purse on her lap. She was familiar, somehow. *I've met her before.*

"You are a Catholic?" the woman asked, surprise in her thickly accented voice.

Susannah followed the woman's gaze to the rosary she clutched in her own hands. "Yes." Much to her parents' chagrin, which had been the original point years ago. "I found the rosary up by the podium. I didn't think anyone would mind if I used it."

"You'll take one of mine," the woman pronounced, digging in her enormous purse. "I have extra." She was Eastern European. Or . . . *Greek.* Okay. Now it made sense.

"You're Mrs. Papadopoulos," Susannah murmured. Luke's mother. "You came to my parents' funeral."

"I did." She took the borrowed rosary from Susannah's hand and replaced it with her own. "You'll call me Mama Papa. Everyone does."

One side of Susannah's mouth lifted. Somehow she couldn't see Luke's mother taking no for an answer on anything. "Thank you."

"You are welcome." Mrs. Papadopoulos drew a second rosary from her purse and began to pray. "Do you not pray for your brother?" she asked abruptly.

Susannah dropped her gaze. "Of course." But she hadn't been, not really. She'd been praying for the strength to do what needed to be done. No matter what the cost.

"Daniel is out of danger," Mrs. Papadopoulos told her. "He will be all right."

Thank you. Her heart whispered the prayer her mind would not allow. "Thank you," she murmured to Luke's mother, still feeling the woman's probing stare.

"Complicated," the woman finally muttered. "So why are you really here, Susannah?"

Susannah frowned. *Nosy woman.* "Because it was quiet. I needed to think."

"About?"

She looked up, her eyes cool. "It's not really your business, Mrs. Papadopoulos."

She expected the woman to flounce away. Instead she smiled, gently. "I know. I ask anyway. Daniel is my family. You are Daniel's family." She shrugged. "So I ask."

Sudden tears burned at Susannah's eyes and again she dropped her gaze. Her throat grew thick, but the words seemed to bubble up. "I'm at a crossroads."

"Life is full of crossroads."

"I know. But this one is a big one." *It's my life, my career. My dreams.*

Mrs. Papadopoulos seemed to consider this. "So you came to church."

"No, I actually came here because it was quiet." She'd escaped here. She'd done so once before, escaping to a church after she'd committed a deed so contemptible . . .

She'd hated herself then, had been too ashamed even to confess to a priest. But still she'd escaped to a church and had somehow found the strength to go on. To do something that approximated the right thing. Today she would do the *one right thing.* This time there would be no turning back. This time she'd have her self-respect.

Luke's mother looked at the rosary in Susannah's hands. "And you found peace."

"As much as I . . ." *Deserve.* "As much as I can expect." More than peace, she'd found strength, and of the two, strength was what she needed most today.

"When first I come in, I thought you were a doctor."

Luke's mother tugged at the scrubs Susannah wore. "What happened to your clothes?"

"My clothes were messed up. One of the nurses loaned me these until I can get some more clothes."

Mrs. Papadopoulos grasped her enormous purse in both hands. "Where is your suitcase? I will get your clothes and bring them here. You stay here with Daniel."

"I don't have any more clothes. I, um, didn't bring any with me."

"You came all the way from New York City and brought not one stitch of clothing?" The woman lifted her brows and Susannah felt compelled to explain.

"I came today on an impulse."

"An impulse." She shook her head. "Complicated. So you did not plan to stay?"

"No. I'll go home . . ." Susannah frowned, suddenly unsure and uncomfortable to be so. "I'm waiting for another patient to wake up. When she's all right, I'll go home."

Mrs. Papadopoulos stood up. "Well, you cannot go anywhere dressed like that. You have not even any shoes." It was true. Susannah wore hospital slippers. "Give me your sizes. My granddaughter works in a clothing store at the mall. She is a fashionable girl. She will get pretty things." She stood up and Susannah followed suit.

"Mrs. Papadopoulos, you don't have to—" A fierce look had Susannah backpedaling. "Mama Papa, you don't have to do that."

"I know." Mrs. Papadopoulos stared down at her and Susannah could see where her son got his probing black eyes that seemed to see too much. "Daniel's Alex told me what you did for that girl, the one you saved."

Susannah frowned. "I don't think anybody is supposed to know about her."

Mrs. Papadopoulos shrugged. "Already I have forgotten her." Then she smiled kindly. "You didn't have to save her."

Susannah swallowed hard. She'd had blood drawn and cultures taken, knowing every possible test would be run to ensure her health. Still it was possible she could pay dearly for what she had done today.

But Jane Doe had paid dearly for what she had not done all those years ago. "Yes, I did. I really did."

"Then yes, I do," Mrs. Papadopoulos said, so gently that new tears sprang to Susannah's eyes. "I really do. So say thank you and allow me this good deed today."

The need to do a good deed Susannah could understand. "I'm a seven petite," she said. "Thank you." Luke's mother gave her a giant hug and left her alone in the chapel.

Susannah squared her shoulders. She'd done what she needed to do this morning when she'd found the box. She'd done what she needed to do that afternoon, when she'd saved Jane Doe from bleeding to death. Now she'd do what she needed to do tonight. Daniel's boss had given her the phone number for Chloe Hathaway, the state's attorney who'd be prosecuting the sole remaining survivor of Simon's club.

Susannah picked up her briefcase and left the haven of the chapel. She had things to do. Calls to make. Her self-respect to regain. But first she'd check on Jane Doe.

Ridgefield House, Friday, February 2, 8:00 p.m.

"They're ready," Rocky said.

Looking up from the personnel files on the computer screen, Bobby stowed the fury that bubbled up at the sight of Rocky, who'd put everything in jeopardy. *I should have gone to the river place myself.* Now Bobby had to find a new doctor to issue health certificates on each shipment and a new cop on the inside of Dutton's sheriff's office.

At least Chili had come through. Finally. The scanner was abuzz with calls for every available firehouse to converge on Granville's house. Mansfield's should be next. Who knew what incriminating evidence those two had kept in their homes?

The business would be protected. And tonight there was money to be made.

Bobby looked over the five young women standing in a row. Two were brand new pretties from the river place and they were clean again, dressed and presentable. The other three were old hands. Every one had her eyes downcast. Every one trembled, two of them shaking so hard their dangling earrings swayed. Good. *Fear was good.*

The outcome of tonight's business venture was a foregone conclusion in Bobby's mind. Haynes liked blondes with that healthy, tanned, all-American look. That look was Bobby's niche in an ever-expanding market of foreign imports. They offered their clients a chance to buy American. "Haynes will choose the blonde. Ashley, right?"

"No." The blonde shrank away while the other four slumped in relief. "Please."

Bobby smiled pleasantly. "Rocky, what is Ashley's home address?"

"Her family lives at 721 Snowbird Drive, Panama City, Florida," Rocky replied instantly. "Her mother died two years ago and her father works the night shift. Now that she's 'run away,' her father's hired a sitter to stay with her

brother while he's at work. Her brother sometimes sneaks
out at night to hang at the—"

"That's good enough," Bobby said when the blonde
began to cry. "I know everything about your family,
Ashley. One misstep, one dissatisfied client, and someone in your house will die. Painfully. You're the one who
wanted adventure and now you have it. So stop crying.
My clients want smiles. Rocky, get them out of here. I
have work to do."

Bobby reopened the personnel files and was deep into
review of a very promising medical candidate when the
throwaway cell phone trilled. This was the number given
to contacts and informers, those who could be convinced
to become Bobby's personnel because they'd done some
very naughty things they didn't want made public.

Information was power. Bobby liked power. The incoming number had an Atlanta area code. "Yes?"

"You said to call if anything happened at the hospital. I
have information."

It took Bobby a few moments to place the voice. *Oh,
yes.* Jennifer Ohman, the ICU nurse with the drug problem. Informants usually had a drug problem. Or a gam-
bling problem. Or a sex problem. Whatever the secret
addiction, the result was the same.

"Well, go ahead. I don't have all day."

"Two patients were airlifted from Dutton. Special
Agent Daniel Vartanian was one."

Bobby abruptly straightened. That Vartanian had been
shot had been on the police scanner, along with the deaths
of Loomis, Mansfield, Granville, and Mack O'Brien, plus
the guard they hadn't identified. Chatter regarding any
other dead bodies the police might have found in the bunker was noticeably absent. "Who was the second?"

"She's a Jane Doe, sixteen or seventeen. She was critical but survived surgery."

Bobby slowly stood, the swirling, bubbling fury within becoming flat dread. "And?"

"She's stable. They're keeping her secret, with a guard posted at her door, 24/7."

Bobby drew a very deep breath. Rocky had been very clear that all the girls left behind were dead. So either this girl was a modern-day Lazarus, or Rocky had lied. Either way, Rocky had made a serious miscalculation. "I see."

"There's more. Two others came in by ambulance, a man and a woman. Bailey Crighton was one. She's the woman who's been missing for a week."

"I know who she is." *Granville, you asshole. Rocky, you idiot.* "And the man?"

"Some army chaplain. Beasley. No, Beardsley. That's it. They're both in stable condition. That's all I know." The nurse hesitated. "So now we're even, right?"

Now there were three people to neutralize and one lone nurse would not be sufficient, but the nurse would still be a valuable asset. "No, I'm afraid it doesn't work that way. I want the girl dead. Poison her, smother her, I don't care. I do not want her to wake up. Do you understand?"

"But . . . *No.* I won't do that."

That's what they all said, initially. Some had to be pushed harder than others, but in the end the outcome was the same. Every one did as they were told. "Yes, you will."

"But I *can't.*" The nurse sounded horrified. They all said that, too.

"Let's see . . ." The file on the nurse was thorough. Bobby's cop on the inside of Atlanta PD had done well, as usual. "You live with your sister. Your son lives with his father, because you lost custody. You let your husband have your son if he wouldn't expose your little problem. How considerate of him. You can't watch them all the time, dear."

"I'll . . . I'll go to the police," the nurse said, desperation pushing the horror aside.

"And tell them what? That you were caught with drugs you stole from your hospital with intent to both use and sell, but my cop let you go and now some evil villain is blackmailing you? How long do you think you'll keep your job when the truth comes out? The day my cop let you go with a warning, you belonged to me. You'll kill the girl tonight or by this time tomorrow one person in your family will be dead. For every day you delay, another person in your family will die. Now go do what you're told."

Bobby hung up, then placed another call. "Paul, it's me."

There was a beat of silence, then a low whistle. "Hell of a mess you got there."

"Really?" Bobby drawled, annoyed. "I had no idea. Look, I need you. Usual pay, usual way." Paul was a useful man—a no-nonsense cop with a wide, reliable information network and absolutely no moral compass other than unwavering loyalty to the highest bidder. "I want to know who in GBI is working the Granville case by midnight, down to the lowest admin assistant."

"Or the guy emptying the trash. Yeah, I got it."

"Good. I want to know which local departments are supporting them and if any of the locals are deep enough to be an ear. I want to know their steps—"

"Before they take them," Paul finished. "Got that, too. Is that all?"

Bobby studied the photo Charles had left that afternoon,

in an oh-so-clever parting jab. In it a stone-faced Susannah Vartanian stood next to her brother at their parents' funeral. Dealing with Susannah would have to wait for now, thanks to Rocky's blunder. But when all the threats to the business were neutralized, it would be Susannah's turn.

"For now, but stay ready. I'll be waiting for your call. Don't be late."

"Have I ever been?" And not waiting for an answer, Paul was gone.

"Rocky! Come here."

Rocky's footsteps thundered down the stairs. "What's wrong?"

"Everything. I have some extra duty for you. It's time to start fixing your mess."

Chapter Six

Luke bolted from his car to where Agent Pete Haywood stood grimly watching Dr. Toby Granville's house—and every speck of evidence inside it—burn. The girls could be anywhere and any links to Granville's partner were going up in smoke.

"What the goddamn hell happened here?" Luke demanded, but Pete didn't respond. He didn't move at all, just kept watching the flames as if hypnotized. *"Pete."* Luke grabbed his arm and had to leap back when Pete whirled, fists clenched at his sides.

Luke backed up a step, hands out. "Whoa, Pete. It's just me." But it was then Luke saw the devastation in Pete's dark eyes and the bandage that ran from Pete's temple halfway around his shiny, bald, ebony head. "What the *hell* happened?"

Pete shook his head. "I can't hear you," he bellowed. "My ears are still ringing. It was a bomb, Luke. Tossed three of us ten feet like we were made of balsa wood."

Pete Haywood was six-four, 250 pounds. Luke couldn't imagine the sheer force it had taken to toss a man his size. Blood was already soaking through Pete's bandage. "You need some stitches," Luke yelled.

"The medics got others to fix first. A shard of flying

metal hit Zach Granger." Pete swallowed. "Might have lost his eye. Chopper's on its way to take him to the hospital."

It just kept getting worse. "Where's the fire investigator?" Luke shouted.

"Not here yet. The local fire chief is standing over there by the truck."

Luke's brows shot up when he saw the man standing next to the fire chief. "Corchran's here, too?"

"Got here about fifteen minutes after our call went out."

Luke led Pete to his car, away from prying ears. "Sit down and tell me what happened, and you don't need to yell. I can hear you just fine."

Wearily, Pete sank sideways onto the passenger seat. "We were waiting for Chloe's call that the warrant was signed. Nobody had gone in or out since we arrived. Chloe called at 7:45 and we went in. I opened the door and all hell broke loose. Literally."

Luke frowned. "What about Mansfield's house?"

"Nancy Dykstra's waiting with her team at Mansfield's. I called her as soon as I picked myself off the ground, told her not to go in. They're waiting for the bomb squad to make sure our little pyro didn't rig both houses to blow."

"Good thinking. Have you seen Granville's wife?"

"If she was in the house, she wouldn't come out when we instructed her to. Zach and the rest of the team got here at 5:15 and had all the exits covered."

"Okay. So whoever planted the bomb did so between 1:38 and 5:15."

Pete frowned. "Why 1:38?"

"That's when Granville placed a call to the person we think was his partner. The news that Granville was dead hadn't hit the media by 5:15. Only Granville's partner would have known he didn't leave the bunker with the rest of them."

"And the partner would be afraid Granville would talk if he got caught or that he'd left incriminating evidence in the house. So he blew it up. What now?"

"Now you get that hard head of yours stitched up. Let me take it from here. We're meeting at Chase's at ten. If you can, join us. If not, try to call in." With a reassuring squeeze to Pete's shoulder, Luke started walking toward Corchran and the fire chief.

The two men met him halfway. "I came as soon as I heard the first calls for fire and rescue over the radio," Corchran said.

"Thanks," Luke said to Corchran. "I appreciate it." He turned to the fire chief. "I'm Agent Papadopoulos, GBI."

"Chief Trumbell. We're fighting this from the outside. Given the explosions, I haven't sent my men inside. I didn't want them stumbling across any other wires."

"So that's how this bomb was triggered?" Luke asked. "Wires?"

"Your arson guys will need to confirm it, but I saw wire tied to the front door's inside doorknob, about six or seven inches left hanging. Looks like a real simple setup. Open the door, wire yanks, bomb detonates. This fire was well in progress by the time we arrived. I'd bet your investigator finds the house doused with some kind of accelerant."

"Got it. Look, Granville has a wife. We don't think she was in the house."

"That's what Haywood said." Trumbell looked over his shoulder at the blaze. "If she's in there . . . I can't risk sending anybody in after her."

As if to punctuate his words, there was a giant crash and everyone instinctively ducked except Trumbell, who ran toward the house, radio in hand, yelling orders for his men to back away.

"I'd say one of the ceilings collapsed," Corchran said.

And any links to Granville's partner with it. "Goddammit," Luke said quietly.

Corchran pointed down the street. "The vultures caught the scent."

Two TV news vans were pulling up. "The cherry on top," Luke muttered. "Hey, thanks for coming out tonight. I know Dutton is not your responsibility."

Corchran looked uncomfortable. "No it's not, but their police force is in . . . disarray."

"Their sheriff and lead deputy are dead, so I'd say that's an understatement."

"If you need support, call, but I don't want to be stepping on any jurisdictional toes."

"Thanks. I expect the governor is appointing a new sheriff as we speak, so hopefully we'll get some order restored in Dutton. Now I need to set the crime scene boundary."

Corchran sent a scathing look toward the TV vans. "Make sure it's real far back."

"You can bet on that."

Luke pushed the reporters back, citing concern for their personal safety as well as the safety of the emergency personnel. He endured the occasional muffled personal epithet, proud he hadn't told one reporter to fuck himself. He'd posted a state trooper patrol to maintain the crime scene line when his cell buzzed in his pocket.

He frowned at the 917 area code on his caller ID, then remembered it was Susannah's Manhattan cell number. *Don't let the girl be dead.* He looked at Granville's ruined house. *She may be all we have left.* "Susannah, what can I do for you?"

"The girl is awake. She can't speak, but she's awake."

Thank you. "I'll be there as soon as I can."

Ridgefield House, Friday, February 2, 8:45 p.m.

"Time to party, Ashley," Rocky said, unlocking her door. "Mr. Haynes is—"

Rocky stopped in Ashley's doorway, shock momentarily robbing her of thought. Then the rage came, blistering and hot, and she rushed into the room to where Ashley lay on the floor, curled in a fetal ball.

"What the fuck have you done?" Rocky snarled, grabbing Ashley by the hair she had left. "Goddammit, what have you done?"

Ashley's lip was bloody where she'd bitten it clean through. Her scalp was red, with at least eight bald patches the size of silver dollars visible along the top of her head. The bitch had pulled her own hair out by the roots.

Ashley's eyes were wet with tears, but full of defiance. "He wanted a blonde. Does he want me now?"

Rocky slapped her hard, knocking her to the floor.

"What the hell are you . . . ?" Bobby stopped. "Holy shit."

Rocky stared down at the bald spots, breathing hard. "She pulled her own hair out. Haynes won't want her now."

"Then he'll just have to take one of the others."

Bobby was not pleased. Which meant Rocky would pay the price. "You want me to give her to one of the guards?"

Bobby studied the girl, eyes narrowed. "Not yet. I don't

want her bruised, just compliant. Put her in the hole. No food, no water. A few days down there will knock some of the defiance out of her. When you bring her out, shave her head. She can wear a wig. Hell, all the rock stars are doing it, why not our girls? And, Rocky, find me some blondes fast. I promised Haynes one tonight, so I'll have to give him a discount on whoever he does choose. I want to be able to deliver what he wants next time. A quarter of our new business comes through him."

Rocky thought of the girls she'd been chatting online. "I have two, maybe three I can pull in now," she said.

"And they're blond?"

She nodded. "I've checked them out myself. But who's going to pick them up? That was Mansfield's job."

"You get them ready. I'll arrange for pick-up. Get this one out of my sight before I change my mind and beat the shit out of her myself. And don't be late for your meeting. I've given you a chance to earn your way back. Don't fuck it up."

Rocky bit the inside of her cheek. She'd known better than to argue over the "extra duty" Bobby had assigned. Didn't mean she had to like it, though. She checked her watch. She had to get this girl in the hole or she'd miss the shift change at the hospital.

Atlanta, Friday, February 2, 9:15 p.m.

"Susannah."

Susannah lifted her eyes to Luke's reflection in the glass that separated her from Jane Doe's ICU bed. He looked tired. "They let me see her for a few minutes."

"Was she lucid?"

"I think so. She recognized me, squeezed my fingers. Her eyes are closed now, but she may be awake."

"She's still got a breathing tube."

"Like I said on the phone, she can't speak. The doctor said she has shock lung."

Luke winced. "Oh, shit."

"You know what that is?"

"Yeah. My brother Leo was a Marine and he had it from a battle injury. More than three broken ribs on one side of the body and the lung collapses." His dark brows furrowed. "Did I do that when I carried her?"

His concern touched her heart. "I don't think so. She had bruising all over her rib cage. A couple that the doctor said looked like the toe of a boot. He said she might be intubated for another few days."

"Well, I've interviewed witnesses with breathing tubes before. If she's lucid we'll use a letter board and she can blink. But I have to find out what she knows."

He took a step closer until he stood right behind her, the heat from his body warming her skin, making her shiver. He leaned over her shoulder to peer through the glass and if she turned her head there would be a scant inch between her nose and his stubbled cheek. This afternoon in his car, before everything had gone to hell, he'd smelled like cedar. Now, he smelled like stale smoke. She kept her eyes locked straight ahead.

"She looks younger than she did this afternoon," he murmured.

"She was covered in blood this afternoon. She's cleaner now. What burned down?"

He turned his head and she could feel his stare. "Granville's house."

Susannah closed her eyes. "Dammit."

"That's what I said." He stepped back and she shivered again, chilled without his heat. "I'm going to try to talk to her." He held out a shopping bag. "This is for you."

There were clothes in the bag and Susannah took them, looking up at him with a puzzled frown. "How did you get these?"

His mouth quirked slightly. "We had an informal family reunion in the lobby. My mother was leaving and my brother and niece had come to pick her up. Leo had picked Stacie up from her job at the mall where she bought your things. Leo's going to drive Mama home and Stacie's going to drive Mama's car home because last time Mama drove at night she got stopped by a cop for doing thirty in a sixty-five zone." He shrugged. "Cops are happy, Mama's happy. So it's all good."

Susannah felt rather sorry for any cop having to give Mrs. Papadopoulos a traffic ticket. "Um, thank you. I'll write your niece a check."

He nodded once, then pushed past her into the small ICU room.

The nurse stood on the other side of the girl's bed. "Two minutes. That's all."

"Yes, ma'am. Hey, honey," Luke said, his voice smooth. "Are you awake?"

Jane Doe's eyelids fluttered, but she didn't open her eyes. He pulled up a chair and sat. "Do you remember me? I'm Agent Papadopoulos. I was with Susannah Vartanian this afternoon when we found you."

Jane Doe stirred and the number on the blood pressure monitor began to rise.

Susannah saw his gaze flick to the monitor before returning to the girl's face. "I'm not going to hurt you, honey," he said. "But I need your help."

The girl's pulse jumped, sending another monitor beeping. She pitched her head, growing agitated, and Luke looked at Susannah with concern as the nurse looked as if she'd throw them out right then.

"I'm here, too," Susannah said softly. She set the shopping bag on the floor and brushed her knuckles softly over the girl's cheek. "Don't be afraid."

Jane Doe's blood pressure began to decrease and Luke stood up. "You sit and I'll wait on the other side of the glass. Talk to her. You know what I want to know. I'll make you a letter chart."

"Okay." Susannah leaned close, covering the girl's hand with her own. "Hey, you're all right. You're safe. Nobody's gonna hurt you anymore. But we need your help. The other girls, they weren't as lucky as you. Some of them have been taken away and we need to find them. We need your help."

Her eyes opened, her expression one of helpless fear and dazed awareness.

"I know," Susannah soothed. "You're afraid and feel powerless. I know what that feels like and it totally sucks. But you can help us win. You can get back at the bastards who did this to you. Help me. What's your name?"

She took the piece of paper Luke handed through the doorway. On it was the alphabet and she held it up in front of Jane Doe's face, running her finger across each letter slowly. "Blink when I get there."

Susannah kept her eyes fixed on the girl's face, feeling a surge of satisfaction when the girl blinked. "M? Your name starts with M? Blink twice for yes."

The girl blinked twice, some of the fear in her eyes was replaced with determination.

"Next letter then."

"I'm sorry, your two minutes are more than up," the nurse said.

"But—" Luke tried.

The nurse shook her head. "This patient is critical. If you want any information, you need to let her rest."

Luke's jaw tightened. "With all due respect, the lives of maybe five girls are at stake."

The nurse's chin lifted. "With all due respect, the life of this girl is at stake. You can come back tomorrow."

Susannah could see the fury snapping in Luke's eyes from where she sat, but he kept his cool. "One more yes/no question," he said. "Please?"

The nurse blew out a breath. "One."

"Thank you. Susannah, ask if she knows an Ashley."

Susannah leaned in close again. "Do you know a girl named Ashley? Blink twice if you do." The girl blinked twice, very deliberately. "Yeah. She does."

He nodded once. "Then we're on the right track."

Susannah caressed the girl's face, swearing the brown eyes that stared up at her snapped in frustration. "I know. I'll be back tomorrow. Don't be afraid. There's a guard right outside and he won't let anyone in that's not supposed to be here. Sleep now. You're safe."

Luke retrieved her shopping bag from the floor. "I'll take you to Daniel's house," he said when they were outside of ICU.

Susannah shook her head. "No, that's okay. I have a hotel. Please," she said when he opened his mouth to protest. "I appreciate your concern, but . . . this isn't your concern." She smiled as she said it, trying to soften her words.

He looked as if he wanted to argue, but he nodded. "Fine. Do you want to change?"

"I'll wait. I'm . . . I want to clean up a little first."

"Fine," he said again and she knew it was anything but. "I'll take you to your hotel, but first I want to check on Daniel."

She followed him across the ICU floor because she knew she'd feel ashamed if she did not. He entered the room while she stood at the doorway, watching Daniel's big chest rise and fall, still shallowly. He'd nearly died today. *And I would have been alone.*

Which was ridiculous, because she'd been alone for the past eleven years, ever since he'd walked out of their house, her life, never looking back. But deep down, she'd always known she was never truly alone. Today, she almost had been.

"How is he?" Luke murmured to Alex, who'd been keeping vigil by Daniel's side.

"Better," Alex said. "They had to sedate him. He started thrashing, trying to get out of bed. He nearly pulled out all his tubes. But he's only here for observation now that the breathing tube's been removed. They'll let him go to the floor tomorrow." She turned, looked over her shoulder with a tired smile. "Susannah. How are you?"

"I'm fine." And if her words were abrupt, Alex Fallon didn't seem to notice.

"Good. I wouldn't care to live through another day like today. I have the keys to Daniel's house. I know he'd want you to be comfortable there."

"I'm going to a hotel." She forced her lips to curve. "But thank you."

Alex's brow furrowed slightly, but she nodded. "Get some rest. I'll watch over him."

You do that, Susannah thought, unwilling to deal

with the tightness in her throat. "And the girl," she murmured.

"And the girl. Don't worry. Susannah, tomorrow will be better."

But Susannah knew differently. She knew what lay ahead, what needed to be done. Tomorrow would be, to borrow Luke's word, difficult. Very difficult. "Yes. Better," she said quietly, because it was the socially appropriate response.

Luke touched her arm, the briefest of contact, and when she looked up, it was understanding she saw in his dark eyes and not the criticism she'd expected. "Let's go," he said. "I'll drop you off at your hotel on my way back to the office."

Ridgefield House, Georgia, Friday, February 2, 9:45 p.m.

Bobby hung up the phone, satisfied. It was wise to have one's eggs in multiple baskets. Luckily there were several hospital employees on the potential personnel list. One of them had been dispatched to take care of Captain Ryan Beardsley and Bailey Crighton. Bailey's demise would please Bobby on a number of levels.

It would have been more pleasing to kill Bailey myself. But it was best to keep personal feelings out of such things. Passion led to mistakes and enough mistakes had been made for one day.

In a matter of hours all the loose threads would be snipped and business could return to normal. A car door slammed outside. Speaking of which . . .

Haynes was here. It was time to make some money.

Atlanta, Friday, February 2, 9:50 p.m.

"Luke, these are for you." Leigh Smithson, Chase's clerk, put a stack of folders on the conference room table. "Dr. Berg sent these over. And Latent identified your dead guard. I pulled his priors for you."

"So who's our mystery man?" Chase asked, putting two cups of coffee on the table.

"Jesse Hogan," Luke read. "Assault, B&E. Beardsley did the world a favor."

"He's awake," Leigh said. "Captain Beardsley, that is. His father called a few minutes ago. Beardsley says you can come interview him any time. I gave him your cell."

"I'll go back over to the hospital when we're done. Anything from Missing Children?"

Leigh shook her head. "No. They're supposed to call you or Chase directly if they find any matches to the prints of the victims. But they said it might take a while. Most of the prints were taken at schools and shopping malls when the kids were smaller and if they were younger than four or five . . ."

"Their prints can change," Luke said. "We're crossing our fingers. What about missing girls named Ashley O-s-something?" He'd phoned her with the partial name from the cot frame as he'd driven to the fire scene.

"They're searching. I also sent requests to missing persons departments in the surrounding states."

"Thanks, Leigh."

She turned for the door. "I'll stay until your meeting is over, then I'm going to call it a night. I'll be back tomorrow and three stenos just came on shift, answering calls. The phone's been ringing off the hook since the press conference."

"We expected that," Chase said. "I've assigned more admin coverage for tomorrow. We'll need to evaluate every call that comes in."

Leigh tilted her head, the argument between two people growing steadily louder—one deep booming voice and one quieter, more melodious. "Pete and Nancy are back."

She left as the two came in, Pete giving Nancy an exaggerated "after you" gesture. "He's a stubborn fool," Nancy declared. "The man has nine stitches in that cueball of his and he won't go home."

Pete rolled his eyes. "I got worse playin' football. Chase, tell this woman to hush."

Chase sighed. Pete and Nancy bickered like old married people. "What did the doctor say, Pete?"

"That I'm cleared for duty," Pete said, disgruntled. "I even got a goddamned note."

Chase shrugged. "Sorry, Nancy. Doctor trumps."

Pete sat down, satisfied, and Luke leaned sideways to mumble, "Did you really get worse playing football?"

"Hell no," Pete mumbled back. "And this hurts like a bitch. But I'm not telling her."

"Smart." Luke was saved from Nancy's ire by the appearance of Ed, Nate Dyer, and ASA Chloe Hathaway.

Chase seemed surprised. "Chloe. Didn't expect you."

Chloe sat, crossing her long legs. Luke thought the move was habit on her part, but he was certain she knew the stir it created. "My boss says I'm part of the team now. He wants to be sure every piece of evidence we bring in will stand up in court."

"We want that, too," Luke said, thinking of the five dead, the five missing, and the girl in the hospital bed across town. "Does everyone know Nate?"

Nate was already studying the autopsy photos and had

pulled Angel's photo aside. He looked up and nodded at the group. "Nate Dyer, ICAC."

Chloe frowned. "ICAC? Why is Internet Crimes Against Children involved?"

Luke tapped the photo of Angel that Nate had set aside. "This one is one we've seen before. Hold on to the question, Chloe. We'll get there. We're all here now. Let's get started."

"I'll start," Chase said. "The brass has been informed, all the way up through the governor. I don't need to tell you all that they will be following every move we make. I'll handle the administrative floor and the press. Tonight I informed the media that Mack O'Brien had been killed and broke the news of the thirteen-year-old rapes. As of seven p.m. tonight, all the victims had been informed of the status of the investigation. Whether any or all choose to testify will be between the victims and the DA's office."

"I've already received calls from six of the victims on your list, Chase." She lifted a brow. "And a voicemail tonight from a victim who wasn't on your list."

Susannah. Luke opened his mouth and closed it. That was between Susannah and Chloe now. But she'd kept her promise. A stirring of pride eased a little of the tightness in his chest. *Good for you, Susannah.*

Chase gave Luke a short nod, acknowledging he, too, understood and would keep Susannah's name out of it until she chose to put it in. "Of course when we described the scene at the bunker, there was a furor of questions. We answered what we could, but it was pretty clear we didn't have a lot of information to give them. Pandora's box is officially open, people. Be watchful for the press. We'll control what is communicated from my office. Do not talk to any reporters."

"Aw, man," Ed whined. "And that's my favorite thing."

Chase smiled briefly, as Ed had intended. "Your turn, Ed. What have you found?"

Ed's forced levity disappeared. "Hell on earth, Chase. The filth, the stench . . . It's indescribable. We've gathered samples of blood and other body fluids from every cell. From the state of the cots and waste left behind in the cells, we think there were five more girls taken. The waste in the twelfth cell was not as recent—we don't think it was occupied, but we took samples just in case. We also found IV bags and syringes—some of them still have legible production lot codes. We're tracing those back to the manufacturer. The manufacturer will know where their products were initially shipped. After that, we're going to have to dig to trace how they ended up in that bunker."

"Good," Chase said. "What about the victims?"

"This one we've seen before," Nate Dyer said, holding up Angel's picture. "On a Web site Luke and I shut down eight months ago. We'll send the photo to our partners worldwide. Maybe they've seen either Angel or the other two girls who were with her on the Web site." He looked at Luke. "We need to go back over our records, see if there is anything we missed the first time."

Luke nodded heavily. "I know. And that was my case. I know it better than anyone. I'll be in tomorrow to look through the old files."

"I'll work on it some tonight," Nate said, then sighed. "Either way, it'll be a bitch."

Luke knew what he meant, because the same thoughts had been flying around his own mind. What if he found something he had missed the second time around? That meant he might have helped Angel and the others then.

What if he didn't find anything new? They'd be stuck at square one. A man could drive himself crazy.

Luke straightened his spine. "So far we have two leads on the female victims in the bunker. Angel and the scratched name, Ashley O-s-something."

"I've got my team looking at that cot frame more closely," Ed said. "Under better lighting, we may be able to see more. I did find what she used to scratch her name, though." He held out a plastic bag. "A chip of broken tooth."

Luke's brows lifted. "Resourceful girl."

"Let's hope she stays that way," Chase said. "Do we have anything on the girl who got away? What's her name? Where is she from?"

"Her first name starts with M," Luke said. "That's all we were able to get. She'd just woken up from surgery and has a breathing tube, so she can't talk. We submitted her prints and photo to NCMEC. So far, no hits, but it's only been a few hours. Worst case, we wait until tomorrow to get the rest of her name."

"Good," Chase said. "Pete, what did the fire investigator say?"

"He's still sifting through the wreckage, but he found traces of accelerant. He hadn't found the detonator as of about twenty minutes ago. When he does, he'll call me."

"How's Zach Granger?" Luke asked, and was relieved when Pete smiled.

"They saved his eye. He may still have some vision loss. We won't know for a few days. The rest of the team has some cuts and bruises, but we're all cleared for duty."

"At least we got some good news," Chase said. "Nancy?"

"The bomb squad had just arrived at Mansfield's when I got here," Nancy said. "If they rigged both houses to blow, we'll have the device to study. Hopefully our arsonist left some kind of signature. If we find the arsonist, we just follow the money."

Chase held up his crossed fingers and turned to Chloe. "And you?"

"I've got the warrant in process for Garth Davis's phone records. I can hold him till Monday, tops. I'll ask for remand, but I'm not holding my breath."

"I'll put somebody on Davis the minute he's released," Chase promised.

"Not Germanio," Chloe said darkly. "Chase, y'gotta stop your guys from picking up the phone and hitting redial unless they have a phone warrant."

Chase winced. "Again?"

"Yeah. You have to make him stop. Especially the phones in Davis's office. Davis is a lawyer. He could have been talking to a client and we'd be hit with a dismissal based on violation of his Sixth Amendment rights. I'm serious, Chase. Fix this."

"I will. You have my word, Chloe."

"Okay." She sighed. "I checked out the name Germanio gave me. Kira Laneer."

"Was she a stripper?" Luke asked dryly.

"Not in recent years, but I'm still betting she was in her misspent youth. She's thirty-four, makes about twenty-five grand a year, and drives a brand new Mercedes. Her car loan was cosigned by Garth Davis. The loan came from Davis Bank in Dutton at well below the going interest rate. She might know something."

"Does she know where Garth's wife went?" Luke asked. "Because right now that's what I want to know. I checked the airlines and there were no tickets sold to Davis's wife or kids and their minivan isn't in their garage, so I'm assuming wherever she went, she drove there. She contacted Davis's sister once, maybe she will again. I'll find out."

"Why is Garth Davis's wife so important?" Ed asked.

"Because Davis knows about a cabin Granville had access to thirteen years ago," Luke said. "They used it for one of the rapes when they had to find a new location."

Ed's brows went up. "And why is the cabin so important?"

"Because Granville had a mentor thirteen years ago. Someone who was teaching him to manipulate others, to control their responses. The cabin's owner could be a link to the mentor. Davis won't give up that information until he sees his kids."

"You think this mentor is his partner?" Nancy asked.

"Maybe." Luke shrugged. "Either way, it's the best we've got right now."

"What about Granville's wife?" Pete asked. "She's still in the wind."

"I checked the airports for her, too, but she hasn't taken any planes," Luke said. "Chase, let's get photos of Mrs. Granville to all the bus stations."

"Daniel grew up in Dutton," Chloe said. "Maybe he knows about this cabin."

"He's still unconscious, isn't he?" Pete asked.

"Sedated actually. But his sister might know," Luke said. "I'll ask her."

Chase nodded. "Sounds like we have a plan. Let's—"

"Wait," Ed said. "What about Mack O'Brien?"

Chase frowned. "He's dead. Daniel killed him."

Luke drew a breath. "Oh my God, you're right, Ed. Remember, Mack O'Brien found out about the rape club because he stole his brother's journals from Jared's widow.

We never found where Mack hid the journals. Jared's widow told Daniel that he wrote about each rape in detail. What if he also wrote about the one night they went to the cabin? What if those journals have the same information Garth Davis refuses to tell us?"

Chase smiled, a genuine smile for the first time all night. "Find them." He pointed to Pete. "You find Davis's wife, just in case we don't find those journals. She had to have left a trail. Nancy, you get back to Mansfield's and as soon as the bomb squad disables the detonator, you search that house from top to bottom. Ed, keep searching the bunker. Nate, you'd be helping us a lot if you could track Angel."

"And I'll interview Beardsley again," Luke said. "He might remember something now that he's had a chance to recover."

"Then let's go. Be back here tomorrow at eight a.m. And be careful."

Chapter Seven

Atlanta, Friday, February 2, 10:15 p.m.

That's her, Rocky thought, relieved she'd come a little early. The shift didn't change for a while. Nursey must have left early and her step was brisk as she walked toward her car. Not the step of a woman who'd just committed her first murder and not a good sign at all. Rocky was now responsible for making sure this nurse killed the girl. It was a test, she knew. If she succeeded, she'd earn her way back into Bobby's good graces.

She pulled next to the nurse and slowed to match the woman's pace. "Excuse me."

"Not interested," the nurse snapped.

"Yes, you are. Bobby sent me."

The nurse stopped abruptly and turned, fear in her eyes. But no guilt. Rocky sighed. "You didn't do it, did you?"

The nurse stiffened. "Not exactly."

"What does that mean, not exactly?"

Desperate fury flared in the woman's eyes. "It means I didn't kill her," she hissed.

"Get in." Rocky drew the pistol from her pocket and pointed it. "Draw a breath to scream and it will be your last," she said calmly, even though her heart was pounding. *Please get in. Please don't make me shoot.* The nurse obeyed, shaking visibly, and Rocky let herself breathe.

"Are you going to kill me?" the woman whispered hoarsely.

"Well, that depends. Start by telling me exactly what 'not exactly' means."

The nurse stared straight ahead. "I couldn't do it. I couldn't kill her. But I made sure she wouldn't talk to anyone else."

"Else? What do you mean, anyone *else*?" Shit.

"She had two visitors tonight. A man and a woman."

Bailey and Beardsley. *Damn that Granville.* Rocky had had no idea he'd brought them to the bunker until Bobby'd confronted her with it—and her lie. *You said they were dead. You said you were sure. You lied to me. This girl could ruin us all.*

She'd thought fast, but her lie that she *had* checked but simply missed the girl's thready pulse hadn't been good enough. Rocky resisted the urge to waggle her jaw. Bobby had hit her hard. Her jaw wasn't broken, but it throbbed like a bitch.

Still, she knew she'd hurt a lot more if the girl talked. The damage would be worse depending on which girl had escaped. Angel had been there the longest, but Monica was the boldest. *Don't let it have been Monica.* "Who were the visitors?"

"He was GBI. Special Agent Papa-something. Papadopoulos. The woman was the one who found her, down at that bunker on the river. Her brother is also in ICU."

Rocky blinked. "Susannah Vartanian found the girl on the side of the road?"

Wonderful. It was, actually. Rocky didn't know why, but Bobby hated Susannah Vartanian. There was a photo of the judge's daughter next to Bobby's computer with a red X penned through her face. Dealing with Susannah might be a way to regain favor. At a minimum the guaranteed wrath that would be generated when Rocky shared this tidbit of news might take some of the heat off herself.

"Did the girl say anything to Susannah?"

"I heard that she only got a few words out when they first found her, that someone had 'killed them all.' I assumed this meant the girls they found in the bunker." The nurse glanced nervously from the corner of her eye. "I heard it on the news."

She'd seen Granville kill the others. *This was very bad.* "And later, in the hospital? What did she say then?"

"Nothing. She still has her breathing tube in. They used a letter board and found out her name started with M. But their time was up and they had to leave."

Monica. This was going from bad to worse. *I should have shoved her in the boat. I should have made room. I should never have left her behind.* "What else?"

"The GBI agent asked her if she knew a girl named Ashley and she blinked 'yes.'"

Ashley? How the hell had Papadopoulos known about Ashley? What more did he know? She kept her voice level. "So how did you keep her from saying any more?"

The nurse sighed out a breath. "I put a paralytic in her IV bag. When she wakes up, she won't be able to open her eyes, blink, move, or say anything."

"How long will it last?"

"About eight hours."

"And what had you planned to do then?" Rocky asked sharply, then laughed bitterly. "You hadn't planned to do anything, had you? You were going to run."

The nurse looked straight ahead, her throat working. "I can't kill her. You have to understand. GBI posted a guard outside the ICU, 24/7. He checks every ID. The minute she stops breathing alarms will go off. They'll catch me." Her jaw cocked slightly. "And when they do, what should I tell them? Your description? What kind of car you drive? Your name, maybe? I don't think you want that, either."

Panic mixed with rage. "I should kill you right now."

The nurse's lips curved. "And in eight hours your Jane Doe's paralytic will wear off and she'll sing like a bird. What will she tell the cops? Nothing about me. She didn't see me." Her head turned slightly. "Did she see you?"

Maybe. Dammit, yes. In that last moment at the bunker. She'd stared at her face, memorizing every feature. The girl had to die, before she spoke to anyone. *And Bobby can't find out I was so damn careless.* "How long before she's out of ICU?"

Satisfaction and relief flickered in the nurse's eyes. "She'll stay in ICU until the breathing tube is removed and they won't do that until they're certain she can breathe on her own. Whoever beat her up did too good a job. She's got four broken ribs on her right side. Her lung is collapsed. She'll be in the hospital for several days, at least."

Rocky ground her teeth. "How long before she's out of ICU?" she repeated.

"I don't know. If she weren't paralyzed, maybe in twenty-four or forty-eight hours."

"How long can you keep her paralyzed?"

"Not long, a day or two, max. The staff will start to suspect and someone will order an EEG. The paralytic will show up." Her chin lifted. "And I'll probably be caught—"

"Yeah, yeah," Rocky interrupted. "Then you'll tell on me and we all go to jail."

Heart racing, Rocky considered her options. The situation was rapidly snowballing from bad to worse to devastating. *Bobby can't find out about this.* She'd made enough mistakes today. One more fuck-up and . . . her stomach rolled over. She'd seen the results of Bobby's "employee separation." She swallowed hard. The last guy who messed up this badly was separated from his head. There had been a lot of blood.

So much blood. She could run. But realistically she knew there was nowhere to hide. Bobby would find her and . . . She made herself focus, made herself remember everything she knew about Monica Cassidy. And a plan began to form. *I can fix this.* It would work. It would have to. Unless she was prepared to walk into the ICU and smother the girl herself, which she was not. "All right. This is what I want you to do."

Atlanta, Friday, February 2, 11:15 p.m.

This statement is hereby given freely by Susannah A. Vartanian and is witnessed by Chloe M. Hathaway, Assistant State's Attorney. Sitting at the desk in her hotel room, Susannah's hands paused on her laptop and she reread the statement she'd prepared. In it were all the details she recalled from that day thirteen years ago, from the most sordid to the most benign. She and Chloe Hathaway had traded voicemails, but they'd meet tomorrow morning to discuss Susannah's statement and subsequent testimony.

Subsequent testimony. It sounded so brisk, so impersonal . . . so like somebody else's life. *But it's not. It's mine.* Restless, Susannah pushed away from the desk. She would not change a word. Not this time. This time she'd do the right thing.

It was just a matter of time before her involvement in

what the media had already dubbed "The Richie Rich Rapists" hit the news. She'd already spied someone with a camera taking pictures as she'd checked in to the hotel. They must have followed Luke Papadopoulos's car when he'd driven her from the hospital.

Luke. She'd thought of him often this day, each time a little differently. He was big, strong enough to carry Jane Doe up a steep hill without breathing hard, but he'd been so gentle with the girl. Susannah knew there were gentle giants out there, but in her experience they were rare. She hoped the woman in Luke's life appreciated his value.

That he'd have a woman in his life was a given. Coupled with his dark good looks, the man vibrated with an intensity most women would find sexually enticing. Susannah was honest enough to admit that she did, that her stomach had gone all tight when he'd stood so close in the ICU, and that she'd thought about pressing her mouth to his jaw.

But Susannah was smart enough not to get involved. Ever. Involvement led to questions, and questions ultimately would require answers. She wasn't prepared to give answers to Luke Papadopoulos or anyone else. Ever.

Still, she remembered the devastation in his black eyes when he'd come out of the bunker. And even then he'd held her up when her own legs buckled. He felt things deeply, but seemed able to partition those feelings away to focus on what needed to be done. She respected that because she knew just how difficult it was to do.

Luke had dropped her off at the hotel without further argument, respecting her wishes, even though he disagreed. Then he'd gone on his way to meet with his team, focused and intense, which seemed to be his resting state.

She envied him. Luke Papadopoulos had things to do, important things, while she'd been sitting on her hands all day. In reality that was less than accurate. She'd had a very busy morning and afternoon. It was the evening that had been empty as she'd sat waiting, powerless, with too much time to think. Tomorrow, she'd do something. She'd sit with the girl with no name, because there was no one else to do so. *Because she's my responsibility.* But first she'd give her statement to Chloe Hathaway.

She glanced at the newspaper she'd bought in the hotel lobby. The headlines screamed of a serial killer at large in Dutton. *Old news.* But below the fold was an article on the Dutton dead, as of the day before. One name caught her eye. Sheila Cunningham. They shared a bond, she and Sheila. Tomorrow Sheila would be laid to rest and Susannah knew she needed to be there. So tomorrow she'd stand in the Dutton cemetery once again.

Tomorrow would be a *difficult* day.

Her stomach growled, mercifully derailing her thoughts and reminding her of the time. She hadn't eaten since breakfast and room service was late. She'd picked up the phone to check its status when there was a knock at her door. *Finally.*

"Thank y—" Her mouth fell open. Her boss stood outside her door. "Al. What are you doing here? Come in."

Al Landers closed the door behind him. "I wanted to talk to you."

"How did you know to come here? I didn't tell you my hotel."

"You're a creature of habit," Al said. "Every time you travel you stay in this hotel chain. It was just a question of calling around until I found the right one."

"But you came to my room. Did the front desk give that information?"

"No. I overheard a reporter trying to bribe the concierge for your room number."

"I guess this was bound to happen. Vartanians are big news in Atlanta right now." Simon had made sure of that. "So did the concierge tell him?"

"Yes, that's how I knew your room number. So I reported him to the manager. You may want to consider a different hotel the next time you come to town."

When this was over, there wouldn't be a next time. "You said you wanted to talk."

Al looked around. "Do you have anything to drink?"

"Scotch in the minibar." She poured him a glass and sat on the arm of the sofa.

He went to her desk and glanced at her laptop screen. "I'm here because of that."

"My statement? Why?"

He took his time answering, first sipping at the scotch, then downing it in a gulp. "Are you sure . . . very sure you want to do this, Susannah? Once you are cast in the role of a victim, your life, your career will never be the same."

Susannah went to the window and stared out at the city. "Believe me, I know. But I have my reasons, Al. Thirteen years ago I was . . ." she swallowed hard, ". . . raped. A gang of boys drugged me, raped me, and poured whiskey all over me, just like they would do to fifteen other girls over the course of the next year. When I woke up, I was shoved in a little hidey-hole behind my bedroom wall. I thought it was my secret hiding place, but my brother Simon knew about it."

Behind her she heard Al's careful exhalation. "So Simon participated?"

Oh, yes. "Simon was the team captain."

"Wasn't there anyone you could tell?" he asked carefully.

"No. My father would have called me a liar. And Simon made sure I didn't tell a soul. He showed me a picture of me being . . . you know."

"Yeah," Al said tightly. "I know."

"He said they'd do it again. He said there was nowhere I could hide." She drew a breath, the terror as fresh as if thirteen years had not passed. "He said I had to sleep sometime, that I should stay out of his affairs. So I did. I never said anything. And they went on to rape fifteen others. They took pictures of all of us. Kept them as trophies."

"Do the police have these pictures now?"

"GBI does. I found them this afternoon, in Simon's hidey-hole. A whole box full."

"So the GBI has incontrovertible proof. There's only one of those bastards left, Susannah. Why put yourself through this now?"

Anger bubbled and she whirled to face the man who'd taught her so much about the law, the man who'd been a shining example. The man who'd been everything Judge Arthur Vartanian had not. "Why are you trying to talk me out of doing what's right?"

"Because I'm not so sure that it is right," he said calmly. "Susannah, you have been through hell. Nothing will change if you come forward. The facts will be the same. They have pictures of this man . . . what's his name? The only one left?"

"Garth Davis," she spat.

His eyes flashed dangerously, but his voice remained level. "They have pictures of this Davis raping you, raping others. If you come forward, you will be known as the victim who turned prosecutor. Every defense attorney you go up against will question your zeal. 'Is it the guilt of my client Ms. Vartanian is trying to prove, or is she trying to get revenge for her own assault?' "

"That's not fair," she said, tears close to the edge.

"Life isn't fair," he said, still calmly. But his eyes were tormented and she could keep the tears at bay no longer.

"He was my brother." She glared at him, blinking away the tears in frustration. "Don't you get it? He was my *brother* and I let him do that to me. I let him do it to others. Because I said nothing, fifteen other girls got raped and seventeen other people are dead in Philadelphia. How do I ever make that right?"

Al gripped her upper arms. "You can't. *You. Can't.* And if that's why you're testifying, it's the wrong reason. I won't let you ruin your career for the wrong reason."

"I'm testifying because it's the right thing to do."

He looked her square in the eye. "Are you sure you're not doing this because of Darcy Williams?"

Everything inside her froze. Her heart stopped. Dropped to her stomach. Her mouth moved, but no words would come out. In a blink, she saw the scene. All the blood. Darcy's body. *All that blood.* And Al knew. *He knows. He knows. He knows.*

"I've always known, Susannah. You didn't think a smart cop like Detective Reiser would take an anonymous tip on something so important, did you? Not on a homicide."

Somehow she found her voice. "I didn't think he ever knew who'd called him."

"He knew. He set up a second call, saying he wanted to verify your initial information. He'd traced your first tip to a public phone booth and when you called a second time, he was waiting down the block, watching."

"I'm a creature of habit," she said dully. "I went back to the same phone booth."

"Most people do. You know that."

"So why didn't he ever say anything?" She closed her eyes, mortification mixing with the shock. "We've worked on a dozen cases since then. He never let on he knew."

"He followed you home that night. You were working for me then and Reiser and I go way back, so he came to me first. You were only an intern, but I already could see the promise in you." He sighed. "And the rage. You were always polite, always in control, but behind your eyes was rage. When Reiser told me what you'd witnessed, I knew you had to be into something very dark. I asked him if he believed you'd done anything illegal yourself and he didn't have anything to say you had."

"So you asked him to keep my name out of it," she said stiffly.

"Only if he found no evidence of your having done anything wrong. He was able to use your tips to get a warrant and found the murder weapon in the killer's closet along with shoes with Darcy's blood in the laces. He made his case without you."

"But if he hadn't been able to, you would have let him call me to the stand."

Al's smile was grim. "It would have been the right thing to do. Susannah, you visit Darcy's grave every year on the day of her death. You still grieve for her. But you turned your life around. You've prosecuted offenders with a passion we rarely see. There was nothing to be gained from your coming forward on Darcy Williams's death."

"That's where you're wrong," she said. "I have to look at myself, every day, and know I did a passable copy of the right thing. This time, I want to be able to live with what I've done. I have to do this, Al. I've lived with the shame of the wrong thing for almost half my life. I want to live the rest of my life able to hold my head up to anyone I meet. If I have to sacrifice my career to do that, then I will. I can't believe *you*, of all people, are trying to talk me out of this. You're an officer of the court, for God's sake."

"I took off my DA hat the moment I walked in this door. I'm here as your friend."

Her throat closed and she resolutely cleared it. "There are lots of other prosecutors out there with pasts like mine. They make it work."

Again his smile was grim. "Their last name wasn't Vartanian."

She winced. "Point made. But my decision is the same. The SA and I have an appointment tomorrow morning at nine. She'll come here. I'll give her my statement."

"Do you want me to be here?"

"No." Uttering the word was reflex. But it wasn't true. "Yes," she said.

He nodded steadily. "All right."

She hesitated. "Then I'm going to a funeral. In Dutton."

"Whose funeral?"

"Sheila Cunningham. She was one of Simon's gang's fifteen rape victims. This past Tuesday night she was going to give my brother Daniel some information about the assaults thirteen years ago, but she was killed before she could talk to him. One of the gang members was our hometown deputy. He arranged for Sheila to be killed, then killed the hit man to keep him quiet. Today the deputy shot my brother."

Al's eyes widened. "You didn't tell me your brother had been shot when you called."

"No, I didn't." And she was too mixed up in her mind about Daniel to understand why she had not. "Daniel will be all right, thanks to his girlfriend, Alex."

"Is the deputy in custody?"

"Of a fashion. After he shot Daniel, he turned his gun on Alex. She shot him dead."

Al blinked. "I need another drink." Susannah pulled another little bottle of scotch from the minibar, along with a bottle of water for herself.

Al tapped his glass to her bottle. "To the right thing."

She nodded. "Even when it's the hard thing."

"I'd like to meet your brother Daniel. I've read a lot about him."

Even when it's the hard thing. Like it or not, ready or not, Daniel would be part of her life for the foreseeable future. "He can have visitors starting tomorrow."

"Do you want me to go to this woman's funeral with you?"

"You don't have to," she said and he gave her a look, as if he were counting to ten.

"You don't have to do this alone, Susannah. You never did. Let me help you."

Relief had her shoulders slumping. "It's at eleven. We need to leave right after I talk with Ms. Hathaway."

"Then I'll let you sleep. Try not to worry."

"I'll try. You . . ." Her throat tightened. "You made me believe in the law, Al. I know it works. It didn't work for me before, because I never gave it the chance."

"Tomorrow at nine. We'll give it a chance this time."

She saw him to the door. "I'll be here. Thank you."

Atlanta, Friday, February 2, 11:30 p.m.

Luke stepped into the elevator in Susannah's hotel, the aroma of food smacking him hard. A white-coated waiter stood behind a room service tray set for two. Luke glanced down at the room service tray longingly. It had been a long time since he'd eaten and all he'd get tonight was a burger from whatever drive-thru was still open.

You could be eating that burger right now. You could have just called her to ask about the cabin. Of course he could have, and should have. Yet here he was.

The elevator dinged and the doors slid open. "After you, sir," the waiter said.

Luke nodded and headed for Susannah's room. *She's probably asleep. You should just have called.* But if he'd called, he definitely would have woken her. Now, he could listen at the door. If he didn't hear anything, he'd leave. *You go right on thinking that, Papa. You just want to see her again, make sure she's all right.*

Just to make sure she was all right. Yeah, that was it. *Uh-huh.*

A door opened at the end of the hall and an older man emerged, someone in the room closing the door behind him. The man was about fifty-five, dressed impeccably in a suit and tie. He scrutinized Luke, directly meeting his eyes as they passed.

Frowning, Luke turned to watch the man and almost collided with the waiter pushing the room service cart— who stopped at the door from which the man had emerged.

Luke frowned again when Susannah answered the waiter's knock. She'd started to sign the bill when she realized Luke was there. "Agent Papadopoulos," she said.

Luke nudged the waiter out of the way. "I'll get this for you. Good night."

Susannah watched as he pushed the cart into the room and closed the door. "What are you doing here?" she asked, though not unkindly.

"I needed to ask you something." But then he got a look at her clothes and a sudden pulse of heat burned his skin. A tight skirt hit her legs midthigh and a clingy sweater dipped low. She looked utterly young and almost carefree. *And I want her. Now.*

"Looks like my niece Stacie bought what she wanted for herself," he said, forcing his voice to be amused. "My sister Demi won't let her dress like that."

Her smile was rueful. "I thought as much, but I had to get rid of those scrubs." She gestured at the cart. "Would you like to join me?"

"I'm starving," he confessed. "But I don't want to take your dinner."

"I'll never eat all this," she said and pointed at the small table in the corner. "Sit."

He maneuvered around the cart, hitting the desk with his hip. Her laptop cleared of its screensaver and he stopped when he saw what filled the screen. "Your statement."

She put the tray on the table. "I'm meeting ASA Hathaway tomorrow morning."

"She said you'd called." He narrowed his eyes at the two sets of silverware on the tray, thinking of the man who'd come from her room. "You ordered dinner for two."

"I always do. I don't want anyone to think I'm here alone." She shrugged, slightly embarrassed. "It's the irrational fears that get you at three a.m. Eat before it gets cold."

Three a.m. fears he understood. Three a.m. rarely found him asleep. They ate in silence, until Luke's need to know overwhelmed. "Who was the man who left here?"

She blinked. "My boss. Al Landers, from New York. I'd called him earlier, told him about the box, and my statement. He came to make sure I was okay." Her eyes widened. "You thought—? Oh, no. Al's married." Her jaw set. "He's a good man."

Luke's gut settled. "That was nice of him to come all this way," he said quietly.

She seemed to settle as well. "And it was nice of your niece to go shopping for me." She got up and got her purse. "Here's a check. Will you give it to her?"

He slid the check into his shirt pocket. "That's not what you would have bought."

"No, but that doesn't make it any less kind. When I go back to New York, she can have this outfit if her mom will let her. I'm sure it would look better on her. I'm too old to dress like this." She sat down and met his eyes. "What did you want to ask me?"

For a moment he couldn't remember, then his good sense kicked in. "Did you ever visit a cabin up in the mountains?"

She frowned. "A cabin? No. Why?"

"I talked to Garth Davis tonight and he mentioned that they normally used one another's houses for the . . . assaults, but that one night they used a cabin in the mountains. Granville made the arrangements and drove them there in secret."

Her eyes had flickered at his hesitation. "Does Davis know who owned it?"

"I think so, but he's not saying until we find his kids. His wife took off with them yesterday when she found out Mack O'Brien had targeted their family."

"Garth's cousin was murdered. I read about it in the paper." She sat back, thinking. "My father didn't have a cabin that I knew of. He bought a ski chalet in Vale, but to my knowledge he never used it."

"Why did he buy it then?"

"I think to torment us, especially my mother. She wanted to go out West, but he wouldn't take the time. He bought the chalet so they owned it, but she couldn't use it."

"But no cabin in the mountains here?"

"No. But I do remember him going fishing with Randy Mansfield's father."

"He and Mansfield's father were friends?"

She shrugged. "When it suited either of them. Mansfield's father was the county prosecutor and would come around when he had a case that wasn't going well. They'd whisper in my father's office and suddenly the tide would turn the prosecution's way."

"So Mansfield's father bribed your father."

"Sure. Lots of people bribed my father. My father bribed lots of people. Blackmailed others." Her eyes flashed. "I wanted to tell, but nobody would have believed me."

"Who could you have told? You had no idea who wasn't in your dad's pocket."

The rage in her eyes subsided. "I know. They were all in it together."

"I'm sorry. I don't mean to dredge all this up."

"It's okay. You were asking about the cabin. When my father and Richard Mansfield went fishing, they did go to a cabin." She looked down, thinking, then abruptly looked up, meeting his eyes. "Judge Borenson. It was his cabin."

"I know that name. I've heard it recently. Can I use your laptop?"

"Of course."

He sat down at the desk and she stood behind him, watching him type.

"Oh my God," she murmured, reaching over his shoulder to point at the screen at the same time the words jumped out at him. "Borenson presided over Gary Fulmore's trial."

"The man falsely convicted for killing Alex Fallon's twin sister thirteen years ago," Luke muttered, focusing on the computer screen and not on her clingy sweater that brushed his shoulder or her scent that filled his head. "Coincidence?"

"No," she murmured. "It can't be a coincidence." She stepped back, lowering herself to the edge of the bed. "Gary Fulmore served thirteen years for a murder he didn't do."

"Mack O'Brien's older brother Jared killed Alex's sister," Luke told her, both relieved and disappointed at the distance she'd put between them. "But nobody else knew that back then. All the boys in the gang thought the other had killed Alicia Tremaine, because she was alive when they left her after raping her. Jared O'Brien went back, raped her again, and killed her when she tried to scream for help."

"Frank Loomis was the sheriff then. He tampered with evidence. Framed Gary Fulmore for the murder. Why?"

"I know Daniel wants to know."

"Frank treated Daniel like his own son, gave him his first job at the police station. Finding out Frank had done such a terrible thing must have killed him."

Luke looked over his shoulder abruptly. "Frank treated Daniel like his own son. Could he have treated Granville the same way?"

"Frank Loomis as Granville's *thích*?" she asked doubtfully. "I guess it's possible."

"Were Sheriff Loomis and Judge Borenson friends?"

"I don't know. They could have been. Dutton politics forged strange bedfellows."

Luke searched through the rest of the Borenson search hits. "He's pushing seventy, but I don't see a death notice, so he's probably still alive. We need to talk to him."

"If Borenson's cabin was known to Granville, it could be known to whoever is his partner now." She drew a breath. "And . . ."

"The girls could be there. It's a long shot, but it is a possibility, and right now, it's all we have." He looked over his shoulder. "Do you know where Borenson's cabin was?"

"Somewhere up in North Georgia. I'm sorry. I wish I knew more."

"No, you've been a big help. I can find the cabin if it was in his name." He typed in another search and sat back. "The cabin's up past Ellijay on Trout Stream Drive."

"That area is remote. It'll be hard to find, especially in the dark. You'll need a guide."

"I've fished at cabins up in Ellijay. I should be able to find my own way." Luke paused at the door, then gave in, turning for a last look. "You're wrong, you know."

"About what?"

His mouth was suddenly dry. "You're not too old for that outfit. Stacie chose well."

One side of her mouth lifted. "Good night, Agent Papadopoulos. Good hunting."

Ridgefield, Georgia, Saturday, February 3, 12:30 a.m.

Bobby smiled at Haynes. "It's always a pleasure doing business with you, Darryl."

Haynes slipped his money clip back in his pants pocket.

"Likewise. I have to say I'm disappointed the blonde took sick, though. I kind of had my hopes up, there."

"Next time. I promise."

Haynes's lips curved into a politician's smile. "I'll hold you to it," Haynes said.

Bobby walked the rich man to the door and watched as he drove away, his new purchase stowed safely on a fluffy blanket in the trunk of his Cadillac Seville.

Tanner appeared. "I dislike that man."

Bobby smiled. "You just dislike politicians and so do I. Haynes is a good customer, and once he's elected, we'll have one more powerfully placed . . . personnel."

Tanner sighed. "I suppose. Mr. Paul is on your business line."

"Thanks, Tanner. You can go to bed now. I'll ring if I need you again."

Tanner nodded. "I'll check on our guests before I retire."

"Thank you, Tanner." Bobby smiled as the old man made his way up the old stairs. Tanner had a mile-wide streak of southern gentility, despite his rather checkered past. Tanner had been Bobby's first "personnel acquisition," at the ripe old age of twelve. Tanner had been old even then, but still young enough not to want to spend the rest of his life behind bars. They'd forged a relationship that had lasted more than half of Bobby's life. There wasn't anyone Bobby trusted more. Not even Charles.

Especially not Charles. Charles was a cobra, slithering around in the underbrush, hanging from trees, waiting for the optimal moment to strike.

Shrugging back a shiver, Bobby picked up the phone. "Paul. You're late."

"But I got your information, plus a few extras. Take

down these names. Luke Papadopoulos is lead agent on the Granville case. He's reporting to Chase Wharton."

"That I knew. Who's the support staff?" Bobby frowned as Paul recited all the names. "I don't know any of them."

"Oh, I do," Paul said smugly. "One of them will fit your needs nicely because one of them has a secret worth hiding. It should have been a major arrest for me, but I figured I'd just bide my time."

"Smart. This one is more useful to us on the job than in prison." Bobby recorded the name and the secret. "Now I'll have a well-placed mole on the GBI team. Fantastic."

"And if you play your cards right, not just for this case, but for years to come."

"You did well, Paul. What about the other matter?"

"That you're going to be less happy about. Rocky met the nurse in the hospital parking lot and they chatted in her car."

"And you were where?"

"Two rows over. I had to get that close for my mike to pick them up. Turns out your nurse hasn't done the deed. She had your assistant pretty rattled."

Bobby's jaw tightened. "I thought as much. Where is Rocky now?"

"Driving north on I-85. I'm trailing about a half mile behind."

"Why?"

"That I don't know because she didn't say."

"Did Rocky at least get a description of the girl?"

"All the nurse knew was that her name started with M."

Fuck. Monica. "I see. So the girl is awake and talking?"

"No. The nurse made it so the girl is paralyzed, gave

her something in her IV. She can't open her eyes, move, or speak."

Bobby breathed an easier breath. "So at least the nurse isn't a total failure."

"Rocky told the nurse to give the girl one more dose, which would keep her paralyzed until about two this afternoon. She said she'd be back with more instructions, then let the nurse out. Rocky waited, then followed a car to one of the local hotels. A woman went into the hotel, the car kept going. Rocky started driving north."

"What did the woman look like?"

"A doctor. She got out of the car wearing scrubs and carrying a computer bag in one hand and a shopping bag in the other. I can keep following Rocky. Your call."

"I've got her car wired. Just use the GPS. I have other things for you to do tonight."

"Can't. Rocky must've ditched the transmitter because I'm not picking her up."

Bobby sighed. "I've always known she was bright. I'll just have to have Tanner hide the transmitter better next time. Follow her. I want to know every move she makes."

"It's your dime. Oh, one more thing. Rocky was very interested when the nurse said the woman who found the girl was Susannah Vartanian. She saved the girl's life."

Bobby tensed. "What did the doctor look like, the one that went into the hotel?"

"Thirty. Dark hair in a ponytail. Maybe five-three. Real pretty," he added slyly.

Susannah. "How nice. Call me when Rocky gets to where she's going."

Bobby hung up and stared at the photo of Susannah that Charles had left, wondering if he'd known about Susannah finding the girl, then rejected the notion.

Charles would have been here, playing chess when the girl escaped. Charles knew a lot, but even he didn't know everything. *Damn the old man, playing with my mind.* Susannah Vartanian. The woman had been a festering thorn for years, simply by breathing. Today she'd done a hell of a lot more than breathe. Because of Susannah, the girl had survived. The girl could bring them all down.

For now the girl was neutralized. The nurse would need to be brought into line, that was a given. But Susannah had crossed the line. It was way past time to pull out the thorn. Way past time for Susannah to stop breathing.

But first, Bobby would deal with Rocky. It would not be pretty. *Father always told me it was a mistake to go into business with family. I really should have listened.*

Chapter Eight

Ellijay, North Georgia, Saturday, February 3, 2:15 a.m.

Luke, wake up. We're here."

Luke blinked his eyes open. Special Agent Talia Scott was slowing the car to a stop at the edge of a tree-lined dirt road, which according to their map should lead to Judge Walter Borenson's cabin. "I wasn't asleep," he said. "I was just resting my eyes."

"Then you are the loudest eye-rester I've ever heard. Your snores could wake the damn dead, Papa. No wonder you can't keep a girlfriend. So wake up."

"Maybe I did sleep a little." That he had was testament to just how much he trusted Talia. They'd been friends for a long time. He glanced in his rearview. Chase was behind them, and two vans brought up the rear.

One van was filled with the SWAT team Chase had assembled, the other held a crime lab team from the local GBI field office. "We got a signed warrant?" Luke asked.

"Yeah," Talia said. "Chloe grumbled about some early morning meeting and needing her beauty sleep, but she came through."

Chloe's morning meeting was with Susannah, Luke knew. He'd almost told Talia about Susannah's statement before he'd fallen asleep. Talia had been interviewing the surviving victims of Simon and Granville's rape club for the past two days. At some point she'd know that Susannah had been a victim, too. But he'd held his tongue. Susannah deserved her privacy until she formally signed that statement.

"Chloe usually does come through," he said and got out of the car. "If Granville's partner is here, he's boxed himself in. There isn't any way out, except this road."

Talia shined her flashlight across the dirt. "The ground's too hard to show any tire tracks if a vehicle did come through." She sniffed the air. "No fire in any woodstove."

Chase came close, tightening the straps on his Kevlar vest, two pairs of night goggles and two earpieces in his hand. "For you two. Let's approach through the trees. I'll go left. Talia, you go right, and Luke, you come around and cover the back. If they are in there, I do not want them to see us coming."

Luke thought of the bunker, the vacant eyes, the bullet holes centered on their foreheads. No, he didn't want to give the bastards any advance notice. "Let's go."

They organized, splitting the SWAT team into three groups, and set out, creeping through the trees. As they grew closer to the cabin, Luke could tell no one was there. The place was dark and had the feel of abandonment. No one had been here in days.

Luke came out of the trees on one side of the road as Chase emerged on the other. Silently, Chase pointed around to the back of the house and Luke followed the order. All was quiet until he got about five feet from the house, then he heard a low growl.

A bulldog struggled to stand, a low growl coming from its throat. The dog limped to the edge of the back porch, its teeth bared.

"We're in position," Chase's voice murmured in his ear.

Luke carefully approached. "Easy, boy," he said softly. The dog began to back up step by step, teeth still bared, but made no move to strike. "We're ready, Chase."

"Then *move*."

Luke knocked the back door in, then gagged at the stench. "Oh my God."

"GBI, freeze," Chase ordered from the front door, but the cabin was empty.

Luke hit a light switch and immediately saw the source of the odor. Three fish lay on the kitchen counter, rotting. One looked like it had been in the process of being deboned. A long, thin filleting knife lay on the floor, covered in dried blood.

"Bedroom's clear," Talia called.

Chase looked at the fish, his mouth twisted in a grimace. "At least it's not Borenson."

"Looks like he got interrupted," Luke said. "Somebody was looking for something."

Drawers in the living room had been yanked, contents strewn. The sofa had been slashed, stuffing everywhere. Books had been pulled from the shelves. Pictures had been pulled from the walls, the glass shattered in the frames.

"Hey, Papa," Talia called from the bedroom. "Come here."

Luke winced. Blood covered the bed, soaking the linens. "That had to have hurt."

Again, drawers were pulled, contents strewn. A framed photo lay in a pile of broken glass on the floor next to the bed. It was an old man holding a fly-fishing rod, standing next to a dog. "It's the bulldog from outside," Luke said, "and the old guy is Borenson."

"Talia, stay with the crime lab," Chase said. "We'll fan out and see if Borenson's been dumped anywhere around the cabin, then we'll talk to the folks in town, see if anyone saw anything. The girls are not here, nor do they appear to have been here. We're not back to square one, though. Somebody didn't want Borenson to talk."

A whimper had them looking down. The bulldog had lain down at Luke's feet.

"What about the dog?" Talia asked wryly.

"Find him something to eat," Luke said. "Then have the lab crate him and transport him back to Atlanta. Maybe he bit a suspect with those teeth." Luke hesitated, then crouched to scratch behind the dog's ears. "You're a good boy," he murmured. "Waiting for your master like that. *She's* a good dog," he corrected, then jumped when his cell phone buzzed in his pocket.

His heart quickened when he saw the caller ID. "Alex, what's happened?"

"Daniel's fine," Alex said. "But three minutes ago they rushed Beardsley to ICU."

"Beardsley's in ICU," he said to the others. "What happened? He was stable."

"None of the medical staff are talking, but I'm standing here with Ryan's father, who said they'd just changed his IV. A minute later he was convulsing."

"Oh, hell," Luke muttered. "You think he was poisoned?"

"I don't know," Alex said, "but his father said he'd remembered some things you'd want to know. His father said he called your cell, but got your voicemail."

Luke's jaw tightened. He'd fallen asleep in the car and missed the call. *Dammit.* "I'm ninety minutes away.

I'm going to call Pete Haywood to come. He's one of Chase's."

"I'll wait with Daniel and keep an eye on Ryan Beardsley. Tell Agent Haywood he'll want to take that IV bag in for testing. You should hurry back, Luke. Beardsley's dad said he flatlined. They had to bring him back with the paddles."

"I'll be there." He hung up. "Looks like someone tried to kill Ryan Beardsley."

"In the hospital?" Chase asked incredulously.

"In the hospital," Luke confirmed grimly. "I have to head back."

"You two both go back," Talia said. "I've got this covered and I'll start looking for neighbors at daybreak. Don't worry. We're good here."

"Thanks." Luke started for the door and the dog followed at his heels. "Stay, girl," he said firmly. The dog obeyed, although she quivered, ready to follow at a word.

"Yes," Talia said, her tone longsuffering. "I'll take care of the dog, too."

Luke slumped in Chase's car. "It just doesn't stop." He grimaced. "And I reek."

"A little sweat, a little smoke, a little rotting fish. Chicks love it."

Luke snorted a tired laugh. "No woman would come within a mile of me." But Susannah had. She'd come within inches. If he concentrated, he could still remember how she'd smelled. Fresh. Sweet. *Just leave it alone.* "I'll call Pete. We still have a guard on ICU. I'll post a guard outside Bailey's room, too. Dammit, I was hoping this was it. But it's been ten hours and we still have no idea where those girls are."

"Granville's partner is still pulling the strings," Chase said quietly.

Luke glared at the passing trees. "Well, I'm damn tired of being his puppet."

Dutton, Saturday, February 3, 3:00 a.m.

"Tell me," Charles said, his mild voice covering up a fury that was almost ready to explode. Still his hands were steady as he held a new scalpel Toby Granville had given him just last Christmas. It was important to have the best tools. "Tell me where it fits."

Judge Borenson shook his head. "No."

"You're a stubborn old man. I'll just have to start cutting deeper and perhaps cutting off things you might otherwise like to keep. I know the key fits a safe deposit box. And I know Toby hurt you pretty badly up at your cabin and you still wouldn't talk. I'm prepared to do much worse." Charles sliced a ribbon deep into Borenson's abdomen as the judge cried out in pain. "Just the name of the bank and the name of the city. Box number would be nice, too."

Borenson closed his eyes. "Bank of Hell. You'll never find it."

"That's a sad attitude, Judge. I need that statement you prepared. You know, the one that could ruin us both if it falls into the wrong hands?"

"Like I give a shit."

Charles's lips thinned. "You like pain, Judge?"

Borenson moaned as the knife dug deeper, but he said no more.

Charles sighed. "At least I love my job. I wonder how long you'll hold out."

"Check your crystal ball," Borenson said from between his teeth. "I'm not telling you."

Charles laughed. "It says you'll die by Sunday noon. And I'll make sure my prediction comes true, just like I always do. Some might say I'm cheating, but I just call it strengthening the house advantage. You can die quickly and painlessly or very slowly. It's your choice. Give me what I want and I'll go away. So will you, but you knew that was going to happen as soon as either I or Arthur Vartanian died, didn't you? You made a deal with the devil, Judge. Free lesson—the devil always wins."

Atlanta, Saturday, February 3, 3:00 a.m.

Susannah got out of bed and turned on the light. Sleep would not come and she'd learned long ago not to fight it. She sat down at the desk and turned on her laptop.

She had briefs to write. Work to catch up on. But none of that seemed real tonight.

She thought of Luke Papadopoulos and wondered what he'd found in Borenson's cabin. If he'd found the missing girls, he would have called her, of that she was sure.

She thought about the way he'd looked at her when he'd walked out the door tonight and a shiver ran down her back. He was a potent man. She was sure of that, too.

What she wasn't so sure of was the way she felt about it.

But that wasn't something she had to settle tonight. Tonight Luke was out there, doing something, while she sat, doing nothing. From her briefcase she pulled her cell phone and studied the photo she'd snapped of M. Jane Doe.

What's your name, girl? she wondered. Mary, Maxine, Mona? *If only I'd gotten a second or third letter.* Had M. Jane Doe been a runaway? Kidnapped? She knew the girl's fingerprints had been taken when she'd arrived at the hospital. The nurses had confirmed that much. But so far M. Doe's identity was still a mystery.

Is someone waiting for you, M? She'd asked for her mom, just before she'd been placed in the helicopter, so she had at least one parent who, one hoped, loved her.

Susannah brought up the Web site for missing children and searched the database for girls. There were hundreds and hundreds. She narrowed the search to those whose names began with M. Now there were fewer than fifty. She studied every face with a heavy heart. Every girl on the screen was gone.

No matter how bad it had been at home, she'd never been taken away. At least not for longer than the one night Simon and his friends had . . . *raped me.* It was still no easier to say, even in her own mind. She wondered if it ever would be.

She got to the end of the pictures and sighed. M. Jane Doe was not listed. Most of the girls listed in the database were classified as "endangered runaways," and runaways weren't investigated in the same way abducted teens might be. It was sad, but in a world of strained budgets and overworked resources, it was reality.

She wondered if M. Jane Doe had been a runaway, endangered or otherwise. There were online clearinghouses for teen runaways. Some of them had photos. She brought up a Web site for runaways and sighed again. Lots of photos. All individually listed. There would be no searching based on age or gender or names that began with the letter M. She settled back and began opening each photo file, one at a time.

It was going to be a long night.

Charlotte, North Carolina, Saturday, February 3, 3:15 a.m.

Rocky slowed as she pulled into the parking lot, grateful for her nearly photographic memory. She hadn't wanted to go back to Ridgefield House to check her notes. She hadn't wanted to face Bobby. *Not until I've fixed this.* Luckily she was able to remember the facts on all the girls she'd lured from their beds during the past eighteen months.

Tonight's prey would serve a dual purpose—she'd give Bobby a new blonde and she'd ensure Monica Cassidy's silence, until the girl could be moved out of the heavily guarded ICU, at which point Rocky would make the nurse kill her.

She wasn't sure how she'd do that, but she'd cross that bridge when she got there.

She'd made good time, but the four-hour drive had left her no more prepared to do this thing alone. She released her grip on the steering wheel to check her pocket. Her gun was still there, of course. But it was reassuring to know for sure.

Don't be stupid. You've done this before. But not alone. Twice she'd accompanied Mansfield on pickups, but he'd done all the work. Rocky had simply navigated the drive.

Tonight she went solo. *Oh, God, there she is.* A teenaged

girl had inched her way out of the shadows and stood waiting. *This is it. Don't fuck it up now.*

Ridgefield House, Saturday, February 3, 3:15 a.m.

The ringing of the phone pulled Bobby from sleep. A few blinks had the caller ID coming into focus. Paul. "Yeah? Where the hell are you?"

"In the parking lot of an all-night diner in Charlotte, North Carolina."

"Why?"

"Because that's where Rocky stopped. She's sitting in her car, headlights off. Wait. Somebody's coming."

"Can they see you?"

He made a scoffing sound. "You know better than that. Nobody sees me that I don't want to see me. It's a girl, about fifteen. She's coming toward Rocky's car."

"Is she a blonde?"

"What?"

"Is she a blonde?" Bobby carefully enunciated each word.

"Yeah. Looks like it."

Bobby yawned. "Then it's business. Rocky said she had a few blondes ready to harvest. I told her I'd arrange for pickup, but it looks like she's trying to make amends. I wish she'd followed my instructions on the nurse. I'll deal with her when she returns."

"Then I just turn around and go home?"

"Turn around, but don't go home. I need one more job."

Paul sighed. "Bobby. I'm tired."

"Don't whine. I need a body found tomorrow morning."

"Anybody I know?" Paul asked dryly.

"Yeah, the nurse's sister. I need it to look like she fought off a mugger. But make sure she's found. I've sent the sister's address and photo to your hotmail account. She should be leaving her house around eight. Be there a little early. Make it hurt."

"So Bobby takes the gloves off," Paul said, amusement lacing his tone.

"Absolutely. I always keep my promises. The nurse will be far more willing to follow my instructions in the future. So how is Rocky doing with the blonde in the parking lot?"

"Not bad. The girl struggled a little, but your kid wonder was prepared. Looks like she knocked her out. She's got a great right hook. No wonder you call her Rocky."

Bobby laughed softly. "No, that's not why. Thanks, Paul, I'll make sure you're paid well for this evening."

"Always a pleasure, Bobby."

"Text me when the sister's dead. I have a special delivery for the nurse."

Atlanta, Saturday, February 3, 4:30 a.m.

Luke's brother Leo brought his car to a stop outside the gated GBI lot. "We're here."

Luke opened his eyes, refreshed by the brief rest. He gave his ID to Leo, who slid it through the card reader, sending the gate silently upward. "Thanks for driving me to get my car, man."

Leo shrugged. "I wasn't doing anything else."

Luke grunted as he sat upright, working the kinks from his neck. "That's sad, Leo."

"Ain't it though?" Leo studied him, eyes worried. "Are you all right?"

"I'm here." He wasn't going to lie to Leo. He couldn't if he tried.

"Well, at least you don't smell like a dog that's been rolling in rotten fish anymore."

"There is that. I appreciate the breakfast." Luke had been unsurprised when Leo had silently materialized from the shadows of his living room as soon as Luke had let himself into his apartment. Leo had seen Chase's press conference and knew Luke would come home sometime, tired and hungry. Leo was good about anticipating the needs of others. Luke wished his brother was as good about taking care of himself.

"You're lucky. Those two eggs were the only thing in your fridge that were edible."

"I haven't been to the grocery in a while." Not since his Internet Crimes unit had picked up the scent of those three kids for whom they'd been too late last Tuesday. "I think the milk's expired, too."

"It's solidified. I'll run by and get you some bread and milk when I take your suit over to Johnny's later today. He's getting good at salvaging your clothes."

That their cousin Johnny had his own dry-cleaning business was both a bane and boon. "Tell him to go light on the starch on my shirt, okay? Last one was so stiff it almost rubbed the skin off my neck."

Leo smirked. "He did that on purpose."

"I know." He needed to move, but his body wasn't co-operating. "I'm so tired, Leo."

"I know," Leo said quietly, and Luke knew his brother understood it was more than physical fatigue.

"Those girls could be anywhere. God only knows what they've had done to them."

"You can't think like that," Leo said brusquely. "You can't think of them as Stacie and Min. So stop it."

As he had been. Luke pushed the pictures of his sister Demi's pretty, smiling, teenaged daughters from his mind. "I know, I know. Eyes on the goal. It's just that . . ."

"You're human," Leo said quietly. "You see their faces. And it eats you up."

And a little more of you dies each day. How right Susannah Vartanian had been. "It's like a sea of faces. They're always there. Some days I think I'm losing my mind."

"You aren't losing your mind. But you can't be human right now. If you think of them, of their suffering, you'll lose your edge and you'll be no good to any of them."

"How do you do that? Stop thinking of them?"

Leo's chuckle was void of humor. "I have no idea. That's what they used to tell us before we went door to door, but I never learned how to."

Luke thought of his brother in full battle gear, searching out insurgents in Baghdad. It had been a very tense time for his family. Their mama. Every day they'd waited for word that Leo had been one of the lucky ones, that he'd survived another day. The day he came home, they'd rejoiced. But one had only to look at Leo's eyes to know he had not been one of the lucky ones. A piece of his brother had died over there, but it was not something Leo ever discussed, *even with me.* "So you got out?"

Leo's eyes shuttered. "You thinkin' of getting out of the GBI?"

"Every goddamn day. But I don't."

Leo tapped his steering wheel lightly. "And that's what makes you a better man."

"Leo."

But Leo shook his head. "Don't. Not today. You don't need my shit piled on top of yours." He settled in his seat and Luke knew that topic was closed. "So how is she?"

"Who?"

"Susannah Vartanian." Leo shot him a look. "Come on, it's me you're talking to here. I saw how you looked at her at her parents' funeral. You didn't think you were hiding anything, did you?"

Not from Leo's eagle eye. "I guess not. She's . . ." *Fine.* Of course on a physical level that was true. Susannah Vartanian was very fine. Too fine. Too tempting. On an emotional level it couldn't be more false. "She's holding on."

"Why did she come back today?"

"I can't tell you. I'm sorry."

Leo's expression turned contemplative, then he shook his head hard. "No. No way."

Luke sighed. "What?"

"In that press conference, your boss said that you'd broken the case of those thirteen-year-old rapes today, that they'd happened in Dutton. She was one of them."

"I can't tell you." But in not denying it, he'd confirmed it and they both knew it. "I'm sorry."

"It's okay. Are *you* okay?"

Luke blinked. "Me?"

"You're interested in a woman who comes with heavy baggage. Can you deal?"

"Before or after I do what I want to do to the one son-ofabitch that's still standing?"

"I'll open up the range day or night if you need to take out a paper man or two."

"I appreciate it." Luke had taken out many a paper target at Leo's shooting range. Many days it was all that enabled him to keep a lid on his temper. "But not right now. I've got too many things I should have already done." First of which would be a visit to the hospital where Ryan Beardsley was, thankfully, in stable condition. He also needed to get to the morgue to check autopsy results before the eight-o'clock meeting.

"You've got a couple things going for you," Leo said when Luke got out of the car.

Luke grabbed his gym bag full of clean clothes from Leo's backseat. "Like what?"

Leo grinned. "Mama likes her. And she's Catholic. Everything else is just details."

Luke threw the bag in the trunk of his own car, chuckling. "Thanks. I feel better now."

Atlanta, Saturday, February 3, 4:40 a.m.

Monica woke up. It was dark. And quiet. And she couldn't move. *I can't move. Oh, God.* She tried to open her eyes and . . . couldn't. *Help! Help! What's happening to me?*

I'm dead. Oh, God, I'm dead. Mom. Susannah.

"Doctor." It was a woman's voice, urgently calling.

She wanted to drag in a breath, but couldn't. The tube was still in her throat. *No, no I'm not dead. I'm in the hospital. That's a nurse. She'll help. She'll help.*

"What's going on?" A deeper voice. A doctor. *A doctor.*

Stop. He's a real doctor. He won't hurt you. Still her heart raced like a wild horse.

"Her BP's up. So is her pulse."

"Let's get her comfortable. Call me if her pressure doesn't go down."

I can't move. I can't see. Help me. She heard the rattle of instruments, felt the quick prick of a needle. *Listen to me.* But the scream wouldn't come, echoing only in her mind. *Susannah, where are you?*

She started to drift, to calm. And then she heard a voice, low and gruff, and right next to her ear. *Male? Female?* She couldn't tell.

"You're not dying. You've been given a drug to make you paralyzed."

Paralyzed. Oh my God. She fought to open her eyes, to see who spoke. But she could do nothing. Say nothing. *Oh God.*

"Sshh," the voice said. "Don't fight it. They'll just give you more sedative. Now you listen to me. In a few hours, this is going to wear off. When it does you'll be able to move, to see again. When the cops come back, you will tell them you remember nothing, not even your name. You will say nothing of your time in the bunker. They have your sister and they will do to her what they did to you if you say anything."

She could feel warm breath against her ear. "Say nothing and your sister will be free. Say one word and she'll be their whore, just like you were. It's up to you now."

The heat disappeared and Monica heard the shuffle of shoes as the person walked away. Then she felt the wetness on her temples as tears leaked from her eyes.

Genie. They had Genie. *She's only fourteen. Oh, God, what do I do?*

Atlanta, Saturday, February 3, 4:50 a.m.

Pete Haywood was waiting in the hospital lobby when Luke came in.

"Status?" Luke asked.

"Beardsley's awake and lucid, asking for 'Papa.' We thought he wanted his father, but then I realized he was asking for you. He wouldn't talk to me."

"What about the IV bag?"

"Sent it to the crime lab a couple hours ago. Haven't heard anything yet. The doctors did a CT scan and a tox screen. The scan was negative, but the tox screen hasn't come back yet. I interviewed the nurse who changed the IV bag. She's ripped up. Every doctor and nurse on the floor has vouched for her, but I've got Leigh pulling her financials, just in case. I don't think she did it. The nurses stage their IV bags up to two hours ahead of time, so anybody who went into that room could have had access."

"Wonderful."

"Not so bad, actually. The hospital has a tracking system. See those blue antennae?" Pete pointed to what looked like two blue stalactites hanging from the ceiling outside the gift shop. "They're everywhere. Employees wear a badge that tracks their location 24/7."

"Holy Big Brother, Batman," Luke murmured, and Pete chuckled.

"Hospital security was running a list of everyone in the area. They should be finished any minute. I think the doctor who responded to Beardsley's attack suspected foul play, too, and that he took Beardsley up to ICU because he knew there was a guard up there. But nobody's confirming that. I think the hospital admin is being careful about liability."

"We'll know more when that bag is analyzed. Where are you going?"

"I just got a call from the fire investigator at Granville's house. He's found the bomb's trigger. Now that you're here, I'll head to Dutton. I'll be back by the eight-o'clock meeting."

Pete headed out and Luke headed up, stepping out of the elevator to find a new state trooper standing guard. "I'm Papadopoulos," Luke said, flashing his badge.

"Marlow. I just put a call in to Haywood. He said you were on your way up."

"What's happened?"

"Your Jane Doe had some kind of seizure or something. Her BP spiked and they sedated her. The doctor said it was nothing unusual, that this kind of thing happens after surgery, but given Beardsley's condition, I thought you all should know."

"Thanks, man."

Alex met him at the door. "Ryan Beardsley has been asking for you."

"I heard. Has he said anything to you?"

"No. He's waiting for you."

"What about the girl?"

"She woke up very agitated. Sometimes that happens when a patient wakes up in a strange place after surgery. And who knows? She might have been having a nightmare about the bunker. I know I've had a few. She's resting comfortably now, but her nurse is that one over there, the tall woman with gray in her hair. Her name's Ella. She can also tell you more about Ryan Beardsley."

"Thanks. How's Daniel?"

"Still asleep, but stable. I'll call you as soon as he wakes up."

Luke glanced into Daniel's cubicle as he walked by, wondering how much his friend knew about Judge Borenson, if anything. He wondered if they'd find Borenson alive.

But Beardsley was still alive. Luke approached the tall nurse named Ella. She hadn't been on shift earlier when he and Susannah had talked to Jane Doe. "Excuse me, I'm Special Agent Papadopoulos. I'm here to see Ryan Beardsley. How is he?"

"Stable. The team that worked on him downstairs got to him quickly and that's in his favor. Plus, he's in good physical condition. He's up here primarily for observation."

And for the guard. "Does that mean he'll go back to a regular room?"

Ella nodded. "Yes, but when he does, we'll be sure to tell you first."

"Thanks. Please call me if there's any change in condition on any of our patients up here." Luke went into Beardsley's cubicle. "Ryan, it's Luke Papadopoulos. Can you hear me?" Beardsley's eyes opened and Luke was relieved to see he was coherent. "Agent Haywood said you wanted to talk to me. You could have talked to him. I trust him."

"I didn't know him," Beardsley said, so faintly Luke had trouble hearing him. "Someone tried to kill me. Under the circumstances, I thought it best I wait for you."

Luke leaned closer. "I suppose I can understand that. So what did you recall?"

"A phone call that Granville got on the third day. From somebody named Rocky."

"Rocky?" Luke murmured. "Like the fighter?"

"Yes. Rocky was a boss, gave Granville orders. Made the doc very unhappy."

Luke's pulse shot up. *Finally.* "Granville didn't like getting orders from this Rocky?"

"No. Made him angry. He beat me harder."

"What order did Rocky give Granville that he didn't like?"

"Don't know, but when he hung up he said he wouldn't take orders from 'a little shit.'"

"Okay. That's helpful, Ryan. Did you hear anything else?"

Beardsley's face grew grim. "Yeah. The first day I was there, I woke up and heard noises outside my wall. On the outside, not in the hall. Sounded like digging. Burying."

Luke got a sick feeling in the pit of his stomach. "Burying something or someone?"

"Someone." Beardsley's gaze was weary. "One of the men called her Becky."

"Hell." Luke sighed. "Anything else?"

"No. That's all I remember."

"Can I get you anything? Do anything for you?"

Beardsley didn't respond at first. Then, just when Luke had thought he'd drifted back into sleep, he murmured, "BBQ. I'm so hungry I could eat the whole pig myself."

"When you're out of here, I'll bring you all you can eat." He got up to go, but Beardsley grabbed his arm.

"Is Bailey okay?" he asked, serious again.

"Bailey's fine. I put a guard on her door. Don't worry." He squeezed Beardsley's hand and went back out to the nurse's station. "He wants a barbecue sandwich."

Ella nodded. "It's always a good sign when they start asking for food."

"Can you tell me where I can find the head of security?"

Luke was headed for the elevator when his cell phone buzzed in his pocket.

"It's Chase. We have a match on one of the homicides. Kasey Knight. Sixteen, five-eight, red hair." He hesitated. "The one that only weighed eighty pounds."

The one he'd found Malcolm Zuckerman crying over as he'd gently bagged her hands and feet. The one whose red hair had come out in Malcolm's hands. Luke cleared his throat. "Have her parents been notified?"

"Yes. I just got off the phone with the father." Luke could hear Chase draw an unsteady breath. "I asked them to bring her hairbrush or some other DNA source. They, um, they want to see her."

"God, Chase. They don't want to see her. They really don't."

"It's closure," Chase said. "You know that as well as I do. They won't believe their daughter's dead until they see her for themselves. She's been gone two years, Luke."

Two years of waiting, agonizing. Hoping for the best and visualizing the very worst. "I'm on my way to the morgue. I'll ask Felicity Berg if she can make her look any better. I've got news, too. We have a potential sixth homicide."

"Aw, Christ," Chase muttered wearily. "Who?"

"Only a first name. Becky. Have Ed's team check for a body buried in the area outside the cell where Ryan Beardsley was being held."

Chase's sigh was heavy. "Do we know there's only one?"

"I thought the same thing. Have them do a scan before they start digging."

"God, this gets better every hour."

There was dread in Chase's voice. And grief. "What happened?"

"Zach Granger's dead."

Luke felt the air leave his lungs. "But it was just an eye injury."

"He had a brain hemorrhage about an hour ago. His wife was with him."

"But . . . I was just in the hospital. Nobody told me."

"We're keeping it quiet."

"Does Pete know?"

"No, not yet. Don't tell him. I will."

"He's on his way to meet with the fire investigator in Dutton."

Chase's oath was hoarse and vile. "I wish I'd never heard of that damn town."

"Join the ever-growing club. But we do have a lead on Granville's partner. Beardsley heard Granville talking to some guy named Rocky."

"That's delightfully vague," Chase said bitterly.

"It's better than we had an hour ago. I'll see you at eight. I'm going to the morgue."

Chapter Nine

Atlanta, Saturday, February 3, 6:00 a.m.

Ma'am? We're here. Ma'am? This is the airport. *Ma'am*?"

Susannah woke up, momentarily disoriented. She'd fallen asleep, finally. Too bad that it had been in the backseat of a taxicab and not in her hotel bed. "I'm sorry. I've had a long night." She paid him and slid from the backseat. "Thank you."

"No luggage?"

"No, I'm actually here to rent a car."

"You'll have to take a shuttle to any of the rental car joints."

"I wasn't thinking." When she'd left her hotel room, she'd had one purpose—to escape the faces of the hundreds of runaways she'd been searching for nearly three hours. But there was no escape. She still saw the faces, some happy, some miserable.

All gone. What a waste. Of potential. Of hope. Of life.

She'd started out comparing each face to M. Jane Doe, but at some point her mind had wandered and she realized it was Darcy Williams's face she saw in each picture.

Rattled, she'd pushed away from her computer. She'd needed a break and a car if she was going to get to Dutton for Sheila Cunningham's funeral. So here she was.

"I can drive you there," the cabbie said. "Get back in."

She got back in, shivering. "Thank you."

"It's okay." The cabbie was quiet as he drove the short distance to the rental car row. But when he stopped the cab, he sighed loudly. "Lady, this ain't none of my business, but I think you gotta right to know. We've had a tail since we left the hotel."

Annoyance had her frowning. Another reporter. "What kind of car?"

"Black sedan, tinted windows."

"How original," she said tightly and he glanced up in his rearview mirror.

"I just thought . . . maybe you were running from somebody."

Only from myself. "I don't think they're dangerous. Probably just a reporter."

He squinted at her as he took her money. "Are you some kind of a celebrity?"

"No, but thank you for telling me they're back there. It was kind of you."

"I got a daughter your age. She travels all the time for her job and I worry."

Susannah smiled at him. "Then she's a lucky girl. Take care."

As he drove away she looked back. Sure enough, the black sedan hovered back, but definitely close enough to be seen. She'd turned to go inside the rental car office, when the sedan began to move, slowly. Susannah backed up, one step, then two, then stopped. The sedan wasn't stopping. Instead, it continued by at a slow roll, and a shiver of apprehension raced down her spine.

Georgia license DRC119. Committing it to memory, she turned again for the rental car office, then it clicked.

She whirled, her heart pounding, but the sedan was gone.

DRC. Darcy. It might have been simply a coincidence. Except for the number. One-nineteen. Six years ago, on January nineteenth, was the day she'd found Darcy, beaten and bloodied and very, very dead. And thirteen years ago, on January nineteenth, she'd woken in a hidey-hole covered in whiskey, raped and terrified.

Charles smiled. He'd finally gotten her attention. Susannah had always been the aloof one, sophisticated. At least that's what everyone thought. But he knew better.

He'd always known there was a dark side to Susannah Vartanian. He could always tell. There was a look. A smell. An aura. He'd tried to lure her, all those years ago, but she'd gotten away, far away. At least that's what she thought. But he knew better.

He knew everything about little Susannah Vartanian. Everything.

Wouldn't the world be shocked by what he knew? *Tsk, tsk*, naughty girl. He chuckled. Soon he'd have her, one way or another. But he'd play with her a little first.

He waited until she exited the rental car garage, driving a sensible sedan. Nothing flashy for the good Vartanian girl. He pulled out behind her, knowing she saw him. He followed her to a Wal-Mart. Well, she had left New York the morning before with only the clothes on her back, so a little shopping trip made sense.

Staying back just far enough, he waited until she parked and started walking into the store before gliding past her one more time. He laughed aloud. The look on her face was priceless.

Charles had planned to wait one more year before

taunting her with the DRC license plates, making it an even seven since Darcy's death, but Susannah was here and vulnerable and he'd be a fool to waste the moment. When she was in the store, he parked, having no fear that she would call the police. She'd never tell what happened on January 19, either time. He opened his ivory box, this time pulling out one of his greatest treasures, a simple photograph. But it was so much more. It was a moment in time, frozen forever.

A younger version of himself smiled in black and white, standing next to Pham. Pham was old in the picture and knew he was nearing death even then. *But I was blissfully unaware he was so sick. I was simply enjoying the day.* Pham had been a big believer in enjoying the day but he'd also preached patience. *The patient bird breakfasts on the juiciest worm.*

But Charles believed in the American ideal of striking while the iron was hot, and over time, Pham had come to see the usefulness in the concept as well. An amazing team, the revered Buddhist monk and his Western bodyguard were admitted to homes everywhere they went. Whether Pham told fortunes, held healing services, or simply dealt in the fine art of blackmail, the homes in which they stayed were always much poorer after they'd departed.

I miss you still, my friend. My mentor. He wondered what Pham would have done if Charles had died first, as Toby had. Then Charles laughed aloud. Pham would have been whoever and done whatever would have made him the most money on that day, as if it were no different than any other. Pham was all about cold, hard cash.

Charles no longer needed the money, so his enjoyment

at Susannah Vartanian's expense was purely pleasure. Pham would have approved.

Atlanta, Saturday, February 3, 6:15 a.m.

Dr. Felicity Berg glanced up briefly when Luke entered, then again focused on the body on the table. "I was wondering when you'd get here. I was about to call you."

"I've been a little busy," Luke said, unoffended at her brusque tone. He liked Felicity, although many considered her cold. Luke imagined many considered Susannah cold as well, but he wondered how many people truly knew her. "What have you got so far?"

"A hell of a mess," she snapped, then sighed. "Sorry. I'm tired. I know you are, too."

"Yeah, but I haven't had to look at this all night," he said softly. "You okay, Felicity?"

Her swallow was audible in the quiet. "No." Then she continued in a businesslike tone, "You have five females, all between the ages of fifteen and twenty. Two suffer from extreme malnutrition. Victim two and victim five here on the table."

"We think we have an ID on number five," Luke said. "Kasey Knight. Her parents are coming to do an ID. They should arrive sometime around two."

Felicity abruptly looked up, horrified. "They want to *see* her? Luke, no."

"Yes." Luke came closer, steeling himself, then swallowed the bile that rose in his throat. "Can't you . . . Can you make her look any . . . better?"

"Can you convince them not to look at her? I can do a DNA ID in twenty-four hours."

"Felicity, they've been waiting two years. They need to see her."

She stood glaring at him, then her sob broke the silence. "Goddammit, Luke." She stepped back, crying, her bloody gloved hands held stiffly in front of her. "Dammit."

Luke pulled on a pair of gloves, pushed her goggles up to her forehead, then dabbed at her eyes with a tissue. "You've had a long night," he said quietly. "Why not go home and get some rest until the parents get here? She's the last one, right?"

"Yeah, and I'm almost finished with her. Fix my goggles, would you?"

Luke did so, then stepped away. "I won't tell anyone," he said conspiratorially, and her laugh was watery and self-conscious.

"I don't usually let them get to me, but . . ."

"I feel the same way. So what can you tell me besides two were malnourished?"

She set her shoulders, and when she spoke, it was all business again. "Victim five, Kasey Knight, has gonorrhea and syphilis."

"But the rest don't?"

"Right. Victim one has sickle cell, so that might help narrow down her ID. Victim two has had her arm broken, in the last six months. It wasn't set very well. The other arm had radial fractures and looks like the events occurred in the same time period. I'd assume the breaks are due to abuse." She looked up again, her brows bunched. "It's weird. The two emaciated girls had high levels of electrolytes in their blood. And I found needle marks in their arms—like someone had administered fluids via IV."

"We found IV bags in the bunker and some syringes and needles."

"So this doctor that was killed, Granville. He was *treating* them?"

"I'm wondering if he wasn't trying to get them ready for resale. Anything else?"

"Yeah. I saved the best for last. Come here."

He came closer as she gently rolled the body of Kasey Knight to one side. He squinted, then bent closer to see the small area high on the right hip and his jaw tightened. "A swastika." He looked up. "Is that a brand?"

"It is. All of them have one, same place, on the right hip. Size of a dime."

Luke straightened. "Neo-Nazis?"

"There's a bag over on the counter that might help."

Luke held it up to the light. It was a signet ring with the AMA snake symbol. "So?"

"It came off Granville's finger."

"Okay. He was a doctor, this is the AMA symbol. Not to be obtuse, but so?"

Her brows lifted. "It's got a false front. Trey found it by accident when he was taking it off the good doctor. There's a little button on the side."

Luke flicked it and inside the bag, the top of the ring swung open revealing the same swastika design. "I'll be damned. Did this make those brands?"

"I don't think so. The design is set too deep and there doesn't appear to be any cellular residue on the surface, but the lab can tell you for certain."

"I'll see if I can track down this design. Felicity, one of the others can do the ID."

"I'll do it." Carefully she pulled the sheet to cover Kasey Knight. "I'll see you at two."

Atlanta, Saturday, February 3, 7:45 a.m.

Susannah stood at the door to Luke's office, willing her hands not to shake. After the black sedan had disappeared, she'd rented her car and driven to the local Wal-Mart to buy toiletries. Then she'd driven back to the hotel, growing more rattled with every mile, because DRC119 had appeared in the store parking lot, on the highway as she was driving back, even passing by the hotel as she gave her keys to the valet.

For a split second she wondered if Al Landers had told someone, but she instantly dismissed the possibility. Besides, if Al had known she visited Darcy's grave every year, someone else might, too. She had to find out who'd registered that license plate.

Luke. She trusted him. So she'd stopped the valet, taken her car, and driven here.

She knocked and he looked up from his computer, the surprise in his dark eyes quickly followed by interest. For a moment their gazes locked and her mouth grew dry. Then his eyes grew shuttered and polite and the moment was broken. "Susannah?"

It didn't matter if she wasn't sure how she felt about his interest, she thought, because it would disappear if he knew the truth. *He wouldn't want me anymore. No decent man would.* "I met Leigh coming in from her break and she walked me up."

"Come in." He moved a stack of folders from the chair on the other side of his desk. "I have some time before our morning meeting, so I'm doing paperwork from yesterday. Have a seat. I've been meaning to call you all night, but things got crazy. We got to Borenson's cabin last night and he was gone. There was evidence of a struggle."

Her chin jerked up as she sat down. "Do you think he's dead?"

He slouched in his chair. "The struggle was a few days ago, minimum. If he's wounded somewhere, it won't be good. He'd have to have lost a lot of blood by now."

"A few days ago was before all this broke loose with Granville. You were still tracking O'Brien then."

"I know, but I can't ignore it. He was connected thirteen years ago. He could very well be connected now." He frowned. "Speaking of connected, did you notice any kind of mark or scar or anything on Jane Doe?"

"Like what?"

He hesitated. "Like a swastika."

For the second time in two hours Susannah's blood ran ice cold. "No. She was gowned and under a sheet by the time I saw her in ICU." *Good, you're staying calm.* "I would've thought the hospital would have pointed something like that out."

"Me, too, but they were a little busy yesterday saving her life."

"I suppose they were. Why not just ask them today?"

"Because." He hesitated again. "Because someone tried to kill Beardsley last night."

"Oh my God. Are you sure?"

"I have the crime lab's analysis right here. Someone tampered with his IV."

"Is he okay?"

"He's fine. He had a bad few moments there, but he's fine."

"What about the girl? And Bailey?" *And Daniel?*

"And Daniel?" he asked quietly, with only a trace of reproach.

Which I deserved. "And Daniel. Are all of them all right?"

"Yes, but I'm not sure who I can trust. I hoped you'd seen a mark on Jane Doe."

Her heart was pounding, but her voice was calm. "What's the significance?"

"Every girl in the morgue has one branded on her hip."

She swallowed hard, forcing her heart back down to her chest. *It's not possible. This is not happening.* But it was possible. It was happening. *Tell him. Tell him now.*

In a minute. First, DRC119. "So it was Granville's mark."

"It appears so. But, you came all the way down here. What can I do for you?"

Calm, Susannah. "I hate to bother you with this, but a car followed me this morning."

His dark brows crunched. "What do you mean?"

"I went to the airport to rent a car this morning. I'm going to Dutton for Sheila Cunningham's funeral today."

"Sheila Cunningham. I'd almost forgotten about the funeral," he murmured, then looked back at her. "So what happened with the car that was following you?"

"I took a cab from the hotel to the airport, and a black sedan followed me. I went to the store afterward and it followed me there, too. I have to admit . . . I was a little rattled." *Utterly unnerved.* "Can you run a check on the license plate?"

"What is it?"

"DRC119. It wasn't the normal layout, you know, with the peach in the middle. All the characters were together."

"A vanity plate, you mean."

"Yeah. I guess so." Holding her breath, she waited as he typed it into his computer. And waited some more as he stared at the screen, his expression inscrutable. Finally she could stand it no longer. "Luke?"

He looked up, eyes guarded. "Susannah, do you know a Darcy Williams?"

Don't you dare run away this time. "She was my friend. Now she's dead."

"Susannah, the vehicle is registered to Darcy Williams, but the picture in her DMV record . . . it's yours."

Her throat closed. No air came in. No words came out.

"Susannah?" He lurched to his feet and came around his desk to take her shoulders in his hands, his grip firm. "Breathe."

She sucked in a breath, nauseous. "There's something you need to know." Her voice was no longer calm. "It's the swastika. I have one. On my hip. It's a brand."

He exhaled carefully. His hands remained on her shoulders, kneading. "From the assault thirteen years ago." It wasn't a question. It should have been.

She gently pulled away and walked to the window. "No. It happened seven years later. On January nineteenth."

"One-nineteen," he said. "Like the license plate. DRC119."

"January nineteenth was also the day of my assault by Simon's gang."

In the glass, she watched him go still. "Susannah, who was Darcy Williams?"

She leaned her forehead on the cool glass. Her head burned, but the rest of her was ice cold. "Like I said. She was my friend and now she's dead."

"How did she die?" he asked gently.

She kept her eyes fixed on the parking lot below. "I've never told this. To anyone."

"But somebody knows."

"At least three people. And now you." She turned around, met his eyes. "Whoever followed me today knows. Last night I found out my boss has known since it happened. Part of it anyway. The other person is the detective who led the investigation."

"Investigation into what?"

"Darcy was murdered in a cheap hotel room in Hell's Kitchen. I was in the next room." She kept her eyes on his, an anchor. "I was in law school at NYU. Darcy was a year or so younger, a waitress in the West Village. We'd meet in a bar. That night, we'd met some guys."

"In Hell's Kitchen? Did you go there often?"

She hesitated for a fraction of a heartbeat. "It was a one-night thing."

Liar. Liar. Liar.

Shut up. I have to keep something *secret.*

"But something happened," he said.

"I passed out. I think the guy put something in my drink. When I woke up, I was alone and . . ." *I had sticky thighs. He hadn't used a condom.* "My hip burned like fire."

"The brand."

"Yes. I got dressed and knocked on the room next door, where Darcy was. The door just . . . swung open." And suddenly she was there again. Blood. Everywhere. On the mirror, on the bed, on the walls. "Darcy was crumpled in a heap on the floor. Naked. She was dead. She'd been beaten to death."

"So what did you do?"

"I ran. I ran to a phone booth two blocks away and called 911. Anonymously."

"Why anonymously?"

"I was in law school. I was clerking in the district attorney's office. If I'd gotten mixed up in that kind of scandal . . ." She looked away. "I sound like my mother. She used to say that to my father when Simon would screw up. 'We just can't have a scandal, Arthur.' And my father would go 'fix' it."

"You are not like your parents, Susannah."

"You have no idea what I am," she shot back, then stopped, startled. She'd said the same thing to Daniel. Word for word.

Why did you come back? he'd asked.

The others will testify, she'd told him. *What kind of coward would I be not to do the same?* He'd insisted she wasn't a coward and she'd nearly laughed in his face. *You have no idea what I am, Daniel.* And he didn't. She'd like to keep it that way, but her secrets were leaking out, one by one.

"What are you then?" Luke asked quietly.

She drew a breath, returned the conversation to the past. "I was a coward."

His eyes flickered. He'd caught her parry. "You called 911. That was something."

"Yeah. Then I followed up with another anonymous call to the detective who'd landed the case. I described the guy who'd picked Darcy up at the bar and gave him the bar's address. He said he'd need to verify some things, and for me to call him back in four hours. I did, and he was watching for me to make the call."

"You used the same phone booth."

"All three times." She forced a taut smile. "That's why we catch so many bad guys, Agent Papadopoulos. They do stupid things."

"Luke," he said levelly. "My name is Luke."

Her taut smile faded. "Luke."

"Then what happened?" he asked, as if she weren't telling him something sordid.

"Detective Reiser caught the guy based on my leads. He was able to corroborate independently once he knew where to start. He didn't need to bring me in, but told my boss, I think more to cover his ass. So my reputation, and my career, were saved."

"It's a good reputation, a good career. Why are you beating yourself up over this?"

"Because I was a coward. I should have faced the guy who killed Darcy then."

"So you're facing Garth Davis now? To make up for what happened then?"

Her lips thinned. "That seems to be the popular conclusion."

He slid his finger under her chin, nudging until she met his eyes again. "What about the other guy?" he asked, his eyes intense. "The one that drugged you."

She lifted a shoulder. "He left. I never saw him again. I got over it."

"Did he rape you?" he asked, his voice carefully controlled.

She remembered the blood, the stickiness of his semen on her thighs. "Yes. But I went to that hotel room willingly."

"Did you *hear* what you just *said*?" he asked, his tone just shy of a snarl.

"Yes," she hissed. "I hear it every time I think it. Every time I tell a victim she didn't deserve to be raped. But this was different, dammit. *It's different.*"

"*Why?*"

"Because it happened to me," she cried. "Again. I let it happen to me *again* and my friend *died*. My friend *died* and I was a coward and ran away."

"So you deserved to be raped?"

She shook her head, wearily. "No. But I didn't deserve justice either."

"You Vartanians are so *fucked up*," he said, the fury snapping in his black eyes. "If your father weren't already dead, I'd be tempted to kill him myself."

She raised up on her toes, holding his gaze. "Stand in line." She took a step back, pulled her emotions into check. "So, what does this mean? The same night my friend is murdered in New York, I get assaulted and branded. Six years later five homicides are branded with the same symbol in beautiful, scenic Dutton. Connected? I vote yes."

She watched him bank his fury, partitioning it away. "Let's see it," Luke said.

Her eyes widened. "Excuse me?"

"Let's see it. How will we know if it's the same symbol?"

"Show me yours first and I'll tell you if they're the same."

"Mine are in the morgue," he snapped. "For God's sake, Susannah, I saw you in your bra yesterday. My meeting started a few minutes ago. Just do it. Please."

He was right, of course. This was no time for modesty and she had no right to it anyway, given what she'd just disclosed. "Close your eyes." Rapidly she unzipped the skirt and pushed her underwear down far enough to show him. "Look."

He crouched, staring at the mark, then closed his eyes. "Zip back up. It's the same design. Slightly larger in diameter." He straightened, eyes still closed. "You decent?"

"Yeah. So, now what? Somebody here in Atlanta knows about Darcy. Somebody in Dutton has a swastika brand. Did that same someone brand me and kill my friend? If so, who and why?"

"I don't know. All I know is that we need to start looking at white supremacy groups."

"Because of the swastika? Maybe, maybe not."

He stopped, his hand on the knob of his office door. "Why not?"

It was easier to think details than dwell on an act she could not change. "My brand isn't a German swastika. This swastika is bent at the tips. It's a symbol used in many Eastern religions." She lifted her brows. "Including Buddhism."

"So we're back to Granville's *thich*."

"Maybe. Maybe not. I can research it for you if you want."

"Yes. Sit here and do it while I'm in my meeting. I'll come back for you."

"I can't stay. I'm meeting Chloe Hathaway at nine."

"She's here in the eight-o'clock meeting. She can meet with you when we're done. It'll save her a trip to your hotel."

"But my confession is on my laptop. I left it in my hotel room."

"We have a small army of stenographers out there answering calls from the tip line," he said impatiently. "We'll pull one of them in to take your statement. I have to go."

"Luke, wait. My boss, Al—he was going to sit in on the meeting." Her lips curved in a self-mocking smile. "For moral support."

His eyes softened. "Call him then, and tell him to come down. But I don't want you driving around by yourself until we understand who that person was in the black sedan. It all fits. We just have to figure out how." He hesitated. "I've tried to keep your name out of the investigation until you gave your statement."

"Why?" she managed, knowing what was coming. *He's going to have to tell. Everyone will know what I've done. And what I have not.* It was what she deserved.

"You deserve your privacy. Just like you deserve your justice."

She swallowed, his choice of words striking her hard. "Tell them whatever you need to. Tell them about thirteen years ago. Tell them about Hell's Kitchen, Darcy, and the brand. I'm so damn tired of my privacy. It's been choking the life out of me for thirteen years." She lifted her chin. "So tell them all. I don't care anymore."

Ridgefield House, Saturday, February 3, 8:05 a.m.

Bobby picked up the phone on the first ring. "Is it done?"

Paul sighed. "It's done."

"Excellent. Go to bed, Paul. You sound tired."

"Y'think?" Paul asked sarcastically. "I'm on duty tonight, so don't call me."

"Got it. Sweet dreams. And thanks."

Bobby flipped open the cell, checked the photo of the eight-year-old boy whose mother was about to discover that nobody disobeyed Bobby and walked away unpunished. The note was to the point. *Obey or he'll die, too.* Bobby hit send. And it was done. "Tanner, can you get my breakfast, please?"

Tanner appeared from the shadows. "As you wish."

Chapter Ten

Atlanta, Saturday, February 3, 8:10 a.m.

Luke stopped at the door to the conference room. He was so angry he was shaking.

I didn't deserve justice either. He'd wanted to scream, shake some sense into her. But he hadn't. He could only do what needed to be done. So here he stood.

He'd been shocked yesterday to learn she was one of the gang's victims. He'd been shocked even more to learn she'd been raped again. On the same date, no less.

He wondered why she hadn't connected the two events. And he wanted to know what the hell she'd been doing, going to cheap hotels with one-night stands. And he wondered how he could possibly tell a room of other people her most intimate secrets.

"What's wrong?" Ed came around the corner carrying a box. "You look whipped."

"I am. What's in the box?"

"Lots of stuff, including the keys we found in Granville's pockets yesterday."

Luke straightened. "Why?"

Ed's brows waggled. "Open the door and we'll all find out."

The conference room table was already crowded. Nate Dyer from ICAC was there, along with Chloe, Nancy

Dykstra, and Pete Haywood. Next to Nate sat Mary McCrady, one of the department psychologists. Hank Germanio sat next to Chloe, jerking his chin up when Luke entered. He'd been staring under the table, probably at Chloe's legs. Chloe wore a look of general distaste. There was no love lost between the two.

Chase looked mildly perturbed. "You're both late."

"It'll be worth it," Ed promised.

Chase tapped the table. "Now that we're all here, let's get started. I asked Mary McCrady to join us. She'll be building a psych profile of Granville's partner. I'll go first." He held up a leatherbound volume in a plastic bag. "Jared O'Brien's journal."

Luke stared. "Where did you find it?"

"Mack's last victim," Ed said. "She had GPS on her car and we traced it. We found where Mack had been holed up and that journal was with his things."

"It's fascinating reading," Chase said. "I did find mention of Borenson's cabin, Luke. Seems like all the boys knew where they were once they'd arrived. Toby Granville hadn't bothered to take any of Borenson's personal pictures or plaques off the walls. I'll be going through the journal today to see if we can glean any more on Granville's mentor. More updates? Luke?"

Luke needed to lead with Susannah's brand, but somehow he couldn't make himself. Not yet. "I got the lab report on the fluid in Ryan Beardsley's IV. The concentration of stimulant in his IV was enough to have killed him. Hospital security says a guy named Isaac Gamble's ID was tracked close to Beardsley's room."

"We've got four agents out looking for Gamble," Chase said.

"Good. When we find him, charge him with attempted

murder. If they hadn't gotten to Beardsley with the pad-
dles when they did, he'd be dead. He's okay now, luckily.
He remembered hearing the name Rocky. We think that's
Granville's boss."

" 'Rocky' isn't very specific," Nancy said doubtfully.

"Since it's a nickname it could indicate body size, or
lack thereof," Mary said. "He could sound like Rocky
Balboa. It's a piece of the profile."

"And it's better than we had," Chase said. "Beardsley
also remembered hearing men digging outside the wall of
his cell. The men said the name 'Becky.' "

"God," Chloe murmured. "Now we've got bodies outside, too?"

"I've got someone from the university coming out to
Dutton," Ed said. "They're going to do a scan with ground-
penetrating radar to see where the grave is."

"Try to hang a tarp," Chase said. "I don't want the
media seeing anything with their flyovers. We also have
an ID on one of the homicides, Kasey Knight."

"Her parents will be here by two," Luke said. "Felicity
will have her ready."

"She's finished the autopsies?" Ed asked.

"Yeah. Besides one of the girls' having sickle cell,
there's nothing specific to identify any of them. She did
find that the two most emaciated girls had high electrolyte
levels, consistent with the IV bags we found in the bunker.
One of the girls had some pretty serious STDs. Beyond
that the autopsies showed nothing."

"But one of the homicides we've seen before—Angel,"
Chase said. "Anything, Nate?"

"I was up all night reviewing case files. I couldn't find
anything new on Angel or the two other girls she was with
on the old Web site we shut down. I've sent a photo of

her face and her description to partnering agencies. I'll keep looking."

Nate looked drawn and Luke understood. There were few things as emotionally draining as having to view pictures of human beings being violated. When they were children . . . It was a million times worse. "I haven't been able to help," Luke said, apology in his voice. "I'll be there today to look with you."

"I could use a break," Nate admitted wearily. "But I can keep looking if you're needed elsewhere. It's not like you haven't been busy, too."

"We all have," Chase said. "Pete, what did the fire investigator say?"

"He found the timing device used in Granville's house," Pete said, very quietly, but there was menace beneath the calm. One of his team was dead, and Pete was pissed.

Luke frowned. "I thought it was set off with a wire connected to the front door."

"It was," Pete said. "But this guy wanted to be certain the firebomb went off. His double planning tripped him up. The fire investigator said the mistake was a common one among arsonists. Sometimes they'll leave an extra starter just to be certain, and one doesn't go off, leaving the investigator with a trail to follow."

"And we were this lucky?" Chase asked.

"We were. This arsonist left two devices, one with a timer and one connected to the door. The one with the timer wasn't set to go off for another two hours."

"Did the fire investigator recognize the timer?" Chase asked.

Pete nodded. "He thinks it belongs to a Clive Pepper. He's got two priors for arson-for-hire. He goes by Chili."

Nancy rolled her eyes. "Chili Pepper? Puh-lease."

Pete's eyes flashed. "Sonofbitch better hope I don't find him first."

"Pete," Chase cautioned, and Pete drew a breath, his expression still menacing. "Tone it down." Chase looked at Chloe. "Can we charge him with murder?"

She nodded once, hard. "You bet."

"Murder," Germanio said disbelievingly. "Why?"

Everyone but Pete and Chloe looked confused. Chase sighed. "Zach Granger died tonight." There was a hush around the table. Even Germanio looked stunned. "He hit his head in the explosion. Apparently it caused a blood clot and . . . he's gone."

Nancy paled. "Pete, I'm so sorry." She reached across the table and covered his clenched fists with her hands. "Not your fault, partner," she whispered fiercely.

Pete said nothing. Luke wasn't sure the big man could without losing it.

"So we're charging him with murder," Chase said. "I'm sorry, Pete." Clearing his throat, he redirected the conversation. "Nancy, what did you find at Mansfield's house?"

"Lots of porn," she said grimly. "Whips and chains. Rape. Kiddie porn, too."

Luke steeled his spine. "I'll look through it."

"We both will," Nate said. "Where is it, Nancy?"

"On his computer mainly. Computer forensics is checking it out now. We also found a very well-stocked arsenal in a concrete bomb shelter in his basement. Guns and ammo and enough food to feed an entire town for a month. I'm checking through his bills and other files. Nothing's popped so far. Except . . ." From next to her chair she grabbed an evidence bag. "I found this right before I came back for this meeting."

"A highway atlas?" Luke asked.

"You got it." It was the large variety, dog-eared and very well used. "He's marked routes on the pages for Georgia, the Carolinas, Florida, and Mississippi. One hundred thirty-six routes are marked," Nancy said. "I'll have each route detailed. I don't know what all the destinations are for, but I'm assuming none of it's good."

"We're going to find out," Chase said. "Good work, Nance. Hank?"

"I may have found Granville's wife," Germanio said. "Helen Granville bought a train ticket for Savannah."

"Does she have family there?" Luke asked, and Germanio shook his head.

"I checked with neighbors and nobody seemed to know where her family was from. They said she was a quiet woman who didn't say much. Almost all of them said they were shocked by all the events, except for one neighbor who said she wasn't surprised to find that Granville was so depraved. She suspected Granville abused his wife."

"Why did that one neighbor think differently?" Mary asked.

"She was an attorney in a legal aid clinic before she retired. Did lots of work with abused women. She said she never saw any bruises on Helen Granville, but that there was something 'off' about the woman. She once asked her if she needed help and Helen never spoke to her again. Here's her card if you want to talk to her."

Mary wrote down the woman's name and number. "I will. Thanks, Hank."

Germanio threw an arch look at Chloe. "I requested a *warrant* to check Helen Granville's cell phone records, since none of the house phone calls look odd. And now that I got a *warrant* for Davis's phones, I'll be following up on Kira Laneer, Davis's mistress. And when I get a *warrant*, I'll check Mrs. Davis's cell phone records to see where she's gone. It'll be harder for her to just disappear with two sons. I went to see Davis's sister Kate, but she wasn't answering the door. I'll go by again tomorrow."

"Drive to Savannah first," Chase said. "I want Mrs. Granville here. Ed, you're next."

Ed opened his box and pulled out a rusted piece of metal. "This is part of the cot we found in one of the bunker rooms. We cleaned it and looked at it under the microscope. That O isn't completely closed."

"So it's not Ashley O-s, it's C-s-something," Luke said excitedly, and Ed nodded.

"Leigh's doing a check with Missing Kids and the tristate missing person divisions."

"Excellent," Chase said, looking into the box. "What else?"

Ed looked at Pete, who'd pulled himself together. "Granville's keys."

Pete moved a copy paper box to the table. "Which hopefully fit Granville's fire safe."

Pete lifted the firebox to the table. Its outside was charred, but the lock was intact. "The fire investigator found this when he was poking around what used to be Granville's study." He tried the smallest key and everyone at the table leaned forward as it turned.

"This could be your ticket to fame, Pete," Nancy teased lightly. "Geraldo tried this once, and look what happened to him."

Pete gave her a ghost of a smile as he lifted the lid. "Passport." He lifted his brows. "Another passport." He opened them both. "Both Granville's face, but two different names. Michael Tewes and Toby Ellis."

"Our boy was mobile," Ed drawled.

"Looks like. Stock certificates and a key." Pete held it up. It was small and silver. "Maybe to a safe deposit box."

"Simon Vartanian had a box at the bank in Dutton," Luke said. "Granville might, too. Hopefully it's not as empty as Simon's was." There had been no incriminating photographs documenting the gang's rapes in Simon's box as they'd hoped. "I'm going to Dutton for Sheila Cunningham's funeral later this morning. I'll check while I'm down there. Does the warrant cover the safe deposit box, Chloe?"

"No, but it won't take long to get a new warrant as the key is covered under the original. What else, Pete?"

"Marriage license. Helen's maiden name is Eastman, by the way. In case you want to track her family. Birth certificates, and last, this." He pulled out a flat amulet on a silver chain and Luke's eyes narrowed. The amulet was engraved with the swastika. Susannah had been right, the edges did bend. Each side was topped with a heavy dot. It was not a Nazi design.

"Oh, hell," Chase muttered. "Neo-Nazis."

"I don't think so," Luke said. "I have a lot more to tell. That design matches a brand Felicity Berg found on the hip of each of our homicide victims."

Everyone around the table perked up.

"This amulet is too flat to make a brand," Pete said, studying the engraving.

"Felicity also found a ring on Granville's finger. Same design, also probably not the branding tool." Luke drew a breath. "The symbol has shown up once more. On Susannah Vartanian."

This drew surprised glances from everyone.

"Perhaps you'd better explain," Chase said quietly.

Ridgefield House, Saturday, February 3, 8:20 a.m.

Rocky pulled her car into the garage. She was so tired. An accident outside Atlanta had brought traffic to a stand-still for over an hour, during which she'd been on tenter-hooks, just waiting for someone to hear the thumping in her trunk. Luckily it had been cold and everyone stayed in their vehicles with their windows up.

She would undoubtedly have found it difficult explaining the bound and gagged teenaged girl in her trunk. And like on the old *Mission Impossible* show, she knew Bobby would have disavowed any knowledge of her had she been caught. *But I wasn't caught.* Perhaps now Bobby would believe in her again.

Before she explained all to Bobby, she needed an update from the nurse. Rocky hoped the nurse hadn't given Monica Cassidy another dose of the paralytic. The sooner they got Monica out of ICU and into a regular room, the sooner they could kill her without all the fuss. Then the gem in her trunk would be just another item on the inventory. She dialed, anticipating the approval in Bobby's blue eyes.

She'd done quite a lot for that approval over the years. Luckily she'd always been able to avoid murder. The thought of murder left her sick.

"You bitch," the nurse screamed before Rocky could say a word. "We had an agreement. You fucking bitch."

Her stomach rolled over. "What? What happened?"

"My sister," the nurse hissed. "As if you didn't know. Bobby killed her." The nurse began to sob. "Beat her to death. Oh God, this is all my fault."

"How do you know it was Bobby?" Rocky asked, trying to stay calm.

"Because of the picture, you damn idiot. On my phone. Of my *son*. He's *eight*."

"Bobby sent a picture of your son to your phone?" Rocky repeated.

"With a note. 'Obey or he'll die, too.' *Too*," she spat. "I rushed over here and . . . I just found her. I found her in the alley like the garbage. They left her like garbage."

"What are you going to do?"

The nurse laughed hysterically. "What do you think? Whatever Bobby wants."

"Did you give the girl another dose of paralytic?"

"No." Rocky heard the nurse take deep breaths, trying to calm herself. "There was too much security in ICU last night after they brought that army chaplain in."

"What did you say?"

"The army chaplain. Somebody tried to kill him last night, but they failed." Her chuckle was raw. "Didn't know about that either? Your boss must trust you, Rocky."

The sarcasm fell flat because Rocky knew her boss didn't trust her at all. Rocky was smart enough to know where she stood. That cop Paul was higher on the totem pole than she was. A lot higher. A fact Bobby had made abundantly clear on many occasions. Rocky's temper began to boil. "So have you spoken to her? To Monica?"

"I told her what you said to tell her."

Rocky popped the trunk, snapped a picture of Genie Cassidy. "I'm sending a picture to your phone. Show it to Monica. It'll keep her quiet until you can kill her."

"If I go down, I'm taking you down with me."

"Tell the police. You can't prove anything and the cops will just think you're insane."

"I hate you. And I hate Bobby, too." The phone clicked as the nurse hung up.

Rocky sighed. *I was handling this. That nurse's sister didn't need to die.* It would just bring more attention to them and that they didn't need. She found Tanner in the kitchen, preparing Bobby's tea. "I've got a new guest in the trunk of my car," she said. "Can you get her warm and clean? Where's Bobby?"

"In the study." Tanner raised a bushy gray brow. "And none too happy with you."

"Feeling's mutual," Rocky muttered. She knocked on Bobby's door and entered before being given permission.

Bobby looked up, eyes ice blue. "You're a little late. I sent you on a simple errand last night and you return eight hours later."

"You had that nurse's sister killed."

Bobby's brows lifted. "Of course. The girl's still alive."

"Yeah, she is. And so is Beardsley."

Bobby shot up, furious. "What?"

Rocky laughed. "So the swami doesn't know everything." Then her head was knocked sharply to the left as Bobby's hand connected with her cheek.

"You little bitch. How dare you?"

Rocky's cheek stung. "Because I'm angry. I guess I just got angry enough."

"Sweetheart, you don't know the meaning of the word. I gave you a job. You *failed*."

"I *reconvened*. There was no way the nurse was going to be able to kill Monica Cassidy in ICU."

"So she told you. And you believed her," Bobby said with contempt.

"And I found another way to achieve the goal, which is more than I can say for whichever flunky failed to kill the army chaplain."

Bobby sat slowly, features like granite. "Beardsley flatlined."

"Obviously they brought him back," Rocky said coldly. "Now ICU is locked up tighter than Fort Knox."

"Tell me what you did."

"I drove to Charlotte and snatched Monica's little sister. She's in the trunk of my car."

Bobby actually paled, sending Rocky's pulse skyrocketing. "You did *what*?"

"I took her sister. I've been chatting her up for two months now. Monica sold so well, I thought her sister would sell well, too."

"Did you stop to think about the repercussions? One child running away with a guy she met on the Internet is believable. Two . . . Now the cops will be all over this. You'll have a grieving mother on the TV sobbing for her child's safe return. We might as well kill the sister now. Nobody's going to want her with her face on every damn milk carton."

Rocky sank into a chair. "I hadn't thought about that. But it's okay. I went to the bus station wearing her hoodie and bought a ticket to Raleigh, where her father lives. If the cops do investigate, it'll look like she went to live with him."

"I see," Bobby said coolly. "I *see* that I gave you a simple task—to ensure the nurse's compliance. I *see* you failed to do so. And I *see* you've taken a failure and compounded it with this unauthorized procurement. I will deal with the new girl and the nurse myself. You are dismissed."

Rocky stood, willed her body not to tremble. "The new girl is here. You might as well use her. She's even prettier than her sister. You can ship her out of the country where they don't have milk cartons. She'll bring a good price."

Bobby tapped the desk, thinking. "Perhaps. Now go."

Rocky stood her ground. "What will you do to the nurse?"

"What I promised."

"*No.* You promised to kill her son next. He's only eight. Just like your—"

"*Enough.*" Bobby rose, eyes ice blue with fury, and Rocky could no longer control her trembling. "I will have obedience, from the nurse and from you. You are dismissed."

Bobby waited until Rocky was gone, then redialed Paul.

"I thought I told you not to call me again today," Paul snapped.

Insolent man. I'd kill you, but I need you. "I need you to go up to Raleigh."

"I'm on duty tonight."

"Call in sick. I pay you triple what Atlanta PD does, anyway."

"Dammit, Bobby." Paul's sigh was frustrated. "What do you want me to do?"

"I need you to clean up Rocky's mess."

"Rocky's made quite a few messes lately."

"Yes, I know. When you've cleaned up this one, we'll discuss disposition of Rocky."

Atlanta, Saturday, February 3, 8:40 a.m.

Luke told the team Susannah's story about the black sedan, Darcy Williams, and the day six years ago in Hell's Kitchen. Hardly anyone breathed until he was finished.

Chase sat back, stunned. "You mean to tell me that

Susannah was assaulted twice on the same freaking day, seven years apart? And nobody thought this was strange?"

Luke hesitated. "She never reported either assault."

"For God's sake, why not?" Chase thundered.

"She was a victim, Chase," Mary McCrady said in her psychologist voice.

"None of this is easy for her," Luke said, "and now she's got some creep in a black sedan following her around. She's planning to go to Sheila Cunningham's funeral today and I'm concerned for her safety until we find out who this guy is."

"So you're going to the funeral to see if black sedan man shows up," Ed said. "You'll want video surveillance. I'll take care of it."

"Thanks," Luke said. It wasn't the only reason he'd decided to go to Sheila Cunningham's funeral, but it was the main one. "Susannah also said this swastika with its bent edges is a common symbol in Eastern religions. Like Buddhism."

"The *thích* we were searching for," Pete murmured. "It all falls together somehow."

"Let's figure out how," Chase said. "Hank, get down to Savannah and find Helen Granville. We need to know the truth about her husband. Pete, I want you to take over the search at Mansfield's house, and Nancy, you track down this Chili Pepper. I want to know who hired him." Pete opened his mouth to protest and Chase shot him a warning look. "Don't try it, Pete. You're not getting within a mile of this guy."

"I can handle myself," Pete said tightly.

"I know," Chase said, gently. "But I'm still not putting you in the situation."

"I'm still tracking the medical supplies we found in the bunker," Ed said. "We're also running PCRs on the hair samples we found when we swept the bunker's office area. Maybe something will match with the DNA patterns we have on file. We'll search the area outside the bunker for more victims. And we'll dust that road atlas for prints."

"Good," Chase said. "What else?"

"I want to talk to Susannah Vartanian," Mary said.

"I'm meeting her at her hotel in a little while," Chloe said. "I'll tell her to call you."

"She's not at her hotel," Luke said. "She's in my office. She drove here when the black sedan was following her. She's researching the swastika symbol."

Chase waved at the door. "Now go, and good luck. We meet again at five. Luke, stay." When the door was closed and they were alone, Chase met his eyes with a troubled frown. "Why didn't Susannah report either of those rapes?"

"The first time, she was terrified of Simon, who told her she had to sleep sometime."

Chase's jaw hardened. "Sonofabitch. So what about the second time?"

I didn't deserve justice either. "She was scared, and being Daniel's sister, has felt guilty all these years that her friend died and she didn't."

"They are alike, aren't they?"

"Two peas in a fucking pod."

"Is her story documented?"

"Documentable, I imagine. Her boss has known for years and he's an ADA."

"Why are you going to that funeral, really?"

Luke frowned. "What do you mean?"

"I mean I don't have resources to waste babysitting Susannah Vartanian. And from what I can see, she's the last person who'd expect me to."

"You think I'd do that?" Luke felt his blood pressure rise. "Waste resources?"

"I think you wouldn't see it that way. Look, I feel sorry for Susannah, too, but—"

Luke struggled for patience. He was tired and irritable. Chase was, too, and neither one of them wore that combination well. "I'm not babysitting her. Am I concerned? Yes. Think about this. She's raped at age sixteen. The only people who know are either dead or Garth Davis. She leaves home, goes to college. Then at age twenty-three, she's raped again, on the same fucking date. She's branded, her friend beaten to death. She's ashamed and scared and says nothing. Six years later, that same brand turns up on Granville's amulet and on the hips of five girls Granville murdered."

Chase's eyes sharpened. "So?"

Luke's fist clenched under the table. "So there's a connection, dammit. The man who killed her friend was convicted. The man who raped her the second time hasn't been caught. What if that man was Rocky? What if Rocky or Granville orchestrated it? What if the man sitting in prison for killing her friend knows Rocky? What if the driver of the black sedan was Rocky? Do I have to draw you a goddamn map?"

Chase leaned back. "No. I'd already drawn it myself. I just needed to make sure you had, too. Go to the funeral. It'll be a media zoo, coming on the heels of yesterday."

Luke stood, vibrating with temper and annoyed Chase had treated him like a junior G-man. "I'll be sure to pack my chair and whip."

He was ready to slam out, when Chase stopped him. "Good job, Luke."

Luke shuddered out a breath. "Thank you."

Ridgefield House, Saturday, February 3, 9:00 a.m.

Ashley Csorka lifted her head, listening in the dark of the "hole." It was a root cellar, underneath the house, not even big enough to stand up in. Dank and cold. *I'm so cold.*

Her stomach was growling. It was breakfast time. She could smell food cooking upstairs. *I'm so hungry.* She forced her mind to do the math. She'd been huddling in this corner for almost twelve hours.

The woman said they'd keep her here for a few days. *I'll be crazy in a few days.* Plus there were rats. Ashley had heard them scurry behind the walls during the night.

Ashley hated rats. Panic welled, huge and terrifying. *I have to get out of here.*

"Well, sure," she murmured aloud, her voice lessening some of the panic. "How?"

They were near a river. If she could only get to the river, she was certain she could swim across. Her swim team trained in the ocean sometimes, where the currents ran stronger than the river's. And even if she drowned, it would be preferable to what was in store for her when they decided to let her out of the hole.

How do I get out of here? There was only one door at the top of the short staircase and it was locked. She'd tried it already. And even if she did manage to open the door, there was that skinny creepy butler, Tanner, who carried a gun.

Outside there was a guard. She'd seen him when they'd

brought them in yesterday. He carried a bigger gun. It was no use. *I'll die here. I'll never go home.*

Stop. You will not die. She got on her hands and knees and began to feel her way around. Her jaw clenched against the pain in her hand where she'd caught an exposed nail when she'd been shoved down the stairs. *Just ignore it and look for a way out.*

The first wall was cinderblock, as was the second and third.

But the fourth wall . . . Ashley's fingers brushed against something rough. Brick. Someone had bricked in this wall. That meant there was something on the other side. A door? A window?

So what? It's brick. Solid brick. Discouraged, Ashley slid down, her back against the wall. She wrapped her arms around her knees. She couldn't claw her way through brick.

She'd need a sledgehammer to bust through or a file to chip at the mortar. She had neither. Slowly she lifted her hand. But there was an exposed nail on the stairs.

But they might hear me chipping at the mortar.

So what? If they hear you, they'll just drag you out sooner. Her future would be the same unless she got away. *So you might as well try.*

Never say try. She conjured the voice of her coach. *Set your goal. Then do it.*

"So do it, Ashley," she whispered. "Do it now."

Chapter Eleven

Atlanta, Saturday, February 3, 9:20 a.m.

Is it complete?" Chloe asked as Susannah reviewed the stenographer's transcript. Al Landers sat at her side, silent. His hand gripped hers, supportive.

"Yes," Susannah said. "Give me a pen before I change my mind."

"It's not too late, Susannah," Al murmured, and she smiled at him.

"I know, but this is bigger than just me, Al. This is all tied up in what happened in that bunker. Five girls are still missing. I have to do this."

"Thank you," Chloe said. "I can only imagine how difficult this has been."

Susannah huffed a wry chuckle. "Difficult. Yeah. That about sums it up."

"How long before the press gets hold of this?" Al asked.

"We won't tell them," Chloe said. "We never disclose the names of victims of sexual assault, but it's going to get out. One of the other victims, Gretchen French, has already mentioned scheduling a press conference. She wants to control her announcement."

"I don't know her," Susannah said. "I suppose I will, soon enough." She rose and tugged the short skirt, trying to cover another inch of her legs. "We should give Agent Papadopoulos his office back. And I have to get to that funeral. I wish it had been scheduled for noon. The department stores don't open till ten and I didn't have time to shop for clothes this morning." She'd been too unnerved to do so, had there been time.

Chloe frowned. "You look fine."

"I look like a teenager, but my clothes were ruined yesterday and this is all I have. I wish I had something more sober to wear. It *is* a funeral. This feels disrespectful."

Chloe studied her a moment. "I'm way too tall, so my suits won't fit you, but I have a short black cocktail dress that might hit you below the knee. You could use a belt to cinch the waist. I only live a few minutes away. I'll run home and get it for you."

Susannah opened her mouth to politely decline, then changed her mind. "Thanks. I appreciate it." When she was gone, Susannah turned to Al. "Thanks for being here."

"I wish I'd known the rest of it. I would have been there years ago."

"Excuse me." Luke stuck his head in. "I saw Chloe leave. Are you finished?"

"We are." She rose. "Luke, this is my boss, Al Landers. Al, Special Agent Luke Papadopoulos. He's a friend of my brother Daniel."

"You're the guy I saw in the hotel hall last night," Al said as they shook hands. "What are you doing to catch this guy in the black sedan?"

"We're setting up surveillance at the funeral this afternoon," Luke said. "And we'd like to talk to the guy who was convicted for Darcy Williams's murder."

"I can arrange an interview. What about the other guy, Susannah?" Al looked grim. "The one who assaulted you. Did he know Darcy's killer?"

Susannah's cheeks grew hot. "No. They were strangers, too."

"How do you know for sure?" Luke asked gently, and his implication hit her hard.

"I guess I don't," she said. "How stupid were we?"

"Pretty damn stupid," Al said sadly. "What were you thinking, Susannah?"

"I wasn't." She looked away, crossing her arms over her chest. "I met Darcy when she was a waitress in the West Village and I went to NYU. One night I went in for some carryout and we started talking. Turned out we had a lot in common. Both of us had bad relationships with our fathers and mothers who didn't protect us. Darcy had run away at fourteen, done drugs, the whole nine yards."

"Whose idea was it to meet the men?" Al asked, and again her cheeks heated.

"Darcy's. She hated men and then, so did I. She said she wanted to be in control for once. She wanted to be the one to leave the guy in the middle of the night without a thank you. I was appalled at first. Then . . . I just did it." And the second time was easier. And the third time a dark thrill. By the fourth time . . . it shamed her to even think of it.

Al and Luke were looking at each other oddly. "What?" she asked.

"What if Darcy was put up to meeting you?" Luke asked, his voice still gentle.

Susannah's mouth fell open. "Oh my God. I never . . ." Her arms went limp at her sides. "That's crazy."

"Didn't you think it odd that both assaults happened on the same day?" Al asked.

Susannah blew out a breath. "Of course. But I'd gone to that hotel of my own free will." By then it had become a dark obsession. "I chose that date specifically. It was supposed to be my declaration of independence. Later, I told myself it was . . . an omen. God's punishment, call it what you want. I'd royally erred and I was paying the price. The date was a message. Clean up or else. It sounds stupid when I say it out loud."

"You were a victim," Luke said. "Twice. You weren't thinking like an ADA, you were thinking like a human being who had to make sense of something horrific. There isn't any sense to it, though. Bad things sometimes happen to good people. Period."

I wasn't a good person. I wasn't. But she nodded gravely. "I know."

Luke's dark eyes flickered and she knew he hadn't bought her easy acceptance of his words. "What about the man who assaulted you? Can you describe him?"

"Of course. I'll never forget his face. But what will that help? It was six years ago. The trail went cold a long time ago."

"We'll still sit you down with a sketch artist, just in case this guy is still around and involved with that black sedan." He turned to Al. "How can I talk to Darcy's killer?"

"Michael Ellis," Susannah murmured.

Luke frowned. "What did you say?"

"Michael Ellis," Al supplied. "Darcy's killer. Why?"

Luke scraped his palms down his stubbled face. "We found two passports in Granville's firebox. Both had his photo, but neither had his name. One name was Michael Tewes. The other name was Toby Ellis."

"Sonofabitch," Al muttered. "Granville set this up."

"Either with black sedan man or he told him later," Luke confirmed. "Sonofabitch."

Susannah sat down, her heart in her throat. "It was all planned," she said tonelessly, dropping her eyes to her lap. "I was set up. They've been laughing at me. All this time."

Luke crouched in front of her, taking her cold hands in his warm ones. "Granville's paid. This other guy will, too. Does the name Rocky mean anything to you?"

She shook her head. "No. Should it?"

"We think that's Granville's partner's name." He gave her hands a squeeze.

She looked up, met his eyes, another thought taking root, just as crazy as the others. But this wasn't crazy. It was reality. "Simon stalked me. In New York."

"What do you mean?" Luke asked.

"Daniel didn't tell you?" she asked, and he shook his head. "When we were in Philadelphia the detectives had several sketches of Simon. He'd become very good at disguise, one of which was an old man. It was how he lured his victims. I recognized the picture. I sometimes saw the old man when I was walking my dog in the park. It was Simon. He'd sit five feet from me and chat, and I never knew it was my own brother."

"But Simon can't be Granville's partner," Luke said. "Simon's dead."

"I know. But . . ." She sighed. "I don't know what."

Luke squeezed her hands. "Just try to relax and keep your eyes open at the funeral. I'm going to be there, too." He looked at Al over his shoulder. "You're going?"

"You couldn't stop me," Al said grimly.

"Good. We can use all the eyes we can get."

Ridgefield House, Saturday, February 3, 9:45 a.m.

Bobby hung up the phone, feeling elation and trepidation in equal measures. Paul's analysis had been spot on as usual and now, after a minimum of persuasion, Bobby had a new informant on the GBI team. But the informant's information was unsettling. Beardsley not only had lived, he'd talked. The police knew about Rocky. After the nerve she'd shown today, this was Rocky's final straw.

"Mr. Charles is here to see you," Tanner said from the doorway.

Meddling old man. "Show him in, Tanner. Thank you."

Charles came in, dressed in a black suit, his ivory box under one arm. "I thought I'd stop by." He patted the box. "Maybe play a game of chess."

"I'm not in the mood for games." Bobby gestured to a chair. "Sit. Please."

Charles's lips twitched condescendingly. "What's stuck up your craw?"

"DRC119," Bobby said, and had the pleasure of seeing Charles blink in surprise for the first time ever.

But he recovered quickly, his smile returning. "How did you know?"

"I have a source on the GBI team investigating the incident at the bunker." Bobby suspected the GBI mole was holding out, but there had been enough information shared to establish an action plan.

"My star pupil," Charles said mildly.

"Don't change the subject. Were you driving that black sedan?"

"Of course. I didn't want to miss the expression on her face."

"What if you'd been stopped? Caught?"

"Why would I have been stopped? I wasn't speeding."

Bobby frowned. "That was an unacceptable risk."

Charles's expression went from genial to glacial. "You're behaving like an old woman." He leaned forward until their eyes locked. "I taught you better than that."

Chastised and feeling five years old, Bobby looked away.

Charles settled in his chair, satisfied. "What else did your GBI mole tell you?"

"Beardsley heard Granville talking about Rocky, by name," Bobby said, subdued. *I hate you, old man.*

"By Rocky or by her name?"

"Well, by Rocky, but that's still too close for me."

"I agree. What will you do?"

Exactly what you'd do. Kill her. "I'm not sure yet."

Charles nodded, his expression now disapproving. "I drove by Randy Mansfield's house. It's still standing."

Bastard. Just rub it in. "Yes, I know."

"Why is it still standing?" He lifted his brows, reproach in his eyes. "It's not like you to miss a detail as important as that."

Bobby wanted to squirm. "I didn't miss a detail. My guy didn't do the job correctly." And for that Chili Pepper would die as soon as he was located. GBI was already looking for him. *I need to find him first.* God only knew what Pepper would tell them.

"Then you failed."

Bobby started to speak, then looked away again, deflated. "Yes. I did."

"So what happened?" Charles asked, more kindly, in the way one rewarded a dog with affection after punishing it for bad behavior.

I hate you. "Mr. Pepper got too technical. In both

houses he left a firebomb with a timing device, then wired the house to blow if the cops went in before the timer went off. The cops tripped the wire at Granville's, which alerted thcm to the bombs at Mansfield's. The bomb squad disabled both devices at Mansfield's before they could blow."

"There were cops all over Mansfield's place when I drove by."

"I know, but all they've found is his gun collection and his library of kiddie porn."

"His father was so smart," Charles lamented. "Randy was such a disappointment."

"I know. Granville's house burned to the ground. The only thing they found was his fire safe with his fake passports inside."

"Why didn't your firebug just use gas and a match?"

"I don't know. I'll ask him when I find him."

"But you know where Mr. Pepper is now," Charles said.

No, but I'm not about to admit that to you. "Of course. Just like I know where Garth and Toby's wives are, right now." Which was, fortunately, very true. "The cops think the wives can lead them to the infamous Rocky, who they believe is Granville's partner and the brains of the operation."

"And what else?"

Bobby hesitated. "Did you know Susannah Vartanian was raped by Granville's club thirteen years ago?"

Charles lifted a shoulder. "Let's just say it was a . . . private performance."

"Susannah Vartanian just signed a statement accusing Garth Davis of rape."

"Interesting," was all Charles replied. "Anything more?"

"You obviously knew about the incident with Darcy Williams."

"Obviously. And what else?"

"Nothing." Except that Susannah would be at Sheila Cunningham's funeral today. And that there were probably a dozen things the GBI mole had not mentioned.

And I'm scared. There were too many unexpected and unwelcome developments. This had the feel of an iceberg lurking beneath the water. Impact was certain and imminent. Bobby hated to be scared. Charles could always sense fear.

Charles stood up, his lips curled in disgust. "I have to be going."

"Where?"

"The Cunningham girl is being buried today," he said. "I would be remiss were I not to attend." He stepped closer, his shadow falling over Bobby's chair. And he waited.

Despite sincere efforts to not meet his eyes, Bobby finally looked up, and as always, could not look away. *I hate you, old man.*

"You disappoint me, Bobby. You are afraid. And that, more than anything else, makes you a failure."

Bobby wanted to speak, but no words would come and Charles laughed bitterly.

"Your 'guy' did not fail at Mansfield's house, Bobby. Your 'personnel' inside the hospital did not fail. Your assistant did not fail. You did. You sit in this relic of a house, believing you are pulling strings." Contempt dripped from his voice. "That you are a master. But you are not. You sit here, hiding from the world. And from your birthright."

Charles leaned forward. "You wish you were a master, but you're no more than a shadow of what you might have been. All you command is a chain of mobile whorehouses that pander to truckers on the interstate. You play at being a high-priced 'purveyor of fine flesh,' but you're nothing more than a glorified pimp. You were much more interesting when you were a high-priced whore yourself."

Bobby's heart was pounding. *Say something. Defend yourself.* But no words came and Charles's mouth twisted into a sneer. "Have you found out why Susannah came back? Of course you haven't. You'll let her slip away, back to New York City, so far away." He whined the last three words, mocking. "You could have gone to New York at any point and had your revenge, but you obviously don't want it badly enough."

Charles stepped back and Bobby's eyes followed, like a bird hoping for the smallest morsel. *I hate you, old man.* Charles shoved his ivory box of chess pieces under his arm. "I'll not return until you can show me you deserve my respect."

Charles left and Bobby sat stewing. But Charles had been right. *I've become insulated. Completely out of touch.* The decision was clear. "Tanner! I need you. I'm going out. You need to help me dress."

Tanner frowned. "You think this is a good idea?"

"I do. Charles was right. I've been hiding here for two days, pulling weak strings that keep snapping. I don't have a lot of time. Where is that trunk of old clothes?"

"You're going to wear your mother's clothes? Bobby. That's so wrong."

"Of course I'm not going to wear Mother's clothes, she was too short."

"And she had hideous fashion sense."

"Well, that, too. Grandmother was taller. Her stuff should fit. Where is Rocky?"

"Off licking her wounds, I would imagine."

"Find her. She's going with me. But first she's going to show me all the girls she has in the pipeline. Glorified pimp, my ass. Charles will eat those words. But I have given Rocky too much power. *I'll* oversee the new acquisitions from here on out."

Tanner's eyes gleamed. "I know all her passwords and screen names."

Bobby blinked. "How?"

Tanner shrugged. "I'm a thief and always will be, but I keep up with technology. I sent a Trojan to her computer that logs all her keystrokes. I know every mark she's been cultivating for the last six months and where they live."

"You wily old man. I always underestimate you."

"Yes, you do." But he smiled as he said it.

Bobby started up the stairs, then stopped and looked back down at him. "Was I more interesting when I was a high-priced whore?"

"Infinitely. But you can't do *that* anymore, so you adapt and move on."

"You're right. Make sure the girls are shackled to the wall. Who's on duty today?"

"It was Jesse Hogan, but . . ." Tanner shrugged.

"But Beardsley killed him. Hogan was stupid to let a prisoner get the drop on him. Call Bill. If he whines about the overtime, tell him I'll pay him double." The guards were one group Bobby kept well-paid. "We need to hire another guard to take Hogan's place."

"I'll take care of it. Anything else?"

Bobby looked around the foyer. "Charles called this house a relic."

"About that, he was right. This place is drafty and none of the appliances work correctly, especially the stove.

It's impossible to make a good cup of tea when the water never boils."

"So let's find another house. I have enough money. Let's blow this relic."

Tanner's gray brows went up cagily. "I hear the old Vartanian house is empty."

Bobby laughed. "In good time, Tanner. For now, help me dress for this funeral. And make sure my gun is loaded."

Charles looked in his rearview mirror as he pulled away from the curb. Tanner had given him the evil eye as he'd shown him out, but Bobby had become complacent and needed that kick in the ass. He thought of how far they'd come since the day they'd met. He'd known there was something there, something worth molding. The baggage Bobby carried made his job all the easier. There had been a drive, a need to dominate.

Part of it came from the man who'd raised Bobby with an iron fist. He was long dead, having raised his iron fist to Bobby once too often. Bobby raised an iron fist right back and beat the man to death with it, along with his wife. Tanner had somehow been involved, to what extent, Charles had never been able to determine. He did know that Tanner had been charged and Bobby had helped the old man escape. Since then, they'd been inseparable.

But Tanner was old, as much a relic as that house. Bobby needed to move on. To claim that birthright, because the lion's share of Bobby's desire to dominate was genetic. It was an indisputable fact to anyone who took the time to look, but surprisingly, no one had. *No one but me.* Charles often wondered why no one else had seen what had been so obvious the first time he'd looked into Bobby's blue eyes.

It was as indelible as a brand.

Speaking of which, Charles had to admit he was a bit surprised at Susannah. She'd gone to the police and told them about Darcy Williams. He truly had not anticipated that. However, he was certain she'd said no more than she'd had to. Six years ago he'd led her to a place she never even conceived existed. He'd shown her the depth of perversion of which she personally was capable. Not once, not twice, but again and again until she couldn't pretend it hadn't been her idea, until she despised herself for the depths of obsession to which she'd sunk and clung.

That's where Bobby and Susannah were different, he mused. Bobby yearned for the birthright. Susannah spurned it. Both were equally intense in their goal.

Intensity made for vulnerability. This he'd learned the hard way.

This morning he'd pushed Susannah and she'd responded by confessing. In hindsight, he should have seen that coming. She'd turned to her faith after the Darcy episode. Her faith and her career. And in both had convinced herself she was back in control. But Charles knew differently. His mentor Pham always said that once one tasted the forbidden, the flavor lingered. Tempted.

Charles could push Susannah where he wanted her to go. It was a challenge.

Today he'd pushed Bobby. Now he had to stand back and see how his star pupil would respond. He sincerely hoped Rocky would be dealt with. He'd been even less pleased with Bobby's choice of recruit than he'd been with Granville's.

Granville tagged Simon Vartanian young, but even then Charles had seen the insanity in the boy. Then Simon had been proclaimed dead by his father. Simon hadn't been dead, of course, only banished. It was Judge Vartanian's way of neutralizing the impact of Simon's bad deeds on his own judicial career. The Judge told everyone Simon had been in a car accident. He'd even had some stranger's body buried in Simon's grave. And standing by Simon's grave back then, Charles had been relieved. Simon had his uses, but given long enough, he would have brought Granville down.

When Granville tagged Mansfield, he'd been optimistic. But Randy Mansfield hadn't become half the man his father had been.

As for Rocky, she wasn't insane or worthless. However, she had a softness, a pathos that was a definite liability. And now she knew their secrets. *She knows my face.*

If Bobby doesn't eliminate her, I'll have to.

Atlanta, Saturday February 3, 10:15 a.m.

"Wake up."

Monica heard the hissed words and struggled to obey. Her eyelids lifted.

My eyes work again. She moved her arm, gratified when she felt the tug of the IV needle. *The breathing tube is still in. I can't talk. But I'm not paralyzed.*

She blinked and a face came into focus. *A nurse.* Panic sent her pulse scrambling.

"Just listen," the nurse said hoarsely, and Monica could see the woman's eyes were red from crying. "They have your sister. I have a picture." She shoved her phone in front of Monica's eyes and Monica's scrambling heart seemed to stop.

Oh God, it was true. It was Genie, curled into a ball, her mouth gagged, her hands tied. She was in the trunk of a car. *She might be dead. Oh God.*

"She's alive," the nurse said. "But they mean business, make no mistake. I was supposed to kill you, but I couldn't." Tears filled her eyes and she dashed them away. "Now my sister is dead. They beat her to death. Because I didn't kill you."

Horrified, Monica watched the nurse inject something into her IV and walk away.

Chapter Twelve

Dutton, Saturday, February 3, 11:05 a.m.

I can't do this," Rocky said. "I'll be caught."

"You're afraid," Bobby said scornfully.

"Yes," Rocky said. "I am. You want me to walk into the middle of the town and shoot Susannah Vartanian in the cemetery? In front of everyone?"

"There is anonymity in a crowd," Bobby said. "Once you fire, you drop the gun. There will be so much confusion, you'll be able to walk away."

"That's insane."

Bobby grew very still. "I thought you trusted me."

"I do, but—"

"You've shown fear at every occasion," Bobby said harshly. "Yesterday at the bunker. With the nurse. If you plan to hide at every turn, I can't use you." Bobby's brows lifted. "And Rocky, nobody just walks away from me."

"I know," Rocky said. If she refused, she'd die here. *I don't want to die.*

Bobby was watching her. "You're afraid. You're a failure. You are of no use to me."

Rocky stared at the gun Bobby pointed at her. "You'd shoot me? Just like that?"

"Just like that. If you have no more trust than this, after

all I've done for you, all your life . . . You should be grateful. Yet you disappoint me again and again. I have no use for failures. I have no use for you. You've failed too many times. This was your opportunity to show me you're worth saving. Worth keeping."

Bobby sat calm, confident, and Rocky wanted to scream. Insecurity warred with fear. If she were cast aside, where would she go? She'd be alone. "Can I have a gun with a silencer at least?"

"No. A silencer is a crutch. You have to prove to me that you have the courage to be my protégée. If you are successful today, you'll never be afraid again. That is what I need in my assistant. What I must have. So choose. Live and serve, or cower and die."

Rocky stared at the gun in Bobby's hand. Both choices sucked. Dying sucked more. And she was so damn tired of being afraid.

"Give me the gun. I'll do it." *But when I fire, Susannah Vartanian won't be the one to fall. You will. I'll tell them who you are, what you've done. Then I'll be free.*

Dutton, Saturday, February 3, 11:35 a.m.

"Did anybody stay home?" Luke muttered. "Looks like the whole damn town's here."

"They are," Susannah murmured. Standing in the cemetery behind Dutton's First Baptist Church, she was flanked on one side by Luke, on the other by Al. Chase was somewhere in the crowd, watching, supported by ten plainclothes state cops.

"Do you see anyone that looks familiar?" Luke murmured.

"Just the same old people I grew up with. If you need running commentary, just ask."

"Okay. Who was the preacher who did the service?"

"That would be Pastor Wertz," she said softly, and Luke bent his head closer to better hear. He smelled like cedar again today, she thought, the odor of fire and death washed away. She took another breath, filling her head with his scent before turning her focus back to the cemetery in which she'd stood with Daniel barely two weeks before. "Wertz has been pastor since before I was born. My father thought he was a fool. That either meant he couldn't be bought or that he wasn't bright enough to play his games. Wertz doesn't seem much different, except that his sermons used to be a lot longer. Today's was barely twenty minutes."

"He's got a lot of them to do," Al said. "Maybe he's pacing himself."

She thought of all the death inflicted by Mack O'Brien. "You're probably right."

"What about the older gentleman with the entourage?" Luke asked.

"That's Congressman Bob Bowie."

"His daughter was Mack O'Brien's first victim," Luke murmured, and she nodded.

"Standing beside him are his wife, Rose, and his son, Michael."

"What about the thin, old man beside the son?"

"That's Mr. Dinwiddie. He's the Bowies' butler and has been since I can remember. The Bowies had live-in servants, and that made my mother jealous. She wanted a butler, but my father wouldn't allow it. 'Servants have big ears and wagging tongues,' he'd say. He did too much business in the middle of the night to worry about a butler."

"Anybody else I should know?"

"Do you see the older lady with big hair? She's standing three rows back. That's Angie Delacroix. She might be a good resource to talk to about Granville and anyone else. Angie owns the beauty shop. She knows everything that goes on in Dutton, and what she doesn't hear, the barbershop trio see. That's them, coming this way."

Three old men had been sitting in folding chairs at the graveside. As one they'd risen and were now making their way across the grass.

"Barbershop trio?" Al asked as the old men approached. "Not a quartet?"

"No. There are always three, and they sit on a bench outside the barber shop all day and watch the world go by from nine to five, Monday through Friday. They take an hour for lunch in the diner across the street. They're a Dutton institution. The old men in the town have to wait for one of the trio to die before a space on the bench opens up."

"O-kay," Luke murmured. "And I thought my great-uncle Yanni was weird for painting all the eyes of his yard statues blue. Which of these guys is Daniel's old English teacher? He helped us with Mack O'Brien yesterday. He might be willing to give us information again."

"That would be Mr. Grant. He's on the right. The others are Dr. Fink and Dr. Grim. All three of them creep me out," she murmured.

"With names like Fink and Grim, I can understand," Luke said, amused.

"That's their real names, too. Dr. Fink was my dentist. I still can't hear a drill without panicking. Mr. Grant always talked about dead poets. He tried to get me to go out for theater. And Dr. Grim was my biology teacher. He was . . . different."

"Different how?" Luke asked.

"He made Ben Stein in *Ferris Bueller* look like he had ADD."

"That exciting?" Luke asked, a smile in his voice.

"More so." She straightened as the three stopped in front of her. "Gentlemen, please allow me to introduce you to Special Agent Papadopoulos and Assistant District Attorney Al Landers. This is Dr. Fink, Dr. Grim, and Mr. Grant."

The old men nodded politely. "Miss Susannah." Dr. Fink took her hand. "I didn't get the chance to express my condolences at your parents' funeral."

"Thank you, Dr. Fink," she said quietly. "I appreciate that."

The next man brushed a kiss against her cheek. "You're looking lovely, my dear."

"And you're looking well, Mr. Grant."

"We heard the news about Daniel," Mr. Grant said, worried. "Is he improved?"

"He's still in intensive care, but his prognosis is excellent."

Mr. Grant shook his head. "I can't believe twenty-four hours ago he gave me a volume of poetry, and now . . . But he's young and strong. He'll pull through."

"Thank you, sir."

The third man was studying her intently. "You're looking peaked, Miss Vartanian."

She straightened again. "I'm just tired, Dr. Grim. It's been a long few weeks."

"Are you taking B-twelve? You haven't forgotten the importance of vitamins, have you?"

"I certainly could never forget the importance of vitamins, sir."

Dr. Grim's face softened. "I was so sorry to hear about your mama and daddy."

Susannah held back the flinch. "Thank you, sir. Thank you very much."

"Excuse me," Luke inserted, "but I'm sure you gentlemen have heard about the death of Dr. Granville yesterday."

All three grimaced. "It's a terrible shock," Dr. Fink said. "Before I retired, my dental practice was next door to his clinic. I spoke to him every day. I'd have lunch with him sometimes. My daughter took my grandkids to him for their shots. I had no idea . . ."

"He was one of my students," Mr. Grant said sadly. "A brilliant mind. Skipped two grades to graduate early. What a waste. Fink's right. It's a shock to all of us."

Dr. Grim looked most devastated. "He was my star pupil. Nobody absorbed biology like Toby Granville. Nobody knew he had such evil in him. It's unbelievable."

"I understand," Luke murmured. "You three must see a lot that goes on in Dutton."

"We do," Dr. Fink said proudly. "At least one of us is on that bench at all times."

Susannah lifted her brows, surprised. "I thought you had to sit there, nine to five."

"Well, we don't leave unless there's a good reason, of course," Mr. Grant said. "Like my weekly therapy on my knee or Fink's dialysis or Grim's—"

"That's enough," Grim said roughly. "He didn't ask our daily routine, Grant. Do you have a specific question, Agent Papadopoulos?"

"Yes, sir," Luke said. "I do. Did you notice Dr. Granville talking to anyone unusual?"

All three men frowned and looked at each other.

"Like a woman?" Fink asked. "Are you asking if he was having an affair?"

"No," Luke said, "but are you saying he did?"

"No," Grim said. "To say he was a God-fearing man seems ludicrous, but I never saw him in an inappropriate situation. He was the town doctor. He talked to everyone."

"So he didn't have anyone he was especially friendly with, or did business with?"

"Not to my knowledge," Mr. Grant said. "Fink, Grim?"

The three men shook their heads, curiously unwilling to speak against a man who was now known to have been a rapist, killer, and pedophile. But their reticence could also be due to a general mistrust of outsiders, Susannah thought.

"Thank you," Luke said. "I wish we could have met under different circumstances."

The three gave Susannah a stern glare, then started back for their folding chairs.

Susannah let out a breath. "That was interesting. I would have expected them to be cool to Al, just because he's a Yankee, but not to you, Luke."

"I'm glad I didn't say anything then," Al said, mildly affronted.

Her mouth curved a little. "Sorry, Al, but the older generation still holds a grudge."

"I didn't expect them to be happy with my questions," Luke said. "Granville's scandal is a shock and reflects poorly on the whole town. Who's the woman with the camera?"

"That's Marianne Woolf. Her husband owns the *Dutton Review*."

Luke let out a low whistle. "Daniel said she was voted most likely to do everyone. Now I understand. Whoa."

Susannah quashed the spurt of jealousy. Men had always had that reaction to Marianne, and the years had been good to her. Susannah wondered if the plastic surgeons had been good as well, but dismissed the thought as petty.

"Marianne must be covering this for the *Review*," she said. "Jim Woolf and his brothers aren't here. His sister Lisa was buried yesterday."

"Lisa Woolf was one of O'Brien's victims, too," Luke said for Al's benefit.

Susannah didn't want to think about Mack's victims. That they were dead too closely tied to Simon, which too closely tied to her. "The man next to Pastor Wertz is Corey Presto. Mr. Presto owns the pizza parlor where Sheila worked and was killed."

"Presto I know. I was at the scene with Daniel after Sheila was shot." Luke lifted his head to scan the crowd and Susannah felt cold again. "Two-thirds of the people here are reporters. I thought your parents' funeral was a media circus, but this is insane."

She hesitated. "Thank you, by the way, for coming to my parents' funeral. I know it meant a lot to Daniel to have you and your family here."

He squeezed her arm. "Daniel's family. We couldn't let him go through that alone."

She shivered, whether from the contact or the sentiment she was unsure. Studying the crowd, she frowned at the figure standing alone off to the side. "That's odd."

Al Landers instantly tensed. "What?"

"Just that Garth Davis's sister Kate came. I didn't expect to see her here, under the circumstances. I mean,

Sheila was one of Garth's victims. That's her, standing alone."

"Maybe she's just here to pay her respects," Al said.

"Maybe," Susannah said doubtfully. "But how awkward."

"Sshh," Luke cautioned. "They're getting ready to start."

It was a short service, and sad. Next to Pastor Wertz, pizza parlor owner Corey Presto stood quietly crying. Susannah didn't see any other family or friends. She wondered how many people here had actually known Sheila Cunningham.

Based on the avidly curious expressions of nearly every face in the crowd, not many. Sheila was news. She'd be gossiped about around water coolers for days to come.

Once the news of my statement hits, so will I.

Pastor Wertz began reading from the Bible, his face weary. He'd already officiated over two funerals in as many days and there were many more to come.

She thought about Daniel as Corey Presto put a red rose on top of Sheila's casket. Her brother had very nearly died yesterday. Had Alex not acted so quickly Susannah might have been standing here again in a few days, burying the last of her family.

And then I would be as alone as Sheila Cunningham had been. More so, because at least Sheila had Corey Presto. *I have no one.* Susannah swallowed hard, startled to find her face wet. Embarrassed, she quickly wiped her cheeks with her fingertips, stiffening when Luke's hand brushed her hair, settling on her back, warm and solid. For just a moment she gave in to the temptation to lean, resting her head against him.

And for just a moment she let herself yearn for a man

like Luke Papadopoulos, decent and kind. But that was not in the cards. Not after what he now knew. He would be kind because Daniel was family, and he might even be attracted to her, but ultimately the man whose mama still carried a rosary around in her purse would never want . . . *a woman like me*. And who could blame him? *I don't want a woman like me.*

Pastor Wertz said the "Amen" and Susannah pulled away from Luke, physically and emotionally. Al pushed a handkerchief into her hand. "Your mascara's run."

Quickly she wiped her face again. "Did I fix it?"

Al tipped her face up. "Yeah. You okay?"

No. "Yeah." She turned to Luke. "You don't have to babysit me. I'll be fine."

Luke didn't look like he believed her, but nodded. "I do need to get back. I have an appointment at two. Call if you need me or if you see anyone who looks familiar." He looked around. "I did want to talk to Kate Davis. Do you see her?"

Susannah didn't. "She must have left. This had to have been uncomfortable."

Luke looked at Al. "There are cops everywhere. If you need to, yell."

Al watched him go, then looked down at her, brows lifted. "He's very . . . nice."

Way too nice for me. "Let's go back. I haven't spent any time with Jane Doe today."

She'd only taken a few steps when a woman stopped in her path. She was tall, blond, and smileless. "Hi," she said nervously. "You're Susannah Vartanian, aren't you?"

Al's hand closed over her arm protectively. "I am," Susannah said. "Do I know you?"

"I don't think so. I'm Gretchen French."

The victim Chloe Hathaway said was trying to organize a press conference. How could she have found out so quickly? "What can I do for you, Miss French?"

"I met your brother Daniel a few days ago. I heard he was shot by Randy Mansfield."

The knot in her chest loosened. "He was, but he'll be all right."

Gretchen smiled, but it looked like it cost her. "I just wanted to ask you to thank him for me. He and Talia Scott made a very difficult time more bearable. He's a kind man."

Susannah nodded. "I'll tell him."

"It's nice of you to come today, to pay your respects to Sheila in Daniel's place."

Susannah felt Al's grip tighten, bolstering her. "That's not why I'm here."

"Then you knew Sheila?"

"No." *Just say it. Say it. Say it and it will be easier the second time.*

Gretchen's brows crunched. "Then why *are* you here?"

Susannah drew a breath. "For the same reason you are." She let the breath out quietly. "I was a victim, too."

Gretchen's mouth dropped open. "But . . . I . . ." She stared. "I had no idea."

"I didn't know about you either, or any of the others. Not until Daniel told me on Thursday. I thought I was the only one."

"So did I. Oh God." Gretchen took a steadying breath. "We all did."

"I gave my statement to ASA Hathaway today," Susannah said. "I'll be testifying."

Gretchen was still stunned. "It will be difficult."

Difficult. She was beginning to hate that word. "It will be hell for us all."

"I suppose you know that better than any of us. I read that you're a prosecutor now."

"Now," Susannah said, and Al squeezed her arm again. *But maybe not later.* Al was indeed correct that the defense would exploit her status as a victim. But she'd stand with the others now and cross each bridge as she got there. "Miss Hathaway said you're organizing a press conference. If you tell me when and where, I'll be there."

"Thank you."

"Don't thank me, please. I'll give you my card. Call me when the arrangements are made." She'd bowed her head to search her purse when a sharp crack split the air.

In an instant Susannah was thrown to the ground, her breath leaving her in a rush as Al landed on top of her and all hell broke loose in the cemetery. Around her people screamed and ran as police mobilized to bring order to the crowd.

Dazed, Susannah lifted her head, her gaze locking onto a woman who stood still amid all the frenzied movement around her. She was dressed in black, from her veiled hat to the hem of her old-fashioned dress to the tips of her gloved fingers. The black lace of the veil fell below her chin, covering her face, but somehow Susannah knew the woman was staring. *At me.*

And Susannah stared back, momentarily mesmerized.

Red lips. *She has red, red lips.* The color showed through the black lace, creating a startling effect. And then the woman slipped into the crowd and was gone.

"Are you all right?" Al shouted over the panicked screams.

"I'm fine."

"Stay down another few— Oh, shit." Al leaped up

and Susannah pushed herself to her knees as he lowered Gretchen French to the ground. "She's hit."

Twenty uniformed police stormed the area, and Susannah found herself stemming blood flow from a gunshot wound for the second time in less than twenty-four hours. Gretchen was conscious, but pale and shaken. The bullet had pierced the fleshy part of her arm and blood was sullenly oozing from the wound.

"Stay put," Susannah said. "Just don't move." She balled up Al's handkerchief and pressed it to Gretchen's arm. "Al, get me . . ." She looked up to find Al's horrified gaze fixed straight ahead, and her heart stumbled to a stop. "Oh, hell. Oh, no."

Kate Davis lay on the ground between two tombstones, staring skyward, her white shirt already red with blood. One arm lay flung outward, a gun still clutched in her hand.

Two officers were holstering their weapons. Susannah continued to stare, shocked. She hadn't heard the shot. But Kate Davis was dead.

Al looked down, stunned. "She shot Gretchen French."

"Step aside, please." Paramedics were pushing her out of the way, again for the second time in twenty-four hours. She stood up, her legs like rubber.

"Al . . ."

His arms came around her, keeping her from crumpling to the ground again as her knees buckled. He shielded her with his body as cameras began to flash. "Just come with me." He was breathing hard. "Susannah, this is one hell of a fucked-up town."

"Yeah," Susannah said breathlessly. "I know."

Tanner slowed the car and Bobby slid into the passenger seat. "Drive."

He obeyed and in ten seconds they'd cleared the cemetery gates. "Is it done?"

"Of course." And exactly as planned.

"Did anyone recognize you?"

"No."

Tanner grimaced as Bobby removed the veiled hat. "That hat is hideous, but the lipstick is even worse." He passed his handkerchief across the car. "Clean your face."

"Sheila always wore this color. I thought it was a nice touch."

Tanner rolled his eyes as Bobby wiped at the lipstick. "Where's your gun?"

"I dropped the one I used on Rocky in the grass, just like I'd planned. The other one is still in my pocket." Bobby fingered the small hole in the pocket's fabric. "All that training with Charles finally paid off. Two targets hit, using both hands. Ballistics will have a field day doing the matchups."

"So Susannah Vartanian is dead, too?"

"Of course not."

Tanner's head jerked, his frown fierce. "You said it was done. You missed?"

Bobby frowned back. "I don't miss. If I'd meant to hit Susannah, I would have. I never intended to kill her that painlessly. If Charles can play with her a little, so can I."

"So who else did you shoot?"

"I have no idea," Bobby said cheerfully. "Just a woman unlucky enough to be standing next to Susannah at the time." A laugh bubbled out. "I haven't felt like this in . . . well, I don't remember the last time. Maybe not since I killed that sonofabitch Lyle."

"Your father had it coming," Tanner said decisively.

He wasn't my father. "So did Rocky. Let's get back to

Ridgefield now. We have some things to do before you leave for Savannah."

Tanner tensed. "Get down. Police car at twelve o'clock."

Bobby twisted, ducking below the dash. "I didn't see any police cars."

"It was unmarked, but it's gone now. Let's get out of here."

Dutton, Saturday, February 3, 12:05 p.m.

Luke ran from his car, heart pounding. *Shots fired, Dutton Cemetery.* As soon as he'd heard the words on his radio, he'd U-turned and raced back. Susannah was sitting in the passenger seat of her rental car, parked in on all sides. Two state troopers were managing crowd control while an angry Al Landers paced the length of the car.

"What the hell happened?" Luke demanded.

Al shook his head. "I'm still not sure. I don't think your boss knows yet either."

Luke stuck his head in the car. Susannah sat, her hands folded in her lap. Her face, as well as the front of her black dress, was streaked red with clay. "Are you all right?"

She gave him a weary look. "The only thing that hit me was Al. Kate Davis is dead."

Luke frowned. "Kate Davis? You're kidding."

"I wish. The police shot her after she shot Gretchen French."

Luke shook his head to clear it. "Kate Davis *shot* someone? In the *cemetery*?"

"Yes," Susannah said calmly. "Gretchen French. In the cemetery. With a gun."

"The victim Chloe mentioned this morning? The one who's mobilizing the other victims to do a press conference?"

"That's the one. Gretchen's not hurt badly. The medics have her now."

Al stuck his head next to Susannah, his expression grim. "What she's not telling you is that she was standing next to Gretchen at the time."

Luke's stomach rolled over. She could have been killed. "I'll get an update on Miss French," he said roughly. "Then you're going back with me."

She looked surprised. "Kate didn't shoot me. She shot Gretchen. And now Kate's dead. I don't think she'll be shooting anyone else."

"Humor me. Please."

Something shifted in her gray eyes. "You've been very kind, Luke, but you don't have to babysit me. I'll be all right on my own."

She'd pulled away even though she hadn't moved a muscle. "Humor me anyway," he said, his jaw tightening. "Susannah, I'm so exhausted that it's hard for me to focus. It'll just be harder if I'm worried about you." That seemed to make a difference.

She nodded. "All right then. Should I come with you now?"

"No. Stay here until I come back." He and Al straightened and regarded each other over the top of the car. "Can you drive this rental car back?"

"Yes. That young woman, Kate Davis. Her brother Garth is the last surviving member of Simon's club. Is it possible news of Susannah's statement leaked out?"

"And that she was the intended target?" Luke had already considered it. "I'll find out."

Luke found Chase looking down at Kate Davis's body. Chase looked up sourly. "I'm having a very bad day."

"So's Kate Davis," Luke said. "Who shot her?"

"Don't know," Chase said, even more sourly. "Wasn't any of us."

Luke frowned. "You mean it wasn't GBI?"

"No, I mean it was not any law enforcement officer on the premises. No one fired their weapon. Therefore, I do not know who shot this woman," Chase said testily.

Luke looked around, frowning. "We have a second shooter?"

"Looks like."

"The bullet hit her straight in her heart. Somebody has a good eye."

"Yeah, I got that part. At least Kate's eye wasn't so good. Gretchen will be all right."

"That's what Susannah said. I'm taking Susannah back to Atlanta myself. So what *did* happen?"

"Kate Davis was in a pocket of people milling around the graveside. There was a huge line of cars waiting to get out of the cemetery and people were getting impatient."

"I parked on the next access road," Luke said. "I had to walk, but I got out fast."

"You weren't the only one, which was part of the problem. When bullets started to fly, people had already started leaving. It was almost impossible to lock the area down."

There were still a lot of people in the cemetery, many lined up along the yellow tape one of the officers had strung, hoping for a real-life taste of CSI. "Witnesses?"

"The three old men on the folding chairs had a ringside view. They said they saw Kate with a jacket draped over her arm, looking 'antsy.'" He pointed to the jacket lying on the ground about two feet from the body. "The next moment there was a shot fired and people started screaming. Al Landers tackled Susannah, knocking her down, but it was Gretchen French who was hit. Seconds later, two cops had their guns drawn and pointed at Kate. One told her to drop her weapon. The cops said she looked stunned." Chase met his eyes. "And then she said, 'I missed.'"

Luke's blood ran cold. "Shit."

"Yeah. The next second Kate drops like a rock. She was dead before she hit the ground. Like you said, somebody was a damn good shot."

"And had a gun with a silencer."

"Right again."

"Then the other shooter got away." Luke refused to let the panic in his gut rise to choke him. She'd missed and Susannah was unhurt. Gretchen's injury was minor. "I'm glad you're handling the brass. This is going to make us look like fucking monkeys."

"That about sums it up. You don't have to stay, Luke. Ed's got the scene and I'll manage the press." He grimaced. "They all got some great video for their newscasts."

"I'm glad we were here," Luke said pointedly, and Chase rolled his eyes.

"You were right. This was no babysitting job."

"Thank you. I'm going back now. I have to meet Kasey Knight's parents at two. You know, the parents of the first dead girl we've identified. I'm not looking forward to this."

"Wait," Chase said. "Weren't you going to check to see if Granville had a safe deposit box at Davis Bank in Dutton?"

"I went by before the service, but the bank is closed,"

Luke told him. "Rob Davis, the bank manager's grandson, is being buried up in Atlanta today."

"Because Rob Davis pissed off Mack O'Brien who then killed his grandson in retaliation." Chase sighed. "Now his nephew Garth is in jail, Garth's wife and sons are missing, and Kate is dead. I don't think it's healthy to be a member of that family."

"Or a Vartanian for that matter," Luke said quietly.

"Or a Vartanian," Chase agreed.

"Excuse me."

Both Luke and Chase turned to find a pale Pastor Wertz standing behind them. "Yes, Reverend?" Chase asked. "What can we do for you?"

Wertz looked stunned. "I have another funeral this afternoon. What should I do?"

"Whose funeral is it?" Luke asked.

"Gemma Martin," the pastor replied. "Oh, dear, this is not good. Not good at all."

"Mack O'Brien's third victim," Chase muttered. "Are you expecting a large crowd?"

"The family hired security to keep the media out," the pastor said. "But they've been flying overhead, sneaking through. It's been horrible. Horrible."

"We'll be cordoning off this whole section of cemetery," Chase said. "It's a crime scene now. The funeral and burial will have to be postponed."

"Oh my. Oh my." Pastor Wertz wrung his hands. "I'll tell Mrs. Martin, Gemma's grandmother. She won't be happy about this. No, not at all."

"If it'll help, I'll tell them," Chase offered, and the pastor nodded.

"It would, indeed." He looked down with a sigh. "Poor Kate. She was the last person I would have expected to do this. But I suppose even clear heads can get muddied in times like these, with Gretchen accusing her brother of rape. Her parents would have been so disappointed to see how Kate and Garth turned out. So sad. So very sad."

Dutton, Saturday, February 3, 12:45 p.m.

Luke glanced at Susannah before returning his eyes to the road. She'd had her eyes glued to her computer screen since they'd left the cemetery. "What are you doing now?"

"Checking runaway sites for Jane Doe. I spent about three hours on this last night."

"We have people checking all those sites. Why don't you sit back and go to sleep?"

"Because she's mine," Susannah said quietly. "Besides, your people only have pictures of her face all bruised up with her eyes closed. I saw her eyes open. I might see something they don't see. And I'll go crazy if I don't have something to do."

"That I understand. What did you find out about swastikas this morning?"

"Not much earthshaking. The swastika is used in Hinduism, Jainism, and Buddhism. In all cases, it's a religious symbol and can represent anything from evolution of life to good luck and harmony. It can mean something different depending on whether it's right or left facing. Mine faces right, which is strength and intelligence. Facing left," she said wryly, "it means love and mercy."

Luke considered it. "None of the brands faced left."

"I didn't think so. The Nazi swastika does point right, however."

"So this could still be tied to a neo-Nazi group."

"Possibly, but I don't think so. The Nazi form is very straight and almost always presented at a forty-five-degree angle. The ends are never bent."

He glanced at her. "Why did you never get yours removed?"

"Penance, I suppose." She hesitated, then shrugged. "And nobody was ever going to see it, so it didn't matter."

He frowned. "What does that mean?"

"It means I don't plan to show it to anyone ever again."

His frown deepened. "At the beach, or in a relationship?"

"Either."

There was a finality in her tone. "Why not?"

She made an annoyed noise. "You're a very nosy man, Agent Papadopoulos."

"Luke," he said, more sharply than he'd intended, and she shrugged again, making him angry. "Earlier I was kind. Now I'm nosy." He waited, but she said no more. "Is that all you're going to say?"

"Yes. That's all."

He was relieved when his cell buzzed in his pocket. He'd been about to lose his temper, and that was the last thing either of them needed right now. "Papadopoulos."

"Luke, it's Leigh. I have some phone messages for you. Is this a bad time?"

Yes. "No, it's a fine time," he said. "What is it?"

"First is from the Knights. You're supposed to meet them at two, but they won't be here until three-thirty. Second, I got a match to your Ashley C-s name. A Jacek Csorka in Panama City, Florida, filed a missing-person report on his daughter. She's been missing since this past Wednesday. She's not quite eighteen."

"Can you give me the number? Actually, give it to

Susannah." He handed the phone across the car. "Can you copy down the phone number she gives you?" Susannah did and Luke took his phone back. "What else?"

"Alex called. Daniel's awake."

He took his first easy breath in hours "Excellent. What about Jane Doe?"

"Still asleep."

"Can't have everything, I guess. What about tips on the hotline?"

"Hundreds of calls, but nothing credible."

"Thanks, Leigh. Call me as soon as Jane Doe wakes up. No change on Jane Doe," he said to Susannah when he'd hung up. Her eyes stayed locked on her computer screen. "Maybe Jane Doe's not in there, Susannah."

"No, she asked for her mom yesterday. Her mother must have loved her. I can't see a mother not doing everything she can to find her daughter."

There was yearning in her voice he wondered if she heard. It cut at his heart. "I have another nosy question."

She sighed. "What?"

"Have you ever had a boyfriend?"

She frowned. "That's not funny."

"I didn't mean it to be. In college, before Darcy, did you have a boyfriend?"

"No," she said coldly, but he was undeterred.

"In high school, before Simon and Granville, did you?"

"No," she said, angry now.

"And since Darcy?"

"No," she thundered. "Will you *stop*? If this is what I have to listen to so I can stay alive, then just throw me to the evil Rocky and be done with it."

"Why didn't you?" he asked, ignoring her tantrum. "After Darcy, why didn't you?"

"Because," she snapped, then her shoulders sagged. "You want my soul, Agent Papadopoulos?" she asked wearily, and for once he didn't correct her. "Fine. God knows I don't deserve it. More importantly, no decent man deserves it either."

"Am I decent?" he asked softly.

"I'm afraid so, Luke," she said, so sadly it broke his heart.

"So you'll be alone forever? Is that the penance you'll pay?"

"Yes."

Luke shook his head, unwilling to accept it. "That's wrong, Susannah. You're paying for something that was done to you. You were the victim."

"You don't know what I was," she said bitterly.

"Then tell me. Talk to me."

"Why?"

"Because I need to know. I want to help you." He sucked in a breath. "I want to know you. Dammit." His hands clenched the steering wheel, kneading it. "The first time I saw you . . . I wanted to . . . know you." He, normally good with the words women wanted to hear, was stumbling. "I wanted you," he finished quietly.

She said nothing for a long moment. "You don't want me, Luke. Trust me."

"Because you had a one-night stand? So the fuck what?"

"Not one," she whispered so softly he nearly missed it. Then she swallowed hard. "I really don't want to talk to you anymore. This is hard enough. Please."

It was the desperate tremble in her voice that made him stop pushing her. "All right. Will you dial the number Leigh gave you?"

She did, and he talked to Mr. Csorka, who planned to leave right away from Florida, bringing DNA samples from his daughter Ashley. Luke was hoping for his first positive ID on one of the missing girls. Mr. Csorka would arrive sometime after six this evening.

Luke went over every detail of the case in his mind, trying to fill the silence in the car, but every few minutes he'd glance at her, wishing he knew what to say. In the end, he honored her request, and said nothing. When they arrived at the hospital in Atlanta, he hoped she'd say something, but she closed her laptop without a word and walked away.

Feeling very sad and helpless, he let her.

He'd parked so he could go in and visit Daniel, but his cell buzzed again.

"Luke, it's Nate. I've been looking at the pictures on Mansfield's computer."

Luke felt a spear of guilt. "I'm so sorry to have left you with this, Nate. I've got time before Kasey Knight's parents arrive. Let me talk to Daniel and then I'll come help you."

"Actually, I found something," Nate said, his voice energized. "Come now."

Chapter Thirteen

Atlanta, Saturday, February 3, 1:25 p.m.

Susannah had intended to go straight to Jane Doe, but her feet slowed as she walked past Daniel's room. He was alone, awake, and propped up on the pillows.

Their eyes locked, his intensely blue. She didn't know what to say or what he'd do. Then he held out his hand and the dam inside her burst. Stumbling forward she grabbed his hand and he pulled her close. Burying her face against his shoulder, she wept.

Awkwardly he brushed her hair and she realized he was crying, too.

"I'm so sorry, Suze," he rasped. "I can't go back. I can't change what I did."

"Neither can I."

"You didn't do anything," he said fiercely. "I should have protected you."

"And I should have told you," she murmured, and he went still.

"Why didn't you?" he whispered, his voice anguished. "Why didn't you tell me?"

"Simon told me not to. He told me that you were gone and . . ." She shrugged. "Simon said lots of other things. He liked to play mind games."

"I know. Just like Dad." He sighed. "I should have

guessed. Both of them were always so much crueler to you. When I took care of you, it seemed to get worse."

"So you stayed away," she murmured.

"I shouldn't have."

I forgive you. Say it. Say the words. But they stuck in her throat. "It's done, Daniel," she said instead. "I understand." It was the best she could do.

She rose, averting her face as she searched for tissues. She wiped her face, then sat next to his bed. Then she winced. "Yikes. The nurses are going to be mad at me."

He smiled weakly. Her makeup had stained his hospital gown and the red clay from her dress had streaked the sheets. "You're dirty, kid."

"I fell down, kind of. I went to Sheila Cunningham's funeral."

He blinked in surprise. "You did?" he asked, and she nodded.

"I met Gretchen French. She sends her regards and her thanks." She lifted one shoulder. "I wouldn't be surprised if she stops in after they finish with her in the ER."

His eyes widened. "Gretchen's in the ER?"

She told him what had happened and he was stunned. "My God. Kate Davis helped us find Mack O'Brien. She told us Garth's wife had split with the kids because she was afraid for her life. I thought with Mack and the others dead she'd be safe, but now . . ."

"I guess Kate took issue with us accusing Garth. Daniel, I need to say some things and I need you to listen. Yesterday I told you that you didn't know what I was."

"I know. I didn't understand then. I still don't."

"I'm going to tell you and if you want me to go, I will. But I realized standing next to Sheila's grave that if you'd died yesterday, I would be all alone. I don't want to be."

"I won't leave you again," he said harshly.

One side of her mouth lifted sadly. "Well, let's see how you feel when you hear the story. You'd hear it all from Luke at some point, but I'd rather you hear it from me."

Atlanta, Saturday, February 3, 1:25 p.m.

Luke found Nate Dyer in The Room, the place they used to view the vile material that made decent people gag. *Am I decent?* he heard himself ask Susannah.

I'm afraid so, Luke. And she thought she wasn't, because she'd done a one-night stand. Or more. He'd get her to tell it, if for no other reason than for her to hear a *decent person* tell her that she wasn't hopeless. That she did deserve her soul.

But Susannah would have to wait. No matter how long he'd put this off, Luke had known he'd return to The Room as soon as he'd recognized Angel's face yesterday.

The Room was windowless, with one door. Only those with a need to know, a need to see, were admitted. Luke wished he didn't have the combination as he punched in the code. He'd spent far too many hours here. *And a little more of you dies each day.*

Yeah. Steeling his spine, Luke pushed the door open. "Hey, Nate."

Nate looked up, no smile on his face. "You need to sit down for this."

Luke did, preparing for the sick twisting of his stomach that occurred every time he opened a new Web page or viewed a new collection of obscenity. All the preparation, though, never made it easier. "Okay. I'm ready."

"I've only started looking at the material from

Deputy Mansfield's computer," Nate said. "The guy had five external hard drives, Papa. Each drive is five hundred gig."

"Hundreds of thousands of pictures," Luke murmured.

"This stash will keep us busy for months. The computer forensics guys imaged all the hard drives and I picked up the copies just a few hours ago. Mansfield's hard drives are organized. A lot of the folder names are phrases. He'd marked one 'Fine Young American Flesh, Inc.' *This* is what I found inside."

Luke sat in front of Nate's computer and began scrolling through the pictures. Each was a girl, provocatively posed. Each was nude and each held a small American flag in one hand and in the other, a symbol of the state from which she came.

Each picture was labeled with a name and a profile and a "personal message" from the girl. " 'Hi, I'm Amy,' " Luke read. " 'I was born and raised in Idaho.' " Amy clutched a potato some sick bastard had computer-enhanced to resemble male genitalia. There was Jasmine, raised in sunny California, and Tawny, raised in Wisconsin. Each girl was smiling seductively, and Luke wondered what had been done to them to force the smile.

"There's a price list at the end," Nate said.

"It's a catalog," Luke said dully.

"Exactly. And the logo for the company is the swastika with the bent ends."

"Buy American," Luke said. "I had a feeling we'd be looking at supremacist groups."

"Look on page twenty-four."

Luke did. "It's Angel." But they'd named her Gabriela.

"And page fifty-two."

Luke's pulse spiked. "It's Jane Doe. They call her

Honey. I called her that last night. That's why she got so agitated. Are there other editions, earlier ones?"

"Yeah, two more. Looks like the catalogs are done quarterly, and this one is dated about two months ago. Luke, further on in this catalog are the two girls that were with Angel on the Web site we shut down eight months ago."

"We lost track of those girls. Couldn't find them anywhere on the Web."

Nate pointed to the screen. "Now, we know where they went."

"So either Mansfield was somehow involved with that Web site or he knew who was. How else could he get all three girls?"

"Don't know. George and Ernie are coming in so I can grab some sleep. Maybe they'll find something that'll take us to the perv that ran the site. I'd give a lot to get my hands on him." Nate searched Luke's face. "You look as tired as I do. Get some rest."

"No. I've got an hour before I meet Kasey Knight's parents. Give me one of those hard drives." He sat in front of a computer and closed his eyes, mentally preparing.

"You need anything? Lunch, maybe?" Nate asked, and Luke realized he hadn't eaten since Leo's eggs almost twelve hours before.

"Yeah, I forgot to eat."

"You always do," Nate said, and gave him a container from their small fridge. "Moussaka."

Luke blinked at it. "How . . ."

Nate smiled. "Your mother came by with food for the office yesterday. She was worried we weren't eating right with you off helping Daniel Vartanian's case."

Luke's heart squeezed. *I love you, Mama.* "She's a good woman, my mama."

"And a damn good cook. Eat, Papa. Then search. Your eyes are faster than mine."

So, armed with his mama's moussaka, Luke sat down to view the stuff of which his nightmares were made. He scanned the directory, looking for any name that popped out. Some of the folder names were more self-explanatory than others. *Whips and Chains, No Means Yes, Boys Will Be Boys* ... Luke had a pretty good idea of what he'd find in those folders. Then his eyes froze on one of the names.

Sweetpea, my ass. He clicked it open and his heart rose to choke him. Slowly he put the plastic container of food aside. "Oh my God. Nate, come here."

Nate peered over his shoulder. "Horrible quality pictures."

They were, grainy and blurry and off center. "Mansfield probably took them with a cell phone or hidden camera. Look, it's Granville. With a girl."

"What's he doing?" Nate leaned closer, then sighed. "Aw, fuck, Papa."

"Goddamn bastard." Luke scrolled, each photo more vile than the last. Granville had tortured these girls, unspeakably. And Mansfield had somehow captured it all.

"What does *Sweetpea, my ass* mean?" Nate asked, pulling up a chair.

"You know about the rape club, right?"

"Thirteen years ago. Daniel's brother Simon was the ringleader."

"Not exactly," Luke said. "We think Granville was the leader, but Simon was his partner. Daniel talked to the widow of one of the men who'd been in the club and she told him all the boys in the club had nicknames. Mansfield was Sweetpea."

"Why the 'my ass' part?"

"I don't know. Everything went to hell and Daniel got

shot before I could get any more information. I'll go see him and find out, but my guess is that Mansfield took these pictures as protection, in case he needed to hold something over Granville's head."

Luke continued paging through the photos, then stopped, and what little he'd eaten threatened to come back up. It was Angel. In all the vile perversion he'd witnessed, what Luke now stared at might be the worst. "Aw, hell, Nate."

Nate closed his eyes. "Shit." He swallowed hard, pursing his lips. "Shit."

"We missed something, Nate," Luke said, his voice as dead as he felt inside. "We didn't catch those assholes who ran the Web site, but Granville and Mansfield managed to. That's why those three girls dropped off the face of the earth all of a sudden. Granville had them here. Doing *that* to them. How did they get them?"

"I don't know. But if it's on one of these five hard drives, we'll find it."

Five hard drives. Twenty-five hundred gig. A hundred thousand pictures. "Dammit."

"We'll figure it out, Luke."

"In time for the five girls Granville's current partner took with him?" Luke said bitterly. "We've been at this for twenty hours and nothing fits. We've got a missing judge and swastika brands. We've got a name, Rocky, that means absofuckinglutely nothing. We've got a six-year-old homicide in New York and thirteen-year-old rapes, and they're somehow connected. And we've got a girl who won't *goddamn wake up* and tell us what happened." He looked away, his temper a second away from explosion.

Beside him, Nate drew a careful breath. "And we've got a dead girl named Angel who we should have saved," he said quietly.

A sob rose in Luke's throat and, horrified, he tried to shove it back. "Goddammit, Nate," he choked. "Look what he did to her. To all of them."

Nate squeezed his shoulder hard. "It's all right," he murmured. "It wouldn't be the first time one of us let go in here. That's why we're soundproofed."

Luke shook his head, slowly grappling for his control. "I'm okay."

"No, you're not."

"Okay, I'm not. But I'll do what needs to be done." He checked his watch. "I've got enough time to see Daniel before the Knights get to identify their daughter. Maybe Daniel knows something more."

"You need to sleep, Luke."

"Not now. I can't close my eyes now. I'll see *that*."

Atlanta, Saturday, February 3, 2:30 p.m.

"Hello, Susannah."

Susannah turned in the chair next to Jane Doe's bed, surprised to find Mrs. Papadopoulos holding a big shopping bag in each hand. "Mama Papa. Hello."

"I thought I would find you here, with this girl."

Susannah smiled. "I thought you'd already forgotten about this girl."

Her dark eyes twinkled. "I am mute when I leave. For now, I bring you these. Luka told my daughter Demi what my granddaughter bought for you. Demi was not pleased."

"It was still very kind," Susannah said, but Luke's mother shook her head.

"So I send my youngest daughter Mitra out this morning to buy you proper clothing." She held out the bags. "You like, you buy. You no like, Mitra will return."

Susannah looked through the bags and smiled. "It's all beautiful. Truly appropriate."

"And everything was on sale." Mama's eyes narrowed. "You've been crying."

"I went to a funeral. I always cry at funerals." Which was a lie, but Susannah had to keep some dignity. "Here, come meet M. Jane Doe."

Luke's mama covered the girl's hand with hers. "It's nice to meet you, Jane," she said softly. "I hope you wake up soon." Then she leaned forward and pressed a kiss to the girl's forehead and Susannah felt new tears well. No one, ever, had done that to her. Luke's mama turned to Susannah, her dark eyes shrewdly appraising. "Come, let's change you out of that dirty dress. You'll feel better."

"All right." Susannah brushed the hair from the girl's face. "I'll be back soon."

Atlanta, Saturday, February 3, 2:45 p.m.

She wasn't dead. Monica couldn't move again, but she wasn't dead. *Whatever the nurse gave me wore off before. It will wear off again. So stay calm. It'll wear off.*

When it does, what will you do? Will you tell the cops? If you do, they'll sell Genie.

If I don't, they might anyway. They won't let her go. I have to tell.

At least Susannah was back from changing her clothes, sitting in the chair next to her bed, but something was wrong there, too. *I always cry at funerals*, Susannah had told the woman, the one who'd brought her clothes. *The one who kissed my forehead.*

Funeral for who? They couldn't be burying the others yet. It was only yesterday that they'd been killed. *Who died?* Susannah had left with the other woman, then had returned a few minutes later alone. She'd been quiet. Subdued. So very sad.

Monica tensed. Someone else was here now. "How is she?" a man asked.

It was the agent, the one with the black eyes. Luke. He sounded angry. Upset.

"She woke up for a little while this morning," Susannah said, "but she slipped back under. I suppose it's her way of dodging the pain for a while."

A chair scraped and Monica could feel the warmth from his body. "Did she say anything when she woke up?"

"I wasn't here."

"What about yesterday? Did she say anything else?"

"No. She just looked at me like I was God or something."

"You brought her out of the woods."

"I didn't do anything," Susannah said, and Luke sighed.

"Susannah. You did not cause this."

"I don't happen to agree."

"*Talk* to me," he said, frustrated. Like he'd said it before.

"Why?"

"Because . . . Because I want to know."

"You want to know what, Agent Papadopoulos?" Susannah's voice had grown cold.

"Why you think this is your fault."

"Because I knew," she said flatly. "I knew and I said nothing."

"What did you know?" he asked, soothingly.

"I knew Simon was a rapist."

Simon. Who is Simon? Who did he rape?

"I thought Simon didn't do any of the rapes, that he only took the pictures."

There was a beat of silence. "He did at least one."

Oh, no. Monica now understood. *Whoever Simon was, he'd raped Susannah, too.*

Luke sucked in a breath. "Did you tell Daniel?"

Who is Daniel?

"No," Susannah said angrily. "And neither will you. I only know that if I'd said something, this might have been avoided. She might not be here right now."

Nobody said anything for a long time, but Monica could hear them breathe.

Finally Luke spoke. "I recognized one of the bodies back there yesterday."

"How?" Susannah asked, surprise in her voice.

"From a case I was working eight months ago. I failed to protect that girl. I failed to bring a sexual sadist that preyed on children to justice. I want another bite at the apple."

He sounded so very angry. His voice shook.

"Granville's dead," Susannah said.

Dead? He's dead? Hallelujah. He couldn't hurt Genie.

"But there's still the other. Someone who's pulling the strings. Someone who taught Granville how to be very good at his job," he said bitterly. "I want him. I want to throw him into hell and throw away the key."

The other. The woman who'd given the doctor the order to kill them. The other had Genie. Monica's elation fizzled.

"Why are you telling me this?" Susannah asked. There was a note of impatience in her voice, like *tell me something I don't already know.*

"Because you want the same thing."

There was a long pause. "What do you want me to do?"

"I don't know yet. I'll call you when I do." He got up. "Thank you."

"For what?"

"For not telling Daniel about Simon."

"Thank you for respecting my decision."

Then Luke was gone and Susannah sighed heavily.

Yeah, Monica thought helplessly. *Tell me about it.*

Daniel looked asleep, Luke thought as he stood in the doorway.

"I'm not asleep," Daniel said, opening his eyes. His voice was raspy, but stronger than Luke had anticipated. "I was wondering when you'd come by."

Luke's gaze dropped to the smudges on the shoulder of Daniel's hospital gown. "You'd think for what you're paying that you'd at least get a clean gown."

One side of Daniel's mouth lifted and Luke saw an uncanny resemblance to Susannah. In no other way did they look alike. "Everything went to hell yesterday."

"You have no idea. I don't have much time, but I need some information."

"Shoot." Daniel grimaced. "Actually, on second thought, don't do that."

Luke chuckled, feeling a little better. "I'm sure glad you didn't get yourself killed."

"Me, too," Daniel said. "But I gotta say you look as bad as I feel."

"Thank you," Luke said dryly, then sobered. "You

may not have heard the news. Kate Davis was killed this afternoon."

"Suze told me, but it doesn't make sense. Kate didn't seem like the type to start shooting people."

"I agree, but nothing about this case is the way it seems."

"Alex told me about the bodies you found and the live girls they took with them. She said Mansfield and Granville were into human trafficking."

"She's right. Too much has happened in the last twenty-four. I don't have time to tell you all of it right now, but, Daniel, we found a file on Mansfield's computer. Very graphic photos of Granville torturing these girls. The file is called *Sweetpea, my ass*."

"Sweetpea is Mansfield. Granville gave him the name and he hated it."

"That's what I thought. What do you know about Judge Borenson?"

Daniel looked surprised at the question. "He presided over Gary Fulmore's murder trial. Frank Loomis's clerk said he retired and became a hermit up in the mountains."

"That part I know. What do you remember about him? From when you were young?"

"He sometimes had dinner with us, then he and my father would go into his study and talk until the wee hours of the morning. Why?"

"He's missing. We found his cabin ransacked, blood everywhere. Last I heard Talia was waiting for cadaver dogs to search for his body."

Daniel winced. "Hell. They're all gone, then. Randy Mansfield's father was the prosecutor on Gary Fulmore's murder case and he's dead. The coroner who did the autopsy's dead. Fulmore's original defense attorney is dead—that was a suspicious death, by the way. He had a car accident on a dry road in the middle of the day."

"And now Frank Loomis is dead, too," Luke said, and Daniel looked haunted.

"I know. I keep seeing him die. He tried to warn me at the last minute. He did something horrible, Luke, falsifying evidence. Gary Fulmore's spent thirteen years in prison for a crime he didn't do and for the life of me I can't figure out why Frank did it."

"Loomis wasn't a rich man, so there wasn't any payoff," Luke said.

Daniel closed his eyes. "He was the only father I really ever had."

"I'm sorry."

"Thanks." His eyes still closed, Daniel frowned. "Fifty-two," he said, then opened his eyes and Luke saw renewed vitality. "I was seeing the moment Frank died. He'd come to warn me that it was a trap. There was a gunshot and he just slid down my window."

Luke remembered the bloody streaks on the window. "What's fifty-two?"

"The boat. I tried to back away, but Mansfield had blocked the road and I crashed and hit my head. For a minute I thought Alex was dead, but she was just stunned. Mansfield made me carry her into the bunker and as we were walking around to the door I saw the boat as it passed. Those numbers were on the bow."

"There should have been a GA, four numbers, then two letters."

Daniel closed his eyes, concentrating, then shook his head. "Sorry, I only remember the fifty-two. I only glanced at it. It was moving really fast."

"And you were seeing stars from the crash. This is the closest we've come so far."

Daniel sagged back against the pillows. "Good."

"I've just got one more and then I'll go. Does the name Rocky mean anything?"

Daniel pondered, then shook his head again. "I'm sorry, but no. Why?"

"We think that's the name of Granville's partner."

"There are no pictures of the partner in Mansfield's Sweetpea file?"

"Not that I saw, but there are five hard drives to search, so we might find one." Luke stood. "Get some rest. That nurse outside looks like she's going to take off my head."

"Wait." Daniel swallowed. "I need you to tell me what's going on with Susannah."

"What do you mean?" Luke asked warily.

"Not like that." His jaw tightened. "Although you make her one of your affairs and we will speak, and not kindly."

"Relax, Daniel. Susannah's made it clear she's not interested." Crystal clear.

"But you are?"

Luke considered, then decided he'd been friends with Daniel too long to lie. "I was from the moment I saw her at your parents' funeral, but not in the way you think."

"So not as a time-passer?" Daniel asked, very seriously.

"No. She's been through too much."

Daniel swallowed. "I know. She told me."

Luke's eyes widened. "She did? When?"

Daniel lightly touched the brown stain on his hospital gown. "Before you got here. She told me about her friend Darcy and everything else."

No, my friend, Luke thought sadly. *Not everything.* Susannah would not tell Daniel that Simon had brutalized her. "She's strong, Daniel."

"Nobody's that strong. But I know there was more. More she didn't tell me." His eyes narrowed. "You know."

"She's safe. At this point, that's all I can tell you."

"Because you don't know or because you won't tell me?"

Luke stood up. "Don't push it, Daniel, please. Just know that I'm watching over her."

"Thank you." His eyes moved and a smile bent his lips. "Mama Papa. You came."

Luke's mama came in, her arms opened wide. "I just hear from that nurse that you are awake." She arched an eyebrow at Luke. "*Some* people tell their mamas nothing."

Daniel closed his eyes as Mama hugged him, and the look on his face was one of a man finally warm after months of winter. Luke remembered the yearning in Susannah's voice as she insisted Jane Doe's mother loved her and his heart hurt.

"Did you drive yourself, Mama?" Daniel asked, teasing reproach in his tone.

"No." Mama sat in the chair, her huge purse in her lap. "Leo drove me." She looked up at Luke with a frown. "Your refrigerator was dis*gus*ting, Luka."

Luke's lips twitched. Obviously Leo had called in the Special Forces to deal with his kitchen. "I know. Did you clean it?"

"I did. And stocked it with food." Her frown became a sly look. "So if you bring home any visitors, she will not think you a pig."

Luke's smile faded. He knew what she insinuated and

he knew it was unlikely to ever occur. "Thanks, Mama." He kissed the top of her head. "I'll see you later."

Atlanta, Saturday, February 3, 3:30 p.m.

"I hate that this girl's parents are going to see her this way," Felicity said fiercely.

Luke forced himself to look at Kasey Knight's grotesquely gaunt face. Her cheekbones were razor sharp, nearly protruding through her skin. A bullet hole was centered in her forehead. "They insisted. She's been missing two years. It's closure."

"Then let's get this over with," she snapped, but he took no offense because her eyes were bright with unshed tears. "Go get the parents."

In the lobby both parents sprang to their feet. "We've been waiting, dreading this call for two years." Mr. Knight's throat worked as he gripped his wife's hand. "We need to know what happened to our daughter."

Mrs. Knight was dangerously pale. "Please," she whispered. "Take us to her."

"This way." Luke led them back to the viewing room. It was decorated in warm colors and comfortable furniture, small details aimed at easing the ordeal of grieving relatives. "Does your wife need a doctor?" Luke murmured as Mrs. Knight sank onto the sofa, her body trembling. She looked as though she might pass out any minute.

Mr. Knight shook his head. "No," he said hoarsely. "We just need this to be over."

Luke wanted to prepare them, but knew there was no preparation for what they were about to endure. "This girl doesn't look like the picture of Kasey you gave the police."

"It's been two years. Kids change."

"It's . . . more than that. She only weighs about eighty pounds, but her height is five-eight, the same as your daughter was when she disappeared."

Mrs. Knight stiffened. "Kasey weighed one-thirty."

"I know, ma'am," Luke said gently, and he could see they understood.

Mr. Knight swallowed audibly. "Was she sexually . . ." His voice broke.

"Yes." *Multiple times*, but Luke didn't say that. These parents were in enough pain.

"Agent Papadopoulos," Mr. Knight asked hoarsely, "what did they do to my baby?"

Vile, unspeakable things. But Luke didn't say that either. "You've asked to see her face and the ME will comply with your wishes, but please, focus on other parts of her body. Her hands, her feet, any birthmarks or scars." He knew the waiting was making it worse, so he tapped the intercom button. "We're ready, Dr. Berg."

From the other side of the glass, Felicity opened the curtains. Mr. Knight's eyes were tightly closed. "Mr. Knight," Luke said softly. "We're ready when you are."

Clenching his teeth, Knight opened his eyes, and the strangled whimper that emerged from his throat broke Luke's heart. Felicity had covered the torso with a smaller sheet, affording the victim as much decency as she could. And sparing the parents as much pain as she could.

"Oh, Kasey," Knight whispered. "Baby. Why didn't you listen to us?"

"How do you know this is your daughter, sir?"

Knight barely breathed. "There's a scar on her knee from when she fell off a bike. And her middle toe was longer than the others. She had a mole on her left foot, too."

Luke nodded to Felicity and she pulled the curtains. Mr. Knight knelt so that he met his wife's eyes. Tears were running down her face. "It's Kasey." He uttered the words on a moan and she leaned forward, wrapping her arms around him. Her silent tears became anguished sobs and she slid from the sofa to kneel with her husband. Her sobs became his and together they rocked, leaning on each other through their pain.

"I'll wait in the hall," Luke said roughly. The Knights reminded him of his own parents. Married nearly forty years, they were each other's bulwark, able to withstand every crisis that had come their way. Luke loved them fiercely, but at the same time envied them. Now, listening to the muted sounds of suffering coming from inside the viewing room, Luke pitied the Knights, but envied them as well. In all the world, Luke had never found a woman he trusted enough to allow her to see him like that, defenses down, soul bared. He'd never met a woman who he thought would understand.

Until Susannah. *And she doesn't want anyone.* No, that wasn't true. She didn't trust anyone. No, that wasn't true, either. She'd trusted him today, came to him when she was afraid. Leaned on him in the cemetery.

Susannah didn't trust herself. He listened to the sobs behind him and thought about the brown smudges on Daniel's hospital gown. *Susannah's makeup.* It was a good sign.

The sobs behind the closed door quieted, the door opened, and Mr. Knight cleared his throat. "We're ready to talk to you now, Agent Papadopoulos."

Mrs. Knight looked up, her face ravaged. "Have you caught the man that did this?"

"Not all of them."

Both Knights flinched. "There was more than one?" Mr. Knight asked, horrified.

Luke thought of the Sweetpea pictures. "We know of two. They're both dead."

"Did they suffer?" Mrs. Knight demanded, her teeth clenched.

"Not enough," Luke replied. "We're still looking for the third man."

"You have a lot of agents on this case?" Knight asked.

"More than a dozen agents, which doesn't count all the support personnel answering the tip hotlines. Now, if you don't mind, I have a few questions for you."

The Knights sat up straighter. "Of course," Mr. Knight said. "We're ready."

"Was Kasey involved in any relationships that worried you? Boys, school friends?"

Mrs. Knight sighed. "The police asked us this then. She had a group of girls she'd been friends with since the fourth grade. The night she disappeared she'd gone to a sleepover. The girls said they went to sleep and when they woke up she wasn't there."

"The police were suspicious," Mr. Knight said wearily. "But the police couldn't get any of the girls to tell them what happened."

"Give me the girls' names."

"Are you going to make them tell?" Mrs. Knight asked, her voice thinning.

"I'm going to talk to them," Luke said. "Here's my card. If you have any questions, do not hesitate to call me. And I'll call you as soon as we know more."

Mr. Knight stood, his expression drawn. "We want to thank you. At least we can bury our child." He helped his wife to her feet and she leaned against him.

"We need to confirm your identification. Did you bring the articles that I requested?"

Mrs. Knight nodded shakily. "Kasey's things are in the car."

"Then I'll walk with you." Luke did so, and waited while Mr. Knight opened his trunk. "I know it doesn't help, but I am so very sorry."

"It does help," Mrs. Knight whispered. "You care. You'll find him, the one that did this to our Kasey, the one that still walks free. Won't you?" she added fiercely.

"I will." Clutching their daughter's belongings in the shoe-box in his hand, Luke watched them drive away. He thought of the four unidentified bodies in the morgue, of the five girls still out there, of Jane Doe lying in a hospital bed. *I must.*

Chapter Fourteen

Dutton, Saturday, February 3, 3:45 p.m.

Charles glared at the telephone when it rang for the tenth time in an hour. Damn reporters. Every one of them wanted a new angle on the shootings of Kate Davis and Gretchen French. As if he'd toss them even a crumb. Not.

This call he'd answer, he thought when he saw the caller ID. "Paul, where are you?"

"In Raleigh. Bobby's out of control. Just thought you should know."

There was a sharp edge to Paul's voice. "What's in Raleigh?" Charles asked.

"The father of the girl that escaped from the bunker. Rocky kidnapped the girl's sister and made it look like the sister had run here, to her daddy."

"So Bobby's cleaning up Rocky's mistakes. That shows responsibility."

"It shows loss of control," Paul snapped. "Dr. Cassidy didn't have to die."

"I'll go down to Ridgefield House and have a little talk with Bobby."

"Good, because I'm sick and tired of fetching for your *star pupil*. Bobby thinks I work for money. I came *this close* to saying I only work for you. That you set this whole thing up. That I only pretend to be Bobby's errand boy because you told me to. I'm tired of this, Charles. I mean it."

Paul had always gotten snide when he was tired, ever since he'd been a boy. "You're not my pupil, Paul. You're my right hand, so relax. Get a hotel and take a nap. Call me when you're back in Atlanta."

"Fine, just yank Bobby back into line, will you?"

"I certainly will." He paused meaningfully. "Thank you, Paul."

Paul sighed. "You're welcome, sir. I'm sorry I was rude."

"Apology accepted. Get some rest." Charles hung up, doubly annoyed. First Bobby missed Susannah Vartanian, and from only twenty feet away. *And now, wasting resources like Paul. I taught you better than that.* It was time for a refresher course.

Atlanta, Saturday, February 3, 4:00 p.m.

One of Monica's eyelids was open. It was a strange sensation, being able to see the ceiling through only one eye. Her nurse came in and Monica wanted to scream.

The nurse had another syringe in her hand. Her eyes were no longer red and swollen, but she was tense. The nurse brushed her eyelid closed. "I'm not going to kill you," she murmured close to her ear. "But I can't take a chance on you saying anything to the police until my son is out of danger. This should be the last one."

Monica felt the warmth of the nurse's body as she bent low again, whispering in her ear. "When this one wears off, I'll be gone. Do not trust anyone. Believe me. There is someone else in this hospital that works for the people who hurt you. Yesterday they tried to kill one of the others that escaped from the bunker. The man."

Beardsley. He'd helped them escape from the bunker. Bailey had told her so, when they'd been in the woods. Monica had heard the nurses talking during the day. He'd been rushed into ICU during the night, but was lucky. They'd saved him and he was sent back to a regular room. With a guard.

"As soon as you're out of ICU, you'll be vulnerable," the nurse continued. "I've tried to keep you alive as long as I could. But my son is in danger. I'm sorry, but I can't help you anymore. I think you can trust Susannah and Nurse Ella. Now I have to go."

Raleigh, North Carolina, Saturday, February 3, 4:15 p.m.

Special Agent Harry Grimes looked around the Raleigh office of the North Carolina State Bureau of Investigation fondly. He'd been transferred to the Charlotte office the year before and missed the staff, especially his boss, who'd taught Harry so much.

His old boss was at a new desk, having been recently promoted to special agent in charge. Harry knocked and an instant grin lit Steven Thatcher's face.

"Harry Grimes. How the hell are you? Come in, come in."

"Hope I'm not interrupting," Harry said as Steven came around the desk, hand outstretched in welcome.

"No, no." Steven grimaced. "Just paperwork."

"Comes with the new desk, huh?"

"Yeah, but I'm home more and Jenna likes that, especially with another baby on the way." Steven pointed to a chair. "How's Charlotte?"

Harry sat down. "Great. Not here, but still great."

Steven studied his face. "You're not here on a social call, are you?"

"I wish. I got a call this morning from a frantic mother. Her fourteen-year-old daughter went missing from her bed in the night."

Steven grew serious. "Like, abducted, or left?"

"No sign of forced entry. The locals started out calling her a runaway."

"But they're not now?"

"No. And the confrontation wasn't initially smooth, but they're on board now."

"So bring me up to speed and tell me how I can help."

"This girl's older sister went missing six months ago. She's listed in the NCMEC database as an 'endangered runaway.'" He handed Steven a photo from his briefcase.

"Beatrice Monica Cassidy," Steven read.

"She goes by Monica. She had what her mother considered a normal relationship. They fought about clothes and curfews and school. Then one day six months ago Monica tells Mom she's going to visit a friend and doesn't come home. The friend eventually confessed Monica had asked her to lie, that she was meeting a boy. By then the trail was cold. Monica was gone. Her mother insists she wouldn't have run away."

"Parents normally do," Steven said quietly.

"I know. Apparently Monica had been spending a lot of time on the computer."

"Let me guess. Chat rooms and IM?"

"Of course. Mom couldn't bring back any of Monica's

conversations, which is where I came in. The principal of Monica's school asked me to do a presentation for the PTO on software that can track chat room and instant message conversations. If parents install it right, the kids never know it's there. I had a rep from the local computer store there as I always do, so that parents can buy the software that night."

"Smart, Harry. So many times parents plan to, and life gets in the way."

"Exactly. Mrs. Cassidy was there that night and bought a package because she has a younger daughter, Eugenie Marie. Goes by Genie."

"And as of this morning, Genie is missing."

"Mrs. Cassidy called all her friends, then the police. They came, took a report. Then the mom got online and read Genie's conversations. She's been communicating with someone named Jason through her IM account. He claims to be a college boy."

"You think a pedophile took her?"

"Yeah, I do. Monica's friends said she'd met a college boy online—named Jason."

Steven blinked. "That's quite a coincidence."

"That's what I thought."

"Did Genie's chat log show if she planned to meet this Jason, and where?"

"No, there were no communications yesterday or today, but there are going to be gaps in the log when kids use their cell phones to text. The software only tracks the chats and IMs on the computer itself. I felt so sorry for this woman, Steven, so I went to the bus station and asked around. They said a kid wearing a hoodie from Genie's high school bought a bus ticket to Raleigh in the middle of the night, so here I am."

"So how did you get this case, Harry?" Steven asked cautiously.

Harry's smile was wry. "I'm not being a cowboy, Steven. I'm officially assigned to this case. Mrs. Cassidy lives in a rural area, about thirty miles from Charlotte. The local force is small and asked us to take it after Mrs. Cassidy showed them the Jason parallel. My boss put me on the case since I'd done some of the groundwork."

"So why Raleigh?"

"Her dad lives here. Dad didn't answer my phone calls, so I made the trip. Dad isn't home, and his car is gone."

"Maybe he's just not home, Harry."

"He's a doctor. Didn't show up for his shift today and the hospital staff say that's never happened before. He's reliable to the point of being obsessive."

"You get a warrant for his house?"

"Being signed as we speak. You wanna come with?"

Steven nodded grimly. "Let me get my coat."

Ridgefield House, Saturday, February 3, 4:55 p.m.

"Where's Tanner?" Charles asked as Bobby took his coat.

On his way back from Savannah, Bobby thought, but Charles had no need to know that. "Assisting me." Bobby sat behind the desk without additional explanation. "Well?"

Charles followed, settling himself in a chair. "You could have been caught."

Bobby smiled. "I know. That's what made it fun."

"Where did you get that godawful dress?"

"My grandmother's. You said I was acting like an old woman, so I dressed like one."

"But you missed," he said, and Bobby lifted a

"Au contraire. I never miss. I was taught to shoot by a U.S. Army sniper, you know."

"Yes, I know," Charles said irritably. "I was there for every excruciating lesson."

"So you of all people know my skill. I hit what I aimed at."

Charles looked perplexed. "You intended to hit Gretchen French?"

"*That's* who that was?" Bobby laughed softly. "That makes it even better."

"You didn't know?" he asked, incredulous.

"Nope. I planned to hit whoever was standing closest to Susannah Vartanian the moment Rocky pulled the trigger. I'd kind of hoped to get Agent Papadopoulos, but Gretchen French is even better, under the circumstances."

"So what happened to the shot Rocky fired?"

"A blank. I didn't want her to hit anything. The girl was a lousy shot anyway. But I wanted her to believe she had. I wanted her to think she was killing Susannah Vartanian. And she pulled the trigger. She died knowing she'd obeyed me."

"She died thinking she'd missed."

"Better still. She obeyed me, yet still she failed. She deserved no less."

"Very good," he said, sounding reluctantly pleased. "So what will you do next? I mean about Susannah Vartanian."

"I'll deal with her a little at a time. When I'm finished with her, she'll be more alone than I ever was. She'll be afraid to stand next to a tree stump, afraid it'll be blown up. When I finally decide to kill her, she'll beg me to

strike again?"

the call from the GBI mole that

had come through minutes before Charles arrived. The mole's report had been infuriating, but Bobby had decided to make lemonade from the lemon. And Charles could provide the sweetener.

"In about an hour. I'd like to borrow your car. The black one with the Darcy plates."

"What do you plan to do?"

"I plan to teach a recalcitrant employee a lesson. The nurse called GBI on me."

"So you're still cleaning up Rocky's messes?"

Bobby frowned at his disapproving tone. "What do you mean?"

"You have a lot of loose ends to snip. But there are other ways to do so. So much murder at once is a neon light. I taught you better than that."

"I know. Power in invisibility. But this is a twofer. I send a message that it's unwise to disobey me and I strike at Susannah Vartanian again. You'll see. Trust me."

Charles considered it. "In that case, yes, you may borrow my car."

Atlanta, Saturday, February 3, 4:55 p.m.

"Luke, wake up. Wake up."

Luke's head jerked up. He'd fallen asleep at his desk. "God," he muttered.

Leigh stood next to him, a worried look on her face. "It's almost five. The team's starting to gather in the conference room." She handed him a cup of coffee. "High test."

He gulped half of it down. "Thanks, Leigh. Anything happen while I was asleep?"

"Nope. The calls from last night are starting to taper off. Nothing relevant, not yet."

"You get any hits on that boat registration number Daniel remembered?"

"Couple hundred. But I narrowed it down based on the boat only having room to carry five girls." She handed him a piece of paper. "I just finished it. Here's the list."

"Good work, Leigh. I really appreciate all the time you've put in this weekend. Hopefully it'll be over soon." Luke scrubbed his face, his beard scraping his palms. "I have to shave. Maybe that'll help me feel human. Tell Chase I'll be there in five."

Five minutes later he slumped into a chair between Chase and Ed and looked around the table. Pete and Nancy were there, as were Chloe and Nate. Talia Scott was back from the Ellijay cabin, and she and psychologist Mary McCrady looked fresher than the rest of them. "We ready to start, Chase?" he asked.

"Yep. Germanio is still hunting for Helen Granville, so we're just waiting for you."

Luke straightened in his chair. "We have an ID on Kasey Knight, one of the homicides, and we may have an ID on one of the missing girls, Ashley Csorka. Her dad's on his way from Florida with DNA samples."

"I'll put a rush on the urine samples we took from the mattresses in the bunker," Ed said. "I'll start PCR on the samples he brings. We'll have an ID by tomorrow this time."

"Good," Chase said. "What else?"

"Daniel saw part of the registration number on the boat as it pulled away," Luke said. "Leigh's narrowed possible owners down to a couple dozen."

Chase took the list. "We'll check it out. Anything else?"

"Just what Nate and I found." He gestured to Nate.

"We found catalogs with girls for sale—the company is Fine Young American Flesh and its logo is the swastika," Nate said. "I was able to match photos of three of the five homicides. Kasey Knight wasn't in any of the catalogs."

"How many did you end up finding?" Luke asked.

"Just the three I'd found when you came by. Why?"

"Because Kasey was missing for two years. At three quarterlies, the catalogs only go back a year or so."

"So?" Chase asked.

"So Kasey wasn't part of the Fine Young Flesh business," Nate said. "But she was still in the bunker."

"Just another piece of the puzzle," Luke said, and Chase sighed.

"This puzzle is like one of those round ones that's all yellow," he grumbled. "Can we trace any of the pictures on Mansfield's hard drives?"

"We've got a third of ICAC working on it," Nate said, "but twenty-five hundred gig is a lot of photos."

"The ones I'm most interested in are the ones Mansfield took on the sly," Luke said. "They're not staged, so they're more likely to yield something useful."

Nate nodded. "But they're grainy, so it's slow going. If you don't need me for anything else, I'll get back to it."

"Ed?" Chase asked, when Nate had closed the door behind him.

"Oh, lots of good stuff," Ed said, "to mystify and confuse." He put two plastic bags on the table, each containing a gun. "This one," he said, tapping a revolver, "was found in Kate's hand. The other one was found in the grass." He got up and drew a triangle on the whiteboard. "Kate was standing here, at the top of the triangle. This," he pointed to the point that jutted out to the left side, "was where we found the second gun. It's a semiauto with a silencer. This point at the bottom is where Ms. French was standing."

"What comes next is my favorite part," Chase said sarcastically.

"We found the slug that went through Gretchen's arm over here." Ed pointed to an area outside the triangle, to the far right. "You guys keepin' up?"

Luke frowned. "How is that possible? Unless it ricocheted, there's no way it could have come from Kate's gun."

"Because the bullet that hit Gretchen French didn't come from Kate's gun. It came from here." Ed pointed to where they had found the semiautomatic.

"So the semi shot Gretchen?" Nancy asked.

"No," Ed said. "There were three guns—Kate's, the semiauto, and a third gun that we didn't recover. The third gun shot Gretchen and the semiauto shot Kate, but Kate Davis didn't shoot anybody."

Pete shook his head. "I have a headache now."

"Join the club," Chase said. "Ballistics says the shot Kate fired was likely a blank."

Chloe blinked. "Why?"

"So who shot Gretchen?" Talia Scott asked.

"Nobody knows yet," Ed said. "We're going through the video of that area, but there were people running around everywhere after the first shot was fired."

"So if Kate didn't shoot Gretchen," Luke said, "what did she mean by 'I missed'?"

"We did get a good angle on Kate with our surveillance video," Ed said. "When we realized she'd shot a blank, we went back and looked at the video again. She wasn't aiming for Gretchen or Susannah. She was aiming over here."

He pointed to the area where the semiautomatic had been found. "She was aiming for whoever shot her."

"And if that's not interesting enough, there's one more thing." Chase slid a photo across the table. "Kate's autopsy photo."

Everyone drew a breath.

"She has the swastika brand," Chloe said. "Hell."

"I think we need to get some more information on Kate Davis," Luke said. "It's time for another visit to Mayor Garth. Will you come with me, Chloe?"

"Of course. Do we have any information on his wife?"

"The BOLO on her Chrysler minivan isn't showing up anything," Pete said, "but she's on the move. I've got her cell phone records right here. She's called Kate Davis's cell phone a couple times a day since she left on Thursday. She's headed west. Today she was in Reno. The last call to Kate's phone was at two p.m. today. Lasted five minutes."

Luke frowned. "Two p.m.? Kate was already dead by two p.m. today."

"I know," Pete said. "Did they find a cell phone on Kate's body?"

"No," Chase said. "But somebody answered the call, or the voicemail would have picked up. Let's get that phone account transferred to one of ours. Chloe, can you make that happen?"

"Yeah, but it'll take some time. I think I know a judge that'll help me speed it up."

"Thanks," Chase said. "Pete, does Garth's wife have family out west?"

"No. She has an aunt who lived in Dutton, but whose neighbors say moved away after she married Garth. Nobody has a forwarding address on the aunt. I'm still searching."

"Did you talk to Angie Delacroix?" Luke asked. "The

hairdresser? Susannah says she knows everything that goes on in the town."

"No, but I will." Pete ran a hand over his bald head, trying for levity. "I need a trim."

Everyone smiled, but sadly.

"I checked Mrs. Davis's credit cards," Pete went on. "I found activity in all the places she's called from. I called the local police in the towns where she stopped. They're sending me security tapes from the places the credit cards were used. At least we can try to find out if she's driving a different vehicle. Whoever has Kate's phone might have told her Kate's dead. I'm betting that will make her go even deeper under."

"Maybe the hairdresser will know who else she's calling," Chase said. "Nancy?"

"I've searched all day for Chili Pepper, the arsonist," Nancy said. "His parents say they haven't seen him in years because he's a no-account SOB of a son. The neighbors back up the parents. I found his girlfriend's house and she denies knowledge of his arson activities. She says he's nicknamed Chili because he's hot in bed." She grimaced. "Which is really gross, trust me."

"Lovely individual," Chloe said. "Anything he can't do without, any addictions?"

"Yeah. I found syringes in his girlfriend's house. I asked to use the bathroom and snuck a peek in her medicine cabinet. I know," Nancy said when Chloe looked indignant. "I saw a bottle of insulin with Clive Pepper's name on it."

"Girlfriend's name?" Chloe asked, shaking her head.

"Lulu Jenkins," Nancy said. "I didn't touch anything."

"Yeah," Chloe said, annoyed, "but if we find him, it's fruit of an unlawful search."

"Who's gonna tell him?" Nancy asked, exasperated. "You?"

Chloe turned to Chase, glowering. "Your people are going to get me sanctioned."

"Calm down. Nancy, don't do that again. Chloe, Nancy's not gonna do that again."

"So he's a diabetic," Luke said. "He has to come up for insulin soon."

"Excellent," Chase said. "Ed, did you get that scan of the bunker property?"

Becky, Luke thought. The name Beardsley heard as someone was being buried.

"No. They were supposed to come at three and I was busy with the cemetery crime scene then," Ed said. "Sorry, Chase. It's dark now, so we'll start at daybreak tomorrow."

"I got us some help," Chase announced. "Four new agents."

"When do they start?" Luke asked.

"A few have already started. One of them located Isaac Gamble, the nurse whose tracking badge was closest to Beardsley last night when his IV was tampered with. Gamble said he went to a bar, and the bartender and the security video alibi him."

"So somebody else tried to kill Beardsley," Pete said.

"Looks like. I've got two of the new agents viewing the video we took at the cemetery, trying to find who fired."

Psychologist Mary McCrady leaned forward. "And why he dropped his gun?"

"He made a mistake," Ed said, "or he didn't want to be caught with it."

Mary shrugged. "You could be right. But if you think about the coordination involved to have pulled this off . . . If Kate Davis fired a blank, the shooter had to wait for the exact moment of the shot to shoot Gretchen French. And he'd have to know in advance that Kate planned to shoot. That doesn't seem like someone who'd drop a gun by mistake. I think he wanted you to find it."

"Mind games," Luke said. "He's playing with us."

"I think so," Mary said. "Did Kate Davis know her gun had blanks?"

"Not blanks," Ed said. "Just one blank. The rest of the chambers had live shells."

"Round puzzle, all yellow," Chase said. "You're right, Mary. If Kate intended to hurt Gretchen before she could go public about the rapes, then she wouldn't have had *any* blanks. If she'd planned just to scare her, she would have had *all* blanks. And if she was aiming for someone else, we're missing a yellow puzzle piece."

"Whoever she was aiming at knew Kate would be coming to the cemetery with a gun," Luke said. "Someone was very prepared."

There was a knock on the door and Leigh stuck her head in. "Chase, Germanio's on the phone from Savannah. He says it's urgent."

Chase put him on the speaker phone. "Hank, we're all here. What's going on?"

"I found Helen Granville," Germanio said. "She's dead."

Chase closed his eyes. "How?"

"Hung herself. I found her sister's house, but there were police already here. The sister found Mrs. Granville swinging from a rafter in the bedroom."

"Did you call our ME in the Savannah field office?" Chase asked.

"He's on his way. Helen Granville's sister said she arrived here last night and was very frightened. The sister had to work today. When she came home, Helen was dead."

"Did she say Granville's wife seemed suicidal?" Luke asked.

"No, just 'very frightened.' The sister is pretty shaken up. I may be able to get more out of her when she calms down."

"Keep me updated." Chase ended the call and sighed. "Very, very bad day. Let's finish this meeting. We all need to sleep. Talia, what did you find up in Ellijay?"

"The dogs never picked up the scent. Borenson might have been taken away in a car." She looked at Luke. "Crime lab found nothing on the ugly bulldog. You want her?"

"Me?" Luke said. "Why me?"

"Because she's going to a shelter otherwise. I'd take her, but I already have four dogs and my roommate says we can't have any more."

"I gave Daniel my last dog," Luke said. "I can't take another one."

She shrugged. "She's a nice dog. I hope *somebody'll* want her at the shelter."

Nobody moved and Luke sighed. "I'll take the damn dog."

Talia smiled. "I knew you would."

"But you have to come down to Poplar Bluff with me tomorrow," Luke said. "I have to interview teenaged girls who wouldn't discuss the circumstances of Kasey Knight's disappearance two years ago. You're better talking to girls than I am."

"Okay," Talia said. "I'll go, but you have to bring me some of your mama's food."

"Wait," Nancy said. "Did you say Poplar Bluff?"

"Yeah," Luke said. "It's about two hours south of here."

Nancy took a list from her pocket. "And one of the places Mansfield had mapped."

Chase leaned forward. "What else is on that list?"

Nancy looked up. "Panama City, Florida," she said.

"Ashley Csorka," Luke murmured, and Nancy nodded.

"This is Mansfield's hit list," she said. "This is where he went to grab the girls."

"We can match against last knowns in the missing kids database," Luke said, energized. "And to pictures in the catalog. This list is gold."

"We need to know if Mansfield grabbed them or lured them," Talia said, "and if he lured them, then how? Once we know how they're being taken, we may be able to track them to Rocky."

"And find the missing girls," Luke said.

"Good work, people," Chase said. "Let's go get some rest. I'll get the stenos to work on matching this list to the missing kids database during the night. Once we know names, we can begin informing parents. Be back here to-morrow at eight a.m."

Everyone had risen when Leigh opened the door again, her expression pinched. "A call came in on the hotline, for Luke. A woman claims to have info on the girl in ICU."

Luke jerked around to look at Chase. "We never re-leased her existence to the press. Is she still on the hotline, Leigh?"

"No. She wants to meet you in front of the ER in twenty minutes. Alone."

"I'll go now, but the Csorka girl's father's supposed to be here at six."

"I'll stay," Talia said. "I'll talk with him and get his daughter's DNA sample to the lab."

"Thanks," Chase said. "The rest of you get some sleep. I'll call if anything happens."

Chapter Fifteen

Raleigh, North Carolina, Saturday, February 3,
5:45 p.m

Harry Grimes crouched next to a stain on Dr. Cassidy's garage floor. "It's blood."

Steven turned to the elderly neighbor. "What time did his car leave, ma'am?"

"About noon. The doctor always stops and asks me how I am. He didn't today. I thought he was preoccupied." She wrung her hands. "I should have called the police."

Harry stood up. "Did it look like the doctor driving?"

"I don't know. I don't see so well these days. I'm so sorry."

"Thank you, ma'am. You've been a big help." When she was gone, Harry met Steven's eyes. "Nobody remembers seeing Genie Cassidy on that bus."

"Steven, Harry." A crime lab tech motioned to them. "Kent has something."

Kent Thompson, CSU, was sitting at the doctor's computer. "The doctor got an e-mail from Genie around eleven this morning, saying she was at the bus station and would he pick her up. He says he will and that he's got their plane tickets for Toronto."

"He was going to take her out of the country?" Steven asked.

"That's what we're supposed to think. Look at the envelope info on the two e-mails."

Harry did and immediately saw Kent's point. "Both e-mails were sent over the same wireless router," he said. "The router here, in this house."

"So whoever sent the e-mail was in this house," Steven said.

"Exactly," Kent said. "Genie's message might have been sent from a PDA or a laptop. Either way, Genie was not at the bus station when she sent it."

Harry nodded. "I'll get out an Amber alert."

Atlanta, Saturday, February 3, 6:05 p.m.

"Miss Vartanian, wake up."

Susannah woke with a start. She'd fallen asleep in the chair next to M. Jane Doe's bed. She blinked up into the face of Ella, Jane Doe's night nurse. "What time is it?"

"A little after six. You have a call at the nurses' station. It's the GBI office."

Susannah blinked. "Why are you here if it's only six? Where's Jennifer?"

"Jennifer got sick and had to leave, so I came in early. Your caller is waiting."

Susannah took the phone from a nurse at the desk. "This is Susannah Vartanian."

"This is Brianna Bromley, one of the GBI stenos. I have a message from Agent Papadopoulos. He wants you to meet him at the entrance of the ER. It's urgent."

Her heart began to pound harder. "When?"

"He gave me the message fifteen minutes ago. He should be there any minute."

"Thank you." Susannah ran, shivering when the cold air hit her face. She searched for Luke's car, but instead saw a familiar face. "Jennifer? Ella said you were sick."

The day nurse's eyes were red, her face pasty. "I'm waiting for my ride."

"You don't look well. Have you been waiting long?"

Jennifer's jaw tightened. "He's an hour late."

"How rude." Just then a car entered her peripheral vision, headlights momentarily blinding her. She was blinking from the glare when it hit her that the car was black with its dark tinted windows up. As it approached, the passenger side window began to glide down and too late Susannah saw the glint of metal.

"Down!" she shouted, dragging the nurse to the ground. She heard the shot splinter the air, her head jerking up to see the car's license plate as it peeled away. *DRC119.*

Horrified, she stared after it until a gurgling sound made her look down.

"Oh shit, oh shit." Susannah dragged in a ragged breath, her eyes now locked on the red rapidly spreading on the nurse's scrubs. "Jennifer. *Jennifer.* Somebody *help.*"

Jennifer Ohman's eyes fluttered open. "Bobby," she said. "It was Bobby."

Footsteps smacked on the pavement around them and Susannah leaned closer to the wounded woman. "Bobby who?"

Behind her, tires screeched and a door slammed. "Oh my God."

It was Luke, but Susannah kept her eyes on the nurse's face. "*Who is Bobby?*"

"Move, lady," one of the medics snapped.

Luke lifted her to her feet, his eyes anxiously examining her. "Are you hurt?"

"No." Then she was crushed against him, his arms around her, tight and strong. His heart thundered under her ear. She gripped the lapels of his suit and hung on, pressing her cheek against his chest. He was solid. But he was shaking.

"I heard the shot. I saw you go down." His voice was gruff, breathless. "Are you sure you're not hit?"

She shook her head, wanting to stay where she was, safe, but she needed to tell him. Struggling for calm, she tugged on his lapels until his arms loosened. But he didn't let go. She met those black eyes, once again her anchor. "She said 'It was Bobby.' "

He frowned, confused. "Who's Bobby?"

"I don't know, but she said the name twice. 'Bobby. It was Bobby.' "

His hands moved from her back to grip her upper arms. "Can you stand?"

"Yes." She forced her hands to release his lapels. "I'll be all right."

He leaned over the gurney. "Jennifer. Who is Bobby? *What about the girl*?"

"You have to move, *now*," the doctor commanded. Luke followed them into the ER.

DRC119. "Luke, wait. *Luke.*" Susannah started after him, but stumbled, still dazed.

"Susannah." Chase was suddenly there, holding her up. "What happened?"

"I was just . . . standing here next to Jane Doe's nurse. She was waiting for her ride and the car came. It was the black car, Chase. DRC119." She pursed her lips, trying not to hyperventilate. "I tried to push her out of the way, but I was too late."

"Sshh. Just wait." Chase radioed for all available units

to search for the black car. Then he led her into the ER as Luke came out of the patient care bay, his face grim.

"Jennifer Ohman's dead," he said.

Susannah had to fight to breathe. "She was standing next to me. She's dead because of me. Gretchen was standing next to me. Oh God. Oh God."

Luke took her cold hands in his warm ones, steadying her. "Susannah, take a deep breath and tell me exactly what happened."

"It was the black car. It drove by, the window came down and I saw the gun. I tried to push her out of the way, then I heard the shot. I saw the license plate as they drove away. DRC119."

"The same black car that followed you this morning?" Luke asked.

"You're sure, Susannah?" Chase added.

She glared at them both. "Dead sure."

"I'm sorry," Luke said. "I didn't mean to doubt you."

Her legs felt like rubber. "It's damn hard for me to believe, and I was there."

"*Why* were you there?" Luke asked.

She blinked up at him. "Because you asked me to come down and meet you."

The two men shared a look and Susannah felt a new shiver race down her spine. "You . . . didn't ask me to come down and meet you?"

"Who called you?" Luke asked, very quietly.

"It was a woman. Her name sounded singsong. Brianna Bromley, that's it. She said she was a stenographer in your office and that you'd asked her to call me."

"I didn't ask anyone to call you," Luke said.

"And we don't have any stenos named Brianna Bromley," Chase added grimly.

Susannah's heart had gone from racing to a slow, painful thud. "So I was lured."

"I'll trace the call," Chase said. "Luke, did the nurse say anything before she died?"

"Only what she said to Susannah."

" 'Bobby,' " Susannah quoted. " 'It was Bobby.' Luke, if you didn't call me, what are *you* doing here?"

"I got a call on the hotline from a woman saying she knew information about Jane Doe. It must have been the nurse."

"But . . . If Jennifer called you, then who called me? And why?"

"We now know two names—Bobby and Rocky. One or both had to have been in the black sedan. I think they wanted you to see Jennifer shot."

"So they had to know Jennifer would be standing there, too," Chase said. "Which means either they were watching Jennifer . . ." He paused grimly. "Or we have a leak."

"This doesn't make any sense," Susannah said. "Tonight I'm standing next to Jane Doe's nurse and she's shot. Earlier I was standing next to Gretchen French in the cemetery and she's shot by Kate. Was I the target both times or were they?"

"I don't know," Luke said. "But Gretchen wasn't shot by Kate Davis. There was at least one other shooter. Kate was murdered."

"But . . ." She looked from one man to the other. "I saw the police draw their guns."

"They never fired, Susannah," Chase said gently. "We found the gun that killed Kate Davis. Someone was standing between you and Kate."

"Off to the left," Susannah murmured.

Luke leaned forward until his face was inches from hers. "How did you know that?"

She met his eyes. "The woman in black. Al knocked me down and I looked up and saw this woman, all in black, with lace over her face. She stared at me. Then she was gone, into the crowd."

"Why didn't you mention her before?"

"I thought she was a mourner. I thought Kate had shot Gretchen, that the police had shot Kate."

"Can you describe this woman in black?"

Susannah puffed out her cheeks. "She was very tall. There were people all around her, but she just stood there, like a little pocket of . . . calm. I don't know how long she stared at me. It couldn't have been more than a second or two. It was surreal. Oh, and she had red lips. I saw the red through the lace. Her dress was long. Old. I thought she was old. Creepy." She closed her eyes, visualizing the scene, the frenzied movement around the woman who'd stood still as a statue. "She was wearing a cape, edged in black fur. She looked like someone from an old photo."

"What about her shoes?" Chase asked.

"Blue." She opened her eyes and looked up. "She had on blue running shoes. Her dress stopped above her ankles, like it was too short for her."

"Or him?" Luke asked.

"Bobby," she murmured. "Or Rocky. Oh, hell. Who is Bobby?"

"Round puzzle," Luke muttered.

Chase nodded grimly. "All yellow."

"What the hell does that mean?" Susannah demanded. "Goddammit."

Luke sighed. "It means that every time we peel away a layer, the onion sprouts a new one. You're covered in blood again. I'm taking you back to your hotel."

"I'll go back up to ICU and get my things."

"I'll go with you."

She started to tell him he didn't need to babysit her, then thought of Gretchen and Jennifer and bit back the words. Maybe he did.

Atlanta, Saturday, February 3, 6:30 p.m.

"Is it true?" Nurse Ella demanded. "Is Jennifer dead?"

Monica's mind tensed, waiting for the answer.

"I'm afraid so." Susannah's voice. "She was shot outside a few minutes ago."

Oh, God. Jennifer tried to keep me alive and now she's dead.

She felt a touch on her hand. "It's Susannah. I have to leave, but I'll be back tomorrow morning. I wish you'd wake up. There are so many things we need to know."

I am awake. Dammit, I am awake. Frustration bubbled up and over, then stilled when she felt warmth near her face. Lips. Susannah pressed her lips to Monica's forehead and her frustration mixed with a longing so strong it hurt her chest.

"Sleep," Susannah murmured. "I'll be back tomorrow."

No. Monica wanted to scream it. *Don't go. Don't leave. Please don't leave me.*

But Susannah was gone.

Hot tears trickled from Monica's eyes down her temples where they dried, unnoticed.

Susannah came out of M. Jane Doe's room to find Luke had been watching her, his black eyes intense. She felt her cheeks heat. "She's just a kid. She must be scared."

He cupped her cheek, his palm warm and solid, and for a moment she again let herself lean into him. "You're a good person," he murmured. "You know that, don't you?"

Her throat tightened. When he said it, she almost believed it. She pulled away, her whole body tense, her smile plastic. "You're kind."

Luke drew a frustrated breath and let it out. They rode down in the elevator and walked to Luke's car in silence. When they were both buckled in, he looked straight ahead. "I promised Daniel I would watch over you. I can do that at your hotel or my apartment. I won't ask anything except that you let me keep my promise to Daniel."

She was disappointed, she realized. Which was petty and small . . . and human. What woman wouldn't want a man like Luke in pursuit? But he'd given up. *So easily.*

You told him to. Don't be snide because he listened. Still, she was disappointed. And too tired to argue. "If we go to your apartment, where will I sleep?"

"In my room. I'll take the sofa."

"All right. Let's go."

Atlanta, Saturday, February 3, 6:45 p.m.

"Are they gone?" Bobby asked when Tanner got back into the car.

"Finally." He handed the DRC plates across the front seat. "I changed the plates. Now I'm George Bentley if anyone stops us. Did you have fun?"

"Oh yes," Bobby said emphatically. "I'm glad you got back from Savannah in time to drive me. It would have been too hard to hit Ohman's chest from the driver's side."

"So, back to Ridgefield House?"

"Not yet. I got another report from my mole. GBI is closing in on Jersey Jameson. Apparently Daniel Vartanian saw a piece of his boat registration number on Friday."

"So where do we find Mr. Jameson?" Tanner asked.

"I know some of the places he hangs. You ready to do a little pub crawling?"

Tanner laughed. "It'll be like old times."

"Those were the days. You'd find the marks, I'd go in for the lure. Some of those guys still pay me, cash deposits to my offshore account on the first of every month."

"You were a good whore, Bobby."

"You were good at finding clients who'd pay to keep their perversions secret. I miss those days."

"We could pick up. Go somewhere else. Start over again."

"We could, but I like my life now. Once everything dies down, I still want that house on the hill. It's mine."

"Arthur Vartanian will have left it to his legitimate children, Bobby."

"But I have a legal claim. And soon his *legitimate children* will be resting alongside the judge and his bitch of a wife." The words left a bad taste in the mouth.

"Well, when that happens," Tanner said mildly, "you know what I want."

"Grandmother Vartanian's silver tea service." Bobby chuckled. "Yes, I know."

Atlanta, Saturday, February 3, 7:15 p.m.

"It's nice," Susannah said, looking around Luke's apartment.

"It's clean, thanks to my . . ." The thought trailed when

he saw his dining room table, covered in a white linen cloth and set for two. He didn't need a second look to know the china was his mother's, as was the ornate silver candelabra that stood, ready to light.

Susannah was looking at the table, one side of her mouth turned up. "Your mother?"

"Yeah."

Susannah smiled wistfully. "She nearly smothered Daniel with a hug. I like her."

"Everybody likes my mother."

"What about your father?"

"Oh, she smothers him with hugs, too," he said wryly. "Pop has a restaurant with his brothers. Greek, of course. In the old days, Mama was head chef. Now my cousins take care of the daily stuff. Leaves my dad and my uncles time to finally enjoy life, but Mama misses it. She makes up for it by cooking for all my friends." From his closet he pulled the suit from the day before and gave it a sniff. "Barely a hint of smoke and rotting fish."

"Your dry cleaner delivers inside your apartment?"

"My dry cleaner is my cousin Johnny. He has a key. I get free delivery, he gets to watch the fights on my flatscreen when they're on pay per view."

"I wonder if he can get those red clay stains out of Chloe Hathaway's black dress."

"If Johnny can't, nobody can." His stomach growled and he rubbed it. "I'm starving."

"So am I." She hesitated. "I can cook. A little."

"Mama said she left food in the fridge." He went into the kitchen and she followed.

"Can I do anything?"

"Change your clothes." He shot her a smile as he opened the fridge door. "Again."

She looked down at her blood-spattered shirt. "I'll be back."

His careless smile disappeared along with her. "You do that," he murmured, then began warming the meal his mother had left, still thinking about Susannah.

On the way to his apartment, she'd received a call on her cell phone from Gretchen French, who'd scheduled a press conference for tomorrow afternoon. "You might want to talk to her," she'd told him when she'd hung up. "She still thinks Kate Davis shot her."

"You're sure you want to do this?" he'd asked. "Once you sit with those women in front of a bunch of microphones, there's no going back."

She'd gone very still. "Once I stepped on the plane yesterday morning, there was no going back, Luke. I knew that then. I'm all right with this. I'll do what needs to be done."

He'd been struck with a respect so profound ... And on its heels had come a desire so intense it had taken his breath away. It wasn't her face, or the quiet elegance of her manner. It was deeper. She was, quite simply, what he'd always been looking for.

Now, standing in his kitchen, he knew it didn't matter what he'd wanted or what he'd believed he'd found. In front of the ER she'd been shaking like a leaf. Still she clung to him, trusting him. She was here now, trusting him to keep her safe. But until she trusted him with that soul she claimed not to want, nothing else mattered.

He'd put dinner in the oven to warm and was pulling the cork from a bottle of wine when the doorbell rang. Leaving the wine to breathe, he went to the door and looked through the peep hole. And sighed. "Talia," he said when he'd opened the door.

Talia Scott held the leash of Judge Borenson's bulldog. "You forgot the dog."

"I've been a little busy."

Her smile was sympathetic. "I heard what happened at the ER. Sorry."

He sighed again. "I guess I should ask you in."

"Oh, thank you," Talia said dryly. "Such hospitality."

He opened the door wider. Talia and dog came inside, the dog plopping down on Luke's feet with an even bigger sigh, and Talia laughed. "Her name is Darlin'."

He rolled his eyes. "Of course it is. Does she have food?"

Talia pulled a Ziploc bag filled with kibble from her backpack. "Enough to last you till tomorrow. Here's her leash and bowl."

"*Nobody* wanted her?" Luke pressed as she pushed the dog's things into his arms.

"No. Borenson had hunting dogs the neighbors wanted, but nobody wanted Darlin'. I smell food." Then she saw the table set with the china. "But you have company. I'll go."

She started to leave and he grabbed her jacket. "Susannah Vartanian's here."

Her eyes widened. "Really?"

"It's not what you think. You should stay. Come on in. I've got a bottle of wine."

He went to the kitchen, the dog literally on his heels. Every time he stopped, the dog lay at his feet. Every time he moved, so did she. "I can't keep her. I'm never home."

Talia sat at the counter. "Then she goes to the shelter. Then, who knows?"

Luke scowled. "You're a cruel woman."

She laughed. "And you're a sweet man."

He shook his head. "Don't let it get around. Did you meet with Mr. Csorka?"

She sobered. "I did. He came with dental records, DNA samples, and pictures of Ashley with her trophies. She's a swimmer. She's earned a full college scholarship for next year."

"It's been more than twenty-four hours now. They could be anywhere."

"True, but now we're broadcasting the face of one of the missing girls to every PD in the Southeast. She's seventeen for another few weeks, so I set up an Amber alert." She leaned over, squeezed his hand. "It's better than we had yesterday."

"I used your—" Susannah stopped short, damp towels folded neatly in her arms, her gaze fixed on their joined hands. "I'm sorry. I didn't know anyone else was here."

Smiling, Talia extended her hand. "I'm Talia Scott. I work with Luke and Daniel."

Susannah shifted the towels to one arm so that she could shake Talia's hand. "It's nice to meet you. You talked to Gretchen French."

"And all the other victims," Talia said. "Except you," she added gently.

Susannah's cheeks darkened. "I gave my statement to ASA Hathaway."

"That's not what I meant. I spoke with all the women, making sure they understood their rights and the resources available to them."

Susannah's smile was brittle. "I'm a prosecutor. I know my rights. But thank you."

"You know how to tell other people their rights," Talia said, undaunted. "You might not think about them for yourself in the same way. You can call me any time if you'd like to talk." She held out her card, her easy smile still in place.

Reluctantly Susannah took it. "Gretchen speaks highly of you," she said quietly. Then she lifted her brows at the bag of kibble on the counter. "Is that dinner?"

Luke looked down at his feet and scowled again. "It's hers."

Susannah's face lit up in a smile that made his chest hurt. "Oh, look." She dropped to her knees, setting the towels aside, petting the dog's head. "Is she yours, Talia?"

Talia chuckled and winked at him. "Nope. She's Luke's."

"I don't like you," he muttered, and Talia chuckled again.

Then Susannah looked up at him, the smile still on her face. "She's yours? Really?"

He sighed. "Yeah. I guess so, until I can find her another home. She's Judge Borenson's. If he turns up alive, she goes back to Judge Borenson."

Susannah turned back to the ugly bulldog. "I have a dog. At home in New York."

"What kind?" Talia asked.

"Sheltie. Her name is Thor."

Talia laughed. "A sheltie named Thor? That sounds like a story."

"It is. She's in the kennel, probably wondering when I'm coming back to get her." The dog licked Susannah's face, making her laugh, and the small sound of joy took the pain in his chest and gave it a twist.

"What's her name?" she asked.

"Darlin'," he said softly, and she looked up, meeting his eyes.

"That's nice." Her smile faltered. "Do you always take in strays, Luke?"

"Not usually," he said, then, aware that he'd been staring, looked away.

"We're having wine, Susannah," Talia said, taking pity on him. "Want some?"

"I don't drink, but you go ahead. Dinner smells wonderful. Are you staying, Talia?"

"Yes," Luke said.

"No," Talia said at the same time. "I have to be getting home."

"You're sure you can't take the dog?" Luke asked under his breath.

"Nope," Talia said cheerfully. "My roommate said no more when I brought home the fourth one. I think she means it this time. So it's you or the pound, *Luka*." She reached over the counter, patted his cheek. "Just think what joy a dog can add to your home."

Luke had to laugh at the sparkle in her eyes. "You're enjoying this."

"Walk me to the door. It was nice to meet you, Susannah. Call me any time."

Luke walked Talia to the door, Darlin' at his heels once more. "What?" he asked.

Talia shook her head, her lips twitching. "Oh, baby, you got it bad. And she's not Greek. What's Mama Papa going to say?"

"Who do you think set the damn table?"

"Interesting." She sobered. "Have Susannah call me if she needs me."

"She's just like Daniel," he murmured. "They both just shove it all back down."

"I know," she said. "When do you want to leave for Poplar Bluff?"

"It would be easier to get Kasey Knight's friends during a school day, but we can't wait till Monday. Let's leave right after morning meeting. We'll be there by eleven."

"That's during church." Talia considered it. "Poplar Bluff's a small town. Let me contact the minister and see if they go to his church. That might be the best place to catch them after all. I'll see you tomorrow. Bring me some leftovers, okay?"

"You could just stay for dinner."

She smiled. "No, I really can't. Good luck, Luka."

Rolling his eyes, he went back to the kitchen where Susannah was tearing lettuce. He leaned against the refrigerator, Darlin' at his feet. "She won't stop following me."

One side of Susannah's mouth lifted in the half smile he'd come to anticipate. "Did you bring her out of the woods?"

"I guess in a way I did."

She pushed him aside gently, grabbing vegetables from the refrigerator. "Then, there you go. Darlin' is to you what Jane Doe is to me. And, to a certain extent," she added, cutting the ends off cucumbers with more force than needed, "what I am to you."

He wanted to grab her shoulders and make her look at him, but he stayed where he was. "That's not fair to either of us," Luke said quietly.

She dropped her chin. "You're right. I'm sorry." She swallowed hard, focusing on the vegetables she sliced with quick, expert movements. "Talia called you 'Luka.'"

"My mother calls me that."

"I know. So you and Talia are friends?" she asked carefully.

He kept his voice level, although her question set his heart thumping. "She's Greek."

"So? Do you know all the Greeks in Atlanta?"

He smiled. "A fair number. It's a tightly knit community. My father and his brothers cater a lot of the weddings and parties. We know just about everyone."

She tossed the sliced cucumbers into the salad. "Scott doesn't sound that Greek."

"Her first marriage. Didn't go so well."

"Hmm. I'm surprised your mother didn't pick her for you," she said lightly.

"She tried. Gave up. Talia and I are friends. No more."

She turned then, her arms hugging the salad bowl. Her eyes met his and stayed, intense and filled with longing, and suddenly the simple act of breathing was an effort.

Abruptly she dropped her eyes and pushed past him to put the bowl on the table. He followed her, Darlin' still at his heels, and stopped, staring at her back. "Susannah."

"I need to go. I'll sleep in Jane Doe's room in ICU with the guard at the door if it will make you feel better. I promise."

"What would make me feel better is if you'd look at me." She didn't move, so he gently grasped her shoulders and tugged until she turned around, her eyes level with his chest. He waited, silently, until she finally lifted her eyes. He felt as if he'd been punched in the gut. Her eyes that had been so careful, so guarded, now seethed with emotion, wild and turbulent. Hunger and interest. Denial and dismay. Knowing his next move would be critical, he cupped her cheek as he'd done before.

She turned her face into his palm and drew a breath as if memorizing his scent, and his whole body clenched. He knew he'd never wanted anyone, anything so much.

"How long has it been, Susannah?" he asked roughly.

"For what?"

It was a damn good question. "Since someone touched

you." He swept his thumb across her cheek to show her what he meant. "Since someone kissed your forehead."

He could feel her turmoil. "Never," she finally said.

His heart broke. "Not your mother?"

"No. She wasn't a warm woman."

"Susannah, did your father . . ." He couldn't ask. Not after all she'd been through.

"No. But he wanted to. I could always tell. But he never did." She wet her lips, nervously. "Sometimes I would hide. That's how I found the hidey-hole behind my closet. I wasn't hiding from Simon then. I was hiding from my father."

Luke wanted to scream. To throw something. To kill her father. Ironically, Simon had done it for him. "Did he hit you?"

"No. Most of the time he just ignored me. Like I wasn't there. Then sometimes he'd get this look." She shuddered.

"And your mother?"

Her lips curved, bitterly. "She was a good hostess, kept a nice house. She was never demonstrative. Never paid any attention to us. Except for Simon. It was always about Simon. After he lost his leg, it got worse. And when we'd thought he died, when my father sent him away and told the world he was dead . . . that was bad."

"What happened?"

"My mother was hysterical. She said she hated us, me and Daniel. That she wished we'd never been born. That she wished we'd died instead."

What a thing for a daughter to hear. "So when Simon hurt you, you couldn't tell her."

She looked away. "She already knew."

"*What?*"

She shrugged. "I don't know how she knew, but she

did. She told me that I was loose. What else was a boy to expect? But I wasn't. I'd never even been on a date."

"That's vile, Susannah," he said, his voice trembling.

She finally met his eyes again. "Thank you."

Thank you. Her mother had condoned her own daughter's incestuous rape and she *thanked* him for reviling it. He wanted again to scream, but he reined in his temper and softly kissed her brow. "You think you're alone and you're not. You think you're the only one to do things you're ashamed of, but you're not."

"You haven't done what I've done, Luke."

"How do you know? I've had sex with women I barely knew, sometimes just to numb my mind from what I'd seen that day. So that when I woke up at three a.m. I wouldn't be alone. I'm ashamed of that. I want what my parents have, but I've never found it."

"You don't understand." She started to pull away, reluctantly. "I hope you never do."

"Stop." He whispered the word. "Don't go." He touched his lips to the corner of her mouth. "Don't go." He didn't move, didn't breathe, just held himself there, a whisper away from her mouth.

After what seemed an eternity, she turned her head, just a hair. Just enough.

His mouth covered hers, carefully. Softly. *Finally.* With a whimper she relaxed into him, sliding her hands up his chest and around his neck, and she kissed him back. Her mouth was soft, mobile, and so much sweeter than he thought it would be. And then somewhere, somehow gentleness fled and he took what he'd needed, lifting her feet off the ground, pulling her up against him where his body throbbed and ached.

Susannah ended it too soon, pressing her cheek against

the side of his neck. Then she pushed away until he loosened his grip and her feet touched the floor once more.

She held out her hand to keep him from coming after her, devastation in her eyes. "I can't do this," she said, backing away, then she ran to the bedroom and shut the door.

Luke's teeth clenched as he called himself every name he knew. He'd promised her he wouldn't ask anything more than to let him keep his promise to Daniel. He'd taken advantage of her, just one more person in her life to have done so.

Furious with himself, he grabbed the dog's leash. "Come on, Darlin'. Let's go walk."

Chapter Sixteen

Ridgefield House, Saturday, February 3, 7:30 p.m.

Ashley Csorka drew a breath. She'd been picking at the mortar for hours, until the nail she'd found had dulled. She'd had to pull another stair free to get another nail, and that had taken a long time. Finally, finally she'd freed her first brick, about two feet off the floor. Holding her breath she gave it a push. *It'll be loud, they'll come.*

You've been at this for hours and they haven't come. Maybe they're not home. Hurry, hurry. She pushed the brick harder and nearly sobbed when it worked free, creating one brick-sized hole. The air was fresh on her face. Out there was freedom.

She'd need to loosen at least four or five more bricks. *Hurry. Hurry.*

Charlotte, North Carolina, Saturday, February 3, 9:35 p.m.

Harry Grimes knocked on the door of Nicole Shafer, the third name on the list of friends Genie Cassidy's mother had given him. The door was opened by a young girl. Harry held up his badge. "I'm Special Agent Harry Grimes. Are your parents home?"

"Mom," she called, and her mother appeared, wiping her hand on a dishrag.

"Can we help you?" she asked, and he showed her his badge.

"I'm investigating the disappearance of Genie Cassidy."

The mother frowned. "I heard she ran away."

"No, ma'am. We believe she was abducted. I'd really appreciate the opportunity to ask your daughter a few questions."

"Of course. Come in." He was led to a family room where Mr. Shafer watched TV. "Turn off the TV, Oliver. This man is from the state police. Please sit, Agent Grimes."

Harry did, keeping his gaze on Nicole, whose gaze was fixed on her feet. "Nicole, Genie was chatting online with a boy named Jason. Did you know this?"

Nicole looked at her parents nervously. "Yes. But she didn't want her mom to know. Her mom was so totally overprotective. Genie had, like, no life. Really, Mom."

"Did you know her sister Monica also disappeared after talking to a boy named Jason?" Harry asked, and Nicole nodded.

"Half the boys in our class are named Jason," she said. "It's a common name."

"Do you know where Genie planned to meet him?"

Nicole drew a breath, held it. "Niki," her father said harshly. "If you know, tell him."

Nicole let the breath out. "Mel's. It's a diner."

"I know it," Harry said, then leaned forward. "Nicole, do you chat with Jason?"

She looked at her purple fingernails. "Sometimes. Sometimes if I was with Genie, she'd let me talk to him. Jason was cool. Told her she was pretty."

"Did he ask you to meet him?" Harry asked.

She nodded. "But I was afraid. Genie said we should go together, but I got scared."

"Oh God," Mrs. Shafer breathed, horrified. "Niki. That could have been you."

Nicole's eyes filled with tears. "Is she really missing? Like kidnapped?"

Harry nodded. "We think so. Be careful, Niki. The world presented by guys online is rarely accurate. Sometimes it's even dangerous."

"You'll find her, won't you?" Niki asked, crying now.

"We're sure gonna try. Tell me, does he IM you at a certain time or do you IM him?"

"He IMs me. He's a college boy." She hesitated. "He thinks I'm in college, too."

"I'm going to need all your screen names and passwords," Harry said, his pulse accelerating. If they played their cards right, they might trap the SOB. "And I need your promise that you'll say nothing about this. I don't want your friends tipping him off."

"So I can tell people you came to question me and I told you nothing?"

Harry's lips twitched at the hopeful note in her voice. "Sure. Be cool."

Mr. Shafer quelled his daughter's hope with a look. "I want your phone. You're technologically grounded, young lady."

Nicole started to protest, then closed her mouth, pulling her phone from her pocket and putting it in her father's outstretched hand. "It could have been me," she said quietly.

Mr. Shafer pulled her to him in a hard hug. "Thanks," he said to Harry over his daughter's head. "Anything you need, just ask."

Atlanta, Sunday, February 4, 12:15 a.m.

It was the weeping that woke him. Luke blinked at the light he'd left on in his living room, feeling like he had a hangover even though he'd consumed no wine. He'd been wide awake after that disaster of a kiss, blaming himself every which way he could.

Finally he'd turned his churning mind to "Bobby." Every major player in this case had come from Dutton so that's where he searched, coming up with a list of Dutton residents named Bobby. Then, too exhausted to think anymore, he'd e-mailed the list to Chase and closed his eyes. He'd been asleep four hours and might have slept longer, but for the weeping. He wondered if he'd imagined it. Sometimes he dreamed the weeping.

But tonight it was real. He heard it again, muffled and quiet. Finding his bedroom door ajar, he peeked in and felt lower than shit. Swallowed whole by his old sweats, Susannah sat on the floor, her arms wrapped around Borenson's ugly bulldog. Her shoulders shook as she cried and he scooped her into his arms and sat on the bed.

He thought she would fight him, but instead she grabbed handfuls of his shirt and held on. Just like she had when he'd held her in front of the ER.

He threaded his fingers through the hair at her nape and cradled her head in his palm. After a time, she quieted, her sobs becoming sniffles. She tried to pull away, but he wouldn't let her go. "Just rest," he said quietly.

"I've cried more today than I have in my whole life combined."

"My sister Demi says she feels better after a good cry. You should feel on top of the world right now." He pressed a kiss to her head. "Why were you crying?"

"The hospital's call about our test results."

It took him a second. Then he tensed, his gut turning to ice. Jane Doe's blood. Their HIV tests. "Positive?" he asked, keeping his voice as neutral as he could.

She pulled back, her eyes wide. "No. Negative. I thought you got a call, too."

"If I did, it went to voicemail." He let out a shaky breath. "Whoa. You scared me."

"I'm sorry. I thought you were awake because they just called you."

"I'm awake because I heard you crying. It's negative. We're okay. Why the tears?"

She puffed out her cheeks. "It's hard to explain."

"Try," he said dryly.

She looked away. "I think you're a very nice man."

Luke's brows went up. "So you cry your eyes out? That doesn't make sense."

"I'm *trying* to *explain*. It's just that you're the first man who's paid attention to me. The first decent man. You're kind and interesting, smart, engaging, and . . ."

"Handsome?" he supplied hopefully. "Sinfully sexy?"

She laughed, as he'd hoped she would. "Yes." Then her smile dimmed. "A woman would be a fool not to be flattered." She shrugged. "Or interested."

"Or attracted?"

She looked down. "Yes. So when I got the call from the hospital, my first thought was, 'Yay, I'm not going to die.' My second was, 'Yay, now I can have Luke.'"

He cleared his throat. "Define 'have.'"

She sighed. "You know what I meant. But I can't have you."

"Because of your evil past. Susannah, for a smart woman, that is the most singularly stupid logic I've ever heard."

She gritted her teeth. "It's not stupid."

"It's not smart," he said, exasperated. "If a rape victim came to you with that story, you'd fishslap her and tell her to get therapy and have a life. You know I'm right."

She drew a breath. "I would not fishslap her."

"Fine. But you would tell her to have a life. This guilt you carry around is wrong."

She was quiet. "It's not just the guilt."

"So what else is it?"

"I can't do it," she said between her teeth.

"Yes, you can. You can tell me. I'm engaging and kind."

"I can't do *it. Sex*," she snapped, then closed her eyes. "God. This is humiliating."

Luke mentally backed away, then tiptoed back. "There's a . . . physical issue?"

"No." She covered her eyes with her hands. "Let me go. Please."

"No. Tell me. You want me, you've all but said it. Wouldn't you like to fix whatever problem you have, so then you could have me?"

"Altruistic, aren't you," she said irritably.

"And kind. And handsome. And sinfully sexy."

One side of her mouth lifted sadly. "You're incorrigible."

"Mama always says that." He sobered, stroking the side of her mouth with his thumb. "Tell me, Susannah. I won't laugh. I promise."

"Let me up. I can't talk to you like this. Please."

He opened his arms and she slid back down to the floor. "I miss my dog," she said, petting Darlin'. "She probably thinks I'm not coming home."

"Tell me why you named a female sheltie Thor."

"Thor's the god of lightning," she said. "The night I found her, we had a horrible storm with thunder and lightning. I'd driven out to the cemetery to Darcy's grave. I go every year on January nineteenth."

"In January, you had lightning?"

"It happens, but it's rare. It was snowing like crazy, so I was only going about ten miles per hour. If I'd been going faster, I would have hit her. There was this enormous bolt of lightning and there she was, bedraggled and wet and cold, standing in the middle of the road, like 'Hit me or save me but don't ignore me.'"

"So you stopped."

"It was a rental car. What did I care if it got a little dirty? I'd planned to take her to the vet and leave her there, but then she licked my face, and . . . I'm a sucker for that."

"I'll remember that," he said wryly, and she laughed, but sadly.

"It's not the same. Turns out she was microchipped. She'd escaped from a family up north months before and she'd survived all that time on her own."

He was starting to see the parallel. "Tough little sheltie."

"Yeah. They'd already bought their kids another dog, so they said I should keep her. So I did. It makes a difference, not walking into an empty silent house every night. There have been a lot of nights she sits up with me at three a.m. when I can't sleep. She's a good dog. I'm lucky to have her."

"Sounds like she's just as lucky to have you."

"There you go, being kind again."

"Susannah, tell me why you can't have sex."

She sighed, heavily. "All right. I can, but not the regular way."

"What do you consider the regular way?"

"This is so embarrassing," she muttered, and he had pity on her.

"Missionary, you mean?"

"Yeah. But I can't do it. I can't . . . look at a man. During."

"You mean, during sex?"

"Yeah. It's like I'm trapped. Not enough air. I panic."

He sat on the edge of the bed, stroking her hair. "After everything you've been through? I'm not surprised. So during your . . . encounters before, how did you do it?"

She laughed self-consciously. "Not facing them."

He drew a careful breath, determined she would not know how that turned him on. "That's all? That's your only problem?"

"No. Just one of them."

"What are the others?"

She made a strangled sound. "It has to be . . . unconventional. Has to be. Or I can't."

He frowned. "Susannah, does anything you do hurt?"

"Sometimes. But only me. Nobody else gets hurt."

He closed his eyes. "So you like it . . ."

"Rough. And I *hate* that," she said fiercely.

Have mercy. He opened his mouth to say something, anything, but she went on in an explosion of angry words.

"I hate needing it that way. I hate that that's the only way . . ." She stopped, trembling.

"The only way you can come."

She dropped her chin to her chest. "It's wrong. It's not normal."

"And by needing, and wanting it that way, then doing it that way, you got your friend killed."

"I'm not that complicated, Luke."

Oh, yes, you are. He scooted back, his legs apart. "Come here."

"No."

"You don't have to look at me. Come here. I want to

show you something, and if you don't like it, I won't ever mention it again. I promise."

"You promised before," she grumbled, but she stood.

"Now sit. No, don't look at me," he said when she would have turned around. He pulled her to sit between his legs. "Look over there." He pointed to his dresser mirror. "Look at you. Don't look at me." He put his arms around her waist and pulled her closer. "I'm dressed. You're dressed. Nothing's going to happen here except this."

He pulled her hair back and kissed her neck, her quick intake of breath sending shivers prickling over his skin. "It's just you and me and the mirror," he said.

"This is silly," she said, but she tilted her head to give him better access.

"Does it hurt? Do you feel panicked?"

"No. Not really. Just stupid."

"Just relax. You think too much." He kissed his way down the side of her neck, then ran his tongue along the curve of her shoulder. "Don't I do that better than Thor?" She laughed breathlessly. "You have a very long neck," he murmured in her ear. "This could take awhile."

"But you . . . You can't be . . ."

"Enjoying this? Susannah, I've got my arms around a beautiful woman who thinks I'm sinfully sexy and she's letting me kiss her neck. What more could I want?"

"Sex," she said flatly, and he laughed.

"I'm not that kind of guy. You have to buy me a drink before I hit you a home run."

In the mirror he saw her close her eyes. "I can't believe I told you this."

"I'm engaging. Besides, you were ready to tell someone. I'm just glad it was me. I won't tell anyone. You can trust me."

"I know," she said seriously, and he had to take a moment to control himself, to keep it slow and nonthreatening when he wanted to gobble her whole.

He'd started on the other side of her neck when his cell phone buzzed, making them both jump. He held her, flipping open his phone with one hand. "Papadopoulos."

"It's Chase. I need you back here."

Luke straightened and let Susannah go. "What's wrong?" he asked.

"Lots of stuff," Chase said. "Get in here as fast as you can. And bring Susannah."

Luke pocketed his phone. "We have to go," he said to Susannah. "Chase wants you to come. You should probably change your clothes. I'll walk the dog and then we can go." He had his hand on the doorknob, then decided to take a chance. From deep in his closet he pulled a dusty box and set it on his dresser. "You'd be surprised what's normal and what's not, Susannah," he said, then clicked his tongue. "Come on, Darlin'."

Susannah sat on the edge of his bed, staring at the box for a full thirty seconds before giving in to her curiosity. It obviously had not been opened in some time. She struggled with the lid, then stared when it finally budged.

"Goodness," she murmured, lifting out a set of fur-lined cuffs. There were all kinds of toys in the box. Some she'd used before. Some were tame, some lame, but all enticed her on a level that made her ashamed. But . . . She frowned, dropping the cuffs back into the box and replacing the lid.

Her heart was racing to beat all hell as she changed her clothes quickly. He hadn't been repulsed. He shared her tastes. *But that doesn't make it right. Does it?*

He knocked on the door, startling her. "Are you . . . decent?"

He'd chosen the word carefully, she knew. "You can come in."

He did, glancing at her, then the box. Without a word he put it back in the closet. "Let's go. It's time to get back to work."

Atlanta, Sunday, February 4, 1:45 a.m.

Susannah paced outside the door to the conference room. Luke had been in there for twenty minutes and with every minute her dread climbed. She'd only had to look at Chase's face when they'd arrived to know something was very wrong.

The door opened and Luke came into the hall. There was no smile on his face. "We're ready for you," he said, then took her hand. "Let's just get it over with."

She hesitated before she walked into the room. All those people in there would know. *So? After Gretchen's press conference tomorrow the entire world will know.*

But these people know about Darcy.

It didn't matter anymore. There could be no more secrets, she thought as she entered the crowded room. Chase was there, and Talia and Chloe. And Ed Randall, who she'd met at Sheila Cunningham's funeral. And to her surprise, Al Landers. He patted the empty chair beside him while Chase introduced the team members she hadn't yet met—Pete, Nancy, Hank. Mary, the psychologist.

Uh-oh. They'd brought in the shrink. It had to be bad. "What's happened?"

"A lot," Chase said. "But a few of the things directly affect you, Susannah."

"Chloe and I sent someone to question Michael Ellis," Al said. "Darcy's murderer."

"You talked about doing that this morning. So what did Ellis say?"

"Nothing," Chloe said, "which was odd. He's serving twenty to life and was offered a deal that would take a few of those years off his sentence, but he wouldn't say a word."

"After six years, he's still terrified," Al said. "But, the man has a tattoo."

"The swastika with the bent edges," Susannah said.

Chloe nodded. "On his thigh. But that wasn't the most interesting part." She slid a photo across the table. "This is one of the photos from Darcy's autopsy."

Susannah's stomach twisted in dread, knowing what she'd see before she looked at it. It was a close-up of a woman's hip. "The brand," she said. "She had one, too."

"You mentioned the brand when you were giving your statement this morning, and I remembered it from the pre-trial papers," Al said. "I wanted to confirm before I told you."

"Did this come out in the trial?" Chase asked.

"Ellis never went to trial," Al said. "He took a plea. The police held the brand back in case other victims were found. They didn't want any copycats using the brand."

"So this was all an elaborate setup?" Susannah asked, incredulous. "Somebody *killed Darcy* just to get to me? Why? I'm not that important."

"You are to somebody," Chase said. "Important enough to stage this assault seven years to the day from the first one. Someone who knew you wouldn't come forward."

"This is unbelievable," Susannah said, shaking her head. "Who would do this?"

"Hold that thought," Chase said. "Ed?"

"We recovered a number of hair samples from the bunker," Ed said. "We've been running DNA and found something we didn't expect." He slid two profiles in front of her.

She studied them both. "These two people are related," she said. "Right?"

"Siblings," Ed said. "One of those samples belongs to Daniel."

Susannah was stunned. "Are you saying that Simon was there?"

"Philly PD faxed Simon's profile," Ed said. "This isn't him. Actually, this is a *she*."

"But I never went into the bunker," Susannah insisted.

"The hair wasn't yours," Luke said quietly. "It was short and blond."

She tugged her long, dark hair. "So we have a sibling that we don't know about."

"That's the way it looks," Ed said. "We wanted to know if you knew of one before we asked Daniel. This could be a shock to him."

Susannah's heart was racing. "I don't know of one. It's a shock to me."

Luke cleared his throat. "Ed also ran mitochondrial DNA. No common maternity."

"So my father had illegitimate offspring." Susannah blew out a breath. "Why am I not surprised. I have a half-sister out there somewhere. Shit."

"It could be a motive, Susannah," Luke said. "For Darcy, for everything."

Susannah closed her eyes. "So I have a half-sister who

hates my guts enough to do all this? To taunt me with DRC license plates and shoot people who . . ." Her eyes flew open. "Oh my God. The woman in black at Sheila's graveside."

"One of Chase's agents found her on the video," Luke said.

"Just a glimpse," Chase said. "Not enough to see her face through the black lace. She appears to be a woman, not a man."

"Not Bobby or Rocky," Susannah murmured.

"Are you all right?" Luke asked.

"Yes and no. I mean, I'm not sure if it helps to know I have had some sadist plotting my life like this. I mean, I thought Simon was bad." She rubbed her forehead. "I have a half-sister," she said, still stunned. "That my father had an affair isn't all that shocking, but . . . I wonder if my mother knew."

"Who would know if she did?" Al asked her.

"Angie Delacroix," Susannah said instantly. "If my mother knew, she might have told Angie. They were friends. As much as my mother was friends with anyone."

"The lady who owns the beauty shop," Luke said. "Let's go talk to her."

"Tonight?"

"Tonight," Luke said. "This woman was in that bunker. She was involved somehow with Granville and Mansfield. If she's not directly involved in the disappearance of the girls, she has to have known they were there."

"Maybe she was being tortured, too. Maybe she was a victim, too."

"It's possible," Luke said. "Except that the woman in black likely killed Kate Davis."

Chase hesitated. "We think the man who assaulted you

is involved, may even be Rocky or Bobby. We want you to sit with a police artist. We have one waiting."

"Of course," she murmured.

Luke walked her to the door. "You were wonderful," he said quietly. "The police artist is right there." He pointed to a woman who sat quietly in a chair. "When you're done, go to my office. I'll be with you as soon as I can, then we can see the hairstylist."

"All right."

Luke closed the conference room door. "That went better than I anticipated."

"She's been through hell," Al said, visibly upset. "I hate to leave her, but I have a major trial starting Monday morning. I have to fly back to New York today."

"We'll be with her," Luke said. "Don't worry."

"Thanks, Al," Chase said. "You've been a huge help. Have a safe flight back."

"You'll take care of that other thing we discussed?" Luke asked, and Al nodded.

"You bet. I'll call you with the details."

"What details?" Chase asked when Al was gone.

"Something for Susannah," Luke said. "It's personal."

"I guess she's entitled to something personal," Chase said ruefully.

Luke sighed. "Now to deal with the rest of it. We've got three dead witnesses who might have led us to Granville's partner. Nancy?"

"It was not a pretty sight. I found Chili Pepper at his girlfriend's house. They were both dead, throats slit. Crime lab is still there, looking for leads."

"Thanks, Nancy," Chase said. "Hank, what about Helen Granville?"

"The ME found the ligature marks around Helen's neck didn't match the rope. She was strangled with something thinner, then strung up and made to look like suicide."

Luke rubbed his forehead. "So the man hired by Granville's partner to torch his house is dead. Granville's wife, who might have known the partner, is dead. And the nurse who might have seen Granville's partner is dead. This just sucks."

"Granville's partner is tying up loose ends," Chase said. "Granville's wife is dead. Davis's wife could be next. Pete, have you found the Davis woman and her kids?"

"No, but I did find this. I got the video from three of the gas stations where Mrs. Davis made those phone calls to Kate Davis's cell phone. Garth's wife doesn't show up, but this guy does." He tapped the photo of a burly man with a grizzled beard standing next to an eighteen-wheeler.

"He's a trucker," Luke said, and comprehension dawned. "He's got Garth wife's cell phone. Does he have Garth's wife and kids, too?"

"I've got a BOLO out for this guy," Pete said. "Nothing yet, but if he's on the interstates, some trooper is going to see him sooner or later."

"Let's hope it's sooner," Chase said.

"Maybe she doesn't want to be found," Mary McCrady said from the end of the table where she'd been silently listening. "If she believes her children are in danger . . . A mother will go to great lengths to protect her young."

"It's possible," Chase said, "but we won't know till we find her. What about the mistress, the one who works at the airport?"

"Kira Laneer. I haven't talked to her yet," Hank said.

"What about the nurse?" Luke asked. "Have we found anything among her effects?"

"Cell phone, keys, her tracking badge, all in her purse," Chase said, pointing to a plastic bag on the table. "They're in there."

"Only her prints on the phone," Ed said slowly. "Wait." He pulled on a pair of gloves and took the nurse's cell phone from her bag. "There is something. This phone number. She got a call at 8:20 yesterday morning. This incoming call is from the same number Granville called just before everything went to hell on Friday."

"Granville's partner," Chloe said. "He called her. Was he threatening her?"

" 'It was Bobby,' " Luke quoted softly. "Bobby threatened her, then killed her."

"So who is Rocky?" Pete asked.

"Could it be the same person?" Nancy asked. "Rocky sounds like a nickname."

"Here's the list of Dutton Bobbys," Chase said, referring to the list Luke had made earlier that evening. "We've got Bobbys, Roberts, Bobs, Robs . . ."

"Pass it over," Chloe said, then blinked in surprise. "Congressman Robert Michael Bowie? His son, Robert Michael Bowie, Jr. Rob Davis, Garth's uncle."

"The congressman's son's about the same age as Granville and Mansfield," Ed said. "I met him when I processed his sister's room after she was killed by Mack O'Brien. He was cooperative, but then we were investigating his sister's murder and not his private affairs. The congressman himself is older. Maybe sixty. But he's in good shape."

"Good enough to slit the throats of two people half his age?" Nancy said.

"He could have paid someone," Hank argued.

But Luke was thinking about the Dutton residents he'd

reviewed to compile the Bobby list. He'd consciously discarded one name in particular earlier, but now . . .

"Could Bobby be a woman?" Luke asked, and everyone stilled. "The woman in black killed Kate Davis. She was physically in the bunker. She's involved."

"But . . . Bobby's a man's name," Germanio said.

Luke looked at Pete, whose expression said he'd just come to the same conclusion.

"Mrs. Garth Davis," Pete said slowly. "Her name is Barbara Jean. Bobby Jean."

"Ed?" Luke asked. "How tall was the woman in the video?"

"Five-ten with her running shoes on," Ed said.

"Same as Mrs. Davis," Pete said.

For a long moment, nobody said anything. Then there was a frantic knocking at the door and a second later it opened, Susannah standing in the doorway, her open laptop in her hands, her eyes bright and energized. "I found her."

"Who?" Luke said. "Bobby?"

Susannah blinked. "No."

"Where's the police artist?" Chase asked.

"Finished," Susannah said impatiently. "She gave the sketch to Leigh so she could make copies. Dammit, *listen* to me. I found Jane Doe on the missing kids site." She put her laptop on the table. "I was looking at girls whose names started with M. Then I thought 'What if M was a nickname,' so I started back at the beginning. Here she is, in the Bs."

Luke squinted at the screen. "She doesn't look like the girl in ICU."

"Because she weighs thirty pounds less and her face is all bruised up. I told you your people wouldn't recognize her based on what she looks like now. But I saw her eyes, Luke. She looked up at me in the woods and *I saw her eyes.* This is the girl. Her middle name is Monica. M. Look. Beatrice Monica Cassidy."

"Excellent work, Susannah," Chloe said.

"There's more. I Googled her." She toggled to another screen and Luke stared.

"Amber alert," Luke said. "Her sister Eugenie Cassidy was abducted from Charlotte sometime between Friday at midnight and Saturday at eight a.m. The contact is Special Agent Harry Grimes. Was Charlotte a point on Mansfield's map, Nancy?"

"Yes. Mansfield marked a route to Port Union, South Carolina, south of Charlotte."

Susannah looked around the table. "Well? What are you waiting for? Call him. I'm going to the hospital." She started to move, but Luke gently grabbed her arm.

"Wait." From the pile of photos on the table, Luke found stills of the woman in black and Mrs. Davis. His jaw tightened as he saw what he hadn't seen before. "Look."

Susannah went still. "It's her. Her mouth is the same shape. It was so red, I saw it through the lace. But . . . this is Barbara Jean Davis, Garth's wife. Oh," she breathed. "Bobby Jean. She was in Dutton yesterday morning. She never ran away."

"Look closer," Luke said. "Look at her eyes."

The color in her face drained away. "Her eyes are Daniel's. Our father's eyes."

Chapter Seventeen

Atlanta, Sunday, February 4, 3:00 a.m.

Ella buzzed Susannah and Luke into ICU. "She's awake."

"Good." Susannah looked across the nurses' station to find Daniel's room empty.

"He was moved to a monitored care room on the floor," Ella said. "That's good."

"He's got a guard," Luke murmured in Susannah's ear. "That's better."

Monica was still intubated, but her eyes were alert. Susannah smiled down at her. "Hey." When the nurse had gone, she leaned down to whisper in her ear. "Monica."

Monica's eyes widened, then filled with tears.

"Sshh," Susannah soothed. "We know who you are."

Frantically Monica blinked her tears away.

"Can you hold a pencil?" Luke asked.

"She's still not moving her hands," Susannah said, worried. "Let's use the letter board. Luke, if you point, I'll watch her blink. Monica, do you know who took the girls?"

Between them, the process moved quickly. "*My sister*," Luke said, when Monica stopped blinking. "You know about your sister?" he asked her.

Monica began blinking again.

"*Nurse said they took her. Picture.*" Luke gently

squeezed her other hand. "The nurse took a picture or she showed you a picture?"

"*Cell phone.*"

"There weren't any pictures on the nurse's cell," Luke said, "but she could have deleted them. I'll have the phone sent to Forensics. Maybe they can recover the file."

"*Genie still missing?*"

"I'm afraid so, honey," Susannah said, and Monica flinched even as her eyes filled.

"They called her Honey in the catalog we found on Mansfield's computer," Luke said.

"Beatrice Monica," Susannah said, wiping at Monica's eyes as tenderly as she could. "Honey Bea. Oh, Monica, you must have been so scared."

"*Nurse drugged me. Couldn't kill me. Didn't want me talk.*"

Luke frowned. "How?"

"*Paralyzed.*"

Susannah met Luke's eyes over Monica's bed. "That's why she didn't move."

"A paralytic will wear off in time," Luke said. "Monica, did you see Bobby?"

"*No. Rocky.*"

Luke leaned in. "You saw Rocky? What did he look like?"

"*She.*"

Luke sat back, stunned. "Did you say *she*?"

"*Yes. Rocky woman.*"

"Oh my God," Susannah breathed, poleaxed. "All this time we assumed . . ."

Luke's jaw was tight. "A woman. Hell. We've been chasing our tails for two days."

Monica's eyes filled with tears. "*Sorry.*"

Luke blew out a breath, abruptly relaxing. "No, no, Monica. This is not your fault, sweetheart. I'm sorry. I didn't mean to upset you."

"Luke," Susannah murmured, "do you have a photo of Bobby?"

Luke searched his briefcase and pulled out the picture he'd shown Susannah earlier. "Monica, is this the woman you saw?"

"No. Young. Dark hair. Chin bob."

Susannah's gaze flew up to meet Luke's and she saw he was thinking the same thing. "Do you have a picture of Kate Davis?" she asked.

Frowning, he searched his briefcase again. "Only this one."

Susannah winced. It was Kate lying in the morgue. At least her face wasn't scarred and bloody. Bobby's bullet had hit her in the heart. "Monica, is this Rocky?"

"Yes."

Luke let out a breath. "I'll be damned," he said softly. "Rocky is Kate Davis."

"And Bobby killed her." Susannah's heart pounded hard in her chest. "My God."

"I hate her. Said to kill the girls. Kill me."

"But you escaped," Susannah said, holding her hand. "And now you're safe."

"No. Other here. Hurt rev."

"Rev? Reverend," Luke said. "So Jennifer Ohman didn't try to kill Beardsley?"

"No. Another. Not safe. Killed Jen sister."

"The nurse's sister is dead?" Susannah asked.

"Beat her death. Jen cry. Worry about son."

"Wonderful," Luke muttered. "We'll check on the little boy. But Rocky's dead."

Satisfaction filled Monica's eyes and Susannah didn't blame her a bit.

"Monica," Luke asked, "how did they get you?"

The satisfaction in Monica's eyes disappeared. *"My fault."*

"None of this is your fault," Susannah said firmly. "You're the victim."

"Met boy. Online. Jason. Not. Was deputy."

Luke's eyes narrowed. "So Mansfield lured you, pretending to be Jason?"

"Yes. Made me . . ." She stopped, closing her eyes. Tears seeped from beneath her eyelids, running down her temples, into her hair.

"We know," Susannah said, drying her tears. "I'm so sorry."

"Jason," Luke murmured.

"Just like Agent Grimes said," she murmured back. Harry Grimes had told them about the conversation records he'd found on the Cassidys' home computer. He'd also told them that Monica's father was missing, with foul play assumed, but Monica didn't need to know that now. Not yet. She'd been through enough.

Monica opened her eyes and began to blink again, fast. *"Who is Simon."*

Susannah started. "How did you . . . ? You were awake. You heard everything."

"Simon. Who."

"My brother," Susannah said, and Monica's eyes flickered wildly. "He's dead."

"Good."

Susannah smiled grimly. "I agree."

"Monica." Luke leaned close. "Did you know Angel? They called her Gabriela."

"Yes."

"What about Kasey Knight?"

"Truck stop whore."

Luke's face darkened and a muscle jerked in his cheek. "Bobby, Granville, and Mansfield had a truck stop prostitution business?" he asked.

"Kasey ran away. Deputy caught. Doctor put Kasey river place. Starved."

"We found IVs in the river bunker," Luke said. "We thought he was treating them."

Monica's eyes flashed. *"Fixed us. Hurt again. I wanted die."*

Susannah could feel his temper boiling, barely checked. But it was checked, and when he spoke, it was with a gentleness that made Susannah want to weep. "You can't die, Monica," he said. "You die and they win. Live, and help me throw them into hell."

Monica blinked away more tears. *"Throw away key."*

Luke smiled down at her. "You heard that, too."

"Want bite apple too."

"You'll have another bite at the apple, too," he promised. "We have to go now, but I'm putting another officer on, so they'll be inside and outside ICU. You'll be safe."

"Thank you."

"Thank *you*. You're a very brave young lady. Now try to sleep. We're going to look for your sister and all the others."

"Mom."

"She's on her way," Susannah said. "She said to tell you she never stopped missing you." She smoothed Monica's hair, then pressed a kiss to her brow. "She loves you."

Outside of ICU, Luke pulled her to him. "That was good. We worked well together."

He was right. She rested her forehead against his chest. "I should stay with her."

"I'll bring you back after we go to see Angie Delacroix."

She pulled back to see his face. "But we know about Bobby now." The thought of going back to Dutton still filled her with anxiety. "Why do we need Angie?"

"We don't know where Bobby's hidden the girls—or where her own two sons are."

"All right. Let's go."

Atlanta, Sunday, February 4, 3:25 a.m.

When Luke got behind the wheel, Susannah was digging in her briefcase.

"What are you doing?" he asked when she pulled out a compact.

"I'm fixing my face. My mother never would have dreamed of going to the beauty shop without every hair in place and her makeup on. I never have either."

"Then why go?"

She shrugged. "It's a woman thing. Don't try to understand it, Luke. It just is."

"My sisters say the same thing. I was hoping it was just them."

One side of her mouth lifted. "Sorry to disappoint you."

"You don't," he said seriously. "You couldn't."

The hand applying her lipstick trembled, then steadied. "We'll see," she said cryptically. She shot him an annoyed glance. "Don't you have work to do?"

"I can dial Chase and look at you at the same time," he said, punching buttons on his cell. "I'm a multitasker on top of being sinfully sexy."

"The sinfully sexy came from you." She snapped her compact closed. "Not me."

"But you agreed. Because I'm engaging on top of being sinfully—" He broke it off when Chase answered. "Hey, it's Luke."

"I've got news," Chase said before Luke could say any more. "Ed got a match on the prints on that road atlas of Mansfield's. Guess who else touched it?"

"Kate Davis," Luke said. "Monica Cassidy identified her as Rocky."

"Really? I shouldn't continue to be surprised by anything on this case, but I still am," Chase said. "You still going to talk to the beauty shop lady?"

"Yeah. But you need to check on Jennifer Ohman's son. Monica said the nurse told her that her sister had been murdered and that Ohman was worried about her son."

"So that's how she bullied the nurse. I'll follow up."

"She also said the nurse claimed someone else tried to kill Ryan Beardsley."

"Do you believe that?"

"I don't know why she would have lied about it. Isaac Gamble had an airtight alibi, so he wasn't the one in Beardsley's room Friday night."

"Everyone has a guard outside their room."

"I'm not sure that's enough. We had a guard outside ICU and Jennifer the nurse still managed to give Monica Cassidy a paralytic that's kept her quiet since Friday night."

"You're kidding."

"Nope. We can't just make sure nobody goes in. We've got to make sure nothing is administered that isn't specifically ordered."

"Pain in the fucking ass," Chase muttered. "What else did Monica say?"

"That Kasey Knight was forced into prostitution at truck stops."

Chase cursed quietly. "Every time we clean that up . . ."

"I know. But they're mobile. They just break down and move to the next stop. I was thinking that that might be how the trucker who's been using Bobby Davis's cell phone got it. Maybe he was a client."

"If he kept a clean truck log we might be able to find out where he's stopped around here," Chase said. "We haven't had any hits on his BOLO yet. I'll call you when I do."

"We've seen a rise in interstate truck stop prostitution up north, too," Susannah said when he'd hung up. "It's a frustrating problem."

"I-75 is a problem," Luke said grimly, pulling out of the hospital's lot. "For a long time it was drugs coming up from Miami. Now it's prostitution and a million other things."

"That's going to be hard for Kasey's parents to hear."

"I know. But knowing what happened to her might help Talia loosen the tongues of her so-called friends who wouldn't help the police two years ago."

"My money's on Talia," Susannah said. "I think she can make them talk." She settled into her seat, frowning. "Why won't Darcy's killer talk? What's he so afraid of?"

"Maybe he'll talk once we catch Bobby. Maybe she's threatening him, just like she did Jennifer Ohman."

"Maybe. But . . . I've been thinking. Bobby Davis isn't that much older than I am—maybe a year or two. I was twenty-two when I met Darcy and twenty-three by the time she died. Barbara Jean wouldn't have been more than twenty-four or so herself. It's hard to believe she could have pulled all those details together at twenty-four."

"Not so hard to believe. I investigated a fourteen-year-old who had a Web site and was exposing his seven-year-old sister. We caught him, but it took some doing. Even he knew how to set up the servers so that he couldn't be easily found."

"Is he redeemable?" she asked softly. "Or at fourteen, is he beyond help?"

"The second one," Luke said. "And at seven, the little girl's life is over."

Susannah frowned. "No, it's not," she snapped. "Just because she was . . ." She stopped and looked at him. "You think you're pretty clever."

"And engaging." He glanced at her from the corner of his eye, relieved her frown had smoothed from irate to thoughtful. "I told you that you wouldn't accept a victim thinking her life was over. Why should you be any different?"

"Maybe I'm not," she said and hope surged inside him.

"Damn straight you're not. You'd be arrogant to think you were."

"Don't push your luck, Papadopoulos," she said, quietly serious.

He nodded, satisfied he'd made his point. "Sleep. I'll wake you when we get there."

Dutton, Sunday, February 4, 3:55 a.m.

Charles answered on the first ring. He'd been waiting for the call from Paul. "Well?"

"Bobby killed the nurse in front of about ten witnesses," Paul said in disgust.

"Did they catch her?" Charles asked, bitterly disappointed. He'd hoped Bobby would have more finesse.

"No, they hid for a while. I led the cops away so that they could get away."

"Then where did they go?"

"Jersey Jameson, the drug runner."

"Bobby told Rocky to hire him to move inventory from the bunker. Jersey's dead?"

"Very. Bobby's out of control, Charles. You need to stop her."

"Simon was smart, but so unstable. I was hoping Bobby had the Vartanian brains without the insanity."

"With all due respect, sir, I don't think so."

"I know. I'll deal with Bobby. Be on call in case I need you."

Ridgefield House, Sunday, February 4, 3:55 a.m.

One last *push.* Ashley Csorka put her face against the hole she'd created in the wall, feeling the cold air on her hot face. She rested as she sucked in more fresh air. The hole in the wall was small, but Ashley didn't think her hands could chip away at the wall any longer. She'd used the second brick she'd loosened to pound the nail into the mortar. It was louder than the nail alone, but she was growing desperate enough that she risked discovery by the creepy butler. She'd loosened a third brick, then two more together, and he never came.

If she angled her head, she could see dim light. Moonlight, maybe. That meant a door or a window on the other side. She tensed. A car was coming, crunching up the drive and around the house. Doors slammed and she heard laughter, low and mean.

"I think we've had a good night, Tanner."

"I concur."

It was the woman they called Bobby, and the creepy butler.

"Jersey Jameson shouldn't have tried to tell me what he would and wouldn't do. I might have let him go painlessly otherwise."

"I'd say he'll serve as an example. So are all of our ends now snipped?"

"I think so. Oh, but I'm beat. I think I could sleep through the second coming."

Ashley hoped so. Their voices faded as they rounded the house toward the front. Good. *That means I'm at the back. That's the side the river was on.*

Ashley frowned. They hadn't spoken to the guard. Where was he? She couldn't wait. She'd been lucky to have had all this time to break out. Now it was time to act.

She sucked in her breath and stuck her head through the hole. It was the other half of the room and there was a window. *Hurry.* The sharp edges of the brick cut into her skin as she tried to force her shoulders through the opening. She angled her body, grateful for the yoga her swim coach had made part of their workout. She was flexible.

She was in pain. Biting back the whimper, she shoved through, her shoulders and upper arms burning. Her skin was scraped raw.

It didn't matter. *If you don't hurry, you'll be dead, then some scraped skin won't mean anything.* She wriggled her hips as if she were doing the breaststroke and her hands hit the floor on the other side. She slid the rest of the way out until she knelt on the floor, breathing hard, then looked around her. She nearly laughed out loud. On this side of the wall were all the tools she'd needed to break free. On a table she saw about a hundred doorknobs, some glass, some marble, some still assembled in the old-fashioned cast-iron plate that fit into the door. She lifted one with a marble knob, hefted it in her hand. It fit her hand better than a brick. From the table of tools she chose an awl with a wicked-looking point.

Then she pulled on the door. It creaked loudly and she froze.

"Who's there?" It was the sleepy, slurred voice of the guard.

Run. She darted into the night, appalled to see the moon so bright. She was completely visible. Vulnerable. All this and she was going to be caught.

"Stop!" The thundered order was followed by the crack of gunfire.

It was the guard. *He's shooting at me. Run.* Her feet flew across the back lawn, the footsteps and heavy breathing of the guard getting louder and louder as he got closer.

She grunted in pain when she hit the ground, two hundred pounds of man on top of her. "I got you, baby. I'm going to have you for free," the guard said, and she could smell beer on his breath. That's how she'd been able to work undetected. He'd been drunk. He wasn't so drunk now and really strong. "Then I'm gonna kill you."

I'm going to die. No. No. With a desperate cry she wrenched her hand free and drove the awl into his shoulder.

He howled in pain and she skittered back.

"Tanner!" It was the woman. From the corner of her eye she saw the butler come around the house, a rifle in his hands—just as the guard lunged. Ashley brought her arm around in a hard arc, striking the guard with the doorknob.

For a moment he was stunned motionless.

The moment was all she needed. *Go. Go. Go.* She made it to the woods that separated the house from the river. *God, help me.* The sticks and rocks shredded her feet, slowing her down. *They were coming. Coming.* Uttering a hoarse cry she ran. She could see the water. It would be cold.

Ready. Ready. Big breath. Brace yourself. Now. Jump.

God. She hit the cold water and dove deep. *Go. Go. Go.* She surfaced a few seconds later, the water too cold for her to hold her breath any longer, and she flinched at the sound of the rifle. It had hit the water, somewhere behind her.

Behind her. They were behind her.

But they had no boat. *And I am going to the Olympics.*

Move. She forced her arms to move, to stroke, to work with the current. *It was working. I'm getting away. I'm coming, Dad. I'm coming home.*

Dutton, Sunday, February 4, 4:10 a.m.

Susannah woke with lips on hers, unable to breathe. Panicked, she shrank back, her fist connecting with something solid and warm. That smelled like cedar.

"Ow." Luke pulled back, rubbing his jaw. "That hurt."

"Don't do that," she said breathlessly. "I mean it."

He moved his jaw back and forth. "I'm sorry. You looked sweet. I couldn't resist."

"I'm not sweet," she said darkly, and he laughed.

"At the moment, no." He sobered. "You were dreaming and I couldn't wake you up."

She touched her lips with the tip of her tongue. "So you kissed me."

"And you woke up. We're here. This is Angie Delacroix's address."

"She'll be asleep."

"I hope she wakes up better than you do," he muttered,

and came around to get her door. "Let me talk first. If I need you I'll let you know."

"How, with some kind of signal?" she asked.

"How about I just say, 'Susannah, please help,'" he said dryly, and rang Angie's bell. "You ready for this?"

"No. But we'll do what needs to be done."

Angie opened the door, curlers piled high on her head. "What's this? Susannah Vartanian, what in God's name are you doing here in the middle of the night?"

"I'm sorry to wake you," Susannah said quietly, "but it's urgent. May we come in?"

Angie looked from Susannah to Luke, then shrugged. "Come in." She led them into a living room that shone mainly from the plastic covers on every stick of furniture.

Luke sat on the sofa without hesitation, then patted the cushion next to him. "I'm Special Agent Papadopoulos," he said.

"I know who you are," Angie said. "You're Daniel Vartanian's friend."

"Miss Delacroix," he said, "we need your help on a delicate matter."

Angie's eyes shuttered. "What?"

"Tonight we discovered there is another Vartanian," Luke said. "A half-sister."

She sighed. "I was wondering when this would come out. How did you find out?"

"Then you knew?" Susannah asked, and Angie smiled bitterly.

"Honey, I know things I got no business knowing and things I wish I'd never heard. Yes, I knew. A body only had to look at her to know, even that young."

"Where is she, Miss Delacroix?" Luke asked, and Angie looked confused.

"Now? I don't know. She was just a baby when her parents moved away. We lost touch years ago."

"Miss Delacroix," Luke said. "Who was the baby's mother?"

"Terri Styveson."

Susannah blinked. "The preacher's wife?"

"I thought Wertz was the pastor," Luke said.

"Pastor Styveson was here before Pastor Wertz," Angie said.

"You mean Mrs. Styveson had an affair with my father?"

"I don't know if it was as big as an affair. Terri really wasn't your daddy's type. Your mama was pregnant with Simon and as big as a house. That's genetic, you know."

"Thank you," Susannah said. "So because Mother was pregnant, my father just . . ."

"Men have needs. Except, apparently, Pastor Styveson. Terri was one frustrated woman. He was very much into his daily devotional. She once asked me how to make herself more appealing to him. That sure made Sunday services more awkward."

"I guess it did," Susannah said. "So she and my father had a fling?"

"Yes." Angie sighed. "I'll never forget how hurt your mama was when she found out."

"So my mother knew. How did she find out?"

"Like I said, you only had to look at the baby. One morning your mama was picking up Simon in the church nursery and she got a good look. That baby was the spittin' image of Daniel at the same age."

"What happened?"

Angie was quiet for a moment. "Your mother paid a visit to the pastor. Confronted him. The pastor was . . . angry.

Humiliated. Your mama and I were friends for nearly forty years, but she had a mean streak, Susannah. She told Styveson that he had a choice—he had to go or the baby had to go. She said that she'd see he never got another congregation as long as he lived if she had to look at his wife's bastard baby every week in church. She would've done it, too."

"So they left," Luke said.

"And as far as I know they never had any contact with your father or mother again."

She didn't know about Barbara Jean Davis, Susannah thought. "Thank you for telling me," she said. She started to rise, but Angie sat, her lips pursed.

"So the woman's come forward for the inheritance," Angie said, and Susannah blinked. She honestly hadn't even considered that.

"Yes," Luke said without hesitation.

"Greed drives people to do terrible things." She tilted her head. "So does anger."

"What does that mean?" Susannah asked.

"Just that you might want to submit your own sample for paternity testing."

Susannah's mouth fell open. "Miss Angie, don't play games with me. Speak plainly."

"Fine. When your mother found out about your daddy's dalliance, she reciprocated."

Susannah sat back, stunned. "With who?"

Angie looked down at her hands, twisted together in her lap.

All Susannah could hear was her heart pounding in her head. "*Who?*" she repeated.

Angie looked up, her eyes filled with misery. "Frank Loomis."

Susannah's lungs stopped working. "You mean . . . Sheriff Loomis is . . . was . . ."

Angie nodded. "Your father."

Susannah's hands rose to cover her mouth. Luke's hand slid across her back. Warm and solid. "Oh my God," she whispered.

"You need to understand," Angie said. "Frank loved your mama, for years."

"Did Frank know he was Susannah's biological father?" Luke asked.

"Not till later. Not till Simon got into more trouble than Arthur could fix. Your mother would plead with Frank, ask him to make the trouble disappear. 'For me,' she'd say," Angie said bitterly. "Then one day Simon did something so bad, Frank couldn't make it go away. That's when your mother told him about you. He was so shocked. 'For me,' she said. 'The mama of your baby girl.' So he fixed it. And had nightmares for thirteen years because an innocent man had gone to prison."

"Gary Fulmore," Luke said, and she nodded. "How do you know all this?" he asked.

Her lips twisted. "Frank wasn't the only one suffering from unrequited love."

"You and Frank had a relationship?" Luke asked, and her eyes flashed in pain.

"Twenty-five years we were lovers. He'd come in the night, leave before morning. But he wouldn't marry me. He wanted Carol Vartanian."

"You must have hated her," Susannah whispered.

Angie shook her head sadly. "No. She was my friend. But I envied her. She had an important husband *and* the love of a man who sold his soul to make her happy. But it didn't make her happy. A year after Gary Fulmore went to prison, Simon disappeared and your mother was never quite the same. Neither was Frank. When he learned she was dead . . . that Simon had killed her. It nearly killed him. I guess in the end it did."

"Miss Delacroix," Luke said, "we have one more question. The pastor who left, did he leave any forwarding address? Would there be any way to get in touch with him?"

"Bob Bowie and his wife might know. Rose was always active in the church." Her eyes narrowed. "Why was this so urgent that you woke me in the middle of the night?"

"Someone shot at Susannah today," Luke said.

Angie looked surprised. "I thought they shot the French girl, the one who's going public about . . . well, you know."

"Susannah was standing next to her. We're exploring all possibilities."

"You think Terri Styveson's bastard baby would shoot Susannah for an inheritance?"

"People get shot for a lot less, every day." Luke stood, bringing Susannah to her feet. "Please accept our apologies and thanks. I hope you're able to get back to sleep."

Angie's smile was wan. "I haven't slept in days. Not since Frank was killed."

Susannah looked at Angie, her emotions seething. "Why tell me? Why now?"

"I always wondered what went on in your house. I always wondered what went on behind those blank eyes of yours. I was afraid I knew. I should have said something, but . . . Frank didn't want me to. It would have embarrassed your mother. When he finally learned the truth, that you were his, it was too late. It was too late, wasn't it?"

Susannah nodded, numbly. People had known then. They'd *known*. And they'd done nothing. "Yes."

Angie closed her eyes. "I'm sorry. I'm so sorry."

It's all right. That's what she should say. But it wasn't. It wasn't all right. "Did my father . . . Arthur . . . Did he know? That I wasn't his?"

"I don't know for sure. I do know you were your mother's penance. Now you're mine. I didn't say anything then and I've lived with that all these years. Now, I have to live with knowing I could have helped you, and didn't."

They left her sitting on her plastic-covered sofa, her face filled with regret.

"Come on," Luke murmured. Susannah made it to Luke's car before her legs gave out, and he buckled her in as if she were a child. "That was a shock," he said.

One side of her mouth lifted. "It was difficult."

He hunkered down, his face close to hers. He cradled her cheek in his palm. "If I kissed you now, would you hit me?"

His eyes were blacker than the night around them and fixed on hers. She didn't look away, needing his stability. Needing his comfort. "No."

His kiss was warm and sweet, demanding nothing. Suddenly she wished he would. He pulled away, his thumb smoothing the corner of her mouth. "Are you okay?"

"No," she whispered. "My whole life . . . it was a lie."

"Your life wasn't. Just everyone's around you. You are the same person you were fifteen minutes ago, Susannah. A good person who persevered despite everything to care about other people. You think you became a prosecutor just to erase the stigma of being Arthur Vartanian's daughter? You didn't. You did it because you want for others what no one cared enough to give you. Yet still you persevere."

She swallowed hard. "I hated him, Luke. Now I know why he hated me."

"Arthur Vartanian was a cruel man, Susannah. But he's gone and you're still here. You deserve the life you work to give people you represent every day."

"I always dreamed that Arthur wasn't really my father, that I'd been stolen from gypsies or something . . . But I'm not sure Frank Loomis was much better."

"He died trying to save Daniel. And when Bailey and Monica escaped, he could have turned them over to Granville to save himself, but he helped them. He wasn't all bad."

"Daniel needs to know. That Frank falsified the Fulmore evidence has torn him up."

"I think he'll feel better knowing it tore Frank up, too," Luke said, then pressed a kiss to her forehead. "Let's go back to Atlanta and you can get some rest."

"What will you do?"

"Find out where Bobby is hiding. Angie gave us biographical information we didn't have before." His cell buzzed as he stood. "Papadopoulos."

His back stiffened. "Where is she?" He ran around the car and slid behind the wheel, his eyes narrowing as he listened. When he hung up, he was smiling fiercely. "Guess what a family on a houseboat pulled out of the water downriver?"

"Bobby?"

"No, maybe better. A seventeen-year-old named Ashley Csorka."

"The girl from the bunker. The one who scratched her name on her cot."

He did a U-turn in Dutton's Main Street and sped out of town. "One and the same. She said she escaped from where they're holding the girls."

Dutton, Sunday, February 4, 4:30 a.m.

From his bedroom window, Charles watched Luke and Susannah drive away, then hit speed dial three on his phone. "Well? What did you tell them?"

"The truth," Angie said. "Just like you told me to."

"Good."

Chapter Eighteen

Dutton, Sunday, February 4, 4:45 a.m.

Luke found Jock's Raw Bar in Arcadia with no trouble—its neon sign lit the way from the main road. Watching Ashley being loaded into the ambulance was Sheriff Corchran.

"How is she?" Luke asked him.

"In shock. Based on her core temp, the medics think she was in the water about twenty-five minutes. Jock over there heard a thump against his houseboat. He fished her out and called me. I recognized her name from the Amber alert you folks put out earlier tonight. She's pretty lucid. She fought hard to escape."

"Thanks." Luke climbed into the back of the ambulance. "Ashley, can you hear me?"

"Yes," she managed, although her teeth were chattering.

"My name is Agent Papadopoulos. Are the others still alive?"

"I don't know. I think so."

"Where are they?"

"House. An old house. Boarded windows."

"Did it have a dock?"

"No."

"We need to get her to the hospital," one of the medics said. "Either ride or get out."

"Where are you taking her?" Susannah asked. She was standing in the open doors.

"Mansfield Community Hospital. It's closest," the medic answered.

"Luke, you stay with her and I'll meet you there," Susannah said. "I'll drive your car."

Luke tossed her his keys, then looked at Corchran, who stood behind her. "She's been shot at twice today. Stay behind her."

Susannah stepped back as the ambulance drove away. She looked up at Corchran, her brain humming. "Do you have a computer model of the river currents?"

"I've already given the River Patrol the coordinates. If she was in the water twenty-five minutes she might have floated a half mile. They've marked off a section of river about a mile long and they're already searching."

"Sheriff, can you spare someone to drive me to the hospital?"

He looked surprised at the request. "You can't drive?"

"I can, but I need to do some title searches on my computer. I may be able to find where they are. Time is of the essence."

"Larkin," he called. "The lady needs a lift. Let's go."

Inside the ambulance, Luke bent over Ashley's cold face. "Can you see the house from the road?"

"No. I had to run. A long way. Through the woods."

"Her feet are lacerated," the medic said.

"Describe the house for me, honey."

"Really old. Dark inside. Old doorknobs." For some reason this made her smile.

"What about the outside, Ashley?"

"Just a house. Nothing special."

"How did you get there?"

"First by the river, on a boat. I got sick in the boat. Then a trailer."

"Like a tractor trailer?"

"No. Horse trailer. Had hay."

Luke frowned. "Did the horse trailer look different? Unique?"

"All white. Pulled by a pickup truck. White, too. Sorry."

Luke smiled at her. "Don't be sorry. You got out alive. We'll find the others."

"Where's my dad? He's going to be so worried."

"He's here. We found your name scratched in the cot."

She shuddered, tears filling her eyes. "I was so scared."

"But you did so well, Ashley. How did they get you?"

"So stupid. I . . . I met a boy. Online." Her lips twisted as her teeth chattered. "Jason."

"The ever-popular Jason," Luke murmured. "You weren't the only one, Ashley."

Her eyes were haunted. "They took five of us. Then . . . shot the others."

"I know. We found them. Ashley, did you see your captors?"

"Two women, young. One was thirty, one twenty. Maybe. And the man. Creepy."

"There was a man? Describe him."

"Old. Creepy. Tanner."

"His skin was dark?"

"No, his name. Tanner." She was drifting. "And a guard. I think he's dead."

"Ashley, wake up," Luke said, and she struggled to obey. "What about the guard?"

"Young. Big. White." Again she smiled, but faintly. "I hope I killed him."

"Ashley, don't go to sleep," Luke said sharply. "How far away is the house?"

She blinked, her eyelids heavy. "Don't know. I swam hard. But the water was cold."

He brushed a hand over her battered scalp. "Ashley, what did they do to your hair?"

"*I* did it," she said, clenching her chattering teeth.

"Why?"

"Haynes. He likes blondes. I didn't want to go with him. So I did it."

Haynes. They had a customer. Customers tended to roll on the distributors, at least in the Internet child porn business. It was how they'd been able to unravel Web sites in the past. *Follow the money*. It was as old as time.

"So Haynes didn't want you?"

"Never saw me," she murmured, so softly he had to bend closer to her lips. "Bobby threw me in the hole. I got out. Chipped the bricks until . . . I . . ."

She said no more. Luke looked up at the medic.

"Unconscious. Her body took a real beating in that cold water. If she hadn't been in such good shape, her heart might have stopped."

Dutton, Sunday, February 4, 5:20 a.m.

Susannah was pacing impatiently when Luke emerged from the ER.

"They say she'll be all right," he said. "I'm going to wait for her father to get here."

She tugged his arm. "The doctors can talk to him. Come on, let's go."

"Where?"

"I found Terri Styveson's marriage license in the public record. Her maiden name was Petrie. This address is a house that belonged to her mother."

"Bobby's grandmother."

"The court filed an executed will fifteen years ago when the Styvesons were found murdered in their home in Arkansas. The authorities ruled it a robbery gone bad. Barbara Jean's grandmother was found dead in her sleep a few months later. Barbara Jean inherited the house. It's an old one, built in 1905. It's called Ridgefield House."

He stared at her. "I was only away from you for thirty minutes."

She smiled, triumph in her eyes. "Chase is sending a team. Corchran's closest, so he's probably there already. Well?" she asked. "You waiting for an engraved invitation?"

He put his arm around her shoulders and they ran to his car, his heart pounding like a sledgehammer. "Have I told you that you're amazing?"

"No. I don't believe you have."

He laughed, hopeful for the first time in days. "You're amazing. Get in."

She was grinning as they pulled out of the parking lot. "I like this. I think I might like it better than the courtroom. It's damn exciting."

"Only when you're not too late," he said, sobering.

She sobered as well. "Corchran had search parties with dogs searching a mile from where she was pulled from the water, but this house is another mile past that. I don't know how she managed to get so far downstream."

"She's a swimmer," Luke said. "Her father showed Talia her ribbons."

"Then she just swam the race of her life," Susannah murmured.

"Let's hope we're as fast."

They were ten minutes out when Luke's cell buzzed. "Papadopoulos."

"It's Corchran. They were definitely here, but now they're gone."

"Fuck," Luke snarled. *Too late. You were too late.* "What do you see?"

"It's an old house. They set it on fire before they left, but we got here in time to keep it from destroying the whole house. Oh, and there's a dead guard around the back."

"Ashley really killed him?" Luke asked, his mind racing. *Too late. Too late.*

"Not unless she had a rifle. He's missing a good part of his gut. He has a shallow stab wound in his shoulder and one hell of a goose egg on his head. We found a bloody marble doorknob near his body."

He thought of Ashley's small smile. "Ashley must have hit him with it and knocked him out, then Bobby shot him rather than leave him behind alive. She's nothing if not consistent. Do you see the white pickup and a horse trailer?" He'd called in the BOLO from the back of the ambulance.

"Negative. We found a minivan registered to Garth Davis and a Volvo registered to his sister Kate. And a black LTD."

"Registered to Darcy Williams," Luke said, his jaw taut. "DRC119."

"Yep," Corchran said. "The plates were under the front seat. But no horse trailer."

"Let's get every available unit out searching."

"We're already on it."

Luke snapped his phone shut. "Goddammit. I'm tired of being too damn late."

Susannah said nothing for a full minute. "Where would they go?" she finally asked. "If this was their base of operations, where would they go?"

"She had to have put her kids somewhere," Luke said. "Maybe she went there."

"Luke," Susannah said, straining forward. "Ahead. That vehicle that just merged onto the highway. It could be a trailer."

She was right. Luke sped up, radioing for any backup units in the area to respond. "They're speeding up," he said tensely, driving faster. "Get down."

Susannah obeyed, ducking her head below the window. "What are they doing?"

"Not slowing down. Just stay down."

"I'm not stupid, Luke," she said, aggrieved.

No, she was amazing. "I know."

"He's seen us," Tanner said, his hands clenching the steering wheel. "We never should have come on the interstate. I told you it was too dangerous."

"Shut up, Tanner. You're not helping." Bobby looked in the side mirror. "He's gaining. We either shoot him or we ditch the trailer and run."

"He's too close. We could never get away now. So shoot him. Now."

Bobby heard the panic in Tanner's voice, then considered the options, the odds. *They know about the trailer, but they don't know who I am. I need time.* Time to get away and begin again. Finally Bobby considered the trumping factor—*What would Charles do?* And the plan was decided.

"Tanner, you're going to pull into that rest area ahead and park diagonally, blocking the road. You and I will get out of the truck and jack a car. By the time they stop to see what's inside the trailer, we'll be back on the interstate, ducking into the next exit."

Tanner nodded. "It could work."

"Of course it'll work. Trust me."

Susannah's neck was getting cramped. "What are they doing now?"

"Same thing they were doing the last time you asked," Luke answered from behind clenched teeth. "Not slowing down."

Staying down, Susannah leaned over the center console and took the small backup revolver from Luke's ankle holster.

"What the hell are you doing?"

"Arming myself. And staying down," she added before he could say it again.

"What the . . . ?" Luke muttered. "Hold on." The car careened to the right. "They're getting off at a rest stop. Whatever happens, you stay down. Promise."

"I won't be stupid," was all she'd say.

He growled a curse, then threw on his brakes. Ahead of them she could hear the squealing of tires as the trailer slid to a stop. He was out of the car before it stopped, shouting, "Police. Everyone down. Everyone down. In the truck, *freeze*."

Then a gunshot cracked. *Luke*. Tightening her grip on his backup revolver, she threw open her door and slid out, using the door as a shield. Luke was nowhere to be seen. She almost ran after him, but stopped at the trailer.

All that mattered was the girls.

Tires squealed somewhere ahead of the trailer and

Susannah heard Luke curse. He ran back, fury in his eyes. "Bobby jumped out and hijacked a car," he said. "You stay and wait for the backups. Move."

Susannah jumped out of the way as he drove up on the curb to get around the pickup, which had been parked diagonally across the road. She refocused her attention on the trailer. The pickup's motor was still running. The back was locked, a chain threaded through the handles. She pulled herself up, standing on the back bumper to see in the dirty window. And the breath she'd been holding came out in a whoosh.

Dear God. Ashley had said one girl had been sold to a man named Haynes, so Susannah expected to see four girls, three of the five who had gone missing from the bunker plus Monica's little sister. But before her were more than twice that many, huddled together, tied and gagged. She pounded on the dirty window.

"Are you hurt?" she shouted.

One of the girls looked up, and even through the filth covering the glass, Susannah could see the devastation in her eyes. Slowly she shook her head. Then stopped, changing to an even slower nod as the tears began to stream down her cheeks.

The chain was padlocked, so Susannah ran around to the pickup's cab and stopped, grimacing at what she saw. "Oh, hell," she muttered. What was left of a man sat behind the wheel. Most of his head was sprayed over the cab. Grimacing, she pulled his keys from the ignition, then tried all the keys in the padlock until she felt it give.

Feeling triumphant, she yanked the chain from the back of the trailer, hearing it clank-clank-clank as each link hit the bumper, then the pavement. She threw open the doors and exhaled as ten pairs of terrified eyes sought hers. "Hi," she said, breathless. "I'm Susannah. You're all safe now."

Interstate 75, Sunday, February 4, 6:20 a.m.

Luke walked up to the horse trailer in time to see Susannah shaming a man into shutting off his video camera. She stood in front of the unfortunate documentarian, fists on her hips, a petite prizefighter primed for a bout with the champ. Had he not just had his heart knocked down to his knees, he might have smiled.

In the thirty minutes he'd been gone, someone had freed the girls in the trailer. Now officers were gently moving them to waiting ambulances, two at a time.

It was triumph. And it was tragedy. In the thirty minutes he'd been gone Bobby had taken yet another life. And she'd gotten away. *Too late. Too late.*

"How could you?" Susannah was saying to the filmmaker as Luke got out of his car. "You've got kids in your car—*daughters*," she went on. "How would you feel if some opportunist wanting to make a buck splashed your daughters' pictures all over CNN? Give me that tape. *Now*," she snarled when he would have argued.

The man popped the tape from the camera, then slunk away, sputtering apologies.

"Dumb ass," she muttered under her breath.

Unsettled and needing her, Luke put his hands on her shoulders and she jumped. "Sshh," he murmured, soothing himself as much as he soothed her. "It's just me."

Her frown disappeared when she saw him, a soft smile blooming. "You weren't too late this time." But she sobered when she realized he had not smiled back.

"What happened, Luke? What took you so long? Where's Bobby?"

"Bobby got in a car up at the end of the row. The engine was running with the passenger asleep. The driver hadn't locked the door."

"I knew she'd stolen the car, but she has another hostage?"

"No. She pushed the passenger out going about sixty. She knew I'd stop. Of course I did, but the passenger was dead. She'd shot him first."

Her fingers closed over his arm, lightly. "I'm sorry."

"Yeah. Me, too." He looked to the end of the rest area to where a man sat in the back of a police car. "Now I get to tell that man his son isn't coming home."

"Let someone else do it. Chase will be here soon."

"No. I'll do what needs to be done."

"Then I'll go with you."

He almost said no. But after everything, he needed someone to lean on. "Thanks."

The man got out of the police car as he approached, the color draining from his face when he saw Luke's expression. "No." He shook his head. "*No.*"

"I'm sorry. Your son was shot by the woman who stole your car. He didn't survive."

The man took a step back, denial warring with horror. "But we're going to Six Flags. It's his birthday. He's fourteen. He's only fourteen."

"I'm so sorry," Luke said, his heart so heavy he wasn't sure he could bear it. "Is there someone I can call for you?"

"My wife. I need to call my wife." Stunned, numb, he stared ahead, his cell phone in his hand. "She's home with the baby. This is going to kill her."

The state trooper who'd been waiting with him gently took the phone from his hand. "I'll take care of this, Agent Papadopoulos. You get back to your other victims." The father's shoulders were now heaving, the sound of his sobs like a knife in Luke's gut.

Now Luke had one more face to add to all the others who haunted his mind.

Behind him, Susannah's small hand came to rest on his back, tentatively at first, then with greater pressure. "You saved ten girls, Luke," she whispered. "Ten."

"All that father cares about is the child we didn't save in time."

"Don't do this," she said, urgency giving her voice strength. "Don't you dare do this to yourself." She grabbed his arm and swung him around. "In that trailer were ten girls who would have been forced into prostitution and death. Now they're going home. You stop thinking about the one you didn't save and you start counting the ten that you did."

He nodded. She was right. "You're right."

"Damn straight I am." Her eyes narrowed, full of purpose. "Now walk back to your car. You're going to drive back to Atlanta, sit down with your team, and figure out how to catch Bárbara Jean Davis. Then you can throw her into hell and throw away the key."

He started walking, her arm around his waist. "I'm so tired."

"I know," she said, her voice gentle again. "Let me drive back. You can sleep."

He leaned over until his cheek rested on her head as they walked. "Thank you."

"You're welcome. I think I owed you before. Now we're even."

"We're keeping score?" he asked soberly.

"Not anymore. I think you need somebody as much as I do."

"You're just now figuring that out?" he murmured.

Her arm tightened around him. "Don't be smug, Agent Papadopoulos."

Interstate 75, Sunday, February 4, 6:45 a.m.

Bobby finally drew a steady breath. The car from the rest stop was ditched. This car was a new one, stolen from a parking lot off the highway. *What next? What next?*

Tanner's dead. It had been so much harder than she'd thought, pulling the trigger. *I'm alone. I'm truly alone.* There was Charles, but Charles had never been . . . family.

Tanner was my family. And now he was dead. But he never would have been able to run fast enough. She'd known it when she'd told him to trust her. Tanner had a fear of jail and he was too old to survive prison. He would've wanted it this way.

So now what? Susannah Vartanian. She was the only end left un-snipped. She'd been with Papadopoulos. She'd ruined everything. *My business. My life.* Now Charles would finally get what he wanted. For some reason he'd always hated Susannah, more than even Bobby had.

I could have killed her long ago. But putting it off had annoyed Charles—the only way Bobby had been able to control *him* when it was always the other way around.

Fine, Charles. You're about to get what you want. I'll kill her for you. Then I'm gone.

Atlanta, Sunday, February 4, 8:40 a.m.

They'd all regrouped around the conference room table, a strained mix of euphoria, exhaustion, and despair hanging over the team. Ed and Chloe, Pete and Nancy, Hank, Talia, and Mary McCrady. At Luke's request, Susannah sat with them. Her quick thinking had led them to the girls tonight. She deserved to be in on the accolades.

"So we're still not done," Pete said when Chase finished. "Bobby's still at large."

"We got the girls, *alive*," Chase said. "Not only the ones from the bunker, but Genie Cassidy and six others who had been lured from their homes. And that is huge."

"We also recovered boxes of records from Bobby's trailer," Luke said, "showing proof of financial transactions between Bobby and her customers. Names and locations. We can prosecute dozens of perverts who bought children for sexual slavery."

Chase's smile had edge. "We provided the FBI with the locations of her truck stop whorehouses, which span from North Carolina into Florida. GBI agents right now are raiding ten different homes to rescue the girls Bobby's most recently sold, including the girl sold to Darryl Haynes on Friday night."

Ed's eyes widened. "The guy running for state Senate on a family values platform?"

"The very same," Chase said grimly.

"Haynes wanted a blonde," Luke said. "And a blonde helped bring him down. Ashley Csorka's escape changed everything."

"How is she?" Talia asked.

"Sitting up and talking to her dad," Luke said with a smile. "Who sends his thanks, and his wish that the man who tried to buy his child gets the same treatment in prison."

"We have a lot to be proud of this morning. Every one of you did well." Chase went on, soberly. "Granville killed the five girls in the bunker, but Monica told us it was at Rocky's-aka-Kate's command, and that Kate said, 'Bobby said so.' When we find her, we will be charging Bobby Davis with those five counts of homicide, in addition to the ten who've died directly at her hand. Add to that the attempts on the lives of Ryan Beardsley and Monica Cassidy—"

"*And* the abduction of God only knows how many minors *and* interstate forced prostitution *and* child pornography in that catalog we found," Luke inserted.

"And she's looking at about a million years behind bars," Chase finished.

Chloe frowned. "Wait. *Ten?* There's Rocky/Kate and Jennifer Ohman, the nurse."

"And the nurse's sister," Susannah said.

"Okay," Chloe nodded, "that's three. Helen Granville is four."

"Chili Pepper and his girlfriend make six," Nancy said.

"The boy at the rest area and Tanner, the man who was driving the trailer, are eight," Luke said, then looked at Pete. "And Zach Granger is nine."

"Oh, gosh, I'm sorry, Pete," Chloe said to Pete, distressed that she'd forgotten.

"It's okay," Pete said, fiercely, "but we have to catch this bitch and make her pay."

"Tenth is the guard Corchran found dead at the back of her house," Luke finished.

"If we count Darcy, she's just one shy of an even dozen," Susannah said coldly.

"And we will count Darcy," Chase said quietly. "I'm sorry, Susannah. And there are still four missing. Judge Borenson, Monica Cassidy's father, and Bobby's two sons."

Everyone was silent, then Luke sighed. "I hoped Bobby wouldn't harm her own children, but seeing what she did to that kid today . . . She's capable of anything."

"So what do we know about her?" Mary McCrady asked. "My psych profile is simply a ruthless, intelligent, soulless monster. I'd like to be able to help you more than that."

"The man driving the pickup was Roger Tanner, sixty-eight," Luke said. "He had four outstanding warrants from the eighties—assault, larceny, and two counts of murder."

"How does he link to Barbara Jean Davis?" Mary asked.

"The two counts of murder were Bobby's parents," Susannah said, "the Reverend Styveson and his wife, Terri. They were bludgeoned to death in the parsonage of the small Arkansas church where Mr. Styveson was the preacher."

"Tanner was the church handyman," Luke said. They'd pieced much of this together on the drive back. He'd been too tense to rest, and ended up spending most of the drive on the phone with the Arkansas PD while Susannah searched the public records. "His fingerprints were found in the house, not unusual because he was the handyman. But that's when they discovered his record."

"Everybody assumed he'd done it," Susannah said, "because there were no other suspects and no sign of forced entry—and he had a key to the parsonage. Bobby suffered no injuries, even though she told police he had overpowered her."

Luke shrugged. "The local PD says her story just didn't match up with the evidence, but there was no evidence to implicate her. Now, knowing she's been in league with Tanner, it makes sense that they were in it together even then. After her parents' funeral, Tanner escaped and was never seen again. Bobby was sent to South Carolina, to live with her mother's sister."

"How did they end up in Dutton?" Nancy asked.

"Who knows? Maybe Bobby knew who her real father was and forced the aunt to bring her back. Maybe the aunt blamed Susannah's mother for having the Styvesons banished and brought the girl back as a taunt. We may never know."

"I never heard anything about Bobby's parents being murdered or her being the daughter of the old pastor," Susannah said. "That kind of thing gets around in a small town, but there was never a word. Even Angie Delacroix didn't know Bobby was the Styvesons' daughter. In school she was Barbara Jean Brown, so she took her aunt Ida Mae Brown's last name. And Brown was the aunt's married name, so nobody linked her with Styveson's wife. For whatever reason, her aunt kept Bobby's secrets well."

"Her aunt moved away from Dutton shortly after Bobby married Garth Davis," Pete said. "And that's where the trail dries up. No job, no credit cards, no utilities."

"Maybe Bobby killed her, too," Talia said.

"But where are her two children?" Mary asked. "Who took care of her kids while she ran truck stop whorehouses and sold young girls to rich men?"

"The Davises have a nanny," Pete said. "Immigrant lady, likely an illegal. Her English wasn't too strong. I talked with her when I was trying to track the aunt. She worked nine to five, weekdays. She said Bobby would leave the house every day to work in her interior-decorating business. Sometimes she was asked to work nights if Bobby had a meeting and Garth wasn't home. The nanny seemed to genuinely care for the Davis boys, and if she had any idea what Bobby was actually up to, she hid it well."

"Her only other relatives are Garth's uncle, Rob Davis, and his family," Chase said.

"I asked Rob Davis if they'd seen her," Pete said. "I never searched the house."

"But would Rob hide Garth's kids?" Chloe asked. "I thought they hated each other."

"That's what Kate told us when she came here Thursday afternoon." A piece of the puzzle fell into place. Luke looked at Chase grimly. "Kate led us to Mack O'Brien."

Chase rubbed his forehead. "We were played like a cheap harmonica."

"Kate would have wanted the spotlight off of Garth and the rest of the club, because the closer Daniel got to exposing them, the closer we got to their bunker operation. Kate gave us Garth so that she and Bobby could keep their secrets. We were played."

"Kate also told us that Garth's wife had fled with the children after Rob Davis's grandson was killed by Mack O'Brien," Ed said. "Hell."

"We took her at her word," Luke finished.

"Why wouldn't you?" Susannah asked reasonably. "You had no idea any of this was going on. So get a warrant for Rob Davis's house and check for the boys."

"Next. We got a tip an hour ago," Chase said. "A call to my cell from Kira Laneer, Garth's mistress, the one who works at the airport. She says she knows where Bobby is, that Garth knew all the places she might hide. She might just be angling for publicity, but I'll assign someone to check it out, just the same. Nancy, you're frowning. Why?"

"I've been thinking about Bobby. We're saying she's murdered ten people in the last two days. Logistically, she had to have had some help."

"Tanner is a definite possibility for an accomplice," Luke said. "Ashley Csorka said he ran Ridgefield House. She called him the creepy butler."

"I don't know," Nancy said. "Unless the creepy butler has some major muscles, he didn't slit the throat of Chili Pepper. Chili's a big dude. Was a big dude."

"Maybe she has other minions," Pete said dourly.

"Others," Susannah murmured. "You know, there's another piece missing. I'm thinking about the *thích*. That conversation between Simon and Toby Granville happened when I was eleven years old. Bobby was twelve and still living in Arkansas."

"And so was Tanner," Luke said, "so it couldn't have been him."

"'I was another's,'" Susannah quoted softly. "There's somebody else out there."

"We sent the artist's sketch based on your description up to Manhattan," Chase said. "The ADA's office is going to show it to Darcy's killer. For now we focus on Bobby Davis and her two missing kids. Pete, go to Rob Davis's and find those boys. Hank, you and Nancy search the Davis house again. Talia, find out anything you can about Bobby's friends, now and in the past. Chloe, how much longer can we keep Garth?"

"He gets arraigned tomorrow."

"We'll have him followed in case he's more involved in this than we believe. Ed?"

"We found Becky's body buried outside Beardsley's cell. Beaten to death."

"So we have one more confirmed body." Chase closed his eyes for a moment. "Get me a picture of Becky. I'll ask the media to help identify her. And," Chase looked at Susannah, "Gretchen French has scheduled a press conference for four this afternoon."

"That's right. In the Grand Hotel. She's expecting it to be standing room only."

"We'll need video surveillance and security teams at the Grand, metal detector required. Bobby might be arrogant enough to come and bask in her glory."

"Or get another shot at Susannah," Luke said quietly.

Chase looked at Susannah again. "Where are you going next?"

"To the hospital," she said. "There are some things I need to discuss with Daniel."

Her paternity for one, Luke knew. Frank Loomis's reasons for his falsifying evidence thirteen years ago, for another. "I'll go with her. I still need to find out who tampered with Ryan Beardsley's IV. It could be this 'other' that we're looking for."

"Fine. Be careful, everyone," Chase said. "Keep in contact and meet back here at two-thirty for a briefing before Gretchen French's press conference." Everyone began to file out, but Chase signaled Luke to stay.

"Luke, you've been going 24/7 for the last week," Chase said. "You found the girls."

"Bobby's still out there," Luke began, but Chase waved him silent.

"I've got every agent in this department working to find her."

"Are you taking me off this case?" Luke demanded, anger beginning to boil up.

"Relax. No, I'm not taking you off the case, but I want you healthy and dependable. We've taken the wind out of Bobby's sails for now," Chase said. "She's probably regrouping. So go home, recharge. Come back better prepared to track her down."

"All right. As soon as I've taken Susannah to see Daniel, I'll go home and crash."

Chapter Nineteen

Dutton, Sunday, February 4, 9:00 a.m.

Bobby snapped the phone shut. Her GBI mole had thought their relationship was finished, just because Bobby had lost a little ground. But secrets were still valid currency, especially now. *They know who I am.* It meant she had to be more careful.

She scoffed. *Kira Laneer thinks she knows where I am.* But that Garth had known more than Bobby thought should not be ignored. Her husband was not a stupid man. Bobby didn't plan to take any chances with Kira Laneer.

She dialed Paul's number. "I need you."

"I don't think so, sugar. I've been watching TV and your ass is fried. Susannah Vartanian looked cute on the news stealing your inventory right out from under you."

Fury bubbled up. "Don't get smart. I have a job for you." She gave him Laneer's address. "Make it painless. She kept Garth from pawing at me, after all." Bobby hated Garth, hated his touch. She'd borne his two brats, fulfilling her expectations as a Davis wife. The boys, however, had been a good accessory for her suburban housewife persona, and she'd been good to them. It was smart business to keep one's cover healthy and smiling. "Kill Kira Laneer before she tells GBI what she knows."

"Bobby, this is too much," Paul said. "You can't keep killing these people."

"Just do as you're told or I'll make a call to the police about *you*." It was the first time she'd ever threatened to. First time she'd felt the need. Shaking, she hung up. Garth's victims would be talking to the press this afternoon. Susannah would be there. *I will be, too.* That GBI had increased security was useful information, although it made things more difficult. But Bobby knew how to manage the problem. *Susannah, it's time to die.*

Dutton, Sunday, February 4, 9:03 a.m.

"I told you so," Paul said to Charles, flipping his phone shut. "She's out of control."

Charles filled their cups with coffee. "She could also make good on her threat, and I need you to remain where you are. You're useful to me in the police department."

Paul's jaw squared. "She won't talk if you kill her first. Or let me do it."

Charles lifted his brows. "But I'm not finished with her yet."

"I'm not going to kill Garth's mistress."

Charles regarded him mildly over his coffee cup. "Yes, you will."

Paul's eyes flashed. "We have no idea what the Laneer woman even knows."

"Pillow talk," Charles mused. "We don't know what Garth might have told Laneer. I'll choose where and when to divulge information." His eyes narrowed, pleased to see Paul straightening in his chair. "I want Bobby at that press conference this afternoon."

"Why?" Paul sounded petulant, just as he had as a small boy.

"Because that's where Susannah will be. Bobby won't be able to resist."

"That's why you wanted me to goad her about Susannah stealing her inventory."

Charles pointed to Paul's plate with his fork. "Eat your eggs, son. They're getting cold. Then get over to Kira Laneer's. You can take my car."

Paul jabbed at his breakfast. "Let Bobby do her own damn dirty work for once."

"I don't want Bobby going over there to do her own dirty work," Charles said sharply. "In her current mood, she'll get caught and I'll miss my live show at four."

Atlanta, Sunday, February 4, 9:30 a.m.

Filled with uncertainty, Susannah stopped in the doorway of Daniel's hospital room. The last time she'd seen him, he'd been in ICU and she'd been crying all over him.

Now, standing here, was an awkward moment. He lay in the bed with his eyes closed, Alex by his side reading a magazine. "How is he?" she whispered to Alex.

"He's fine," Daniel answered. He opened blue eyes that could be glacial, warm, or sad. Now they were warm. "I saw you on the news. You found the girls. Congrats."

"Thank you." Susannah sat on the edge of a chair, wanting to flee. Luke stayed behind her, his hands on her shoulders. She folded her own hands in her lap, primly. "Daniel, I have something to tell you and it's going to be something of a shock."

Luke gently kneaded her shoulders. "You're making it worse. Just tell him."

Daniel was looking up at Luke balefully. "What?" he said, carefully enunciating.

"Relax," Luke said easily, a hint of humor in his voice. "I haven't laid a hand on her."

Yet. Susannah could feel the word hover in the air, and her cheeks heated, not in embarrassment or fear, but in excitement. *Yet.* It was seductive. Powerful. She thought of the box in his bedroom. *Yet.* It was a portent of things to come. But not now, she thought, preparing to deliver what would be both balm to Daniel's heart, and a dagger.

"It's about Frank Loomis," she blurted.

"What about him?" Daniel asked stiffly, going very still.

"We visited Angie Delacroix early this morning, hoping for some answers, and got a lot more than we bargained for. It seems Angie has been having an affair with Frank Loomis for years. But he wouldn't marry her, because he loved someone else. Mother."

Daniel blinked, his lips falling open in surprise. "*Our* mother?"

"Yes. And, it was mutual between them, at least once." She drew a breath, let it out. "Arthur Vartanian is not my father. Frank Loomis is."

Daniel slowly sagged. He stared at Susannah, then up at Luke. "Are you sure?"

"I gave Ed a DNA sample before we came here," she said. "We'll know tomorrow."

"But it makes other pieces make sense," Luke said, briefly squeezing her shoulders.

Susannah hesitated, then took her brother's hand. "Angie said thirteen years ago Simon did something so terrible that Frank couldn't make it go away. She said

Mother begged him to take care of 'it' and Frank did. For Mother."

"So Frank falsified evidence and framed Gary Fulmore," Daniel murmured. "And that's why he disappeared this week. He said he needed space. He was mourning her."

Susannah said nothing for a moment, letting her brother think, consider. And she recognized the moment he understood what she had been too stunned to comprehend in Angie's living room. His eyes flew open and locked on hers, intense and horrified.

"Then Mother *knew*," he whispered hoarsely. "She knew Simon was involved in Alex's sister's murder. Oh my God, Suze. She *knew*."

"If not the murder," Susannah said quietly, "then at least the rape."

"I thought that last night," Luke said quietly, and Susannah twisted to look up at him.

"Why didn't you say something?"

"You were so hurt. I figured you'd get there on your own when you were ready."

She held his gaze for another few beats, touched. Then she looked back at Daniel and stiffened her spine. "Daniel, there's more."

He stared at her, pale. "*More?*"

"Yes. Ed found a hair in the bunker office where you were shot. It ... The DNA is a close match to yours, consistent with a half-sibling, sharing paternity." She'd reverted to her just-the-facts prosecutor persona. It was easier that way. "You have a half-sister. Another half-sister, that is. It's Garth Davis's wife, Barbara Jean. She goes by Bobby."

Alex's eyes widened. "The 'other' Granville was talking about before he died."

Daniel's mouth opened and closed several times. "Are you sure?"

"Yes," Luke said. "Your father had a fling with the wife of the former reverend of your church. Barbara Jean was the product."

"And she's . . . bad, Daniel," Susannah said. "Evil. She's killed eleven people, plus ordering the murders of the five girls. She killed Kate Davis, too."

Daniel's breathing was fast and shallow. "But why? Why kill Kate?"

"Remember I asked about Rocky?" Luke said. "We thought that was a man. Rocky was Kate Davis, Garth's sister. Kate was working with Granville and Bobby Davis."

Daniel looked lost. "But Kate came to us. She told us that whoever was killing the Dutton women last week had sent Garth letters threatening her life. That Garth was afraid to talk because a few years ago Jared O'Brien started to talk about the club and was murdered. We found Mack O'Brien because *she* came to *us*. She *played* us?"

"Like a bad harmonica," Luke said dryly. "Chase and I were pissed, too."

"So you need to be careful," Susannah said urgently. "Bobby's still out there."

"That's why I still have a guard on my door," Daniel said. "Oh my God. This is . . ."

"I know," Susannah murmured. "Insane."

"I'm glad you told me." Daniel raked his fingers through his hair. "This answers a lot of questions. I don't like any of the answers, but as you say, it is what it is. You need to go to a safe house, Suze. For your own safety."

She'd already considered the option and rejected it. "For how long, Daniel?"

His eyes narrowed at her tone. "Until she's caught."

"And if that's weeks? Months? What if she's never caught? I've lost thirteen years of my life because of Simon and Granville and Bobby. I don't want to lose any more."

"You could lose your *life*," Daniel said fiercely.

"I'll take every precaution."

He looked like he wanted to argue. "Will you at least wear a vest?"

She'd already decided to do so. "Yes. That I will do. And now I'm going to visit Monica Cassidy, and then I'm going to sleep. I have a busy afternoon ahead of me."

She was at the door when he spoke again, quietly. "Suze. Promise me you won't take any chances like you did in the Rublonsky trial."

Eyes wide, she turned. "How did you know about that?"

His blue eyes flickered. "I know every case you've prosecuted since you joined the DA's office. I've followed each one."

Emotion rose to clog her throat. "But . . ."

"I left you because I thought I was keeping you safe. I couldn't prove Dad's underhanded dealings and I didn't want to drag you under with me. I had no idea you'd already been . . ." His voice broke and he stopped until he could speak again. "I knew when you graduated second in your class in college. I knew when you started clerking with the DA's office. I've read every decision of every trial you've ever prosecuted."

"I didn't know," she said, devastated. "I thought you didn't care."

"I never stopped caring about you," he whispered harshly. "Never. Not for one minute." His eyes flared, intense, and Susannah couldn't look away. "So promise me," he said fiercely. "Promise me you won't do what you did on the Rublonsky case."

Her eyes stung and she blinked hard. "I promise. I have to go."

"I'll watch over her," she heard Luke say as she made her way to the elevator.

Luke caught up to her at the elevator. "What happened on the Rublonsky case?"

She kept her eyes fixed on the elevator. "A college girl was gang raped and murdered by men with ties to the Russian mob. I set up an interview with an informant who had names, dates . . . proof. He wouldn't come to our office, so I met him outside this bodega. He'd been followed. He was shot standing about a foot away from me."

"Did you get the information?"

"No, but the cops caught the shooter and we got him to roll on the others."

"What happened to the informant?"

"He died," she said, still feeling the immense wave of regret. And guilt.

"You couldn't have known that would happen." She said nothing, then heard his sharp intake of breath. "Did you?"

"I . . . suspected."

The elevator opened. She stepped in, but he stood still, staring at her. The door started to close and he jumped in, taking her chin between his fingers and forcing her to look up at him. "You made yourself *bait*," he said harshly.

She shrugged. "It wasn't so dramatic as all that. I worried something might happen, so I asked the police to come with me, to protect us both. He was a bad guy, Luke. He was playing both sides of a dangerous game. He'd informed on the mob before."

"You made yourself *bait*," he repeated. "You might have been shot yourself."

Again she said nothing and he hissed a curse. "You *were* shot."

One side of her mouth lifted. "I was wearing a vest. But I was surprised how much it *hurt*," she added lightly. "I had one hell of a bruise."

He closed his eyes, his face grown pale. "Mother of God."

"I have to admit it scared me, too," she said. "But we won the case. We were able to get justice for the murdered girl and a dozen new indictments based on the verdict."

The doors opened and he took her arm, leading her into the waiting room outside ICU. Before she could utter a protest his mouth was on hers, urgent and dark and . . . scared. He'd been scared, for her. Abruptly he ended the kiss, his breathing strident. "You will not do that again," he said, his arms coming around to hold her close against him. His heart thundered and she smoothed her hands up his back, soothing.

"All right," she whispered. "I promise." She pressed a kiss to his jaw, dark with stubble. "I'm finally getting my life back, Luke. I won't waste it so foolishly. Now let me go. I need to see Monica before I fall off my feet."

He loosened his hold, kissing her more gently. "I'm glad," he whispered.

"What, that I'm exhausted?"

"No. That you're getting your life back. And that I get to be part of it."

She lifted her brows, trying for levity even though her pulse was pounding. "That would be assuming facts not in evidence, Agent Papadopoulos."

He placed his fingertips between her breasts, and every nerve in her body jumped. "Your heart is racing. So either you're having a heart attack, in which case it's good we're in a hospital, or you're interested." His brows arched. "Because I'm engaging."

Her lips twitched. "And sinfully sexy."

He grinned down at her. "I knew I'd get you to say it eventually. It's part of my evil plan to make you need me." His grin faltered, just a little. "How's it working?"

Her pounding pulse skittered. "Very, very well," she whispered.

He pressed his lips to her forehead. "Good. Let's go see Monica."

Monica's mother was sitting at her side when Luke and Susannah were buzzed past the guard into ICU. She met them halfway. "How can I ever thank you?"

Susannah ran her hand down the woman's arm. "You don't have to."

"She doesn't know about her father. Please don't tell her. Not yet."

"We understand. Any word?" Luke murmured, even though he knew there had been none. He'd been in contact with Agent Harry Grimes in North Carolina ever since they'd recovered Genie Cassidy. There was no sign of Dr. Cassidy, and that didn't look good.

"Not yet," Mrs. Cassidy murmured. "This has been a nightmare."

"We know," Susannah said. "How is Genie?"

"Asleep in Monie's room. I'll never let either of them out of my sight again."

"I can understand that," Luke said. "Her breathing tube's removed. She looks better."

"She is. Once they knew she'd been drugged, they ran a bunch of tests and said she could breathe on her own. She's been asking for you both."

Monica pointed to her sister, asleep on a chair. "Thank you," she whispered.

"You just got your tube yanked," Susannah said with a smile. "You shouldn't talk."

"Have to," Monica rasped. "Need to hear myself. Scared I never would again."

"I guess I can understand that." She touched her cheek. "So, how are you?"

"Better than before. Still hurts like hell." Monica drew a breath, resting. "I need to tell you. You asked about Angel. You also asked about Becky. They were cousins. Were brought in at the same time."

Luke hunkered next to the bed, his face even with Monica's. "Are you sure?"

"Yeah. Becky was my friend. The doctor killed her. She kept trying to escape. We whispered . . . under the floor. Made a little hole."

Just as Beardsley and Bailey had done. "When did he kill her?"

"The day before the reverend came. Doctor beat her. Made her an example."

"Why?" Luke asked.

"Doctor couldn't break her. Tried torture." Her eyes filled, tears spilling onto her cheeks. "Took her to the office, made her kneel. For hours. Covered her head, so she couldn't see. Put gun to her head, said he would shoot. Then, he *hurt* her." She looked up at Susannah. "Like Simon did to you. You know."

Susannah wiped the tears from Monica's cheeks, her hand trembling. "I know."

"It's over now," Mrs. Cassidy said. "You're safe."

Monica shook her head. "It's never over. Keeps going over and over in my mind." She turned her face away. "When she was dead, he did it to me."

"I'm so sorry, Monica," Luke murmured.

She kept her face averted. "It's not your fault." She gathered her composure and turned back to him, her eyes steady now. "Once, the doctor asked someone to help break me. He was so angry I wouldn't obey him."

"Was it Bobby?" Luke asked.

"It was a man, I'm sure. Doctor called him 'sir.' Doctor said he had unruly prisoners." She looked confused. "Then he asked what the VC would do. I didn't understand."

Luke did. *VC. Vietcong.* They were back to the Buddhist *thích,* a Vietnamese title. "So Granville and his *thích* are still thick, after all these years," he murmured. "Monica, what did the man say?"

"He got mad. Slapped the doctor. Told him never to mention that again. Then the man said to break me, they had to make me an animal. Make me forget I'm human. But they couldn't," she added with pride.

"You're strong," Luke said, looking her square in the eye. "Never forget that."

She nodded wearily. "You said you knew Angel, that you didn't get justice for her."

When we thought she couldn't hear us yesterday afternoon. "That's right. Did Becky tell you how they came to be in the bunker?"

"Her stepdad. Sold them both to Mansfield. They got too old for the Web site. Got new girls. Becky's sisters. That's why she kept escaping. To get them out."

"Do you know last names? Becky's and her stepdad's?"

"Snyder. Both. Lived in Atlanta." Her eyes narrowed. "Fourteen twenty-five Candera."

Luke's breath caught. "How long ago did they live there?"

"Six months, maybe. I don't know."

"How did her stepdad know Mansfield would buy them?" Susannah asked.

"Truck stop whores." She began to wheeze, and Nurse Ella came in with a frown.

"You all have to leave. This patient shouldn't be talking at all."

"Wait," Monica said. "Becky's stepfather met Mansfield at a truck stop. He sold her and Angel and one other girl there. I think the third girl was their neighbor. Not sure."

"That's all," Nurse Ella said. "Let her rest. Come back later. Please."

"You did good, kid," Luke said. "You get some rest. I'm gonna go to 1425 Candera, see if I can find this stepfather of Becky's. I have someone to throw into hell."

Monica grabbed his hand. "Save Becky's sisters, please. She died for them."

"I'll do my very best."

Atlanta, Sunday, February 4, 12:15 p.m.

Luke had parked in front of a target range. He made no move to go in, just sat behind the wheel glaring straight ahead. Susannah could feel the rage tightly coiled within him since he'd come out of that dingy apartment house at 1425 Candera, empty-handed. Becky Snyder's stepfather and her little sisters didn't live there anymore. Nobody knew where they'd gone. At least that was the story each neighbor had told.

"Why are we sitting in front of a target range?" Susannah finally asked.

"It's my brother Leo's place. It's . . . where I come."

"When the fury overflows, and eats you until you can't think of anything else."

He turned to her then, his eyes blacker than night. "When I first saw you, I knew you'd understand."

"I have the same anger inside me."

"I knew that, too."

"Luke, this wasn't your fault." She put her hand on his arm, but he jerked away.

"Not now," he warned. "I'd hurt you."

"No, you wouldn't. That's not the man you are." He said nothing, and she sighed. "Go and shoot something or take me back to your place where I can go to sleep."

He looked away. "I can't take you back to my apartment. Not yet."

"Why not?" she asked.

"Because I want you," he said harshly.

A shiver ran down her spine, dark and deep. "I can say no."

He looked at her again and her chest grew taut, her lungs constricted. "But you won't," he said. "Because right now I'm what you want. I'm dangerous and I'm risky and I'm out of control. Which makes you in control. Which is what made you in control every time you picked a strange man to take to a dirty hotel room for sex."

She considered him, considered herself. Then pushed her own anger aside. "So?"

"So, I don't judge what you did, because I understand the need for control. I just don't want to be with you like that. When you have sex with me, I want it to be because you want *me*, not this person I am right now."

"Yin and yang," she said quietly. "Darkness and light. Luke, you're both of those people. And *if* I have sex with you, it'll be because I want you. All of you. Not just the kind, gentle you." She got out of the car. "Come on, let's shoot some stuff."

She was met at the door by a younger version of Luke. "You're Leo. I'm Susannah."

"I know. Come in." Leo looked at Luke, still sitting in his car. "He's brooding again?"

"He's had a rough couple of days." Susannah pointed to the gun cabinet. "Can I?"

"You shoot before?"

"Yeah. Let me have that one." She pointed through the glass pane to a nine-mil semiautomatic she knew from experience was the best fit for her smaller hands.

"Good choice. Let's go."

When she was finished with round one, Leo looked impressed. She looked at the paper target whose brain was now a mangled mess. "Again?"

"Sure." He watched as she reloaded. "Where did you learn to shoot?"

"A cop owed me a favor and taught me how. I find it disturbingly relaxing."

"So do I," he said. "Do you carry?"

"In New York, yes. I had an uncomfortable meeting with a bullet a year ago. After that, I got my concealed-weapon permit, but I didn't bring my gun with me. I wish I had."

"I see. What happened to Luke?"

"He got a lead on some kids being peddled online. He found the apartment, but they were long gone."

"Seems to be the story of his life lately," Leo said sadly, and she nodded.

"He keeps pushing himself," she said. "Sooner or later, he's going to crack."

"It happens. Luke pushes himself, cracks, comes here to let off the steam, then goes home and gets superglued back together." He smiled. "It's what family does."

She felt a tug of yearning she didn't try to deny. "You're lucky."

"I know," he said, then pointed at the target. "Have another go. On the house."

The first time had been practice, impersonal. This time she was thinking about the press conference that loomed a few hours away. The target became definitely personal.

"Good aim," Leo said with a wince when she was finished.

The entire pelvic section of the target was gone. "It's Garth Davis."

Luke had finally joined them. "Then it's really good aim," he said wryly.

Leo tossed Luke the keys. "Lock up when you're done. I promised Mama I'd level her washing machine before dinner. Susannah, you're invited, of course."

"Not this week," Luke said. "She needs to sleep."

Susannah could see the pain in Luke's eyes. He needed supergluing. "I've run on less sleep right before a trial. Tell your mama we'll be there," she said to Leo. "Thanks."

Leo left with a backward wave and Luke leaned against a wall, out of her reach. "Chase called when I was out in the car. Pete found Bobby's little boys with Rob Davis's family. Kate had dropped them off a few days ago and asked Rob not to say anything. The kids are all right."

She sighed with relief. "That's good news. We really needed some of that."

"That's the truth. Come on. I'll take you back to my place so you can sleep."

"No, we're going to your mama's." She approached with care. "Are you safe now?"

His cheeks darkened in embarrassment. "Yeah."

"Oh, stop it, Luke. You have a temper. Most people do. Yours happens to be fueled by more potent stuff. So what? You control it."

His eyes flashed. "So, what if someday I don't? What if someday it boils over and I hurt someone?" He looked away. "What if I hurt you?" he finished quietly.

"Did you worry about that with all the other women?"

"No. I never kept any of them around long enough. None of them meant enough to."

"So you really haven't had anybody either, except the women you take to bed one night at a time so you're not alone at three a.m."

He looked disgusted with himself. "That about covers it."

She tugged his jaw until he met her eyes. "Are you trying to scare me away, Luke?"

"Maybe. No. Hell." He sighed. "You're not the only one with insecurities."

She was beginning to understand that. "So what do we do?" she whispered.

He pulled her to him gently. "Now? We go to Mama's. I think she's making lamb."

Dutton, Sunday, February 4, 12:30 p.m.

"Goddammit, that hurts," Paul gritted.

"Don't be such a baby," Charles said. "I've barely touched you."

"Dammit. I've been a cop for twenty years and never got so much as a hangnail."

"It's just a flesh wound," Charles said, although it was more serious than that. "I've seen a hell of a lot worse." *On myself.* He'd had to learn to mend wounds the hard way.

"And you have the scars to prove it. I know, I know," Paul muttered.

Charles lifted his brows. "Excuse me?"

Paul dropped his eyes. "Nothing. Sorry."

"I thought not," Charles said, satisfied. "I'll stitch you up. You'll be fine."

"Wouldn't have happened if you'd curbed your dog," Paul muttered, then flinched again when Charles jabbed him with the needle. "Sorry."

Charles jabbed him again.

"Sir," Paul added, more respectfully.

"All right. You don't have to be jealous, Paul. Bobby is an asset. You are more." The doorbell rang, and he scowled. "If that's another reporter . . . You stay out of sight."

It was a reporter, but a local one. "Marianne Woolf. What can I do for you, dear?"

Marianne lifted her eyes and Charles blinked. "Get inside," he said tersely. He shut the door, then grabbed Bobby's chin. "What the hell are you doing?"

"Seeing if this disguise would fool anyone. It fooled you, so I should be fine waltzing in and out of the Grand Hotel this afternoon for Gretchen French's press conference."

Charles stepped back and assessed her. "Where did you get that wig?"

"Off Marianne's head. Her hair's not real, but nobody ever knew it except me and Angie Delacroix."

"But all those hair appointments," he said. "She went every Thursday."

"Vanity. She's nearly bald. But her boobs are real." Bobby patted her own breast. "Silicone bra implants. Men will be so busy looking at these, they won't look at my face."

"Where is Marianne?"

"Knocked out in the trunk of her car. I needed her press credentials."

"Who did your makeup?" Charles asked.

"I did. One of the job skills of a high-priced hooker. I haven't eaten since last night and I'm starv—" She pushed past him and came to a full stop when she got to the kitchen, staring at Paul, then back at Charles. "What the hell? I don't understand."

"What, that we knew each other?" Paul said irritably. "Or that I got shot doing your damn errands?"

Recovering quickly, Bobby's chin lifted. "Is Kira Laneer dead?"

"Of course. I shot her damn head off."

"Then your pay will buy a lot of Band-Aids." She turned to Charles. "Why is he here?"

"Because he's mine."

She shook her head. "No. Paul works for me."

"You pay him," Charles said, "but he has always been mine. He was never yours."

Bobby's eyes flashed. "I found him. I formed him."

"He found you, because I told him to. You never had him. You never had Rocky, you never had anyone. Except for Tanner, and you killed him."

Bobby took a step back, her cheeks heating in an angry red flush. "I came to say good-bye. Now I'll just say what I've always wanted to. I hate you, old man. Fuck your control. Fuck your mind games. And fuck you."

Paul lurched to his feet, but Charles raised a hand. "Leave her. She's failed in every way imaginable. She's even lost her birthright, now that everyone knows who she is. You'll never have the big house on the hill, the family name. It's all Susannah's now." He met Bobby's eyes. "You have nothing. Not even your pride."

"I have plenty of pride, old man. I hope you choke on yours."

The door slammed behind her, shaking the glass in the window panes.

"That went well," Paul said dryly.

"Actually, it did. She'll get herself into that press conference now."

"They'll have security. If she brings a gun, they'll catch her."

"Heightens the challenge, my boy. She'll rise to the occasion."

"She's unraveling. You really want her in a crowded room with a loaded gun?"

Charles smiled. "Yes."

"She'll never leave alive."

Charles's smile broadened. "I know."

Chapter Twenty

It was controlled chaos, Susannah thought. There were people everywhere.

The women had gathered in the kitchen, the men in the living room. At first everyone had been politely curious when Luke had introduced her, even turning the sound down on the television to check her out.

But Mama had put her arm around Susannah's shoulders and ushered her into the kitchen with the "rest of the girls." The television in the living room went back to its ear-numbing volume and everyone just talked louder to be heard over it.

"Pop is losing his hearing," Luke's sister Demi confided as she chopped vegetables. As the oldest, she was second in command. Mama Papa, of course ran the show.

Mama shrugged. "Papa doesn't think so, so it's not so."

Susannah had to smile. "The beauty of denial. Are you sure I can't do anything?"

"No," Demi said. "We've got a system." Her two youngest tore through the kitchen, Darlin' the bulldog lumbering behind them. "Stop bothering that dog," she scolded.

"I think Luke's just happy Darlin's following somebody else," Susannah said.

"He pretends to be gruff," Mitra said, turning from the stove. "Luke's an old softie."

"I know," Susannah said, and Demi looked up, eyes narrowed in speculation.

"Do you now?" she asked, then lightly smacked the hand of another child, this one about twelve. "Don't you touch my clean vegetables with your dirty hands, young man. Go wash. Go." She looked at Susannah, again speculatively. "Do you like kids?"

"I don't know. I've never been around them much."

Mitra laughed. "She's asking you if you plan to have children someday, Susannah."

The women were all looking at her. "I haven't really thought about it."

"You're not getting any younger," Demi said and, startled, Susannah laughed.

"Thank you."

Demi just grinned. "I live to give advice."

Mama looked up from her lamb. "Leave her alone, Demitra. She's young still."

Susannah looked at the two sisters. "Your name is Demitra?" she asked Demi.

"Yes. And so is hers," Demi pointed to Mitra. "In Greek families, the oldest is named after the father's father or mother. Pop's mother was Demitra. The second child is named after the mother's parent, and so on."

"Mama's mother was also Demitra," Mitra said.

"So you can have two children in the same family with the same name?"

Mitra shrugged. "It happens more often than you'd think. I know a family where three sons are Peter. Actually the Greek names are different, but all translate to Peter."

Demi nodded. "So what are your parents' names, Susannah?"

"Demi," Mitra hissed, making a fierce face.

"What?" Then Demi blushed. "I'm sorry. I didn't think. Your parents were . . . You didn't have a good relationship with your parents."

Demi seemed to be the master of understatement, but she also looked upset, so Susannah smiled. "It's okay. I don't think I'd be naming any children after my parents."

"So you will have children." Satisfied, Demi went back to her chopping.

Susannah considered protesting, then caught Mitra's grin and closed her mouth.

"How are the clothes I bought working out, Susannah?" Mitra asked, deftly turning the topic. "Stacie was thrilled that you gave her that outfit back, by the way."

"I figured she would be. Your clothes are perfect, thank you. But I'm nearly out."

Mitra's eyes widened. "How? I got you five outfits."

Susannah grimaced. "They keep getting bloody."

"Oh, yeah." Mitra shrugged again. "Well, Johnny can clean them for you."

"Johnny can clean anything," Demi said. "An-y thing."

Their conversation shifted to the stains cousin Johnny had removed, then on to other cousins and so many family members Susannah gave up trying to keep them straight. Instead she enjoyed the pleasure of being in a warm kitchen instead of a restaurant, part of the conversation, instead of listening in on others from a table for one.

The meal was the same. Sitting between Luke and Leo, Susannah watched the quiet devotion his father showered on Mama. And there was laughter, so much she wanted to hold it all in.

"What does Lukamou mean?" she whispered to Leo. Mama had called Luke by that name more than once and every time he'd softened. That's when Susannah realized she was seeing him being superglued back together before her very eyes.

"It's a pet name," Leo whispered back. "Like if someone called you SuzyQ."

"But no one would," Susannah said darkly and Leo chuckled.

"Luke's real name is Loukaniko, by the way. Luke is just a nickname."

"Loukaniko," she murmured. "I'll remember that."

Too soon the meal was over. To think that they did this chaotic, wonderful thing every Sunday afternoon. *No wonder Daniel loves it here so much.*

"You come back next week," Demi said with authority. "Even if Luke must work."

"Thank you. I'd like that."

Like a noisy herd, the whole family moved toward the door. Leo was waiting with her coat and purse. He helped her with her coat, then pressed her purse into her arms. Startled, her eyes flew up to meet his. Her purse was three pounds heavier than it had been before she arrived and she immediately understood what he'd done. "Leo."

He caught her in a hard hug. "Feel safe," he whispered. He pulled back, his eyes as black as Luke's and just as intense. "Come back soon."

Her throat tightened. "I will. Thank you."

Mama caught her in another bear hug. "That matter we discussed on Friday night," she said. "Your crossroads. Have you decided which path you'll take?"

Susannah thought of the press conference, now only hours away. "I knew which direction I had to take then," she said. "I just didn't like it."

"Then it must be the right one," Mama said wryly. "As Leo says, come back soon. Luka, do not leave that dog in my house."

Luke sighed long-sufferingly. "Fine. Come on, Dog."

"Call her Darlin'," Susannah teased. He'd not done so in front of his family.

Leo snickered. "Yes, *darlin'*."

Luke glared at him. "It's bad enough I have to take the damn dog," he muttered. But when he lifted Darlin' into the backseat of his car, his hands lingered to pet her head. "Good girl," Susannah heard him murmur. "Good Darlin'."

Her heart cracked open. *I want him. I want this. They're happy. I want to be happy.*

He got into the car, eyes resting on his mother's house. "Chase told me to go home, get recharged," he said. "I just did. Thanks for giving up your sleep. I needed this."

She took his hand, entwined her fingers through his. "So did I."

He brought her hand to his lips. "Let's take the dog home. Then I have a team meeting before your date with the media. Are you ready?"

"Yeah. I'm ready." And she found she really was. "Let's go."

Dutton, Sunday, February 4, 3:15 p.m.

Luke found Chase sitting on a bench in the outdoor break area, staring morosely at a pair of ducks that greedily pecked the ground. In one hand Chase held a bag of popcorn. Between his fingers was a lit cigarette.

"You don't smoke," Luke said.

Chase looked at his cigarette. "Used to. Quit twelve years, four months ago."

"What's wrong?" Luke asked, bracing himself for the next wave of bad news.

Chase looked up, no smile on his face. "Bobby just hit a baker's dozen."

Thirteen. Luke's heart sank. "Monica's dad?"

"No. No, he's still missing, as is Judge Borenson."

"The Davis kids were found, so who is it?"

"Jersey Jameson. He transported the girls from the bunker to Ridgefield House. He tried to clean, but we found one of Ashley Csorka's hairs, along with traces of vomit."

"She said she'd gotten sick in the boat," Luke murmured. "Who was the thirteenth?"

"Kira Laneer."

Luke sat on the bench heavily. "Garth Davis's mistress. She's dead?"

"Theoretically, yes. In reality no."

"Chase, you're not making any sense."

He sighed. "I know. I'm tired. And now I know for sure I have a mole on my team. I mentioned Kira in the meeting this morning on purpose. She didn't really call in a tip."

Luke frowned. "You suspected one of *us*?"

"I suspected somebody. I had Ms. Laneer socked away in a safe house and good thing I did. Someone fired into her home a few hours ago. They hit a mannequin we'd put on the sofa. With a wig, it looked like her from behind. When my agents confronted him, he shot them."

Luke closed his eyes. "And?"

"One stable. One critical. Shooter got away. One of the agents managed to get off a few shots. We think he nicked an arm, but it didn't slow him down."

"God, Chase."

"I know. We made sure we'd watered the flower bed under that window really well. We got a good shoe impression in the dirt. Man's shoe, size fourteen."

Luke shook his head. "No way that's Bobby's size. I can't even wear a fourteen."

"No, she wears a woman's ten. She wouldn't have been able to run if she'd been wearing these shoes, plus the deformation was even in the impression. The shoe was fully filled with a size fourteen foot. We got pictures of the shooter, but he had a mask covering his face."

"So every time we mention someone in team meeting, they get whacked."

"That's about the size of it."

"I can't see it being any of us. Even Germanio."

"Hank wasn't there when we talked about Jennifer Ohman, the nurse. I've alerted my supervisors and we've brought in OPS."

Luke winced. The Office of Professional Standards was a necessary evil, but every cop, good or bad, instinctively hated them on sight. "What are they going to do?"

"Investigate the hell out of everybody. The investigation goes on, but all cell phone and land line calls will be monitored."

"So why are you telling me this? Does this mean you don't suspect me?" Luke tried to keep the annoyance from his voice, but goddammit, he hated OPS.

"I don't suspect *any* of you," Chase said harshly. He took a long drag on the cigarette and started coughing. "Dammit, I can't even smoke right today."

"How long since you slept, Chase?"

"Too long, but with this . . . I can't sleep knowing we've got a traitor in our ranks."

"What do you want from me?" Luke asked, more kindly.

"I need you to keep your eyes open. That's one of the reasons I sent you home. When Bobby killed that nurse, she just as easily could have killed Susannah. I'm wondering why she didn't."

"Am I the only one who knows?"

"Yeah. And if I die mysteriously, OPS will be on your ass like white on rice."

"Thank you," Luke said dryly. "I'll do my damndest to keep you alive, too."

Chase dumped the popcorn. "Knock yourselves out," he muttered to the ducks.

"It'll be okay," Luke said. "We'll figure this out."

"Yeah, but will I have any agents left when we do?"

Atlanta, Sunday, February 4, 3:55 p.m.

From her carefully chosen place on the standing-room-only sidelines, Bobby counted six of them on the stage. Five women Garth had raped plus sweet Susannah, who sat at the far left of the table, closest to the eaves. Fate had smiled.

But the six women didn't. They were sober, some visibly nervous. Gretchen French had her arm in a sling. That made Bobby satisfied. But Susannah looked serene and that made Bobby furious. She must have skillfully applied her makeup because she had no dark circles and Bobby knew for a fact the woman had not slept in days.

It didn't matter, though. Soon she'd be dead, a bullet straight through her heart. The nine-mil in Bobby's pocket would accomplish the task nicely.

She'd passed through the metal detector with a smile, her press credentials hanging around her neck. Even at a hard glance, the makeup, bra padding, and Marianne's wig had enabled Bobby to pass for Marianne with the toughest of critics. Still, her stomach churned, thinking of Charles. Damned old man. *Why do you care what he thinks?*

But half a lifetime of caring was a hard habit to kick. She still wanted to prove herself. She had pride. She had skill. Soon Charles would see it, along with every person watching live and on the endless CNN loop later.

Bobby resisted the temptation to touch the gun in her pocket. It was real. It was loaded. She'd checked it, taking it into a ladies' room stall minutes after it had been passed to her from behind, wrapped in a jacket and stuffed in a backpack. Her contact had done well. *See, I have something, old man.* She had a mole in GBI.

That Paul gave you. And Charles gave you Paul. It left a bitter taste. When she thought back, she realized how she'd been played. That she'd met Paul exactly when she'd needed a cop inside APD had seemed like fate at the time. Now, she knew she'd been just like one of the pawns Charles carried around in that ivory box of his.

But for now, she needed to focus. For the next hour she was Marianne Woolf, ace reporter. Marianne wouldn't be needing the identity for a while, not until she woke up. She wasn't dead after all, just stunned. There had been no need to kill her. Bobby didn't kill everyone, no matter what Paul thought. Paul, that sonofabitch.

Don't think about him or you'll fail. Think about . . . She searched for a topic. *Marianne.* Bobby had always liked Marianne. She'd been the one tight ass at that stuffy private school who had lowered herself to talk to her. Taunted by the rich bitches as "the girl most likely to do everybody," Marianne had been in dire need of a friend back then.

Their friendship had continued over the years, mostly since Garth had been elected mayor. Since then, a lot of the rich bitches who hadn't given her the time of day were suddenly more attentive. She'd gone to their charity lunches and smiled, secretly smirking at the knowledge they had welcomed a murderer and a high-priced whore to their Irish-lace-covered tables where they sipped tea from antique silver teapots.

But the day she'd been invited to tea at Judge Vartanian's house had been very difficult indeed. Sitting amidst the quiet elegance of old money without screaming *MINE* and grabbing Carol Vartanian by the throat had taken every bit of her self-control. It had taken a meeting with Charles beforehand to calm her. It had taken his assurances that her time would come. That someday *she* would be sitting in the big house, drinking from *her* great-grandmother Vartanian's silver tea set.

That would never happen now. Now that the police knew who she was. Now that Susannah had ruined everything by finding that damn girl in the woods. Now she'd have to leave Dutton, leave Georgia. Leave the fucking country.

Now even Charles had abandoned her.

Don't think about Charles. Keep your hate sharp. Think about the Vartanians. She'd so wanted, *needed* to break Carol Vartanian's scrawny neck. The judge's wife had been the reason the Styvesons had been forced to move from the well-paying Dutton parsonage before Bobby's earliest memory. It had been Carol's interference that had kept her father in low-paying churches in the middle of nowhere. It had been Carol Vartanian who'd ruined her life. Her mother had told her so.

And it was Susannah Vartanian who'd lived her life. Up there in the big house with the fine things. The designer clothes, the pearls handed down six generations. It was Susannah Vartanian who would lose it all today. First her dignity. And then her life.

Bobby resisted the temptation to fiddle with Marianne's press credentials hanging around her neck. Marianne had responded quickly to her call for help this morning, just as Bobby had known she would. Garth had been arrested and their bank accounts had been frozen and *what is to become of me?* Marianne had swallowed it hook, line, and sinker. No doubt the promise of an exclusive hadn't hurt her Good Samaritan zeal.

GBI Agent Talia Scott was walking across the stage, clasping the hand of each woman at the table. Agent Scott lingered over Susannah, her expression concerned, but Susannah nodded resolutely. Scott stepped off to the side and Gretchen French pulled her microphone close.

Gretchen cleared her throat. "Good afternoon. Thank you for coming." Conversation died quickly and all eyes were on the stage. "We are six of sixteen women raped by the Dutton men you in the media have called the Richie Rich Rapists. Please understand that there is nothing comedic about this for the six of us sitting here before you, or the seven of us who for reasons of their own chose not to appear. Or for the three of us who did not survive. This is not funny. It is not cute. It is real and it happened to us."

A few reporters actually looked ashamed. *Gretchen's good*, Bobby thought.

"We were sixteen," Gretchen went on, "and we were raped by a gang of young men who used our shame and fear to keep us silent. Not one of us knew that there were others. Had we known, we would have spoken then. We're speaking now. We will take your questions, but be advised that we may choose not to answer them."

It'll be soon, Bobby thought, her pulse beginning to race. An anonymous phone call to a *Journal* reporter known to skirt the boundaries of good taste was about to cause the uproar she would use to her advantage. Casually she edged through the crowd to where she had a clear shot. She planned three clear shots. The first would finish Gretchen French off and cause a commotion. The second would be for dear little Susannah. *The third shot*, Bobby thought, *is for whichever poor sap is standing closest to me*. The resulting stampede was all she'd need to get away. It had worked before and Bobby was a firm believer in not fixing what wasn't broken. And just as before, Bobby had an escape plan all worked out.

She scanned the crowd. The *Journal* reporter she'd called with a tip was sitting in the third row, a feral gleam in his eyes, waiting for the perfect moment to pounce.

So am I.

Susannah was calm. Surprisingly so. She looked out at the sea of faces and knew she'd made the right choice. She also knew the gossip had begun the moment she'd sat at the table. The media knew the victims were going to speak out. They'd had no idea she was one of the victims. They certainly knew now. Her face had been instantly recognized and the buzz had ripped through the room, viral and electric. Reporters had whipped out their Black-Berries and cell phones, each wanting to be the first to deliver this juicy morsel.

Marianne Woolf was standing off to the side, covering the event for her husband's *Dutton Review*. Marianne's pictures of Kate's murder and Sheila's funeral had been splashed across the *Review*'s front page that morning. Susannah imagined she'd be among tomorrow's front-page stories.

Luke was also out there, standing near the back of the room, on edge, on guard. She and the other five victims had been brought in through a back door to avoid the crush, but everyone else in the room had passed through a metal detector. The GBI was taking no chances with their safety. Still she knew Luke measured each face, each demeanor. It was comforting, knowing he was watching over her.

Talia had come by with encouraging words for each of the women on the stage, pausing to ask Susannah one last time if she was sure. Susannah was very sure.

When Gretchen began speaking everyone went still. Gretchen had shared her prepared statement with the five of them beforehand, and her eloquent but passionate words had brought tears to the eyes of more than one of the women. But now their eyes were dry as they prepared for questions.

The first came from a woman reporter. "How did you find out about one another?"

Talia had provided Gretchen with a scripted response to this question. "In the course of a multiple murder investigation in another state, pictures of our assaults were recovered. Over the past week, the GBI determined our identities from those photos."

Cameras flashed and Susannah heard whispers of *Simon Vartanian* and *Philadelphia* intermixed with her name and Daniel's. Leaning on the skills she'd honed through years of living with Arthur Vartanian, she kept her chin up, her eyes impassive, completely aware most of the cameras were pointed at her face.

A man stood up. "How have your lives been impacted by the assault?"

The women looked at each other and on the other

side of Gretchen, Carla Solomon pulled the microphone closer. "The impact has been felt differently by each one of us, but overall, it's been consistent with the aftereffects suffered by most assault victims. We've had trouble establishing and maintaining relationships. A few of us have battled substance abuse. One of us committed suicide. It was a defining, devastating moment in our lives, one that has left permanent scars."

Then a man in the third row stood and Susannah felt an instant prickle of unease. His eyes were on her and there was a . . . satisfaction in his expression that raised the hairs on the back of her neck.

"Troy Tomlinson with the *Journal*," he said. "This is for Susannah Vartanian."

The microphone was passed down the table. From the corner of her eye Susannah searched for Luke, but he was no longer in the back of the room and her unease grew.

"You all were victims thirteen years ago," Tomlinson began, "and I think I speak for us all in saying we have sympathy for what happened to you and understand why you failed to report your assaults then. You were all sixteen years old and far too young to deal with the enormity of your experience." His voice oozed a false sincerity that set Susannah's teeth on edge, and beside her, Gretchen stiffened. "But, Susannah, how can you, especially given your record of pushing rape victims up in New York City to come forward, how can you explain *your failure* to report a *second* assault, seven years later, one in which your friend was brutally *murdered*?" The buzz swelled and Tomlinson spoke louder. "And how do you respond to Garth Davis's denial of your assault?"

Susannah's heart began to pound. *How did he know about Darcy?* As the second question sank in, fury flared, tamping the fear. *Garth Davis denies raping us? With all of those pictures as proof? Son of a fucking bitch.*

No. Stay calm. Tell the truth.

"Mr. Tomlinson, your insinuation that any rape victim who does not report her assault is somehow negligent or immature is both egregiously insensitive and cruel." She leaned forward, no smile on her face. "Rape is more than a physical assault, and victims, including myself, must deal with the resulting feelings of loss of personal safety, control, and confidence each in her own way. This is true whether they're sixteen or sixty.

"When my friend was murdered six years ago, I cooperated with the authorities the best way I knew how. I made sure the facts were known even as I struggled to survive a second assault. My friend's murderer was subsequently caught and is paying for his crime." He opened his mouth, but she cut him off. "I'm not finished, Mr. Tomlinson. You asked two questions. Mr. Davis cannot possibly deny our assaults occurred, nor his part in them. The evidence is irrefutable. Vile and disturbing. But irrefutable."

Tomlinson smiled. "I interviewed Mayor Davis. He doesn't deny all the assaults, Susannah. Just yours. He challenges you to show one photo of him raping you."

You're a son of a fucking bitch, too. But she kept her cool. "Mr. Davis must answer to God and to the people of the state of Georgia for his crimes. I know what happened to me. What Mr. Davis says is immaterial. As I said, the evidence is irrefutable. Now please sit down, Mr. Tomlinson. You're finished."

Bobby drew a steadying breath. *Bitch.* She'd sailed through that minefield like it was a field of fucking poppies. Damn her. *Goddamn her.* Susannah Vartanian had come out on top for the very last time. *Now*. It would be now.

Stop. Breathe. Follow the plan or you'll leave here in handcuffs. Gretchen first. Susannah second. Bystander third.

Her hand was steady as she reached into her pocket, positioning her gun so she could fire from within the pocket. Her aim was sure as she pulled the trigger, the pop of the silencer covered up by the cries of reporters jockeying to ask the next question. Her smile was grim when her bullet hit Gretchen in the chest. Gretchen slumped forward as the next bullet hit Susannah right in the heart, sending her flying backward to the floor.

Her third bullet landed in the back of a man with a video camera resting on his shoulder. He dropped like a rock, his camera crashing to the floor.

Screams filled the air. It was priceless.

She moved through the surging crowd, feeling like a celebrity on the red carpet with cameras flashing all around her. But the lenses were pointed at the stage. The cop who'd been standing guard at the stage rushed forward to kneel by the cameraman.

Calmly Bobby walked past the stage on her way to the back entrance and her way out. Then stopped. Lying on her stomach under the table was Susannah Vartanian, her eyes wide open and alert, her small hands wrapped around a very large gun.

People were screaming. Behind her, Gretchen was moaning and she could hear Chase yelling for a medic. Susannah's chest was burning. *Shit. It hurt. Worse than the last time.* She'd instinctively rolled under the table, her hand diving into her purse for the gun that had not been there before she'd sat next to Leo Papadopoulos at lunch.

Then the burning in her chest was forgotten as she found herself staring into a pair of cold blue eyes. She had only an instant to register the visual disconnect. The hair and the breasts were Marianne Woolf's. But the eyes belonged to Barbara Jean Davis.

Those eyes narrowed, then her lips pulled back in a snarl, and the hand Barbara Jean held in her pocket lifted her coat, revealing the rigid line of a gun barrel.

For a heartbeat Susannah aimed between Bobby's blue eyes, then reconsidered. *Death is too good for you, bitch.* Dropping her aim to Bobby's right arm, she fired.

Bobby's eyes registered shock, then pain, then rage. The crack of Susannah's gun sent new screams through the crowd and the thunder of feet shook the stage.

"Drop it!" came the shouted order above her head as a new wave of camera flashes left spots dancing in front of her eyes. Still, she could see the smirk on Bobby's face as she took several steps backward and was swallowed up into the crowd.

"But—" Susannah cried out in pain when a booted foot came down on her forearm.

"Drop the gun and put your hands where we can see them," another voice barked. Arm throbbing, heart pounding, Susannah placed the gun on the stage and held her hands straight out in front of her. Six uniformed cops pointed guns at her head.

"Listen to me," she said loudly. "Dammit." She winced when the booted foot moved off her wrist, replaced by the cold steel of handcuffs. "She's—"

The cop had grabbed her other arm, twisting it behind her back, when someone vaulted from the floor to the stage and an authoritative voice boomed. "*Officer*. Back away. *Now*." *Luke*. *Finally*. Susannah let out a breath as the six cops took a measured step back and Luke dropped to his knees by her side.

"What the hell happened here?" Chase demanded from behind her.

"I don't know," Luke said. "Susannah, where are you hurt?"

Susannah grabbed his arm and dragged herself to her knees, the handcuff swinging from her wrist. The room spun and she clenched her eyes shut. "It was Bobby. She has a gun. She's here, in the crowd somewhere."

"What?" Luke demanded.

"Where?" Chase snapped.

"That way," she pointed and prayed Mama Papa's lamb would stay put in her churning stomach. Now that it was over, she was shaking like a leaf, her words choppy. "She's wearing a wig. Marianne Woolf. She looked like Marianne." A wave of hysteria was bubbling up and she shoved it back. "She was wearing a black trench coat."

"I've got it." Chase was running, making the stage bounce. "You stay with her."

Susannah swallowed hard as her head spun and her stomach roiled. Luke's hands tightened on her shoulders. "Oh my god. Susannah."

She forced her eyes open to find him staring at her chest in horror. Slowly she looked down and blinked at the Kevlar vest showing through the bullet hole in her sweater, right over her heart. "Shit," she mumbled. "This was my last clean outfit."

Bobby unbuttoned her coat with one hand, cursing Susannah Vartanian. *Goddamn her*. Bullets just bounced off the little bitch, both literally and metaphorically. *My arm burns like hell and Susannah Vartanian should be dead*. Dead. *A vest*. Susannah was wearing a goddamn vest. *I should have known, should have planned. I failed.*

Stop thinking about Susannah. Get yourself out of here. There would only be a few seconds before Susannah raised the alarm, assuming the cops let her speak. Right now they thought she was the shooter. There was some joy in that irony.

Get busy. Get gone. In the middle of the throng of pushing people, Bobby shrugged out of her coat and draped it over her wounded arm. Now she had free passage, thanks to her GBI mole who'd wrapped the gun in a jacket before stuffing it into the backpack she'd passed to Bobby before the press conference began. The jacket with GBI emblazoned across the back was a tad tight, but it would do the job. Quickly she slipped Marianne Woolf's press credentials beneath her shirt.

"Pardon me," she said loudly. "Coming through." The people crowding her took one look at her jacket and moved aside. "Stay calm," she said officially. "Just stay calm."

Cops were shepherding the crowd to the middle of the room, away from the doors. Head high, Bobby walked through one of the rear doors, nodding to the Atlanta cop who stood guard. He nodded back, briefly, then returned his eyes to the crowd.

She kept her chin up as she walked past the police searching in the hallway.

"Anything?" one asked her.

She shook her head. "They caught one of the shooters inside, but they're still looking for the second one. Excuse me." As she walked, coat over her arm, she fumbled her right hand into the pocket that held the gun. Her arm burned like hell, but her hand still worked. The door was in sight. Just a few more steps to freedom.

"Stop! Police!"

Fuck. Turning as she ran the last few steps, Bobby started to fire.

"She shot you." Kneeling on the stage, Luke's heart climbed up into his throat.

Susannah pressed the heel of her palm to her chest, covering the hole in her sweater. "I know. Hurts like a bitch, too." She frowned, trying to concentrate. "Bobby's hit. I shot her right arm. She had a gun in her coat pocket. She was going to shoot me. Again. Damn."

Luke forced his fear back. The cops were still glaring at them and Susannah still wore one of their handcuffs on her right wrist. She'd shot into a crowd. He glanced at the gun on the stage and knew exactly where it had come from. *Leo*. There would be trouble over this, but he'd deal with it later. Now he focused on Susannah. Her face was ashen, her eyes overly bright. She was shaking. She was in pain. In shock.

And the cameras continued to flash. He needed to get her out of here. "Can you stand up?"

She nodded grimly. "Yes." She turned as he lifted her to her feet, staring at the medics who were securing Gretchen French to the gurney. "How bad is she?"

"She wasn't wearing a vest," Luke said. "But she's conscious and that's good." He looked at the cop, who regarded him through narrowed eyes, ignoring the glare and focusing on the man's nameplate. "Officer Swift. I'm taking her out of here. Please take your cuffs off her wrist, right here where the cameras can see you do it. I'm taking over this shooting."

Susannah held out her wrist and Swift unlocked the

handcuffs. "It was self-defense," she said quietly. "I was shot first."

Officer Swift glanced briefly at the hole in Susannah's sweater. "You shot into a crowd of innocent people, Miss Vartanian."

"And if I hadn't, I'd be dead." Twin slashes of crimson stood out against her pale face. She was furious, but her voice remained in control.

Swift's jaw tightened. "I'll be writing this all in my report and making sure my chain of command is copied."

"Be sure to copy me, too." Luke scooped both her gun and her purse from the floor, then took her arm in a gesture of support rather than control. "Walk with me," he murmured. "We're going down these steps and out the back door."

"Where are the other women?" she asked, her voice now trembling.

"Talia hustled them out the back. They're all safe." He walked her through the back door and closed it behind them. The noise level immediately dropped.

Her shoulders relaxed a hair. "It's quiet," she breathed. "I can hear myself thi—"

"*Stop. Police.*" The shout came from around the corner. It was followed by two shots, then more shouting. Through it, Luke heard the chilling words *officer down.*

Chase. Luke pulled the radio from his belt. "This is Special Agent Papadopoulos. Agent Wharton, what's your status?" There was no reply and his heart started to race again. "Chase, what's your position?"

Two more shots cracked from the radio. Then Chase's voice came through and Luke's shoulders slumped in relief. "We have an APD officer down. Suspect escaped."

She got away. Again. *Goddammit.* "I'm coming toward you." Luke led a pale Susannah around the corner and down another hall and met Chase coming through a door from the outside. He was still talking into his radio, his expression murderous. Off to the side sat a uniformed cop, white-faced, clutching his thigh, his hands covered in his own blood. Another officer had started emergency first aid.

On the floor by the rear door was a black trench coat.

"It was Bobby," Chase said. "She fired at the cop, then ran. She had a car waiting for her. We're in pursuit." His gaze narrowed on Susannah's sweater. "You're hit."

"So was Bobby," she said, her jaw clenched. "I got her right arm just before she shot at me again. That's the coat she was wearing."

"Well, she shot with her left hand without much of a problem. Her first two shots hit the cop on his vest, her third, his thigh. I've got medics on the way. The officer fired twice, but she was already through the door."

"You fired at the car?" Luke asked, and Chase's brows crunched.

"Yeah. Missed. The car was weaving like a stunt driver."

Luke pulled a pair of gloves from his pocket and snapped them on, crouching next to the coat. "Three holes in the pocket," he said. "She fired all those shots from inside her pocket." He looked up, met Susannah's eyes. "One hole in the sleeve. Lots of blood."

"She's wounded," Chase said. "She can't go to a hospital. Where will she go?"

"Not back to her house on the river or her house in Dutton," Luke said. "Susannah?"

"I don't know who she'd trust to help her now. Did you see who was driving the car?"

Chase's jaw tightened. "I didn't get a good look." Then he sighed heavily. "Bobby was wearing a GBI jacket."

Luke's stomach turned over as he stood. "Your leak. Bobby has an accomplice."

"You have a leak?" Susannah asked quietly.

"Yes," Chase said heavily.

"You did get a good look at the driver," Luke said, even more quietly.

Chase shook his head. "No, but I recognized the car. It was Leigh's."

"Leigh? Leigh Smithson? Her car was stolen?" Then he saw Chase's face and understood. "Shit. Leigh's the leak. Damn, Chase, I never would have . . . Shit."

"Yeah." Chase rubbed his forehead. "I put out a BOLO as soon as I saw her car."

"It makes sense," Luke said slowly. "Especially the nurse at the hospital. Leigh brought me the message to meet her."

Susannah went still. "Nurse Ohman said she'd been waiting outside for an hour."

"Enough time for Leigh to take her call, inform Bobby, then draw you out with a false message from me," Luke murmured. "Hell. Why? Why would Leigh do this?"

"Blackmail?" Susannah asked. "But what secret could be so bad that she'd do this?"

Chase blew out a breath. "I don't know. Luke, let's get the team together and debrief. We need to figure out where Bobby will go. Where's your gun, Susannah?"

"Luke took it."

"Where'd you get it?"

"It was my father's," Susannah said without missing a beat. "I took it from his house."

Luke held back what would have been a weary sigh. She was protecting Leo and she lied very well. He wasn't sure how he felt about either. He'd worry about it later.

Chase just nodded. "Don't do it again," was all he said.

Susannah lifted her chin. "Catch Bobby Davis, so I won't have to."

Chase's smile was grim. "Fair enough."

Bobby was thrown against Leigh Smithson's car door as they careened around a corner. She bit back the cry of pain as the throbbing in her arm trebled. "I see your driving skills have not improved," she gritted out, and Smithson shot her a glare.

"I hate you."

"Yeah, I know. Then again, I'm not the one who murdered three little kids."

"Sure you have," Smithson said bitterly.

Bobby chuckled. "You can let me off here."

Leigh Smithson stopped the car and grabbed Bobby's arm. "Shoot me."

"So you can pretend I forced you? No. But this might help." She pulled Marianne Woolf's wig from her head and tossed it. "Knock yourself out." Bobby slammed the door and started walking, shivering. It was cold. She'd dropped her coat when that cop started shooting at her. She still had her gun, but not her cell phone. Dammit. She'd have to get another phone and another car. That wouldn't be too hard to do.

Her arm hurt. It continued to bleed sullenly, but at least she'd stopped most of the flow. She'd felt around enough to know the bullet was still in there.

I need a doctor. But a hospital wasn't an option and Toby Granville couldn't help her because he was dead, because of Daniel Vartanian. Damn him to hell.

She thought of Paul sitting in Charles's kitchen. Charles had stitched him up. She hated to call Charles. Hated him.

This time she didn't have a choice. She had to call Charles. *Tanner could have fixed you up.* But he was dead. *By my hand.* Because of Susannah Vartanian. If she hadn't chased them to the rest area . . . Damn the woman. She needed to die. And soon.

But first I need a place to hide. To recharge. To heal.

She knew just the place. *I'm going home.*

Chapter Twenty-one

The cameraman and Gretchen are both in serious, but stable condition," Chase said when they'd regrouped. "The cop Bobby shot is already home and resting."

"Thank God," Talia said. "Poor Gretchen has been through a lot in the last week."

"Haven't we all?" Susannah murmured, very quiet now. Luke recognized the signs of adrenaline crash, knowing he would soon follow. But for now he was still on edge, his heart racing every time he thought about the hole in her sweater, right over her heart.

She now wore a GBI sweatshirt. Luke had entered her sweater into evidence, along with the gun she'd had in her purse. Luke knew from where it had come, just as he knew Leo would have made sure there was no way it could be traced back to him.

Luke would be indebted to Leo for the rest of his life.

"The cameraman was actually thrilled," Ed said. "When he dropped his camera, it fell lens up. He got footage of Bobby's face. It's already on CNN."

"We found Marianne Woolf's car. Marianne was in the trunk, tied and gagged," Luke said. "She'd been there since before this morning's press conference. She got a call from Bobby asking to meet her and when she did,

Bobby overpowered her and shoved her in the trunk. She stole her press pass first."

"How did Bobby get a gun?" Pete asked. "Everyone went through a metal detector."

Luke and Chase shared a look. This would not be pleasant for any of them.

"The gun came from our evidence room," Chase said.

There was dead silence. Every expression was first disbelieving, then horrified, then furious. Then suspicious. "Checked out by whom?" Pete asked darkly.

Hank Germanio's face hardened as Pete and Nancy threw wary glances his way. He said nothing and Luke actually felt sorry for him.

Chloe's eyes narrowed at Chase, then Luke. "You know who it is. Tell us. Now."

The hurt was still in Chase's eyes. "Atlanta PD found Leigh's body in her house, in her bathtub. She'd . . ." He swallowed audibly. "She'd eaten her gun."

For several seconds no one said a word. No one breathed. What had been suspicion on their faces transformed back into disbelief, then utter shock.

"Leigh?" Talia finally asked. "Leigh Smithson?"

"Our Leigh?" Pete whispered.

Chase swallowed again. "Yes."

"But why?" Nancy asked, her voice cracking. "Why did she do it?"

"We don't know," Chase said. His jaw went taut. "Yet. But we will."

"It makes sense," Luke said. "The witnesses or suspects who were killed before we could find them. Leigh was feeding Bobby information. Her LUDS showed she called the phone we found in Bobby's coat."

Talia slumped in her chair. "But how did she know what happened in here?"

"She put a listening device here, in this conference room," Ed said.

"I'll keep you updated on the investigation into Leigh's motives," Chase said. "Now, we need to focus on finding Bobby. She's disappeared. We're watching Ridgefield House, the bunker on the river, and the house she shared with Garth."

"We checked her computer," Luke said. "And her main clients. She doesn't appear to be with any of them. We've checked every Davis relative and nobody's seen her."

"What about Granville's *thích*?" Susannah asked quietly.

Chase sighed wearily. "I'm not disputing he exists, Susannah, but until we have some evidence that he's physically done something to someone—"

"He did," Susannah interrupted. "Monica said he was in the bunker, talking to Granville, that Granville asked him to help break her. Whether this guy laid a hand on Monica or not, he knew she was there. That's conspiracy to commit kidnapping."

"She's right," Chloe said.

Yes, she is, Luke thought, pride and respect for her swelling anew. Even with all she'd been through, her mind still worked with clockwork precision.

"Besides," Susannah added. "Maybe that's where Bobby's hiding."

Chase rubbed his temples. "You're right. Suggestions?"

"We get Darcy's killer to talk," Susannah said. "He knows who he is but he's afraid."

"I'll call Al Landers," Chloe said. "We'll work on getting through to Darcy's killer."

"We've got Bobby's photo posted with every agency

in the tristate area and with Customs in case she tries to leave the country," Chase said.

"Which is only good if she travels under her own name," Susannah countered.

"You're right again," Chase said tightly. "But until we know more, that's all we can do. We meet again at eight in the morning."

"Susannah," Chloe said. "Can you give me a minute? I need to talk to you."

Susannah remained seated as everyone filed out, as did Luke. Chloe lifted her brows and Luke shook his head, not liking the vibe. "I'm staying, Chloe."

Chloe shrugged. When the door was closed she turned to Susannah. "Your gun."

"My father's," Susannah said.

"It's not marked or registered," Chloe said. "Serial numbers are filed off."

"I didn't think to look at serial numbers. I'm sorry."

Chloe shook her head. "Oh, please. You're far too smart to make a mistake like that. But let's move on. You were carrying a concealed weapon without a license."

"She has one," Luke protested. "In New York."

"Not recognized here," Chloe said. "No reciprocity exists."

"What's the point?" Luke asked. He'd known this was coming. Still, it made him mad.

"The point is that every reporter in that room saw Susannah shoot that woman with an unregistered gun she has no license to carry. I can't let that slide by."

"For God's sake, Chloe," Luke snapped, but Susannah put her hand on his.

"It's all right. I knew what I was doing when I put the gun in my purse. I knew Bobby would stop at nothing.

I knew I was vulnerable. I didn't want to die. So I took one of my father's guns and put it in my purse and shot the woman in front of a room full of cameras." She met Chloe's gaze. "Will you charge me?"

Chloe looked uncomfortable. "Dammit, Susannah."

"If I hadn't had the gun, we wouldn't be having this conversation," Susannah said, calmly. "Bobby had her gun pointed at me from inside her pocket. You know she'd already fired three shots, one that hit me. So I shot her and I'm not sorry."

"I'm not going to charge you in the shooting," Chloe said. "It was clearly self-defense. But, Susannah, what kind of example would I be making if I let you get away with breaking the law? What would you do if our roles were reversed? Be honest."

"I'd have to charge you," Susannah said.

Luke gritted his teeth. "Susannah."

"The law is clear, Luke. Chloe doesn't really have a choice."

"I know." Chloe closed her eyes. "Dammit."

"You said that already," Susannah said dryly. One side of her mouth lifted. "You wanna sleep on it, Counselor?"

Chloe let out a surprised chuckle, then sobered. "You could get disbarred."

Susannah's smile faded. "I know. But I'd rather be disbarred than interred."

Luke thought of the bullet hole in her blouse again and had to draw a deep breath.

"I'd have done the same," Chloe murmured. "That's what makes this so hard."

"Chloe, I did what I needed to do. You do what you need to do. I won't fight you."

"If you did I'd feel better," Chloe grumbled.

"It's not my job to make you feel better," Susannah said evenly.

Chloe glared at her. "Goddamn it. Doesn't anything rattle you?"

"Yeah," Susannah said bitterly. "Lots of things, but one in particular comes to mind. What the hell did that reporter mean when he said Garth Davis denied raping me?"

Chloe sighed. "Tomlinson said he got an anonymous tip about the Darcy Williams murder, *and* that Garth Davis hadn't raped you, *and* to check it with Garth himself. He did and Garth confirmed, categorically denying having assaulted you in any way."

"But my picture . . ." Susannah closed her mouth.

"Her picture was in that box with the others," Luke said, stowing his desire to rip Garth Davis's fucking head off.

"I know," Chloe said. "I talked to the tech who's been categorizing the photos. She says there were nude shots and rape shots. She said there were sixteen victims photographed nude, but only fifteen being assaulted. Susannah, you weren't."

Susannah stiffened, but said nothing, and Luke remembered their conversation in Monica's ICU room the day before. *He did at least one*, she'd said, talking about Simon. How had she known?

"Garth's lying," Susannah said softly. Too softly. Her hand that held his trembled.

"We'll talk to him," Luke promised. "But not today. I'm taking you home."

Chloe stood. "I'm gonna sleep on it. I'll give you my decision tomorrow."

When Chloe was gone, Luke pulled Susannah into his

arms. "It'll be all right," he murmured into her hair. "One way or another."

She hung on tight, her whole body trembling. "How do you know?"

He pressed his lips to her forehead before tipping up her chin to meet her gaze. "Because you've survived a hell of a lot worse alone. And you're not alone anymore."

Emotions churned in her eyes. The fury and fear he understood. The gratitude made him angry. But it was the hope that made his own eyes sting. She smiled at him then, and leaned up on her toes to brush her lips over his, sending every nerve singing. "Then it'll be all right. Let's get out of here. I think I could sleep a year."

Dutton, Sunday, February 4, 7:45 p.m.

"Goddammit," Bobby hissed, her lips white with pain. "Be *careful*."

Charles lifted his brows at her. "I can call 911 if you prefer."

Bobby glared. "I said I was sorry for this morning and I've thanked you a thousand times for coming to help me, even though it took you long enough to get here."

"I told you I couldn't just drop everything. I was with a client."

"Which one?" she demanded.

He shot her a sober look. "And this became your business since when?"

She lowered her eyes. "I'm sorry. Just get the damn thing out, all right?"

He chuckled suddenly, remembering the look on Rose Bowie's face when his cell had started vibrating on the table just as he'd started to commune with the spirit world. "You called at a perfect time, actually. I thought Rose Bowie would have coronary."

"Rose Bowie? What did that old bag want?"

"She was worried violence would mar her daughter's funeral tomorrow," he said, pulling Bobby's arm far harder than he needed to. "Rose didn't want a scene like there was at that Sheila Cunningham's service. Since I was reasonably sure you had no more staff to shoot, I told her it would be fine."

"And for this she paid you?"

"A considerable fee, both for the reading and to keep our sessions secret. Her husband's constituency would not approve of her dabbling in the occult, nor would Rose's friends at the Baptist church." Rose was one of his most lucrative clients.

Although Carol Vartanian had paid much more. Charles missed their sessions. Who knew that under that cool exterior beat the heart of a woman who had truly despised her husband? She'd started coming to Charles to see her future and he'd made certain that just enough of it had come true to keep Carol believing every word that came from his mouth. She'd kept coming out of a perverse desire to do exactly what would have enraged her husband the most.

That sex had been Carol's best weapon had been his gain. Yes, he missed Carol Vartanian. Susannah looked a lot like her mother. *It would have been such a pleasure to initiate her, to have her hang on my every word.* But that was no longer in the cards, as it were. That Susannah would die was never in doubt. That she'd die painfully became an inevitability the night she destroyed one of his best and brightest.

An eye for an eye was a fool's trade, Pham had always said. His mentor had never been wrong. Charles bent over Bobby's arm, his movements harsh as he dug the bullet from her flesh. "You took a chance coming here. To this house."

"They won't look for me here and if they do, there are tons of places to hide. Shit," she hissed again. "That hurts."

He imagined it did. He handed her a bottle of Arthur's best scotch. "Drink this."

She pushed it away. "I can't be drunk. If they come looking, I have to be sharp."

"You said they wouldn't look for you here." He tugged, earning more hissed curses.

"Who taught you bullet removal, Joseph Mengele?" she muttered.

"Actually, I learned when I had to pull a bullet out of my own leg," he said mildly.

Her gaze whipped over to the walking stick he'd propped against the table. "Oh."

Charles pulled the bullet out with a twist. He'd actually had it in his grip several times, but playing with Bobby had suddenly become old. He held it in the palm of his hand for her to see. "You want to keep it as a souvenir?" he mocked.

"Did you?" she asked bitterly. "When some Vietcong soldier shot you?"

Charles considered slapping Bobby senseless, but he wouldn't have to slap that hard. There was no sport in breaking her when she was hanging on to control by a thread. But she was hanging on, and a small part of him had to admire her for that, so he answered her. "Actually I did. I kept the bullet to remind me how much hate I felt at that moment. I needed that hate to survive. And I was not shot by the Vietcong," he added. It was a point of pride, after all.

She closed her eyes and took a deep breath. "Then who shot you?"

She'd never asked before. She'd never had the nerve. Toby Granville had asked long, long ago. He'd been only thirteen and far more self-confident than Bobby had ever been. Charles had answered Toby then. He decided to answer Bobby now. "Another American soldier. We'd escaped together."

Her eyes opened, narrow slits as he cleaned the wound. "From where?"

"A hell-hole in Southeast Asia otherwise known as a POW camp."

She let out a breath between her teeth. "That explains a lot." She flinched when he jabbed the needle into her flesh. "Sir. So why did he shoot you?"

"Over a crust of bread," he said, still mildly, although speaking the words aloud brought the cauldron within him to a steady boil. "Then he left me to die."

"Obviously you didn't."

"Obviously." But that wasn't a story he'd share.

She gritted her teeth as he began to suture the wound. "And your revenge?"

"Slow in coming." Charles thought of the man who sat in a New York prison for a crime he had not committed, protecting the family he'd never had the chance to know. The man who deserved every day of his torment, and more. "But long in duration and well worth the wait. Every day I smile knowing that every day he suffers. Mind, body, and soul. For the rest of his natural life."

She was quiet while he stitched. "Why didn't you just kill him?" she finally asked.

"Because in his case, death was too quick."

She nodded, her teeth imprinting her lower lip, but she didn't cry out. *This* was the tough girl he'd met all those years ago. *This* was the backbone he hadn't seen in some time. He pulled hard on the suture. She sucked in a harsh breath, but remained silent, so he pushed her further. "Susannah, on the other hand . . ."

"I want to see her dead," Bobby said between her teeth. "But it won't be quick."

"Good," he said, a little too vehemently, and she looked up at him, eyes narrowed.

"You hate her, too. Why?"

He frowned, angry with himself for being so transparent. "My reasons are my own."

She frowned back. "All these years you've pushed me to hate her. To take back what's mine."

He bandaged her arm. "As you should. Susannah lived the life to which you were entitled." He placed her arm inside a sling and stepped back. "I'm finished with you."

"*I'm* not finished with *you*. You've pushed me for years to kill her for you. Why do you hate Susannah Vartanian? What did she take of yours?" When he didn't answer she grabbed his arm with her free hand. "*Tell me*." She towered over him, blue eyes flashing cold fire, and for the briefest of instants he felt a tiny spear of fear.

Well done, he thought, proud of her once more. Carefully he removed her hand from his sleeve. "Sit down before you fall down. You've lost a lot of blood."

She sat, shaky, pale, but still intense. "Tell me," she repeated, more quietly. "If I'm going to kill her for you, I at least deserve to know why. What did she take of yours?"

Charles met her eyes. She made a fair point. "Darcy Williams."

Atlanta, Sunday, February 4, 7:45 p.m.

"Susannah, wake up. We don't want to be late."

Susannah fought her eyelids open, then sat straight up, looking around. "Why are we here?" *Here* was the airport and Luke was pulling into the parking garage.

"Surprise," was all he'd say. "It'll be worth it. I promise."

"Why are we here?" she asked again when he led her to baggage claim, toward the wall where the oversized luggage had been placed. "You had my clothes sent? But how . . . ?" The question trailed as he took her shoulders and turned her. Susannah stared for a moment, then her heart flooded. "*Oh.*" She ran to the hard pet carrier sitting against the wall, falling to her knees to peer in the little wire door. A familiar face peered out, happy to see her. Thor. "How did you do this?"

"Al and I arranged it with your kennel."

She opened the little wire door wide enough to stroke her dog's silky coat. "Good girl," she murmured. "I missed you. Soon. You can come out soon." She locked the door, then looked up at Luke, and the tenderness on his face closed her throat.

"You missed her," he said. "I thought it might be easier for you if she was here."

She stood, swallowing hard. "You are a very nice man."

His brows waggled. "And?"

She laughed. "And sinfully sexy." And he was, reminding her of a pirate with his stubbled jaw, dark eyes, and devilish smile. Joy bubbled up and she surprised herself by throwing her arms around his neck. She'd surprised him, too, by the sharp intake of his breath. But he caught her to him, lifting her feet from the floor.

Then she sucked in a breath of her own as she felt

him hard against her, suddenly, fully aroused. Her skin prickled and her body answered and that fast she wanted him.

You don't have to stop this time. He knows it all. And he doesn't care. So stop being a coward. She pulled back to see his face and her racing heart accelerated. The tenderness on his face was gone, replaced with raw hunger.

"Thank you." Then she kissed him, full and lush, and felt his big body shudder.

He'd needed this, too. The knowledge made her want to kiss him again, so she did until he made a sound deep in his throat, relief mixed with frustration.

"Not here," he said, leaning his head back and drawing a breath that pressed his chest into her breasts. New shivers shook her and she brushed her mouth along the strong line of his throat, feeling his pulse throb beneath her lips.

Behind them Thor yipped in the crate, yanking Susannah back to reality. "Oh."

Luke's lips twitched as he put her down, setting her well away from him. "Can you thank me again like that later when we're not in a crowded airport?"

Her cheeks heated, but she refused to look away. "Yes."

His hands flexed wide as if he'd reach for her again. Instead he shoved one hand into his pocket and pulled out a nylon leash. "It's Darlin's. We'll have to stop and get another for . . ." He picked up the small crate and grimaced.

"Thor," she supplied helpfully. "What's wrong?"

"It's just not right. A dog named Thor should weigh more than twenty pounds."

She smiled at him. "And ugly bulldogs shouldn't be named Darlin'?"

He huffed. "She's not *that* ugly."

She laughed. "You're just an old softie."

"Thank me again when we get home," he promised, "and I won't be."

Her heart started racing again and she found she liked the feeling, the anticipation. The thrill. "It's a date."

Dutton, Sunday, February 4, 7:45 p.m.

Bobby watched Charles methodically clean his surgical tools. He had quite a collection. She supposed some secrets he learned took a little more force to pry free than others. Having been on the receiving end of his scalpel today, she understood how he'd become so successful at breaking down his opponents' defenses.

"So . . ." She tilted her head slightly. "Who was Darcy Williams?"

"She was one of mine."

She nodded. He'd used that same terminology that morning. "Like Paul?"

He nodded. "Like Paul."

"Is Paul your son?"

He smiled at that. "Of a fashion."

"Did you raise Paul?"

"Yes."

"And Darcy, too?"

"More or less."

"But Susannah didn't kill Darcy Williams."

His eyes went cold. "She didn't beat her to death, no. But Susannah made it necessary for Darcy to die."

"I don't understand."

"I don't intend for you to." He snapped his bag closed. "Call me when you're ready to make your move. I'd like to be there."

Bobby watched him leave, leaning more heavily on his walking stick than he normally did. "Charles?"

He turned, his face hard as stone. "What?"

She touched her bandage. "I pay my debts, so here's some information. I learned from my GBI mole that Susannah Vartanian described the man who raped her in New York to a police artist. My mole was asked to fax that picture to the DA in New York so he could show it to the man who's sitting in prison for the murder of Darcy Williams."

For the first time ever Bobby saw Charles pale. "Did your mole fax this sketch?"

"No." She lifted her brows. "I asked her why today as she was driving me away from the press conference. She said the man in the sketch was the cop who'd caught her, who hadn't arrested her, who'd been holding her crime over her head, biding his time. Since Paul was the cop who'd given her to me, connecting the dots wasn't difficult. And since Paul is important to you . . ."

He nodded, just once. "Thank you, Bobby."

It was the first time he'd ever thanked her. After thirteen years, it was far too little, far too late. "Consider yourself compensated for the bullet removal. Sir."

Atlanta, Sunday, February 4, 8:45 p.m.

"That's so cute." Susannah stood in Luke's bedroom doorway, smiling at Thor, who had curled up next to Darlin' in a laundry basket, on top of Luke's laundry. They'd brought back Chinese takeout and eaten it off his mama's fine china, talking about wonderfully neutral subjects. By mutual unspoken agreement neither had mentioned Bobby or *thích*s or pending concealed-weapons charges.

Neither had they mentioned the kiss in the airport, but the memory of it hung thickly between them. The anticipation had built, sweetly.

Now, Susannah's heart beat hard, wondering what would happen next.

Luke stopped behind her. "No, it's not cute," he protested. "That laundry was clean."

"Next time, put your clothes away."

"Put your clothes away," he mimicked nasally. "You sound like my mother."

His arms came around her, locking over her stomach, which was turning delightful little cartwheels. He rocked her gently from side to side and she leaned her head back against his chest, comfortable with a man for the first time in her life.

"I had a nice time with your family today."

"Good. They were thrilled to have you."

"And you, too? Were you thrilled to have me?" She'd intended her tone to be light. Instead the words came out reedy. Husky. Needy.

There was a beat of tense silence, then Luke tugged the collar of her borrowed sweatshirt from her throat. "I don't know," he said quietly. "I haven't had you yet." His mouth found the curve of her shoulder and she shivered, tilting her head to give him better access, holding her breath to see what would happen next.

"Will you?" she asked but he shushed her, massaging her shoulders.

"Don't talk," he murmured, his lips tickling her skin, his fingers working magic between her shoulder blades. "You just went all tense on me. I want you relaxed. I want that mind of yours to take a rest. Don't think about what will or won't happen. Just feel. Feel this." He twisted her hair around his fist and gently pulled her head forward, brushing kisses down her neck. "Feel good?" he murmured when she sighed.

"Yes," she whispered.

He pushed her head to the other side, and she hummed deep in her throat when he treated her to the same teasing caresses on the other side. "This is how it should be," he said. "You should feel good, want more. Do you want more?"

He was making this so easy. So sweet. Slowly she nodded and he went still for a moment. Then his hands slipped under her sweatshirt, warm on her skin. Her stomach muscles clenched and she felt him smile against her neck. "Ticklish?"

"More like nervous." She tensed as his fingers slowly climbed her rib cage.

She heard him swallow and his hands ceased. "I think we need to stop."

"Why?"

"Because I want you. But I won't push you. I want you crazy for me, not afraid."

"I'm not afraid," she said, but even she could hear the tremble in her voice.

"You don't want to be. And soon you won't be. But I can only hold back so much."

And he was holding back, but he hadn't retreated. Even though his hands had stopped, they hadn't withdrawn. His thumbs were mere inches from the fullest part of her breast, tempting, tantalizing.

She didn't want to be afraid. Today she'd faced a killer without fear. To be afraid of this, her own sexuality, seemed ludicrous and more than a little sad. She was standing in the arms of a good, decent man who knew everything about her and wanted her anyway. She'd walked away from too many things in her life.

There was no way in hell she was walking away from this.

Before he could say another word she pushed his hands up. His groan mixed with hers as he claimed her, covering her lace-covered breasts with his palms. It felt good. Too good. And not nearly enough. She pressed back against him, feeling him hard and ready against her. She wriggled, wringing another groan from his chest.

"No," he said, his mouth on her neck. "Not yet." She pressed harder backward. His thumbs found her nipples and electricity sizzled over her skin. "It's not time." But he was breathing hard in her ear and his hips were thrusting, the rhythm making her crazy for him. "Dammit, Susannah. Tell me to stop. Please."

And he would stop if she asked. She knew it. Just as she knew she didn't want him to. "I almost died today."

"I know. I can't stop seeing it happen again and again. But that's not good enough reason to do this now, tonight. We've got time. Lots of time." ·

"I've waited long enough. I came back here to get my life back. Help me do that."

He hesitated. "How do you want it?" he asked roughly.

The question thrilled her darkly and she thought about the dusty box he'd hidden back in his closet. But this was new. She was new.

"I want to see if I can do it . . . normally."

"Susannah, any way we do it will be normal. I promise you that."

"I . . . want to see your face."

He stilled, laying his cheek on the top of her head. "Give me a minute." She counted the beats of her heart until he slid his hands out from under her sweatshirt. "Go sit on the bed."

She obeyed, watching as he lifted the basket, dogs and all. He put them outside the door, closed it firmly. Then he knelt in front of her. "You're sure this is what you want."

She nodded, meeting his eyes. "I'm sure."

"All right."

She expected him to rise then, but he stayed where he was, running his hands up and down her calves. "What?"

He smiled. "You New York women," he teased. "Slow down, Susannah. Stay a while." He looked up, his eyes gleaming. "I intend to."

Her chest tightened and she had no response, which made him smile.

"The first time I saw you, you were wearing a skirt like this."

"At my parents' funeral. Last week," she managed, and he nodded.

"I wondered then what it would be like with you. What it would take to get you out of that proper suit. What would it take?"

She swallowed. "Ask me. Nicely."

He sat back on his haunches. "Take off your skirt for me. Please."

Her heart thundering, she slid off the bed. His hands played up and down her legs as she struggled with the button at her back. He watched, black eyes intense. Finally she simply yanked the button off and his lips twitched. "That was your last clean skirt."

"You're enjoying this," she accused unsteadily.

He lifted his brows. "Aren't you?"

She was, she realized. "Yes." She stood, her hands stilled on the zipper, making him wait this time. His eyes went dark and his hands tugged at the hem and she complied, easing the zipper down and pushing the skirt past her hips.

He took it the rest of the way, staring at the lace underwear Mitra had so skillfully chosen. "Pretty," he said, huskily. She started to take them off but he stopped her. "Not yet. Sit back down." He leaned in close and pressed his lips to the inside of one thigh, then the other, until her legs quaked.

"Luke," she whispered, waiting for his mouth to touch her where she throbbed, but he didn't, bypassing her panties entirely. He pushed the sweatshirt up only far enough to kiss her stomach.

"I keep thinking about you kneeling in the woods in your bra." His voice was ragged. "Show it to me now. Please."

Again she complied, knowing he was exciting himself as well as her. She pulled the sweatshirt over her head and dropped it on the floor, waiting. He drew a breath, let it out. "Nice. Very nice." Gently he pushed her knees apart and knelt between them, running his hands up her back. He kissed his way up her stomach, then between her breasts. She waited, holding her breath, but he kept going up, kissing the hollow of her throat. Her laugh was strangled.

"Luke." She felt him smile against her throat.

"Are you having a nice time, Susannah?"

She wanted to throttle him. "Yes. No. Dammit, what are you waiting for?"

"I'm wooing you," he said lightly. "You want to rush through. I've waited for a long time for this." He nuzzled her breast through her bra and she gasped.

"You met me last week."

"But I've waited for you forever." He looked up suddenly, his eyes sharp. "I have. That sounds like a line, I know. But it's the truth."

She ran her thumb across his jaw, feeling his stubble tickle her skin. "I know." She leaned forward, touched her lips to his. "I have, too."

"I want you," he whispered, his voice shaking.

"Then stop teasing me," she whispered back. "Do it."

A muscle twitched in his cheek. "What do you want?"

"Your mouth." She swallowed. "On me."

His smile was fierce. "Where?"

"Everywhere." God, she felt like she was going to explode. She flattened her palms on his cheeks and pulled his face to her breast. Hungrily he took her in his mouth, sucking hard through the lace. His hands twisted the clasp at her back, popping it free with startling ease. But she didn't think about where he'd learned the trick, because he was pulling the bra away and his mouth was on her flesh. She held him close, her head thrown back, eyes closed, absorbing.

He pulled away, just enough to see her face. "Susannah."

She dropped her head forward, focusing on his face, already missing him. "What?"

"Watch," he said thickly. "Watch us."

She lifted her eyes to the mirror over his dresser and her breath caught in her throat at the sight of his dark head at her breast. Erotic. Sweet. The combination left her breathless. His hands clutched her thighs, his thumbs teasing at the lace edge of the panties she knew had to be soaked clean through. "Luke."

He looked up, his mouth wet from sucking her breasts. "What do you want?"

She was shivering uncontrollably. But the words simply would not come.

His eyes dropped to her panties, then looked back up, hungry. "Well?"

"Please," she whispered.

"Ask me," he said. "Nicely."

She pursed her lips. Her cheeks flamed hot. But he wasn't moving. He was waiting. She leaned forward to whisper in his ear. "Taste me. Please."

He threw her legs over his shoulders, then groaned, and whatever she'd intended to say evaporated because finally his mouth was on her. He kissed and licked and nipped, all through the lace until she thought she'd die. She pushed at the panties, until he shoved them down her legs. His tongue went deep and she groaned, long and loud. But orgasm shimmered frustratingly out of reach. "Luke. I can't."

He worked two fingers up into her. "Yes you can. Come for me, Susannah. Let me see you." He opened her up and kissed her again, sweetly, slowly building her back until she was gasping once more. She was so close, teetering on the edge.

So close and not there. "I can't." Tears burned her eyes. "Dammit."

He lurched to his feet, kicked off his trousers, and ripped open a condom. "Stand."

She blinked away the tears and looked up at him, breathing hard. "What?"

He grabbed her hand and dragged her to the dresser. "Look at me," he said harshly, wrapping her hair around his fist, forcing her chin up. "Look at my face."

She did, staring at him in the mirror as he spread her legs with his knee and entered her in one hard, deep stroke and on a low cry she came, convulsing around him. His face tightened and he thrust hard once, twice, and on the third time he threw his head back and groaned her name. Then he sagged, pressing her against the dresser.

She laid her cheek on the cool wood. "Oh my God."

He was breathing hard, every breath pushing her into the dresser. "You came," he said, satisfaction in his tone.

"Yeah." She struggled up on her elbows and stared at him in the mirror. "Thank you."

He smiled, still puffing. "My pleasure. Any time. I mean that."

A laugh bubbled up. "I did it. My God, I did it. Without . . ." She faltered.

"Paraphernalia of any kind," he supplied cheerfully. "No whips, chains, or cuffs."

Her cheeks heated. "Yeah. That. I did that."

He lifted his brows. "I helped."

She laughed again. "I'd say so. Now, if I don't go to sleep soon, I'm going to die."

He backed away, then lifted her into his arms easily, carrying her to the bed. He tucked her under the covers. "Where should I sleep?"

She looked up at him. "Do you want to be alone at three a.m.?"

His eyes flickered. "No."

"Then sleep here." She smiled. "I'll leave you alone. I promise."

He chuckled. "Damn."

Dutton, Monday, February 5, 12:45 a.m.

The throbbing in her arm woke Bobby with a start. She poured herself a cup of water from Grandmother Vartanian's silver tea service, swallowed the Ibuprofen Charles

had left, then tried to relax in the sleeping bag she'd liberated from the basement. The sleeping bag had Daniel
Vartanian's name neatly printed on the label, along with
the number of his Boy Scout troop. Of course he'd been a
Boy Scout. She rolled her eyes.

The bag smelled musty, but it was clean. She'd spread
it out on the box springs in Susannah's old bedroom after
dragging the remnants of the mattress from the bed.
Someone had come through and trashed the house, slash-
ing every cushion and mattress with methodical care.
Toby Granville or Randy Mansfield, she thought. He'd
been looking for Simon Vartanian's key to the damn safe-
deposit box.

Toby and Simon had hidden their incriminating rape
pictures there, she knew. She'd liberated the pictures a few
years ago. It had been handy having Rocky working in her
uncle's bank. Bobby knew what was in the safe-deposit
boxes of a number of the townspeople of Dutton. Knowing their secrets when they all still treated her like white
trash who'd had the good fortune to marry into wealth had
made her feel powerful.

None of that mattered now. What she needed was money
to get away. She'd be able to sell several of the Vartanian family heirlooms, like Grandmother Vartanian's
silver tea service. The thought of it made her smirk. After
all this time, she finally possessed the family silver. She
knew there were more treasures. When she got her hands
on Susannah, she'd force her to show her all the hiding
places in this old house.

She'd use some of the cash she'd get for the Vartanian
treasures to buy a passport with someone else's name.
Someone else's face. Hers was now plastered over every
news program in the country. Maybe even the world.

Dammit. What was I thinking this afternoon? I could have been caught.

She'd been thinking the way Charles had wanted her to think. She'd been single-mindedly focused on humiliating Susannah Vartanian and seeing her die in a very public way. Because that's what Charles wanted.

He hated Susannah, which was interesting, to be sure. But what Charles wanted or Charles felt didn't really matter now, either. *What matters is what I want.*

And I want Susannah Vartanian dead. If it's a private event, so be it.

But now Bobby knew Susannah was far stronger than she'd given her credit for. *I need to heal. Then I'll finish what I started.* Let Charles think she was killing Susannah for him. Bobby knew the truth. *I'll kill her for me.* Then she'd get away.

Atlanta, Monday, February 5, 2:45 a.m.

The weeping woke her. Susannah lifted her head from the pillow, momentarily disoriented. The bed wasn't hers and her body was sore in all kinds of places. But the smell of cedar and the sound of Thor's muffled snoring immediately calmed her.

She was in Luke's bed. But he wasn't.

Gingerly she slid from the bed, suddenly feeling every one of the bumps and bruises from the last three days. Wincing, she shrugged into the shirt he'd thrown on the floor. It smelled like him, cedar and a little sweat.

I boarded that flight out of LaGuardia Friday morning hoping to change my life.

That, she thought as she rolled up Luke's shirt sleeves, she certainly had done.

Darlin' had stationed herself outside Luke's spare bedroom. The door was ajar and Susannah pushed it open enough to peer inside. It was his home gym and in one corner hung a punching bag. Draped around the bag, his shoulders shaking, was Luke. Susannah's eyes stung at the sight. So many times over the past few days he'd been moved or his eyes had even grown bright, but this . . . This was soul-wrenching grief and it tore at her heart.

"Luke."

His bare back went rigid. He pushed against the bag until he stood straight, but didn't turn around. "I didn't mean to wake you," he said stiffly.

"It's almost three a.m.," she said. "Par for the course. Can I come in?" He nodded, still not looking at her. She rubbed her hands over his back, feeling every muscle tense. "What happened?" she asked softly.

"Nate called."

"Nate, from ICAC." Dread pooled in her stomach. "They found Becky Snyder's little sisters?" The little sisters who Monica's friend Becky had died trying to protect.

"Yeah. On a podcast. Pay per view. Nate sent out pictures of the children after we left the empty apartment this morning." The apartment whose address Monica Cassidy had committed to memory, keeping her promise to help Becky's younger sisters. "One of our partners in Europe contacted him. They'd seen the kids. Nate saw them tonight. Online." He rested his forehead on the punching bag. "He's ripped up."

"I can understand that."

"We see these kids, Susannah . . . We know they're out there and they're suffering but we can't *find* them."

She pressed her cheek to his back, wrapping her arms around him. She said nothing, refusing to minimize his grief with platitudes.

"Nate," he went on, "has been there for days, watching tape, looking at pictures. I should have been there. Should have been watching. I've left it all to him."

"While you've been vacationing in Bali," she murmured. "Luke, you've saved so many. Ten girls, not twenty-four hours ago. Don't beat yourself up like this."

"I know. Why isn't that good enough?"

"Because you're you and you care, too damn much. You know you've done your best because you're not capable of doing any less. You have to hold on to that."

His hands covered hers. "That helps. Really."

"You'll find Bobby Davis, then you can help Nate find the Snyder kids and the others that keep you awake at three a.m. Did Nate track Becky's stepfather?"

"No, but we know Snyder had those kids here in the city once. Nate's going to take face shots of the kids to the area schools, see if he can find them that way. But they could be anywhere in the world by now. There's nothing keeping him here in Atlanta."

"Maybe there is. Maybe this scumbag Snyder has roots you don't know about. What made you know he was in Atlanta to start with? When he still had Angel and Becky?"

"Things we saw in the pictures, things around the room where the kids were kept. A Braves cap, a tomahawk, the kind you get on free day. Stuff like that."

"Untraceable stuff that thousands of people have," she said quietly against his back.

"Yeah." The single word was bitter and hopeless.

"Come back to sleep," she said. "You need to rest. You'll be sharper."

"I can't sleep."

"Then come back to bed anyway." She tugged and he followed, stopping when he got to the bed. She was wearing his shirt and it shifted when she climbed on the mattress, revealing the dark bruise on her breast, courtesy of Bobby's bullet. His temper flared higher, remembering how close he'd come to losing her.

He shook his head. "You go to sleep," he said. "I'll go watch some TV." He knew his moods, knew he was too savage right now to risk getting into the bed with her. She was bruised. She had to hurt like hell.

And I'm ready for round two. He swallowed when she knelt on the bed, her small hands reaching for his. *Very, very ready.*

"Don't shut me out," she said softly. "I didn't do that to you."

"It's not the same."

She frowned. "Because you're on the dark side now?" She slipped her fingers inside the waist of his jeans and tugged him closer. "It doesn't matter to me."

He pushed her away, as gently as he was able. "It matters to me." He turned to leave, but she was quick, getting to the door before he could and leaning against it, her chin lifted, challenge in her eyes. "Susannah," he warned. "This is not the time."

"That's what you said last night. You were wrong then, too."

With a curse he tried to move her out of the way, but she put her arms around his neck, and her legs around his waist, attaching herself to him like a limpet. "Don't," she hissed. "Don't push me away."

He braced his hands on the door and they hung there. "Don't you know I'll hurt you?"

She kissed his jaw. "Don't you know I need to help you?"

"You can't." He was knowingly goading her, but he couldn't seem to stop himself.

"Watch me," she murmured, kissing his cheeks, his lips, which he held firmly closed. Undaunted, she moved to his shoulder, kissing and licking her way down to his chest. Still he resisted, until she sank her teeth into his shoulder and bit. Hard.

The rubber band of his restraint snapped. With a growl he shoved his jeans off, and hands shaking, grabbed another condom from the drawer. Without thinking he dropped them both to the bed, her arms still locked around his neck, her legs around his waist, and he thrust into her hard.

She was tight and wet and he pounded into her until the simmering pit of his temper boiled over and the world went black. His body went taut, arching back as he was slammed with the most powerful orgasm he'd ever experienced. Too late he realized she hadn't been with him. He'd left her behind without a care.

Shuddering, mortified, he dropped his head, unable to meet her eyes. He'd used her viciously. "Oh God," he said, when he could speak. "I'm sorry. I'm so sorry."

"Why?"

She didn't sound mad or hurt. He lifted his head and looked down at her. She was smiling at him. Perplexed, he frowned. "Didn't I hurt you?"

"A little. I'll live. How do *you* feel?"

"Good," he said cautiously.

She rolled her eyes. "Please. I was here, don't forget. It was damn good."

He let out a breath. "For me, yes. I was selfish. I didn't take care of you first."

"I know that. I'm sure you'll fix that oversight next time. So how do you *feel*?"

Her grin was contagious. "Damn good."

She leaned up, kissed his chin. "And I saw your face," she added, triumphant.

"You saw my face before."

"Mirrors are cheating. This was real." Her grin softened, her smile luminous. "You think you robbed me of pleasure. You have no idea what this means, Luke."

"Then tell me," he said quietly.

Her smile faded completely, leaving her eyes full of yearning. "Do you know what it meant to sit at your family's table? Do you know I've never done that before? Never. Not once, in my entire life have I had a family dinner with people who loved each other. You gave me that." He opened up his mouth to speak, but she pressed her fingers to his lips. "You gave me more than that. You gave me back myself. I wanted to do something for you. If you were selfish, it was in making me work so hard to do that."

"I didn't want to hurt you."

She studied his face, then shook her head. "No, you didn't want to be hurt."

He looked away. "You're right."

"I know," she said dryly.

He dropped his head. "I'm so tired," he said. "And it never stops."

"I know," she said again. "Go to sleep. It'll still be there when you wake up."

"Will you?" he asked, and one side of her mouth lifted.

"Be here when you wake up? Where am I gonna go? I'm out of clothes."

Reluctantly he withdrew from the warmth of her body, repositioning her so that she snuggled, spooned against him. "There's always the outfit Stacie bought you."

"I gave it back to her. Besides, I can just see me wearing that to my arraignment if Chloe decides to charge me. The judge would think I'd been busted for hooking."

Her wry tone didn't fool him. "What will you do?" he murmured, tightening his arm over her waist. "Can they really disbar you?"

"Sure. I can appeal it, but Chloe's right. A room full of reporters was the wrong venue to break the law. I'll be on the front page of the morning paper in a few hours. I was already all over the TV last night." She sighed. "I'll be the subject of discussion over coffee and water cooler breaks. And I knew it would be so from the moment I stepped on that plane Friday morning. I'll be okay. The worst that can happen to me is a lot of publicity and maybe a misdemeanor. Chloe'll cut a deal, no time served. It's what I would do."

"You didn't find that gun in your father's house," he said quietly, and she said nothing. "Susannah?"

"Some things are best left unanswered, Luke. If you know, you could be subpoenaed. You'd have to tell. Either way, I wouldn't change a thing. Would you?"

"No. Except now Leo gets an even better Christmas present for the rest of his life." He tugged at the shirt she wore, kissed the shoulder he'd bared. "So what will you do if you can't be a lawyer anymore?"

"I don't know. I was thinking about what I said to that reporter today, about every woman having the right to disclose her assault or not. I push these women to disclose every day as a prosecutor."

"That's your job, to get convictions."

"I know, and I've served the state well. But during the

trial . . . I always think about what it would have been like had I come forward. I would have been so scared. They are, too. They have to live it all again. The state stands against the perpetrator, but nobody really stands *for* the victim."

"You're thinking of victim advocacy."

"If I get disbarred. Even if I don't, it'll be hard for me to go into a courtroom and not have the focus be on me and not on the victims. I'm going to have to do something different, no matter what Chloe decides. Hell, maybe I'll set up a Kool-Aid stand."

He yawned hugely. "Will you sell cherry flavor?"

"Grape," he heard her reply sleepily. "Nobody hates grape. Sleep, Loukaniko."

His eyes popped open. "Excuse me? What did you just say?"

"That nobody hates grape. And go to sleep," she said, annoyed. "So go to sleep."

"No, the Loukaniko part."

She craned her neck to look up at him over her shoulder. "Leo said that was your real name. That's why your mama calls you Lukamou."

Luke bit his lip to keep from laughing. "Um. Lukamou is like . . . 'my dear.' Loukaniko is a big fat sausage."

She winced, then her eyes narrowed. "Oh. Sorry. I blame Leo."

"Brother Leo just dropped a rung on the Christmas present ladder."

She snuggled back against him. "Although, I suppose under certain circumstances Loukaniko could apply, too."

He snickered. "Thank you. I think."

"Go to sleep," she said quietly. "Lukamou."

His arm tightened around her, and on a contented sigh, he let himself drift off.

Chapter Twenty-two

Atlanta, Monday, February 5, 7:45 a.m.

What's in these boxes?" Susannah asked, sitting in Luke's office the next morning.

Luke looked up from his reports. She looked fresh and beautiful in the black dress Chloe had loaned her the Saturday before. The dress had magically appeared in Luke's closet while they slept, free of the dirt, blood, and clay she'd accumulated at Sheila Cunningham's funeral. It was nice to have family in the dry-cleaning business.

"Yearbooks," he said, "from all the schools in a twenty-five-mile-radius of Dutton. We used them last week to identify the victims in Simon's pictures."

Kneeling on the floor, she opened the box. "Is my senior annual in here?"

"No. I gave it to Daniel. It's probably in his office. Why?"

"Just curious to see if I looked like I remember. Perspective is an interesting thing."

"You don't have any pictures of your senior year?"

She leveled him a look. "Why would I? I just wanted to forget it."

"I have your picture. Kind of." He pulled his wallet from his pocket, feeling foolish. "I was going through the yearbooks and saw your picture. I'd been thinking about you for days, since I first saw you at your parents' funeral. I . . . photocopied it. I even thought about going to New York to meet you. Priced airfare and everything."

She sat back on her heels, grinning delightedly. "You didn't."

"I did." He gave her the folded photocopy and watched as she opened it, tentatively.

Her smile dimmed. "I look sad."

"I know," he said softly. "I thought so, too."

She swallowed hard and gave him back the copy. "So why did you copy it?"

"Because I thought even sad, you were the most beautiful thing I'd ever seen."

She blushed, charming him. "That's sweet." She went back to the box and he returned to his paperwork. All was quiet for minutes, then she spoke again. "Luke, I know why Kate Davis was called Rocky." She put a yearbook on his desk, looking over his shoulder as he studied the page. It was a picture of a young girl with a very bad overbite and thick glasses. "That's Kate Davis," she said, "aka Rocky."

Luke tried to reconcile the gawky child with the sleek woman Kate had become. "You're kidding."

"Nope. It's a wonder what braces and a makeover will do. I'd forgotten about it until I saw this picture, but the kids used to call Kate 'Rocky.' For the squirrel. You know, the one on the cartoon. With Bullwinkle," she added when he looked up at her blankly.

"Oh. Why?"

She frowned, thinking back. "It started at one of the plays back in high school. Our private school was K through twelve, so they had little kids, too. They did *Snow White* and cast some of the younger kids as woodland

creatures. Some thoughtless teacher cast Kate as a squirrel. She couldn't have been more than eight or nine at the
time."

Luke looked at the buck teeth of the young Kate in the
photo. "That was cruel."

"They started calling her Rocky Squirrel after that, and
because Garth was so big, they called him Bullwinkle. He
didn't mind, but Kate did. I remember her crying." She
sighed. "I should have said something then, but that was
right after . . . well, after Simon and the others did what
they did. I was keeping to myself a lot then."

"I can see why." Luke swiveled in his chair and looked
up at her, deciding to confront his question head on.
"Susannah, how did you know Simon raped you?"

She winced. "He showed me a picture. Somebody must
have taken the picture, because it was definitely Simon,
artificial leg and all."

"What happened to the picture?"

"I don't know. He made his point, then took it back.
But I saw it, and for Garth Davis to call me a liar . . . It
makes it worse."

He hesitated, then spoke when she gave him a look.
"It's just that I'm surprised it wasn't with Simon's collection. Either the one Daniel found or the box you found."

Her eyes narrowed. "You don't believe me?"

"Of course I do," he said quickly and her frown
smoothed. "I definitely believe you. I'm just wondering
where the picture went." He sandwiched her hand between his. "Don't worry about it. I'll go with you to see
Garth when morning meeting is finished. He may know
where Bobby is hiding. Now I gotta go." He dropped a
kiss on her lips.

"Luke." He turned at the door. Her eyes were wide, her

hands clutched together so tightly her knuckles were white. "Tell Chloe to make up her mind. I'd rather just know."

Atlanta, Monday, February 5, 7:55 a.m.

"You look better," Chase said to Luke when he sat at the conference room table.

"You don't," Luke replied. "Any news on Leigh?"

"No. I talked to her family. Nobody seems to know why she would have done this."

The rest of the team filed in. With the exception of Ed and Chloe, all looked rested, but worn. Ed slipped Luke a note as he passed. *Loomis paternity*, it read. *Positive*.

That was one question confirmed. He met Ed's eyes across the table with a nod.

"You want to share the note with the rest of the class?" Chase asked sarcastically.

Susannah had already given her okay to share the information, now that she'd told Daniel first. "Angie Delacroix, the hairdresser in Dutton, told Susannah that Arthur Vartanian wasn't her father. That her mother had had an affair with Frank Loomis. Ed ran the tests and it's true. Frank Loomis is Susannah's biological father."

Chase blinked. "Well. I didn't see that coming."

"Neither did she," Luke said. "Seems like Frank Loomis fixed a lot of Simon's legal problems, including falsifying evidence in the Gary Fulmore case."

"That explains a lot," Chloe said. "I'll make sure that gets included with the record. We'd started an investigation into Loomis the day before he was killed."

"Speaking of investigations," Luke said. "She needs to know, Chloe."

Chloe looked miserable. "I didn't sleep a wink. But, Luke, I have to file charges."

He bit back what would have been a sharp reply. "At least she'll know. Tell them," he added, when the team looked confused.

"Susannah Vartanian was in possession of a firearm illegally yesterday," Chloe said.

"Oh my God," Talia snapped. "*Chloe.*"

"That's stupid," Pete added. "Talk about adding insult to injury."

"No time served. Right, Chloe?" Chase said wearily.

"No time. Community service, but no time." She looked at Luke and for the first time he saw the sassy Chloe on the verge of tears. "I'm sorry."

He patted her hand. "She's okay with it. She said she'd do the same thing."

Chloe blew out a breath. "It still sucks."

"Nothing about the last week has done anything other than suck," Chase said. "Ed, you were busy during the night. Tell them what you've got."

"A couple things." His eyes grew bright in his worn face. "We lifted some prints off the syringes we found in the bunker and got a match with the hospital's records." He pulled a photo from his folder. "Jeff Katowsky, thirty-nine years old. He's a nurse at the hospital. We picked him up this morning, hiding in his mother's basement."

"He tried to kill Ryan Beardsley?" Luke asked.

"He's confessed," Chase said. "He was contacted by a woman and threatened that she'd reveal his drug habit if he didn't kill Beardsley. Just like Jennifer, the nurse."

"How did Bobby know these people's secrets?" Nancy asked. "Bobby had to have a source. Who knew about Jeff Katowsky's drug problem?"

"He won't say," Chase said. "Chloe offered him a deal, and he still wouldn't say."

"He was genuinely terrified," Chloe said. "We said we'd protect him. He laughed."

"Just like Michael Ellis, Darcy's killer," Luke said. "Not a coincidence."

"Chloe, did you ask Al Landers about pressing Darcy's killer again?" Chase asked.

"I called him before I came in this morning, but he wasn't in yet." She took her BlackBerry from her purse. "I also e-mailed him after last night's meeting." She scrolled through her messages, then looked up with a frown. "Here's his reply. He says he'll go up to the prison himself today, but he didn't get the police sketch we faxed up to him. The one Susannah gave of the man who raped her the night Darcy was killed."

Luke closed his eyes. "Susannah said the artist gave the sketch to Leigh."

"Fuck." Chase called for the new clerk sitting at Leigh's desk. Minutes later, he was scowling. "No record of a fax to New York. Leigh didn't send it and it's not in her desk."

"The artist will have a copy," Pete said. "We can send it again."

"Yeah, we can," Luke said. "But why would Leigh not send it? She seemed to be playing both sides of the fence, giving information to Bobby and to us. I wonder what else she held back from us."

"I've been going through the record of calls to her office phone as well as the hotline records all night," Chase said. "Seems like she shared everything that came through."

"Maybe she knew him," Luke said. "Or maybe Bobby told her not to send it."

Chase stared for a moment, then sighed. "You could

be right. I asked the new clerk to contact the sketch artist. We'll get the sketch sent out and see what shakes out. For now, we focus on identifying the unknown man Monica Cassidy heard in the bunker. He could be the only one left who was willing to help Bobby escape."

"Mansfield took pictures of Granville in the bunker as insurance in case Granville ever crossed him," Ed said. "Maybe this guy is in one of them."

Luke's stomach turned, bile rising in his throat at the thought of having to look at those pictures again. "I'll look at them."

Chase shot him a look of sympathy. "I can get somebody else to do it."

"No. I want this guy. I'll do it." And if it got to be too much, he now had somewhere to turn. He wondered if Susannah understood exactly what she'd offered to do, then he remembered that first afternoon in his car. *And a little more of you dies each day.* She knew. From experience she knew. It made her need to help him all the sweeter. "But first I want to talk to Garth Davis. He may know where his wife is hiding."

"He gets arraigned this afternoon," Chloe said. "He'll be transported by eleven."

"Can you get remand?" Talia asked.

"I'm going to try, but I don't think so. I'll probably get a pretty high bail, though, which may amount to the same thing. Garth Davis's bank account is empty. It appears Bobby cleaned him out right before she supposedly ran away."

"Won't he get that money back?" Nancy asked, and Chloe shrugged.

"If we could separate Garth's money from Bobby's revenue," she said innocently. "We found her bank accounts on her hard drive, no problem."

"That hard drive of Bobby's was just packed with information," Ed said, his jaw hard. "She was getting rich selling children to rich perverts. Right now we're too busy trying to document her business transactions to find Garth's money. He can sit a while and rot."

"Amen," Luke said. "Are we done? I want to see Garth before he gets transported."

"In a minute," Chase said. "Pete, get that artist's sketch and pass it around. Show it to Leigh's friends and family, see if they recognize him. I want to know who he is. Talia, get with the police in Arkansas. Find out whatever you can about Bobby's childhood, anybody she might go to for help. Ed, what do you have going?"

"We're tracking concrete manufacturers."

"Why?" Pete asked.

"Do you remember me telling you that the floor of that bunker was really old, but that the walls were new, prefabbed? Well, guess who also had prefabbed concrete walls in his house that are identical in composition?"

"Mansfield," Nancy said, snapping her fingers. "It was that structure off his basement, where he'd stored all his munitions and kiddie porn."

"Yep. I've got a list of concrete companies who'd have this mineral composition," Ed said. "If Mansfield bought a bunker, who knows who else they've served?"

"What about Granville's safe-deposit box key?" Nancy asked.

"Track it," Chase said. "The banks are all open today. See if Granville had a box at any of them. Germanio, I want you in Dutton by ten. Congressman Bowie's daughter Janet's funeral is at noon."

"She was the first of Mack O'Brien's victims last week," Chloe said. "There will be a media circus in

Dutton today. Politicians and reporters everywhere. Bobby might show."

"I know. I've arranged to have video surveillance and plainclothes agents at both the funeral and the cemetery afterward." Chase looked at Germanio. "I'll get you a list of the agents who'll be there. I want you there to coordinate. We'll do searches going into the church for the funeral, but the cemetery will be harder to control. Apparently there's also a luncheon of some kind afterward for the media. I'll see you're admitted."

Germanio nodded. "Will do."

"Good. Everyone, meet back here at five. You're all dismissed." Chase pointed to Luke and Chloe. "You two stay."

"What is it?" Luke asked impatiently when the others were gone.

"When I wasn't going through Leigh's phone records last night, I was reading the rest of Jared O'Brien's journal. Luke, he describes every rape those boys did in great detail. There is nothing about raping Susannah in that journal." Chase sighed. "And Jared was enough of an asshole that he would have bragged about it, if only in his journal. He wanted to . . . choose Susannah, but Simon always said no."

"Because he'd already done it," Luke murmured, and Chase frowned.

"What do you know, Luke?"

Luke sighed. "She doesn't want Daniel to know. Simon participated in at least one rape. He showed her a picture of him raping her."

Chase shook his head. "Jared was *clear* Simon never participated. Where is this picture?"

"She doesn't know."

"So it was Simon and at least one other," Chase said. "Whoever took the photo."

"Granville," Luke said, clenching his teeth. "It had to have been Granville."

"Then it's possible Garth Davis is telling the truth," Chloe said quietly.

"I know," Luke said. "And if he is . . ."

"He's not guilty of her rape," Chase said. "He's the only one of the seven left alive."

"So she came forward for nothing," Chloe said dully. "Godammit."

"Not for nothing." The three of them whipped around to look at the door where Susannah stood clutching a yearbook to her chest. "I came forward for me, to take my life back." She met Luke's eyes and smiled. Luke made himself smile back, even though his heart was cracking. She cleared her throat. "I found something you should see." She put the yearbook on the table and opened it. "I was too nervous to sit still, so I started paging through all the yearbooks in that box in your office. This one is from Springfield High, about twenty miles from Dutton." She pointed to a picture. "Look."

"Marcy Linton." Chase looked up at her with a mild frown. "I don't understand."

"I didn't know her as Marcy Linton," Susannah said. "I knew her as Darcy Williams."

There was a moment of stunned silence, then a collective sigh. "So she grew up twenty miles from you, but met you in New York," Luke said slowly.

"Not a coincidence," Susannah said. "She was somehow part of the plan. I want to know how, and why, and what went wrong the night she was murdered."

"I agree," Chase said. "We need to find out more about Miss Marcy Linton. I've got Talia calling the police in Arkansas about Bobby's past. When she's finished, I'll have her track down the Linton family."

"I'd like to go with her," Susannah said. "Please, Chase. The Darcy I knew said she was a runaway, that she had no family. She was my friend, or I thought she was. I had her buried in New York."

"You paid for her burial?" Chloe asked.

"I couldn't let her be dumped in Potters' Field. If she has family somewhere, they need to know what happened to her. Please let me go with Talia."

"Until we find Bobby, I want you safe in this building," Luke said fiercely.

Susannah shook her head. "What if she's gone, run away? What if we never find her? I can't hide forever, Luke. Talia's a good cop. I'll be safe with her and I promise I'll be careful. First though, I need to speak with Garth Davis."

Charlotte, North Carolina, Monday, February 5, 8:45 a.m.

Special Agent Harry Grimes was putting the finishing touches on his closed report on the abduction and recovery of Eugenie Cassidy when his phone rang. "Grimes."

"Harry, it's Steven Thatcher. We found Dr. Cassidy's car."

Genie and Monica's dad. "Oh, hell, Steven. Where?"

"Lake Gordon. There was a bass tournament yesterday and some guy found Cassidy's car with his fish finder. He called it in this morning when he saw the news on Genie being found, but her father is still missing. We've got a team dragging the lake."

"I'm on my way."

"Hey, how's the girl, by the way?" Steven asked.

"Genie's untouched," Harry said. "Physically anyway. She's still in shock. Monica . . . well, that's a different story. I talked to her mother this morning. Monica's got a long row to hoe. I wish . . . I wish we could have done something to prevent this."

"She's alive," Steven said. "Remember that. What about this Jason character?"

" 'Jason' was a team of two madams, a doctor, and a deputy sheriff. All are dead except for the older madam. Genie identified the younger madam as her abductor."

"Could any of them have killed Dr. Cassidy, assuming this is his car we found?"

Harry checked his notes. "No, none of the four could have done it. Given the time Cassidy's neighbor saw his car drive away, it can't be either of the women. The younger madam was dead by noon, in Georgia. The older woman was seen at the scene and likely killed the young one."

"What about the deputy?"

"He was killed Friday, the day Monica escaped. The doctor was killed then, too."

"Shit," Steven said. "They got a real mess down there."

"I don't think we know the half of it. I talked to Luke Papadopoulos down in Atlanta. He says there's still at least two more out there—the older madam and one other."

"What do you know about Genie's abduction?"

"She was taken from an all-night diner called Mel's."

"If I were you, I'd check it out."

"I did, a few hours before Genie was found. She said the younger madam did it, and she's dead now."

"But you also said the younger madam couldn't have been involved in the abduction of Genie's daddy, so we have at least one more player. Maybe it's the same other player this Papadopoulos in Atlanta's looking for. Did this diner have security video?"

"Only at the cash register. But . . ." Again Harry flipped through his notes. "There's an ATM across the road. The angle on their security camera might be about right."

"There you go," Steven said. "Have at it, boy. I'll call you if we pull up Dr. Cassidy."

Atlanta, Monday, February 5, 9:35 a.m.

Susannah's stomach churned as she stood outside the interrogation room in which Garth Davis waited. "I'm scared, Luke," she murmured.

He slid his arm around her waist. "You don't have to do this. I can talk to him."

"No, I do need to do this." She drew a deep breath. "Let's get it over with."

Chloe was waiting inside the room, along with Garth Davis and his lawyer.

"Garth," Susannah murmured and sat in the chair Luke pulled out for her.

"Susannah," he said warily. "It's been a long time."

"Yes, it has." She studied his face, not with the eye of a prosecutor, but with the eye of a woman whose life had been turned upside down for way too long. Garth looked drawn, haggard. At barely thirty-two years old, he looked . . . old. As old as she felt.

Garth looked up at Luke. "You found my sons. Thank you."

Beside her, Luke nodded once. "We said we would."

"I saw the news. I swear, I didn't know what Barbara Jean had done."

"She tried to kill me yesterday," Susannah said.

Garth met her gaze, his eyes haunted. "I know."

"Did you know she hated me?"

"No."

"Did you know she was Arthur Vartanian's daughter?" she asked.

His eyes widened in shock. "Really?"

"Yes." And then she knew what she wanted to ask. "Did you rape fifteen girls?"

"Garth," his lawyer warned, but Garth held up his hand wearily.

"Enough. It's enough already. I'm not getting out of this. They have pictures, a journal. My sister is dead, along with half of Dutton. Enough people have died for the sins of a handful of stupid boys."

"My original offer stands, Mr. Davis," Chloe said. "Fifteen years."

"The deal sucks, Chloe," Davis's lawyer said. "He was a juvenile, for God's sake."

"He was seventeen."

"Only for half of them," the lawyer argued, and Chloe rolled her eyes.

"There's a mandatory sentence for every count. If a judge orders those served consecutively your client would be in prison for the rest of his life."

"But no judge would," his lawyer scoffed.

Garth shook his head. "Stop, Sweeney. You can't get me out of this."

"We'll request a change of venue," his lawyer said, and Garth laughed bitterly.

"Where? To Mars? There is no place that doesn't know the Richie Rich Rapists." His mouth twisted. "I'm going to take Miss Hathaway's deal. I'll get out in time to see my grandchildren. Yes, Susannah, I raped fifteen girls thirteen years ago. I was caught up in this game . . . this idea that it would make us men. But I swear, I did not rape you."

She believed him. Still . . . "Maybe you were left behind once."

"I don't think so." He shrugged. "The others would have bragged. Everyone wanted you then. You were cool and sophisticated and . . . unattainable."

"I was withdrawn and traumatized," she said evenly. "I was a rape victim."

"I'm truly sorry. But it wasn't me or the others. I'm telling you they would've bragged, especially Jared O'Brien." He paused, sighed. "It could have been Granville."

"Why do you say that, Mr. Davis?" Chloe asked.

"He was always the one in charge and we knew it, although no one ever said it. Everyone was too afraid of Simon to say he wasn't the leader. But it was Toby Granville calling the shots. He picked the girls, the dates, the places."

"But that doesn't explain why you thought Granville did it," Chloe said.

He closed his eyes. "I don't want to say this."

"Mr. Davis," Chloe said harshly, "if you're angling for a better deal, then—"

"I'm not," he snapped. "Dammit. We always wanted to do Susannah, all right?"

Susannah tensed and Luke offered his hand. She

grabbed on tight, listening now, because Garth had seemed to forget she was in the room, addressing Chloe instead.

"What stopped you?" Chloe asked him coolly.

"Granville. Simon would say 'Not my sister,' like he was protecting his turf. Turf, my ass. We always said Simon would do his own mother because he could. And had."

Horrified, Susannah stared, barely registering Chloe's warning glance.

"Are you saying Simon had a relationship with his mother that was inappropriate?" Chloe asked, still cool.

"Yes, that's what I'm saying, because that's what Simon said. And he had *pictures*," he added in disgust. "Simon didn't care about Susannah. He only cared about Simon."

"But still the rest of the boys wanted to choose Susannah," Chloe said evenly.

"Yeah. Finally one day Granville pulled us aside one at time. Told us to stop asking. He said, 'Susannah is taken.'"

"By whom?"

"By *him*. Toby Granville. It's what we understood him to mean." His shoulders sagged and he turned back to Susannah. "I'm sorry. We thought you were Granville's. That you knew. When I heard you'd accused me, I was stunned. And that's the truth."

She was breathing too rapidly because there didn't seem to be enough air in the room. And not a single word would come. Luke's hand tightened around hers.

"I have a few questions, Mr. Davis," Luke said. "First, do you know where your wife is hiding?"

"If I knew, I'd tell you. She could come and take my boys and I'm stuck in here. I can't protect them. So, if

I knew where she was, I would tell you to protect my children."

"What about her friends?" Luke asked.

"She was tight with Marianne Woolf, but my lawyer told me Barbara abducted Marianne, too. She had a weekly hair appointment at Angie's. You could ask Angie who she talked to. She said she had friends in Atlanta. She used to have lunch with them pretty frequently." He gave them some names and Luke shook his head.

"Those are the names of clients we found in her computer."

Garth shrugged. "She had lunch with clients often. That makes sense."

"What kind of clients did your wife have?" Chloe asked carefully.

Garth looked from Chloe to Luke. "She had an interior design business."

The man had been so deluded, Susannah thought. Had he not been such a monster himself, she might have felt a stirring of pity.

From the set of Luke's jaw, Susannah could tell he felt absolutely no pity for Garth, either. Luke ripped off a sheet of paper from his note pad and, still holding Susannah's hand, drew the swastika she wore on her hip. "Do you recognize this?"

Garth's eyes flickered. "Yes."

"Well?" Luke asked.

Garth looked at Chloe. "Before I say any more, I want a concession. I'll allocute. But I want to be able to be sentenced somewhere close by, so I can see my sons."

"Depends," Chloe said. "We already know Granville had the symbol on his ring and on a pendant. Do you have anything different?"

"Yeah," Garth said. "I do."

Chloe nodded. "Then I can petition you serve your time more locally."

"'More locally.'" His lips twisted at her evasion. "Lawyers," he murmured. "Gotta love us. I didn't know Granville had a ring, too. But my wife had one. It was big, a man's ring. I only saw it once. She said it had belonged to her father. I told her I didn't want it in my house, that I didn't think it was good for the kids. She agreed, said she'd get rid of it. I never saw it again."

"Describe it," Luke said.

"Heavy, silver, I think. Raised design."

"How big was it?" Luke asked. "The raised part."

"Size of a dime at least." His eye narrowed. "Why?"

"Did you know," Chloe asked, "that Kate had that design branded on her hip?"

His eyes widened in shock once again. "What? No."

"What was the relationship between your sister and your wife?" Chloe asked.

His mouth fell open. "Are you saying they were . . . *sexually* involved?"

"No," Chloe said. "Are you?"

"*No*," he said, horrified. "They were like sisters. Barbara made Kate beautiful. She made sure she wore the right clothes, taught her to walk and talk. My God." He looked sick. "My *wife* and my *sister*?"

"You are aware that your wife ran a prostitution business in which she peddled minor girls, aren't you?" Chloe asked mildly.

"I read about the girls, yes . . ." His shoulders sagged. "I never knew before. I never knew what was happening under my own roof. Did she . . . Did she molest my boys?"

"We have no indication of that," Chloe said. "The court will order counseling for them when custody is awarded. You've been candid with us, so I'll be candid. We've had reports that your wife operated as a call girl up until your election as mayor of Dutton."

Garth fell back in his chair. "What?"

"We found records on her computer. She took in as much as five hundred an hour. One of her former clients came forward to report she'd blackmailed him afterward. The names of the 'friends' she had in Atlanta match some of the names on her client list."

Susannah looked up at Luke. He looked surprised, too.

Garth grew pale. "All that time . . ." he whispered. "She said she had an interior design business. My uncle Rob always said she was white trash. I should have listened."

Susannah rubbed her temples. "Garth, I was looking through the yearbooks this morning," she said. "There were only a few kids at Bryson Academy whose families weren't wealthy. Barbara lived with her aunt, right? They were far from rich."

"She was there on scholarship," he murmured. "One of the teachers helped her get it. I can't do anymore. Take me back."

When he was gone, Chloe shook her head. "His wife sells children to perverts, kills his sister, and he's most rocked by the fact she cheated on him."

Luke tipped up Susannah's chin. "Your mother and Simon. That was a shock."

"But it explains a lot." Her mouth curved bitterly. "Fine stock Daniel and I come from."

"Sounds like your whole town is one big, festering Peyton Place," Chloe said. "But they say wildflowers that sprout up in weeds are stronger than any rose."

Susannah smiled ruefully. "Thank you, Chloe."

Chloe stood. "I'm off to another heart-to-heart with an inmate. If you hurry, you might meet Daniel coming into the lobby on your way out."

"Daniel's here?" Luke asked.

"He got discharged from the hospital this morning," Susannah said. "I didn't know he was coming here, though."

"Alex has some unfinished business with her stepfather," Chloe said. "They can tell you about it. I'll see you two later."

When she was gone, Luke pulled her to her feet. "I'll take you back to meet Talia so you can search for Marcy/Darcy's family." He hesitated. "You don't really buy that tripe about bad stock, do you?"

"I don't know. But it doesn't seem to matter if it's nature or nurture in this case. Both suck, for Daniel and me. It's no wonder Simon became such a monster."

"But you and Daniel became good people."

She made her lips curve even though her stomach churned worse than before she'd come in. "Two outta three ain't bad?"

Dutton, Monday, February 5, 10:00 a.m.

Charles was laying out his black suit when his cell phone rang. "Paul. Well?"

"It's done. I appreciate the heads up. That sketch artist had done a damn good job. Anybody at APD who saw that sketch would have recognized me in two seconds."

"You got her original sketch and all copies?"

"Yes. The artist had already uploaded it to GBI's server,

but she erased it before I erased *her*. And today," he said
with a smile in his voice, "I got a new assignment."

Charles stopped fussing with his tie selection. "What
are you talking about?"

"Well, it seems the GBI Investigative Unit is a little
shorthanded at this time, since so many of their agents
are either dead or hospitalized."

"Yes, I imagine their ranks are rather depleted at the
moment. So?"

"So, they've asked APD to help guard those they think
are still at risk from Bobby. I volunteered for duty."

Charles sat down, his pulse increasing. "You're guarding Susannah?"

"Not quite. Papadopoulos kept that job. But close. I'm
guarding the venerable and brave Daniel Vartanian."

Charles's smile broadened. "Excellent. Where will you
be?"

"I'm stationed outside his house while he convalesces.
I'm supposed to keep the press away as well as any potential bad guys."

"We'll see that he has a lot of peace and quiet," Charles
said. His smile vanished. "I assume his personal nurse
will be with him, that Alex Fallon."

"I assume so."

"They killed Toby Granville."

"Mack O'Brien killed Granville, Charles, not Daniel
Vartanian or Alex Fallon."

"I don't care. The events were set in motion because of
Vartanian and that nurse of his. He and Fallon killed one
of mine. They'll pay for that. I have to go now. There's
another funeral today and I have to dress."

"Who's getting buried this time?"

"Congressman Bowie's daughter, Janet. We're expecting the press to descend like locusts. The traffic will be unbearable. The funeral, burial, and the lunch in the church afterward will make this an all-day affair. Text me if you need me. I won't be able to use my cell phone in the church."

"Will do."

Charles eyed the surgical kit he'd used to patch Bobby up the night before. It had been a Christmas gift from Toby Granville. Charles had gotten a lot of use from it this week already between Judge Borenson and Bobby Davis. He thought Toby would have been happy to know that. "And Paul, don't kill Vartanian yourself. Bring him to me."

"Put him in the usual place?"

"Yeah. You'll need to dispose of Judge Borenson, though."

Paul grunted in disgust. "How long has he been dead, Charles?"

"He might still be alive. I haven't checked on him in a few days."

"Have you gotten everything you needed to know from him?"

"Yes. If he's not dead yet, do what you wish to him. And make Daniel watch."

"What about the sister?"

"I'll take care of her in my own way."

"Do it fast. When GBI discovers that the sketch artist is dead, they'll just have Susannah work with another artist. She could bury me. You promised she wouldn't."

"And she won't."

"You should have killed her years ago, Charles."

"She'll die today," Charles snapped. "I have to go. Keep in touch."

Atlanta, Monday, February 5, 10:45 a.m.

Luke and Susannah found Chase in his office with a uniformed officer, a young man with a sketch pad under one arm. "We're back," Luke said.

"Come in," Chase said, tersely. "Susannah, too."

Luke and Susannah shared an uneasy glance. "What's happened?" she asked.

"The sketch artist didn't show up for duty this morning. Pete found traces of blood in her apartment. Ed's there now."

Luke blew out a breath. "Hell."

Susannah pursed her lips. "Her sketches were gone?"

Chase nodded. "From the apartment and from our server. They were wiped before the server did its nightly backup. This is Officer Greenburg. He's one of APD's sketch artists. Susannah, we need another description. You can use the conference room."

"Of course," she murmured. She stood, straightening her shoulders. "Let's go."

"Did Garth give you anything?" Chase asked when she was gone.

Luke hesitated. "Nothing on Barbara Jean we didn't already know except she had a swastika ring that probably branded all the girls in the morgue. Susannah's is twice as big, though, so there's still another branding tool out there."

"What else?" Chase asked shrewdly. "There's more."

Luke sighed. "Garth wasn't involved in Susannah's assault. He said the same thing you did—that Jared O'Brien would have bragged about it. Apparently Granville had claimed . . . possession of Susannah. He said she was his and for the others to stay away." He looked away. "Garth also said there was more between Simon and Carol Vartanian than there should have been."

"Oh God," Chase said in disgust. "How'd Susannah and Daniel turn out okay?"

"Must've been raised by wolves," Luke muttered. "They'd have done a better job. But that was mostly it. Garth gave us names of people Bobby lunched with in Atlanta, but they were just her johns. So we're nowhere closer to finding Bobby. I'm going to go over to Nate's office to search Mansfield's hard drives. Maybe Mansfield did get a shot of the man Monica Cassidy heard. Besides, Nate'll need a break. He had a hard night."

"I heard he'd found those kids on a podcast. I'm sorry, Luke."

"Yeah," Luke said bitterly. "Me, too. But one thing at a time. If you need me, use the land line in The Room. My cell phone doesn't always pick up in there. And Chase . . ." Luke shook his head. "Never mind."

"Yeah, I know. I also know Talia won't take any unnecessary risks."

"I know." He closed his eyes. "I just keep seeing Susannah getting shot out of her chair yesterday. Bobby Davis is still out there."

Chase's words were hard, but his voice gentle. "So go do your job and find her."

Chapter Twenty-three

I hate this job," Luke muttered. He'd been staring at the door to The Room, feeling claustrophobic before he even opened the door. The door opened and he jumped back.

A startled Nate stood in the doorway, an empty coffee carafe in one hand. "Don't do that," Nate said tightly. "You nearly gave me a heart attack."

Luke looked at the pot. "How much coffee have you had, man?"

"Too much and not enough. What are you doing here?"

"Mansfield's hard drives. The Sweetpea files. We're hoping Mansfield got a picture of the man Monica Cassidy heard with Granville."

"The mysterious *thíc*. I'll make a fresh pot."

Luke hesitated, the pressure on his chest suddenly so heavy it was hard to breathe.

"You won't find him standing there," Nate said quietly. "It'll be easier to breathe once you step inside."

Luke looked up, met Nate's weary eyes. "You, too?"

"Every goddamn day."

And a little more of you dies each day. "Make the coffee strong," Luke said. He stepped inside and pulled up the Sweetpea files. It was harder than the first time, knowing what he'd find. But he steeled himself against the images of brutality and looked instead for details, backgrounds, shadows, anything that might belong to the occupants of the room there at that damn bunker. Anything except the victims and their suffering.

But he could never see one without the other. That was his problem. It was also, he knew, what made him good at this godforsaken job.

The door opened, closed behind him, and Nate put a mug of steaming coffee on the desk. "What are you looking for, exactly?"

"A man, probably in his sixties. Monica said Granville asked him about how the VC broke its prisoners. Monica said the man slapped Granville for asking."

"Emotional response. You're thinking he was a soldier, captured maybe?"

"Maybe. Susannah heard Granville mention him when she was a little girl, so he had to be living around Dutton then. I had stills made from the video of Sheila Cunningham's funeral. Susannah said the whole town was there." He spread the pictures out.

"Hell, half the town is over sixty, Luke."

"Yeah. Looks like anybody with brains got out of Dodge right after high school."

"Can you blame them?" Luke separated out the photos with older men and pinned them to the board above the monitor. "We could be looking for one of these men. Granville had access to this guy when he was a young teenager. This guy was a religious figure to Granville."

"The whole Buddhist thing."

"Yeah." Luke frowned. "But there isn't a Buddhist congregation in Dutton. I checked."

"He didn't have to be a real cleric," Nate said.

"He just had to be able to have access to a teenager without it being obvious."

"Meaning he could be a teacher, a preacher, a doctor . . . All the usual suspects."

"All of which have lived there since Susannah was a little girl. I have a list of the town's residents from when I was looking for men named Bobby on Saturday." Luke looked over the list he'd studied the night before as Susannah lay sleeping and he could not. "I ran military checks on all the men over fifty."

Nate looked surprised. "When did you do that?"

"Last night. It was what I was doing when you called to tell me about seeing Becky Snyder's little sisters on the Net."

Nate's eyes shadowed. "Any of those men serve in 'Nam?"

"Not one. If I'd found one, I would have hauled my ass over here last night." Instead, he'd taken a few hours of comfort in Susannah's arms, in her willing body. Respite. He'd needed it more than he'd realized.

"Well, your ass is here now, whether it wants to be or not." Nate pulled up a chair. "Let's get started. Four eyes are better than two."

Luke shot him a grateful look. "Thanks."

Charlotte, North Carolina, Monday, February 5, 11:45 a.m.

Harry Grimes sat next to CSU tech Mandy Penn, staring at the grainy stills taken by the ATM across from Mel's Diner where Genie Cassidy had been abducted.

"What are you looking for, exactly?" Mandy asked.

"I'm not sure." Harry leaned forward. "That's the kidnapper's Volvo pulling past the camera, into the parking lot. There's another car. It's stopping, *watching*."

"It's a Ford Crown Vic," Mandy said. In the distance, two figures grappled. The smaller figure was dragged to the back of the Volvo. Through each still, the Crown Vic maintained position, and Mandy whistled softly. "You're right, Harry. He's watching."

"Can you zoom on the license plate?"

"I can try." Mandy zoomed, focused, then sat back, satisfied. "There you go."

"Excellent." He squinted at the photo. "Is the guy in the Crown Vic talking on a cell?"

"Looks like. Maybe calling 911?"

"Nobody called 911 from that location. I checked. Can you run an ID on that plate?"

Mandy did, then went still, eyes wide. "He wasn't calling the cops. He *is* a cop."

Harry looked at her screen, stunned. "Paul Houston, Atlanta PD. He just sat there, watching while Genie was snatched."

"Maybe the car was stolen."

"I sure hope so. Thanks, Mandy." Harry started back for his desk. "I owe you one."

Springdale, Monday, February 5, noon

Talia parked in front of the house belonging to Carl Linton, Marcy Linton's father. "You ready for this, Susannah?"

Susannah stared at the house. "Darcy told me she'd come from Queens, that her father beat her and her mother. That she'd run away from home."

"The Lintons reported her missing when she was nineteen."

"She'd gone to New York by then. I didn't meet her for another two years. Why did she leave her family? Why did she target me?"

"We won't find out sitting here," Talia said. "Let's go."

Talia's knock was met by an older man with graying hair. "Mr. Linton?" Talia asked.

"Yes." He studied Susannah with a frown. "What do you want?"

"I'm Special Agent Talia Scott of the Georgia Bureau of Investigation. This is Assistant District Attorney Varta-nian, from New York. We need to talk with you."

His frown deepened and he opened the door. "Come in."

A woman came from the kitchen and froze. "You're the Vartanian woman. We saw you on the news. You shot that woman. The one who'd kidnapped all those girls."

"Yes, ma'am."

"Why are you here?" Carl Linton asked, more harshly.

Talia's head tilted, just a hair. "We need to talk to you about your daughter, Marcy."

Both Lintons drew shocked breaths. "Sit down," Carl said.

Talia took the lead. "After you reported Marcy missing, did you hear from her again?"

"No," Carl said. "Why? For God's sake tell us what this is about."

"Your daughter is dead, sir," Susannah said quickly. "I'm sorry."

Both parents sagged. "How?" Mrs. Linton whispered.

Talia nodded and Susannah drew a breath. "I grew up in Dutton."

"We know," Carl said coldly.

"When I was in graduate school in New York, I met a woman who said her name was Darcy Williams. She and I became friends. She told me she was from Queens, that she'd run away from an abusive family. Today I saw a photo of Marcy in her high school yearbook. She was the woman I knew as Darcy. Darcy was murdered."

"Murdered?" Mrs. Linton had grown paler. "How? Where? When?"

"A man beat her to death." Susannah's stomach turned over at the pain on the Lintons' faces. "We'd gone to a hotel in the city. When I found her . . . it was too late. It was six years ago, January nineteenth. Her killer confessed and is serving his sentence. I'm so sorry. If I'd known about her real family I would have told you years ago."

Carl shook his head, denial clear in his eyes. "Why would she tell you those lies?"

"We think she may have been hired to," Talia said quietly. "Or perhaps forced to."

Mrs. Linton's lips trembled. "Where is she now?"

"In a cemetery about an hour north of New York City. It's a pretty place. Peaceful." Susannah felt the sting of tears and pushed them back. "I thought she had no family."

"ADA Vartanian paid for her burial," Talia said gently.

"We want her back," Carl said, so hostilely that Susannah blinked.

"Of course. I'll arrange for it immediately."

Talia put her hand over Susannah's. "Just a minute," she said, keeping her voice mild. "ADA Vartanian was also assaulted the night of your daughter's murder. Later, she paid to bury your daughter from her own pocket, believing she had no family."

Carl's jaw went hard as stone. "We want her back," he said, enunciating every word.

"I sympathize with your grief, sir," Talia said. "I need to understand your hostility."

Carl straightened abruptly. "Our daughter was taken from us, forced to do God knows what, then murdered, and you have the nerve to criticize me?"

"I'm not criticizing you," Talia said.

"*The hell you're not.*" Carl lurched to his feet, pointing a trembling finger at Susannah. "My daughter had a future, but your father took that from her. She meets you and now she's dead. You want gratitude for a goddamn burial plot? You can go to hell."

Susannah sat, stunned. "What did my father have to do with your daughter?"

Carl's fists were on his hips and his face was florid. "Don't pretend you don't know. Don't pretend you cared about her. I've had enough from *Vartanians* to last me the rest of my goddamn *life*." He slammed the front door so hard the whole place shook.

Susannah stared after him, unable to think of a thing to say.

Mrs. Linton remained, whether by choice or simply because she was trembling too hard to move Susannah was unsure.

"Mrs. Linton," Talia said smoothly. "What connects your daughter to Judge Vartanian? I checked her file. There were no arrests, no appearances in court."

"She was a minor," Mrs. Linton murmured. "Her record was sealed."

"What was the offense?" Talia asked.

Mrs. Linton's eyes flashed. "Soliciting. She didn't do it. She was an honor student. She tutored kids after school.

Her teachers said she'd earn scholarships. But her life was ruined because she was arrested and we couldn't afford to keep her out of jail."

Talia frowned. "Soliciting. You mean prostitution?"

"Yes," Mrs. Linton said bitterly. "That's exactly what I mean. She served six months in a juvenile facility. We couldn't afford any less."

A chill ran down Susannah's spine. "You couldn't afford less? Less what?"

"Less *time*," Mrs. Linton spat. "Your father sentenced her to *two years*. She was only sixteen. Your father wanted money to keep her out of jail. We mortgaged our house, but he said it wasn't enough. He said she'd still serve a whole year."

Susannah looked at Talia, stricken. She'd known it was true, known it was happening, but she'd been too young to act. Now she was seeing the effects of her father's handiwork. *No, I've been seeing the effects for the last six years. Every time I close my eyes and see Darcy, dead in a pool of her own blood.*

Talia patted her hand, turning all her attention to Marcy's mother. "Mrs. Linton, this is important. You said she'd been sentenced to two years, but you paid the judge enough to get it down to a year. But Marcy served six months. What happened?"

Mrs. Linton was studying Susannah uncertainly. "Someone in the juvenile system helped her. She got a new trial, a different judge. He let her go, time served."

"Who was the judge, Mrs. Linton?" Susannah asked, already knowing the answer.

"Judge Borenson. He's retired now."

Talia blew out a breath. "When did the new trial happen, ma'am?"

"Almost thirteen years ago."

It was like a kick in the ribs. "Not a coincidence," Susannah whispered.

"I agree," Talia said quietly. "Mrs. Linton, who helped your daughter get a new trial?"

"A lawyer from Legal Aid." She looked from Talia to Susannah. "A different one than Marcy had the first time. His name was Alderman."

Susannah closed her eyes. "He represented Gary Fulmore."

"He died soon after he got Marcy out," Mrs. Linton said. "He had a car accident."

"Mrs. Linton," Talia said, "were any others involved in your daughter's release?"

"No, I don't think so. I'll have to ask my husband. He's gone for a walk. It's what he does when he gets angry about Marcy. I'll ask him when he comes back."

"Thank you," Talia said. "Here's my card. Please call me if you remember anything, no matter how small it seems. We'll see ourselves out."

Susannah followed Talia, turning when Mrs. Linton said her name. "Yes, ma'am?"

"Thank you," Mrs. Linton said hoarsely. "For burying my daughter in a nice place."

Susannah's throat closed. "You're welcome. I'll make sure she's moved to a nice place here. Pick the spot and let me know."

Susannah waited for Talia to start the engine, conscious of Mrs. Linton watching them from the window. "Go back to Main Street," she said. "But head away from town."

"Where are we going?" Talia asked.

"To my parents' house. Hurry, before I lose my nerve."

*Charlotte, North Carolina, Monday, February 5,
12:05 p.m.*

Still reeling from the discovery of an Atlanta cop observing Genie Cassidy's abduction, Harry called the one person he trusted to guide him through what could be a sticky situation. "Steven, it's Harry."

"Hey. I was just getting ready to call you."

Harry's heart sank. "You found Dr. Cassidy in Lake Gordon?"

"Only his car. Now we're searching the shoreline. Harry, what's wrong?"

"God, Steven. I've fallen into a mess." He told his old boss about the Crown Vic.

"Holy hell, Harry. Are you sure?"

"That the car is registered to Houston, yes. Who's behind the wheel I can't say."

"Have you called APD?"

"Not yet. I was wondering where to start. I could call the administrative office and get Paul Houston's boss, but his boss might ask him directly. If Houston is dirty, I don't want to risk tipping him off. I could call Atlanta's Internal Affairs, but . . . hell, Steven."

Steven was quiet a moment. "Do you trust this Papadopoulos?"

"Yeah. I think so. More than IA, anyway."

"Then call him. Tell him what you found. Let him field the flak."

"Seems cowardly."

"Well, door number two is IA."

"I'll call Papadopoulos."

"I thought so. Call me if you need anything more."

Springdale, Monday, February 5, 12:25 p.m.

Talia waited until they were on the main road. "Why are we going to your parents' house, Susannah?"

"My father kept records. Borenson came to our house often. They scratched each other's backs."

"But in Marcy's case, Borenson reversed your father's initial ruling."

"Right after Borenson presided over Gary Fulmore's trial, which we know was dirty. My father wouldn't have been happy about being overruled."

"Do you remember an argument between them?"

"No. But when Alicia Tremaine turned up dead in that ditch, my mother somehow knew Simon was involved. She went to Frank Loomis and begged him to 'fix it.' So he framed Gary Fulmore, a drifter who just happened to be in the wrong place at the wrong time and too high to know what was happening. Alderman was Fulmore's defense attorney. The only evidence Loomis had was Alicia's ring in Fulmore's pocket and a little blood on his clothes. There were huge holes in the case. Judge Borenson should have seen. He should have seen."

"A jury convicted Fulmore, Susannah. Borenson may not have been involved."

"We both know a jury convicts based on the evidence they're allowed to hear. Who knows if Borenson allowed Alderman to present a proper case?"

"And a few months later, Alderman stands before Borenson again and gets Marcy Linton released."

"I wonder if Alderman knew Fulmore's case was tainted and somehow threatened Borenson." Susannah pulled her laptop from her briefcase. "I wonder how many cases Alderman won between Marcy Linton and the day he died." Talia drove as she searched. "Looks like Alderman defended five people between Marcy Linton's second trial and his death. He drew Borenson two of those five times and won both cases. He lost the other three."

"Not definitive," Talia said. "And we can't ask him, because he's dead."

"Let's say Alderman knew something—why didn't he use it to get Fulmore off? That was a much more high-profile case. It would have been a huge feather in his cap."

"Either Alderman didn't find out till later or he chose to leverage what he knew on future cases."

"That's what I think." Susannah stiffened as her old house came into view. The bile started to rise in her throat and she resolutely, audibly, swallowed it back.

Talia glanced over again, her expression worried. "You okay?"

"No. But we're going in anyway. Because even if Alderman had information that Borenson ran a dirty trial, it doesn't explain Darcy's death and the fact that Granville's *thich* was at the bunker within the last few weeks. There's a connection. I know it."

"My gut says you're right. I hope we find something concrete to back it up."

"My father kept detailed records on everything, and Daniel and I know most of his hiding places. I knew I'd have to come back here and find his records. I've been dreading it, just like Luke is dreading those pictures on Mansfield's hard drive."

"Do you have a key?" Talia asked.

Susannah nodded grimly. "Frank Loomis gave it to me after my parents' funeral."

Talia just sighed. "Let me call in our location, and we'll get started looking."

Bobby froze, her hand poised on the frame of a very expensive painting hanging in an upstairs parlor. She'd found four wall safes behind equally expensive paintings throughout the house and another safe in the floor of the judge's bedroom. Now she slid her hand away from the frame at the sound of car doors slamming outside.

Women's voices. Carefully she crept to the window, and nodded, satisfied. One of the women had been at the press conference the day before, standing next to the women on the stage. She was GBI. The other was none other than Susannah.

A thrill ran down Bobby's spine. She'd been wondering how she'd force Susannah to open the safes. Now Susannah had been dumped in her lap, like a gift. She'd have to get rid of the agent, but that's what guns were for. Bobby was well-stocked, having found a stash of weapons in the attic while searching for heirlooms. Untraceable guns, switchblades, tasers, all hidden beneath yards of Christmas garland.

Peace on earth, indeed.

Atlanta, Monday, February 5, 12:25 p.m.

Luke continued to click through each picture in Mansfield's Sweetpea file. After an hour, all he'd seen were Granville and the victims. So many victims. He had to focus on the background detail to keep his sanity.

"He took these with a hidden camera," Luke said, just to hear his own voice and not the cries he imagined coming from each victim as she was tortured.

"Granville's clothes change seasonally a couple of times," Nate said. "The angle also changes. I wonder what Mansfield had the camera hidden in."

"I'm betting the camera was in a pen clipped to his pocket. He mostly gets shots of Granville's torso and shoes. I wish he'd date stamped the damn things. We could have cut right to pictures taken during the last two weeks."

"That's the problem with all of his pictures. They're organized by predilection, but not by time. It'll be hard to figure out when the pictures were taken and how old the kids would even be by now."

Luke stiffened as his mind registered a detail in the next photo. "*Wait*."

Nate was leaning forward, eyes narrowed. On the edge of the picture were a man's trousers, the legs bent at the knee. "Whoever's wearing them was sitting down."

"But look at the shoes." Luke pointed with his pen. "The soles."

Nate sucked in a breath. "One's thicker than the other. Special shoes."

Luke's mind had run through all the men in the town and already come to a conclusion before his eyes lifted to the board behind the monitor to where the stills hung. He pointed to the still of the three barbershop bench men, sitting in folding chairs near Sheila's graveside. "The one on the end, with the walking stick. His name is Charles Grant. He was Daniel's English teacher." Quickly he dialed Chloe. "It's Luke. I think I have an ID on the man Monica Cassidy heard in the bunker. Charles Grant."

"Grant?" Chloe repeated, stunned. "Isn't he Daniel's teacher? The one that gave us information on Mack O'Brien?"

"Just when we needed it," Luke said bitterly. "Just like the information supplied by Kate Davis, aka Rocky."

"This is going to kill Daniel," Chloe said.

"Let's get word to him, so that it doesn't," Luke said tersely. "I need a warrant."

"You got a clear ID?"

"Not his face," Luke said. "Just his shoes."

"I don't know if I can get you a warrant on shoes, Luke."

"Dammit, Chloe . . ."

"Luke," Nate said. He'd clicked through a few more pictures. "Look."

The camera angle was different. "Wait," he said and zoomed in. "How about the head of a walking stick identical to the one Charles Grant used at Sheila's funeral?"

"Much better. You get started for Dutton. You'll have a warrant when you get there."

"Thanks, Chloe." Luke hung up and dialed Chase, filling him in.

"Good work," Chase said. "I'll contact Germanio. They should be at the cemetery and hopefully Grant is there. Germanio can watch him while you get down there and search his house. Bobby could be hiding there. Oh, and Luke, I just hung up with that agent in North Carolina. Harry Grimes. He's been trying your cell for over an hour."

"My cell doesn't work in The Room."

"I told him that. He refused to tell me what he wanted, just that it was urgent."

"I'll call him. Chase, have you heard from Talia and Susannah?"

"Yes, she's safe. Now go."

Luke turned to Nate. "Can you send these pics to Chloe for the warrant?"

"Already done. I just e-mailed them to her. Go. Good luck."

"Thanks." A glance at his call log revealed six calls from Harry Grimes. Luke dialed him as he ran down the stairs toward his car. "Harry, it's Luke Papadopoulos."

"I have news for you. It's sensitive and I wasn't sure who I could trust."

"What is it?"

"I found video of Genie Cassidy's abduction. Someone observed the whole thing. Someone driving a Crown Vic registered to an Atlanta cop. Name's Paul Houston."

"A cop?" Luke didn't have time for pause, although a major chunk of the puzzle had just fallen into place. "My God. Now it makes sense."

"It docs?" Harry asked.

"Yeah, it does." Now he knew how Bobby was able to force Nurse Jennifer Ohman to keep Monica silent and the male nurse to try to kill Ryan Beardsley, and maybe even how she was able to force Leigh Smithson to aid her. Bobby was working with a cop. A cop would know about drug addictions and other secrets, and a dirty cop would use those to blackmail. "I'm running to an emergency. I need you to call my boss back. Tell him what you told me, fast. Thanks, Harry, we owe you one."

"Glad to help. Good luck."

Yeah, Luke thought as he reached his car. *I need all the good luck I can get.*

Dutton, Monday, February 5, 1:00 p.m.

Susannah sat in her father's chair, frustrated. "I know he kept records, Talia, but they're not anywhere I've looked.

I'm going about this wrong. If he had records, he wouldn't store them where they could be easily found." She closed her eyes. "I remember hiding at the top of the stairs when I was little, knowing people were meeting with my father, in this office. Even then I knew there was something wrong going on."

"You were a child," Talia said softly. "You couldn't have done anything."

"I know that, just like I know I'm not responsible for Darcy's death. But knowing is different from *knowing*." Susannah kept her eyes closed. "I'd sit at the top of the stairs and listen, then they'd leave and my father— Arthur—would lock the front door."

"What did your father do after he locked the door?"

"He'd go back into his office. Once I got brave and crept down the stairs to listen. There was a rustle, then a pop." She looked over the room, her gaze falling on the thick Persian rug that had covered the carpet for as long as she could remember. She knew there was a floor safe in her parents' bedroom, but that floor was hardwood and this one was carpeted. Still . . . She went to the Persian and pulled back the edge.

"It didn't rustle," Talia said, still standing in the doorway. "Pull it harder."

Susannah did, making a whipping noise as the Persian rolled on itself. "That's the sound." She dropped to her knees and examined the carpet. "God, he was a wily piece of work. This carpet below is pieced." Carefully she pulled it up. "Another floor safe."

"Can you open it?" Talia asked.

"Probably, if I think hard enough. Arthur used to use birthdays of relatives for his combinations. He thought he was being clever and we never knew." She tried her mother's birthday, then Simon's, then any others she could remember. Grandmothers, grandfathers, aunts and uncles. None worked.

"Maybe he picked something different for this safe," Talia said. "Not a birthday."

"Maybe, but he was a creature of habit. I guess I got one thing from him honestly." Then she knew. "Honestly," she murmured again, then twisted the dial and popped the door. "Daniel's birthday. Daniel will get a kick out of that." *The judge used the birthday of the one man he couldn't corrupt, but who tortured himself over the sins of his father.*

Arthur had thought Daniel weak. *He thought the same about me.* The judge was mistaken, she thought as she drew out several bound ledgers and journals. *Bingo.*

Talia came to sit on the floor beside her. "He must have thirty years of records in here. Why not use a safe-deposit box?"

"He didn't trust banks. Marcy should be in this one." Flipping pages, she found the entry. "My God. He wanted seventy-five thousand dollars from the Lintons. No wonder they couldn't come up with the money."

"So what happened with Borenson?" Talia asked.

"Hell." She ran her finger down the page. "He says that the girl's 'handler' stepped in and threatened Borenson and he 'folded like a house of cards.' "

"Handler?" Talia asked. "So she really was soliciting?"

"Sounds like it." Susannah read on. "Marcy was soliciting, but for more than sex. It says here that she'd pick rich men who liked young girls, seduce them, then threaten to tell their wives if they didn't pay her. She'd give the money to her handler and he'd pay her a cut." She met Talia's eyes. "Bobby did that for years, too, in

Atlanta. Chloe told Garth Davis that she'd found the transaction records."

"Another connection," Talia murmured. "Does your father say who the handler is?"

Susannah read it, then read it again, then stared at the page, stunned. "He says Marcy's handler was Charles Grant. That . . . that doesn't make sense."

"It fits. Chase called me when we were driving from the Lintons'. Luke found one of Mansfield's pictures from the bunker—a man with a walking stick, like Charles Grant's."

Susannah's eyes narrowed. "Why didn't you tell me?"

"Because you were so pale I thought you'd pass out, and you got paler as we got closer to this place. I figured I'd let you deal with one stress at a time."

"You're right, I guess. But *Charles Grant*?" She was still numb. "He was Daniel's favorite teacher. He was everybody's favorite teacher."

"He also may be a killer. What else does the journal say, Susannah?"

Susannah kept reading, past stunned. *"Little prick, trying to squeeze me. He might scare Carol with all his Asian voo-doo, but all his talk of occult and* thíchs *doesn't scare me. Grant's a fucking opportunist. He'll use whatever it takes to get what he wants. He thought he could use Simon to get to me, but I took care of Simon's sins. He thought he'd use Susannah to get to me. Like that was ever going to work. She's . . ."* Susannah faltered. *"She's nothing to me."*

"I'm sorry, honey," Talia whispered. "You can stop now."

"No. I need to know. *But today . . . this . . . He's turned Borenson against me and this will not stand. The next time I make a demand, the defendants will just whine to Borenson and he'll let them off with a damn slap on the wrist. Borenson's weak. I told him to just get rid of that upstart Legal-Aid idiot Alderman, but did he listen? Hell no. Before it was his own business when Alderman threatened him. Now, he's cutting into mine. Dammit, this place costs money to keep. The bills are staggering. They will not cut off my income."*

Dread was pooling. "He did it for money. For this house." *And he'd known.* "He knew what happened to me." With trembling hands she flipped pages until she got to the January when she'd woken up in a hidey-hole, bruised, bleeding, forever changed.

"Apparently, Charles Grant had been trying to blackmail my father out of the money he'd blackmailed from the defendants in his courtroom." Her lips curved bitterly. "It's ironic in a totally twisted way," she murmured, then went still, her dread confirmed.

"That prick Grant came by tonight with pictures of Simon fucking Susannah. I was supposed to be ashamed. Incest. I told Grant to go to hell and take his pictures with him, that Susannah got what she deserved. Plus, she'd never go to the cops, the girl doesn't have the guts. So again I won. Charles left with his tail between his legs, threatening me, like always. 'You'll regret this. Simon will do something so terrible even you won't be able to get him off.' Yeah, right. And he's gonna get me and my little dog, too. I told him he could have Susannah. I have no use for her. He said, 'Thank you.'"

Susannah closed her eyes. Tears splashed on her hands and she hastily wiped them away. "I'm going to damage the evidence."

Talia pressed a tissue into her hand, then took a

tissue for herself. "I'm so sorry, Susannah," she whispered unsteadily.

Abruptly Susannah laughed, bitterly. "This is evidence against nobody. We can't prove that Charles Grant did anything more than *know* about my . . . assault."

"He instigated it," Talia said fiercely. "I know it."

Susannah shook her head, objectively. "But it's not proof."

The two of them sat quietly for a long moment, then Talia looked over at her. "It sounds like your father and Mr. Grant were in an all-out war, with Judge Borenson a pawn they traded. But then, nothing happened. No fireworks, no accusations. Borenson retires to the hills, Grant goes on teaching, your father goes on judging and they both go on extorting. No murdering rampages." Talia paused. "Not until Simon rose again."

Susannah let the words sink in and then it was clear. "The three of them had some kind of a truce." Her hands no longer trembled as she flipped pages. She knew what she'd find. She flipped past Alicia Tremaine's murder and Gary Fulmore's trial in Borenson's kangaroo court. "My mother pushed Frank Loomis to manipulate evidence, but Grant's hand is in this as well. Toby Granville was Charles Grant's protégé. If the truth came out about Alicia's assault, Toby would have been charged, imprisoned."

"So Grant pushed Borenson to look the other way, to ignore sham evidence."

"I think so. Then Marcy Linton gets arrested and the battle comes to a head. Maybe my father knows Mr. Grant's involved with Marcy or maybe it's just really bad karma, but Grant uses what he's got on Borenson to get Marcy a new trial and reduced sentence."

"Your daddy wasn't happy. So how did they achieve this truce?"

Susannah turned to a year after Alicia Tremaine's murder, to the day Simon "died." "The day Simon disappeared, I heard him and my father arguing. My father had found the pictures, the ones Daniel ended up using to track down the victims of Simon's rape club. My father told Simon either he'd turn him in or Simon had to disappear. A few days later we heard Simon was dead. He'd run to Mexico and had a car accident."

"But Simon wasn't dead."

"No. My father made it look like he was because he knew my mother would never stop looking for him unless she believed he was dead. My father went away and came back with a coffin he said held Simon's remains. There'd been a Mexican autopsy and the body inside was burned beyond recognition. But they still needed a death certificate, signed by an ME."

"I read that the body inside the coffin was under six feet tall and Simon was six-six."

"No ME would have mistaken that body for Simon's, even with the charred skin." She held out the book for Talia to see. "Arthur recorded receipt of one death certificate, signed by the ME, who was also the town doctor."

"The ME was complicit."

"Had to have been. The date Arthur says he received the death certificate was the day after Simon disappeared. The day *before* we got word Simon had died in Mexico." Susannah was unsurprised and stunned all at once. "They all knew Simon was alive."

"So after he sells the death certificate, Borenson retires and goes into seclusion."

"My father had neutralized the threat and Mr. Grant

had to back down, again. A few months later I went to New York, to college."

"But Charles Grant wouldn't let you go," Talia murmured. "You were his."

"I can only guess he'd influenced Marcy over the years until she sought me out. I guess she would have hated me because of what my father did to her and her family."

Talia's sigh was heavy and sad. "Now we have our connection. I'll call Chase and give him the update. Gather up the journals and I'll help you carry them out to the car."

Talia rose and walked to the foyer to make her call, but Susannah simply sat motionless, staring at the journals. So much pain, so much misery. All for greed, for mastery. It was a damn game to them. *And I was their pawn.*

Wearily she brought the journals and ledgers up from the deep floor safe, then stared. Beneath the ledgers were bundles of cash. Lots of cash. "Talia? Come h . . ."

The word trailed off as Susannah looked over her shoulder and her heart stuttered to a stop. Talia wasn't standing in the doorway. Bobby was. She wore a malevolent grin and in her left hand she held a gun with a silencer. "Welcome home, little sister."

Chapter Twenty-four

Charles Grant sat in a folding chair at Janet Bowie's graveside service, his hands somberly folded atop his walking stick. At the other funerals he'd had ringside seats, but today he and the two old men from the barbershop bench had been relegated to the back. Which was better, actually. From here he could see everyone. From here, he could surreptitiously check his cell phone when it buzzed in his pocket.

It was a text message. From Paul, he hoped, saying Daniel Vartanian and Alex Fallon were ensconced in the interrogation room in his basement. But disappointment speared. It was the throwaway cell he'd given Bobby last night. Disappointment abruptly became anticipation. The text read *SHOWTIME.*

Bobby had Susannah. *I have to get out there*. He feigned a wince, clenching his walking stick. "My sciatica," he murmured to Dr. Fink, the dentist, on his right. He rose stiffly, grimacing in affected pain. "I need to move." He did so, murmuring apologies as he moved through the crowd. It was finally time to see Susannah die.

But then he'd have to deal with Bobby. He'd lost control of her, so he'd have to kill her. He rubbed the head of his walking stick. *Just like I killed my Darcy six years ago.*

Dutton, Monday, February 5, 1:30 p.m.

"Goddammit," Luke snapped. Bobby was not hiding in Charles Grant's house.

Pete looked around Grant's living room. "Ready to start tearing out the walls?"

"Not quite. At least Grant's still at the cemetery." Germanio had confirmed that ten minutes before. "He still doesn't know we're here or that we're on to him."

They'd approached in stealth, difficult when the media had converged on Dutton for Janet Bowie's funeral. He and Chase had debated having Dutton's new sheriff secure Grant's house in the event Bobby had been hiding, but they couldn't be certain there weren't more dirty deputies who'd alert Bobby or Grant. Instead, Luke once again called on Arcadia's Sheriff Corchran, who'd put himself and a trusted deputy on silent patrol.

Corchran had also told Luke's team how to approach without getting snarled in the funeral traffic. Luke's hopes had been high entering Grant's modest frame house off Main Street. Now . . . he could only hope the house itself would hold an answer.

His team waited impatiently. "The warrant covers Bobby's whereabouts and the crimes in the bunker." It had been the best Chloe had been able to do. "Keep looking."

The team scattered, Pete going upstairs, Nancy down. Luke tackled the living room, but there was nothing to indicate this man was anything other than what he purported himself to be—a retired high school English teacher.

Luke stared at one wall. And a community theater director. The wall held playbills from productions Grant had directed, including a school production of *Snow White* in which he'd cast Bobby in the lead. Luke thought of little

Kate Davis being "thoughtlessly" cast as a squirrel, earning the nickname "Rocky." How thoughtless had it been? Garth had told them that Bobby had "made Kate beautiful." Destroying Kate's self-esteem only to build her back up was a great way to guarantee loyalty.

Grant's bookshelves sagged under the weight of hundreds of books, and Luke began checking each one. Homer, Plutarch, Dante . . . He sighed. Nothing but a lot of words.

"Luke!" Nancy called from the basement, urgency in her voice. "Come and see."

Luke took the stairs two at a time. "Is it Bobby?"

Nancy stood by a steel-reinforced door set in a wall of concrete. "No, it's a bunker, just like the one we found in Mansfield's basement," she said. "Mansfield used his to store his guns, ammo, and kiddie porn. Charles Grant . . . well, look for yourself." She opened the door and the smell was intolerable. The sight was worse.

It was a torture chamber, with shackles in the walls and shelves of carefully sorted knives. In the middle of the room was a raised slab, making Luke think of Frankenstein's lab. On the bed was a man. Or he'd been one, before he'd been carved into ribbons.

"Borenson's dead." Luke crossed the threshold and stared. In the corner were an easy chair and a lamp on a doily-covered table. "My God. Grant sat there and watched."

Nancy pointed to a CD player on the small table. "While he listened to Mozart."

Luke studied Borenson's body. "What did Borenson have or know that Charles Grant wanted? He was tortured over a period of time. Some of these cuts look days old." He backed out of the room. "Close the door so we can breathe. Good work, Nancy."

"Thanks. This bunker was hidden." She shut the heavy steel door, then pulled a second pocket door from the wall. "It looks like a real wall when it's pulled all the way across. Mansfield had his sliding wall half open, so we found his bunker fast. When I saw this wall I knew it was the same. There might be other hidden rooms in this house."

"Bobby could still be here, hiding. Keep looking." Luke climbed the stairs, but before he had a chance to dial Chase, his phone began buzzing. It was Chase, and from the road noise, he was in his car. "It doesn't look like Bobby's here," Luke said, "but Borenson's body is. He's been tortured. Germanio can arrest Charles Grant."

"Contact Germanio, have him make the arrest. Did you find *anything* on Bobby?"

"No, but we're still looking." Luke heard a tenseness in Chase's voice that had his pulse scrambling. "Is Susannah all right?" The thought of her facing that house again made him sick. But Talia believed they'd found a connection to Darcy, so Chase had okayed it. Luke didn't think he could have, so it was a good thing Chase was in charge.

"She's fine," Chase said. "It's that cop Agent Grimes saw in Charlotte, Paul Houston. We got his photo. Luke, it's the guy Susannah described to the sketch artist."

Luke's jaw dropped. "*What?* An Atlanta cop raped Susannah in New York?"

"That's what it looks like. But there's more. This morning Paul Houston was assigned to guard Daniel's house when he got home from the hospital. Houston specifically requested it."

Luke's blood ran cold. "Oh my God."

"Daniel's fine. I called him as soon as I knew. Apparently there was a problem with his dog making a mess in his house. Your mother called one of your cousins."

Luke exhaled in relief. "Nick. He's got a carpet-cleaning business. Is *he* all right?"

"He's fine. He hadn't gotten there yet, so Daniel and Alex went to stay with your mother. Your mother's fine, too. Everybody's fine, except me. I'm working with APD's IA, but I want this guy watched *now,* so I drove out to Daniel's. Five minutes ago Houston got a call on his cell phone and left. I'm following. He's headed west, driving very fast."

"Toward us."

"Maybe. I've pulled together a tag-team pursuit, so he won't detect the tail. I'm hoping he's going to meet Bobby. Call Susannah, make sure she knows about him. Finish your search and stay within the limits of the warrant. I don't want Charles Grant slipping off our hook. I'll call you when I know where Paul Houston is going."

Dutton, Monday, February 5, 1:30 p.m.

Bobby couldn't stop grinning. Susannah was exactly where she wanted her, kneeling. That Susannah was kneeling next to piles of cash was the sugar on top.

"Where is Agent Scott?" Susannah asked stonily.

Bobby had to hand it to her. After the initial shock, Susannah didn't show a flicker of fear. "She's not dead, if that's what you're asking. I didn't even shoot her. Yet."

Susannah's eyes narrowed. *Gray eyes*, Bobby thought, *not blue like our father's. Or like Daniel's or Simon's and mine.*

"How much money is in the safe?"

Susannah shrugged coolly. "Couple of thousand. Maybe more. Take it and go."

Bobby smiled. "I will. But first you're going to open every safe in this house."

Susannah's chin lifted. "Open them your goddamn self."

Bobby's foot shot out, kicking Susannah under the chin. She landed on her back, Bobby's foot on her throat. "I said," Bobby snarled, "you'll do it." Bobby applied pressure to her throat, aiming her gun at Susannah's head. "Now get up. The next time you give me lip, I put a bullet in Agent Scott."

Bobby grabbed a fistful of Susannah's hair and yanked her to her feet. To her credit, Susannah didn't whimper. The little woman had proven to be tougher than she looked and not to be underestimated. Bobby shoved her out of the study, past Talia Scott, who was only half conscious after being tasered, gagged, handcuffed, and hog-tied.

Halfway up the stairs, Bobby heard a faint ringing and Susannah stopped short. "That's my cell. It's probably Agent Papadopoulos. If I don't answer it, he'll worry."

Bobby considered it. Once she'd killed Susannah, she'd have to kill Papadopoulos sooner or later. He was the kind of man who wouldn't rest until she, Bobby, was punished, especially if Susannah was dead. Which she soon would be.

However, Bobby preferred to deal with Papadopoulos at a time and place of her own choosing. Dealing with two small women was one thing. Papadopoulos was a big man and would likely come with a posse of his own. "Does your cell phone have a speaker?"

"Yes."

"Then answer it." Bobby knelt next to Agent Scott and put the gun to her head. "Be very careful what you say, little sister, or her blood will be on your hands."

Bobby had the satisfaction of watching Susannah grow pale.

"It's stopped ringing," she said.

"Then call him back. Tell him you found the records you were looking for. Tell him that you and Agent Scott are starting back to Atlanta. And be convincing."

Susannah reached for her purse.

"Uh-uh-uh," Bobby scolded. "I remember your purse from yesterday."

"I'm not armed," she said quietly. "Not anymore."

"Well, I'm not taking any chances. Bring the purse here and dump it on the floor in front of me. Do it now." Susannah obeyed and Bobby looked through her things. No gun. "Fine. Put out your hands."

Susannah glanced at Agent Scott, then held out her hands. Bobby found the sound of snapping cuffs satisfying. "Now call your man. Use the speaker."

Susannah obeyed once more. "Luke, it's me. Sorry, I wasn't close to my phone."

There was a sigh of relief. "I was getting nervous. Where are you?"

"At Mama and Daddy's, but not for much longer. Talia and I found what we were looking for, so we're just about to head back to Atlanta."

"You found the records, then? A connection back to Darcy Williams?"

"We sure did. I'll see you back at the office."

"Susannah, wait. Am . . . am I on the speaker phone?"

"Yeah, I'm sorry. My arms are pretty full, so I hit the hands-free button."

"Where is Talia?"

"Out at the car," she improvised, and Bobby nodded approval. "She took a load of books we found in Daddy's office. Ledgers and diaries."

"Then why are your hands full if Talia's got all the books?"

Susannah faltered. "I . . . I've got a box," she said, injecting a note of brightness into her voice, "filled with some of Mama's things that I want to keep." She hesitated. "I love you, Lukamou," she said quietly. "I'll see you later." She hung up, her hands trembling.

"How sweet," Bobby said with a sneer. With her strong arm she dragged Agent Scott to a crawlspace beneath the stairs and locked her in, then on second thought, opened the door and shot her in the leg. Scott's cry was muted by the tape on her mouth. Bobby cast an amused glance at Susannah, who looked as horrified as she'd hoped. "Leigh Smithson gave the rundown on the GBI team. She said Talia Scott was extremely formidable and not to be underestimated. A veritable Houdini at escaping."

"You shot her," Susannah said furiously. "She was no threat to you."

"Like I said, I'm not taking any chances. A shot in the leg will slow her down if she decides to run. Now get up those stairs and start remembering the birthdays of all the Vartanian relatives I never got to meet. We have four more safes to open."

"Six," Susannah said dully. "There are six."

Luke hung up, barely breathing, trying vainly to remain calm. "No. Pete. Pete."

Pete came running, a bound notebook in his big hands. "Look what I found behind Grant's bedroom closet. The wall had a sliding panel, just like in the movies. There have to be a hundred bound volumes just like this one. What's wrong?"

"Susannah." He swallowed hard. "I think Bobby is there with her."

Pete grasped Luke's shoulder. "Breathe. What exactly did she say?"

"That she and Talia were at her 'Mama and Daddy's' and they had found all 'Daddy's' records and were on their way back, but she was on her speaker phone because her hands were full of things she was taking away to remember her mama."

Pete swallowed. "Shit."

And then she said she loved me, like she'd never get the chance to say it again. "I was going to tell her about Paul Houston, but I didn't know who was listening."

"Smart."

Luke nodded. "I'm going out to the Vartanians'."

"Not smart," Pete said, then sighed. "So I'll go with you."

Luke was already running. "Call Germanio, tell him to arrest Charles Grant."

Pete closed his car door as Luke peeled way, tires screeching. "What's the charge?"

"Start with murder of Judge Borenson."

"We can add extortion," Pete said, tapping the notebook he'd brought from Grant's house. "Charles has the dope on every rich man and woman in this town and they were all paying him through the nose to keep their nasty secrets."

"I'm not surprised, but I don't think we can use that yet. That notebook isn't covered by the warrant. Borenson's murder is enough for now," Luke added as Pete dialed.

"Hank, it's Pete. Pick up Charles Grant and bring him—" Pete frowned. "What the *fuck* do you mean you lost him?"

Luke grabbed Pete's phone, his foot punching the accelerator. "*Where. Is. He?*"

"He left the cemetery," Germanio said, "but headed out of town."

"And you didn't goddamn *call* me? Fuck."

"I had him in my sights, but he pulled off to a side road and I had to pass him so I didn't give myself away. When I doubled back . . . he was gone. I'm sorry."

"You're sorry? You're goddamn *sorry*?" *Breathe*. "Where are you now?"

"About five miles from the cemetery, heading back toward town."

"No, turn around and head for the Vartanians' house. It's another few miles, an old antebellum mansion. Talia's car should be parked out front. Approach silently and wait for me. Bobby's inside with Susannah and Talia.".

"All right."

"Germanio, listen to me. You *wait* for me, okay?" Luke handed Pete his phone. "Damn cowboy. Now Grant knows we know."

"He's not the only cowboy," Pete muttered.

Luke shot him a glare. "What if Ellie were being held captive by a murderer?"

Ellie was Pete's wife, a tiny, little woman. Pete treated her like spun glass. "Why do you think I'm here?" he asked quietly. "Now focus on driving. I'll call Chase."

Dutton, Monday, February 5, 1:35 p.m.

Charles was pissed. He'd had a tail, some clumsy GBI guy who'd been child's play to lose. But that meant he'd been discovered. They knew. Dammit.

He'd known deep down that it was only a matter of time. He'd tried to stick his finger in the dike when he'd helped Daniel Vartanian catch Mack O'Brien. Mack had been calling lots of unwanted attention to Toby Granville and the other boys.

But all good things must come to an end. He could leave behind no loose ends. Bobby was a loose end. So was his house. He wasn't arrogant enough to believe that once the GBI started looking they wouldn't find his records. Everything truly valuable he carried with him in his ivory box, but the house had to go. He'd tell Paul to burn the sucker down. He dialed Paul's cell. "I need you in Dutton," he said.

"Well that's good," Paul said, "because that's just where I'm headed. I've been trying to call you for an hour."

"I *told* you I couldn't take calls at the cemetery," Charles said sternly. "I *told* you to text me. Even Bobby got that part right."

"I can't text and drive at the same time," Paul said, clearly annoyed at the jab. "I got a call from your alarm system. Somebody's in your house."

Charles drew a breath. "What?"

"You heard me. I have the alarm system set to call me and not the security company. Somebody entered your house through the back door at 1:17."

"I just lost a GBI tail," Charles said quietly. "They must be searching my house. It's too late to burn it down. They'll read my books, they'll know what I've done."

"So where are you going?" Paul asked, a thread of panic in his voice.

"Mexico, then back to Southeast Asia. But first, I'm going to the Vartanians'. Bobby is there. I need to be sure neither she nor Susannah survives to tell anyone about you. After I'm done, I'll wait behind the house. You can pick me up and we can drive south. Once I'm in Mexico, you can go back to your life, or you can come with me."

"I'll come with you," Paul said. Of course, Charles had known he would.

Dutton, Monday, February 5, 1:35 p.m.

Pete closed his phone. "Backup's coming. Now you need to know what's in this notebook. You'll be angry. Just keep your cool, all right?"

"All right," Luke said carefully. "You said Grant was extorting rich people. Who?"

"Lots of people, but you really want the tale of two judges."

"Borenson and Vartanian," Luke said grimly.

"Yep. I found at least fifty of these notebooks in the hidden shelf behind Grant's closet. They're alphabetized. He has three V volumes, one for Simon and Arthur, another for Daniel and his mother. Susannah gets her own, and it's nearly full. Listen."

Luke listened, his knuckles gone bone white as he clenched the wheel. Black bile churned within him, fury so intense he shook with it. It was unbelievable. Unforgivable. Inhuman. Susannah's life had been ruined because both Charles Grant and Arthur Vartanian wanted control of a dickwater town that didn't mean shit. Susannah had been a pawn in a high-stakes game she'd never understood. "My God," Luke whispered.

"Can we use the books?" Pete asked. "They don't mention the bunker, but . . ."

"We have to ask Chloe," Luke said. Inside he burned. Each breath physically hurt. "Of course, should Charles Grant die in the meantime, it becomes a moot point."

Pete was quiet for a moment, considering. "So it does. I've got your back."

Luke swallowed hard, moved. "Someday I'll find a way to make it up to you."

Pete huffed a mirthless chuckle. "Not in this lifetime, pal. Drive faster."

Dutton, Monday, February 5, 1:45 p.m.

"None of the Vartanian birthdays I remember are opening this safe," Susannah said, flinching when Bobby jabbed the butt of the gun into the back of her head.

"Shut up. Just keep dialing, little sister."

Susannah's jaw clenched. She'd managed to unlock three of the six upstairs safes. One was empty, one held estate documents, and the third had held Carol Vartanian's best paste diamonds. Bobby had thought they were real and had chortled over her good fortune. Susannah was not about to disillusion her.

Bobby was storing her loot in Grandmother Vartanian's tall silver teapot, which seemed critically important. Again, Susannah was not of a mind to try to understand.

However, Susannah was of a mind to try to stall for time as she knelt on the floor of her parents' bedroom trying unsuccessfully to open another safe. "I'm not your sister," she said, gritting her teeth. "And I'm telling you this safe is empty. Daniel emptied it three weeks ago when he went looking for my parents."

"Then Daniel must have known the combination, which means you should. You seem to have the birthdays all memorized." Bobby smacked her head with the gun butt again. "And I *am* your sister, whether you want to admit it or not."

Susannah sat back on her haunches, blinking against the pain in her head. *Where are you, Luke?* She knew he'd understood her message. Never in her life had she

called Arthur "Daddy," and the idea of taking anything
to remember her mother made her sick to her stomach.
She thought of Talia, bleeding beneath the stairs, and
prayed Luke would get here before Talia bled to death or
Bobby truly did blow their heads off.

So stall. Give him time. "You are not my sister. You are
not even my half-sister. We are not related." And her head
flew to one side when Bobby slapped her, hard.

"Is it so damn hard to admit?" Bobby asked, her eyes
flashing with anger.

Susannah hoped giving Bobby the upper limbs on the
Vartanian family tree might diffuse her anger. She worked
her jaw side to side, her eyes stinging. "Yes, because it's
not true. Your father is Arthur Vartanian, but my mother
did the same thing your mother did. She slept around.
Arthur Vartanian was not my father."

Bobby blinked at her. "You're lying."

"I'm not. I had a paternity test done. Frank Loomis was
my father."

Bobby looked unsure, then threw back her head and
laughed. "Sonofabitch. All this time, sweet Suzie Vartanian has been a bastard, too." She then sobered meanly.
"Dial the safe, Suzie, or I go downstairs and blow your
friend's head off her shoulders."

Susannah swallowed. "I don't know the combination to
this one. I'm not lying."

Bobby frowned. "Then get up."

Susannah obeyed, relieved, then went rigid at the sound
of a car pulling up outside. *Luke. Please be Luke.* Bobby
heard it, too, and, eyes narrowed, crept to the window.

"Fuck," she muttered. "We have company. Who is
he?"

Susannah stayed where she was, then cried out when

Bobby yanked her hair, pulling her to the window. Hank Germanio was carefully approaching the house, his weapon drawn. "I don't know," she lied smoothly. "I've never seen him before."

"Oh, you're good," Bobby said softly. "Butter wouldn't melt in your mouth. Luckily Leigh Smithson told me about him, too. That's Hank Germanio. He's the impetuous type, a real one-man show. Go." She pushed her to the top of the stairs. "Call for help."

"No," Susannah said. "I won't lure another person in here. You can kill me first."

"Oh, I will. After you finish opening all the safes. For now, I'll pick the GBI guys off one at a time." Bobby dragged her so that she stood in front of her on the top step, put her gun to Susannah's temple, then screamed at the top of her lungs, "Help! She's got a gun. Oh my God, she's got a gun and she's going to kill Susannah!"

Through the side windows along the front door Susannah could see Germanio. He looked up, saw her standing on the stairs. Germanio hesitated.

Susannah screamed, "No! Don't come in. It's a trap."

But it was too late. Germanio crashed through the front door and calmly, Bobby fired and Germanio's head . . . came apart. He was dead before his body hit the floor.

Horror and shock exploded into rage. "Fuck you," Susannah screamed. "Damn you to hell." She threw her handcuffed hands to the right and yanked Bobby's wounded arm as hard as she could. Bobby howled in furious pain and Susannah kept yanking, throwing Bobby off-center. When Bobby stumbled, Susannah turned, throwing her weight into the bigger woman and sending them both down the staircase.

They grappled on the stairs, Bobby grabbing at Susannah's hair, dragging her down. Bobby's hair was too short. There was nothing to hang on to, so Susannah kicked and scrambled back up the stairs. Bobby grabbed her leg, yanking her down.

Where was the gun? Did Bobby still have it? *No. If she did, she would have shot me by now.* Susannah kicked with her other leg, twisting to look over her shoulder, trying for a glimpse of the gun. She saw it at the same moment Bobby did, on the bottom stair. *There's no way. I can't get it before she does. She'll kill me now.*

Bobby let go, crawling backward to where the gun lay, and Susannah scrambled up, her breath backing up in her lungs. *Get away, get away.*

Dutton, Monday, February 5, 1:50 p.m.

They were almost there. Luke pushed the anger aside, focusing on Susannah and Talia in Bobby's hands. He'd deal with Bobby, then Charles Grant was a dead man, wherever the hell he was. Charles hadn't gone home, so he was out there somewhere.

Luke bore down on the accelerator, jumping when his cell buzzed. "Papadopoulos."

"Luke, it's Chase. Where are you?"

"About two minutes from the Vartanians' house. Where is Paul Houston?"

"He was headed toward Dutton, but took a detour."

Luke recognized the route. "That's how Corchran told us to come in so we could avoid the traffic, but the opposite way. He's coming here. Why, to help Bobby?"

"Not Bobby. Charles. Put me on speaker so Pete gets

this, too. Al Landers went to the prison to meet with Michael Ellis. Showed him Susannah's sketch and Ellis broke. Paul Houston is *Ellis's son*. Houston and Charles Grant killed Darcy, not Michael Ellis."

Luke frowned. "His son? Ellis took the fall to save his son? Why?"

"And why would Houston set up his father?" Pete added.

"Payback. Ellis was in Vietnam, in a POW camp, and so was Charles Grant."

Luke shook his head. "No, I checked. Charles Grant had no military record."

"Because he was Ray Kraemer, then. Kraemer was an army sniper, captured in '67, met Ellis, and the two ended up escaping together. Ellis was desperate to get home. His girlfriend had his son, but gave him up for adoption. That was Paul. Ellis and Kraemer were down to the last of their food. Ellis shot Kraemer, stole the food, and left him in the jungle to die."

"Sonofabitch," Luke murmured. "Obviously Kraemer didn't die. What happened?"

"Ellis said Kraemer resurfaced eighteen years later in Dutton, calling himself Charles Grant. He chose Dutton because that's where the mother of Ellis's child had moved after giving birth. Paul's mother is Angie Delacroix. She's one of Grant's people now."

Luke blew out a stunned breath. "My God." His mind spun, thinking about all the things she'd told them. "But she told us the truth. DNA showed Loomis is Susannah's father and the tip on Bobby's birth mother panned out. Why would she try to help us find Bobby? Bobby worked with Charles, too."

"That I don't know yet. I had her picked up, but she

isn't talking. Ellis talked a lot, though, when Al Landers told him we knew about Paul being a cop. He said somehow Kraemer located Paul when he was eight. He became his tutor through an after-school volunteer program, but brainwashed Paul against his birth parents and his adopted parents. Paul ran away when he was ten, went to live with Charles. Looks like Charles has been molding Paul all his life. Ellis said Paul will be loyal to Charles to the death."

"So why did Ellis confess to Darcy's murder?" Pete asked.

"To protect Angie and Paul. Charles threatened to have Paul kill Angie if he didn't."

"That's Charles's revenge," Luke said, "owning Ellis's son, using him against him, while Ellis sits in Sing-Sing. He pled guilty to killing Darcy, but he's really paying for what he did to Charles Grant forty years ago."

"Exactly," Chase said. "I'm about twenty minutes out, still following Houston. He's still using his lights to bypass traffic, so he doesn't know we know about him yet. I diverted most of our agents from the cemetery out your way. Wait for them."

Luke came around the bend, his focus immediately reverting to Susannah. *Let her be alive. Don't let me be too late.* "We're coming up on the Vartanians'." Three Arcadia cruisers and an ambulance were slowly approaching from the other direction and Luke sent mental thanks to Sheriff Corchran. "We have backup. We're going in."

Chase blew out a breath. "Be careful. Good luck."

"Thanks." Luke was slowing to instruct the backup when he heard the shot. "That came from the house." *Susannah.* He jammed the gas and flew into the driveway screeching to a stop next to Germanio's car, his heart in his throat. He started running, Pete right behind him.

Chapter Twenty-five

Get away. Frantically Susannah scrambled up the stairs as Bobby scrabbled for the gun. The carpet was slick and her cuffed hands couldn't hang on. A hand clamped on to her ankle and the sound of Bobby's pleased laughter chilled her blood.

"Got it," Bobby crowed. "You're dead, Vartanian."

A shot split the air and Susannah froze, waiting for the pain. But there was none.

She twisted around, and for a second only blinked, stunned at what she saw. Bobby lay on the stairs, her chin propped on one of the stairs so that she stared up at Susannah, blue eyes wide, a surprised look on her face. A blood stain was spreading on the back of her shirt. Frozen, Susannah watched Bobby lift her gun once again. A second shot rang out and Bobby's body jolted, then slumped, her blue eyes now blank.

Nearly hyperventilating, her gaze locked with Bobby's dead stare, Susannah crawled up a few more steps before looking up. Luke stood in the doorway, pale, breathing hard, the gun he clutched hanging limply at his side. Behind him Pete knelt next to Hank's body. Stiffly, mechanically, Luke walked over to the stairs, reached over Bobby, and took the gun from her hand. He checked her pulse, then looked up to meet Susannah's eyes, his dark and seething with fear and fury. "She's dead."

Relief stripped the air from her lungs, rendered her boneless, and Susannah slumped against the stairs, shaking uncontrollably. Then Luke was lifting her up, wrapping his arms around her, his hold desperate, his whisper fierce. "Did she hurt you?"

"I don't know." She burrowed into him, needing him, so scared, shaken. "I don't think so." The wave of terror ebbed enough so that she could draw a breath. She pulled back to see his face. "Hank is dead. She killed him. I saw him die."

"I know. I heard the shot. I thought it was you. I thought you were dead." Luke's dark eyes flashed, fury and grief combined. "Hank was supposed to wait for me."

"No, no. Bobby lured him in. I tried to warn him but it was too late. He was trying to save my life and now he's dead." She looked at Pete, who still knelt next to Germanio, his expression stricken. "Bobby shot Talia. She's under the stairs."

Pete was heaving his shoulder into the door in the staircase when two uniformed police cautiously approached the open front door.

"Agent Papadopoulos?" one asked, and Luke gently let Susannah go, lowering her to sit on the stair. Beneath them, wood splintered as Pete broke the door free.

"She's alive," Pete said, breathless from the effort. "Shit, Talia, you're a mess."

Pete leaned into the crawlspace while Luke unlocked Susannah's handcuffs and rubbed her wrists gently. He let out a slow breath before turning to the officers. "We're clear," Luke said, his voice steady again. "We'll call the crime lab and the ME. Can you call that ambulance up to the house? We need to get Agent Scott to a hospital."

"No!" Talia's refusal burst from inside the closet. Susannah heard angry whispers, then Pete crawled out holding the strip of duct tape that had covered Talia's mouth.

"We're okay here," he said to the officers. "Thank you." When the officers were gone, he pulled Talia from the crawlspace. Her hands and feet were still cuffed. She was still hog-tied. Her slacks were covered in blood, her eyes filled with mortified rage.

"Just get the damn cuffs off," she gritted. "Please."

Pete unlocked the cuffs and rolled her to her back. "The medics are coming."

"No." Talia pushed herself up to a sitting position. "Bad enough she got me. I'll walk out on my own two feet." Luke and Pete each took one of her arms and lifted her. She grimaced, her cheeks red. "This is humiliating," she muttered.

"What happened?" Luke asked carefully.

Talia's glare was defiant. "Bitch got the drop on me. Tasered me."

"How did she get the drop on you?" Pete asked.

Talia lifted her chin, daring them to push her further. "I had something in my eye."

Tears, Susannah thought, remembering the hitch in Talia's voice as she'd offered comfort. "Now the bitch is dead," Susannah murmured. "So is Germanio."

Talia's glare faded abruptly. "I heard. I also heard you on the phone with Luke. That was fast thinking. Luke, get Arthur's journals out of the study. They explain everything. Pete, get me out of here, please, and make me look like I'm walking on my own."

Pete helped her out, hesitating before he lifted her over Germanio's body. "Damn it, Hank," he murmured. "I'll update Chase, and get a location on the others."

"What others?" Susannah asked. "Does he mean Charles Grant? I know about him. It's all in Arthur's journals. You didn't find him?"

"Not yet. Can you walk?" Luke asked Susannah.

"Yeah." Hanging on to the banister, Susannah eased her way past Bobby's body, resisting the urge to kick her. Luke helped her down the final step, then dragged her close again, arms hard around her. "I'm okay," she whispered.

"I know." A shudder shook him. "I just keep seeing her pointing a gun at you, again and again. Susannah, we found some things you need to read."

"Later," she said wearily. "I've read enough for one day."

"I'll take you back to my place. You can have some peace and quiet."

"I don't want quiet." She looked over at Germanio's body, then quickly looked away. "I don't want to think. I want . . . I need supergluing."

He frowned, puzzled. "What?"

She looked up at him. "Can you take me to your mother's house, please?"

This made him smile, although his eyes remained worried. "That I can do. Stay here. I'll get Arthur's journals, then I'm getting you out of here." He walked down the hall into the study. "Holy shit," he exclaimed. "Susannah, there's thousands of dollars in this safe."

"The journals are worth more," she said. "They're worth justice," she added in a murmur, just before her body went rigid, a scream froze in her throat, and a hand clamped over her mouth. A gun was shoved against her temple. *Again. Goddammit.*

"Which is why those journals will never leave this house."

The words were whispered silkily into her ear. *Mr. Grant.*
"Which is why *you'll* never leave this house, my dear."

Luke went down on one knee to gather the journals
from Arthur's study floor and let his shoulders sag. *Oh
God.* His stomach was rolling. He didn't know if he'd ever
be able to wipe from his mind the picture of Susannah
clawing up those stairs, Bobby's gun aimed at her head.
She's safe. He heard the words, but his heart was still
thumping to beat all hell. *She's safe.* Maybe in a million
years, he'd be able to believe it.

Drawing a deep breath, he stood, arms filled with journals and ledgers, then frowned when the sharp smell of
gasoline filled his nose. He turned and froze, raw fury rapidly replacing the shock of seeing one more gun pointed
at Susannah.

Charles Grant stood in the doorway, his gun to Susannah's
temple. At his side was a gas can. Over his shoulder was a
backpack, and Luke could see the outline of sharp corners
through the canvas. The bag held a box that appeared to have
some weight. Hooked through a strap on the backpack was
Grant's walking stick. A glance down at his feet revealed the
same shoes Luke had seen in Mansfield's grainy photo.

"Agent Papadopoulos," he said mildly. "I'm sorry I
wasn't home to welcome you this afternoon. Your visit
was rudely unannounced."

Luke's mind raced. *Use what you know.* He didn't look
at Susannah. One look at her would leave him shaken
with fear. He had to stay focused on Grant. "We didn't
need a guided tour. We found what we were looking for.
We know it all, Mr. Grant."

Charles smiled. "I'm sure you think you do."

Luke regarded him carefully. "Maybe you're right.

Maybe I don't know everything. Like, how the hell you got in here. We have cars guarding the entrance."

"There's a road that comes in from the back of the property," Susannah said quietly.

"It's how Judge Vartanian would welcome his midnight callers," Charles said.

"Is that how you intend to get out of here?" Luke asked. "Sneak out the back way like all the other criminals?"

"Not exactly. Drop the journals and place your weapon on the floor."

He's waiting for Paul Houston, Luke thought, and hoped to hell Chase still knew where Houston was. "No, I don't think I will."

"Then she dies."

"You're going to kill her anyway. It's what you've always wanted to do."

"You have no idea what I've always wanted to do," Charles said with contempt.

"I think I do. Because I know a great deal more about you than you think I do." He paused, lifted a brow. "Ray, isn't it? Ray Kraemer."

Charles stiffened, eyes flashing in anger. "Now she'll die painfully."

"I know you know how to do that. I found Judge Borenson. You're a sick bastard."

"Then I have nothing to lose, do I?" Charles asked. "You'll charge me with murder."

The man's voice was mild but the hand that clutched Susannah's shoulder was white-knuckled. "Multiple murders, Ray," Luke said. "We found your journals."

Again Charles's eyes flashed, but his voice remained calm. "So what's one more?"

"*You* kept journals?" Susannah asked. "You and Arthur were both that arrogant?"

"Perhaps," Charles said, amused. "Your father was a lawyer. He kept impeccable records. And I *am* an English teacher, my dear. Journals are kind of my thing."

"Arthur was not my father and you are a cold-blooded killer," Susannah said stonily.

"You say that like it's a bad thing," Charles drawled. "Killing is an art. A passion. When done well, it's extremely satisfying."

"And when you can manipulate others to do your killing for you?" she asked.

"Ahh, now that's the cherry on top. Agent Papadopoulos. Your weapon." Charles jabbed the gun harder and Susannah winced, her jaw squaring with pain. "Now."

Luke knelt, carefully putting the books on the floor. He chanced a glance at Susannah and saw her gray eyes narrowed, watching every move he made. He moved slowly, betting that Grant wouldn't shoot Susannah, that he planned to use her as a hostage once Paul Houston arrived to take him away.

"You're stalling, Mr. Grant," she said. "Or Mr. Kraemer, or whatever your name is. What are you waiting for? You've got a gun to my head. Why not just kill me?"

Luke knew she was baiting Charles on purpose. She'd understood Luke's plan to push the man and was helping. Still her words left his mouth bone dry.

"You want to die, Susannah?" Charles asked smoothly.

"No. But I'm wondering why you seem like you're . . . killing time. Instead of me."

Charles chuckled. "You were as smart as Daniel and much saner than Simon."

"Speaking of Simon," she said grimly, "did you know he was alive all those years?"

He laughed softly. "Who do you think taught him to play the role of an old man so well?" Luke's stomach turned over. Simon Vartanian had lured his victims dressed as an old man. Simon had also stalked Susannah in the same guise.

"You?" Susannah breathed. "You taught him?"

"Oh, yes. Simon thought it was all his idea to stalk you in the park in New York. It was always easiest to allow Simon to believe things were his idea, but it was indeed me. You, on the other hand . . . I could have done great things with you, my dear." His smile disappeared. "But you didn't want to play with me. You avoided me."

"I was a rape victim." Her voice shook with outrage. "And you *knew* that."

"I have to say I was surprised you confessed the whole Darcy affair. That couldn't have been easy for you, admitting to everyone how depraved you are. How hard the mighty have fallen. It didn't take Darcy more than a few months to turn you."

Her hands tightened into fists. "You recruited Marcy Linton, used her to extort rich men who liked sex with underage girls."

"It beat waiting tables as a way for her to pay for college," Charles said blandly.

"She never got to college. You killed her. Why? Why did you have to kill her?"

Charles's bland façade was replaced with cold fury "Because of you. You ruined her. Made her soft."

"Darcy changed her mind, didn't she? I remember tha last night. She tried to talk me out of going, but it was special date, the anniversary of the day I became a rap

victim," she said bitterly. "I was going to show myself and
the world that I had control. I never had control. You did.
You orchestrated the whole damn thing, you sonofabitch.
All of it. You put Simon and Toby Granville up to raping
me. *You fucking coward.*"

Luke saw the minute movement, the slackening of
the hand on Susannah's shoulder just as Susannah jerked
away. But Charles wasn't that off guard. He grabbed her
with a snarl, jabbing the gun into her head so hard she
cried out. His forearm closed over her throat. Her hands
clawed at his arm so that she could breathe. Luke took an
involuntary step forward, still on one knee.

"Little bitch," Charles muttered. "Papadopoulos, *now*.
Gun on the floor *now* or I'll break her goddamn neck.
She'll still look alive and I'll still have my human shield."

Luke placed his gun on the floor, then held his hands
out. "There. I'm unarmed."

"Your backup, too."

"Don't have one," Luke lied. "I'm wearing boots, not
shoes like you. I like your shoes, Ray Kraemer. They're
what helped us identify you." He was talking fast, not al-
lowing Charles to calm down. "Mansfield took some pictures in the bunker, for insurance. Maybe even revenge.
Got one of a man with a walking stick, whose left shoe
has a higher heel. It's because Michael Ellis shot you in
'Nam. Shot you in the leg and *left* you to die like a dog.
It messed up your leg and that's why you walk with the
stick." Luke hoped Susannah was paying attention.

"Shut up," Charles said through clenched teeth.

"So you got your revenge on Ellis. You took his son,
made him yours. He's still yours, isn't he, Ray Kraemer?"
Every time he used Charles's real name, the man flinched.
"He's useful to you, being a cop and all. You think he's

coming to get you now, but you're wrong. We have Paul Houston in custody and he's going to prison for a very long time." The custody was a lie, but it did the trick.

Charles's face became florid and his breathing hitched. "No. You can't have him."

Stay with me, Susannah. "It's too late, Ray Kraemer. I have him already. Paul is *mine*. You have nothing *left*." And on the last word Susannah kicked Charles hard on his left leg, sending them both to the floor. Charles landed on the backpack, the sharp corners of the box he carried knocking the breath from his lungs. Susannah took the advantage, thrashing and clawing like a trapped cat.

The moment she broke free, Luke lunged, grabbing Charles's wrist with both hands, his elbow digging into Charles's throat. But the old man was much stronger than he appeared. Luke's arms burned from the struggle until he heard a snap of Charles's wrist bone and a hoarse cry. Charles's hand released the gun and, fueled by adrenaline and rage, Luke sat on his chest, clutching the old man by the throat.

"Fucking sonofabitch," Luke snarled. His hands tightened, shaking Charles until he gasped for breath. Luke bore down, feeling the give of throat cartilage. *Kill him.* He drew back his fist, then froze. The old man was incapacitated. Injured. Unarmed. *Kill him.* Luke could hear the words in his mind, a primal chant that throbbed through every inch of his body. *Kill him. Kill him with your bare hands. Kill him for Susannah.* For Monica and Angel and Alicia Tremaine and every other victim.

Wait. The small voice in his mind was soft, but firm. *This is not the man you are.* Yes, it was. But it wasn't the man Luke wanted to be. Disgusted both with Charles and with his own still, small voice, Luke grabbed Charles by the lapels, hauled him into a sitting position, and leaned in close. "I hope some prison con kills you like the dog you are."

Charles's mouth curved as a searing pain ripped through Luke's biceps and too late he saw the short blade in Charles's other hand. *Sonofabitch.*

"*You're* the coward, not me. Never me. You're weak," Charles grunted, twisting, going for the gun with his unbroken hand. "Weak," he repeated, and clumsily Luke grabbed at him, abruptly halting at the sickening sound of crushing bone.

Charles flew back, his head striking the carpet so hard it bounced. His body went still, his mouth wide open. Stunned, Luke looked up. Susannah stood over him, Charles's walking stick clutched in her hands like a baseball bat. Her eyes were wild, turbulent, as she stared down at the man, who with so many others, had ruined her life.

"I'm not weak," she said. "Not anymore. Not ever again."

Luke grasped her wrist gently, tugging until she met his eyes. "You never were weak, Susannah. Never. You're the strongest woman I've ever known."

Her shoulders sagged, her breathing strident. "Did I kill him? Please say I did."

Luke pressed his fingers to Charles's throat. "Yeah, honey. I think you did."

"Good," she said fiercely. She let the stick fall. For a moment they simply stared at each other, catching their breath. Then a voice called from the back of the house.

"Hello? Anybody here?" It was Chase.

Luke blew out a relieved breath and rose, his sliced arm burning like hell and bleeding sullenly. Luckily Charles hadn't hit anything vital. "Back here, Chase." With his good arm, he brought Susannah close, burying his face in her hair. "It's done."

She nodded against his chest. "You're hurt."

"I'll live."

She lifted her face, her lips curving in a trembling smile. "Good."

He smiled back. "You could do some first aid, though. Rip off your blouse to make me a bandage, something like that."

Her smile finally reached her eyes. "I think the medics have regulation bandages. But I'll keep the blouse request in mind for later."

"Oh my God." Chase stopped in the doorway, shock on his face. "What happened here?"

"What? What happened?" Another man pushed past Chase, and Luke opened his mouth in warning, but caught Chase's warning stare.

"This is Officer Houston," Chase said soberly. "He's searching for a suspect he tracked here. Of course we offered support. Houston, is this your man?"

Houston was stumbling forward, horrified. "No."

"It's not your man?" Chase asked carefully.

Houston fell to his knees next to Charles's body. "Oh God. Oh no." He looked up, the rage and fear in his eyes focused completely on Susannah. "*You*. You killed him."

The remaining color drained from her face. "You. You raped me." She looked at Luke, then Chase in confusion. "It's him. Do something. Arrest him."

"You killed him." Houston lunged to his feet, reaching for Susannah. "You bitch."

Chase was on him, suddenly joined by four agents. Quickly subdued, Houston still struggled, now sobbing. "You killed him. You bitch. He was mine. Mine. Mine."

"Well, now he's dead, dead, dead," Susannah said with contempt.

"Take him," Chase said. "Don't forget to read him his rights." Shoulders sagging, he turned to Susannah. "I'm so sorry. We had to link him with Charles or all we might have had would have been accounts from the criminals he was blackmailing. IA wanted him red-handed so we let him come here, hoping we could catch the two of them together."

"Susannah hit Charles after he tried to grab the gun," Luke said. "Self-defense."

"I know," Chase said and pulled an earbud from his ear. "Pete reported the whole thing." He pointed to the window. Pete stood outside, glaring as Houston was dragged away. "Pete saw Charles drag you in here. He mobilized the GBI backup, including a sniper who had Charles in his sights almost the whole time. We were just waiting for a clean shot." He noticed Luke's arm and the bloody knife on the carpet. "You're cut."

"A scratch." It was a lie, but he was more worried about Susannah. "How are you?"

"I'm okay," she said, which was also a lie. She was pale but alert as she examined the walking stick. "The top comes off." She worked it free, then sucked in a breath. Inside was a swastika brand, the same size she wore on her hip. "He was there that night." She looked at Charles's backpack. "I want to see what's inside. I need to know."

"And you will know," Chase said. "As soon as the crime lab is done with the scene, the ME is done with the bodies, we take statements, and you both get checked out at the ER. And don't even *consider* arguing with me. I knew Grant had a gun to your head, but I had to pretend nothing was happening to keep Houston off guard."

And the haggard exhaustion in his eyes was testament to how hard that had been.

"I'm sorry, Chase," she said. "You're right. Luke needs medical attention first. I've waited thirteen years to understand. I can wait a few hours more."

Atlanta, Monday, February 5, 5:30 p.m.

"Knock, knock," Susannah said, and Monica Cassidy looked up, smiling.

"Mom, look."

Mrs. Cassidy stood, considerably more relaxed than the last time they'd seen her. "Susannah, Agent Papadopoulos, come in. What happened to you two?"

Luke's arm was in a sling after receiving twenty stitches to what he'd called "just a scratch." Susannah had a black eye and a broken rib, courtesy of her fight with Bobby.

"We tangled with the bad guys," Susannah said lightly.

Monica's eyes went wary. "And?"

Susannah sobered. "We kicked their sorry asses."

Monica's lips curved. "And sent them to hell?"

"Forever and ever," Luke said. "The woman who was transporting Genie and the man you heard in the bunker that day. Both gone to hell without a key."

"Good," Monica said. "What about Becky's little sisters?"

Luke's smile faded. "We're still looking. They'd moved away. I'm sorry."

Monica swallowed. "I know you can't save them all, Agent Papadopoulos, but could you look real hard? Please?"

Luke nodded. "I give you my word."

"Thank you," she whispered.

"But we have good news," Mrs. Cassidy said, patting Monica's hand. "We got a call from Agent Grimes in Charlotte an hour ago."

"They found my dad. His car was at the bottom of a lake, but he managed to get out of the car and swim to shore."

"He was found with no identification," Mrs. Cassidy said. "Some Good Samaritan took him to the hospital and he was unconscious until this morning. He's on a ventilator, too, so he couldn't tell them anything. One of Agent Grimes's colleagues took his photo to all the area ER's until he found him."

"Agent Grimes said the man who hurt my father was the subject of an ongoing investigation," Monica said, "and he couldn't tell us anything yet. Can you?"

Luke nodded. "The man's in custody. As soon as I leave here, I'll call Agent Grimes and tell him. I'm glad your dad is okay, Monica. You're looking pretty good, too."

"They let me out of ICU this morning. I might get to eat some real food soon." Her smile faltered. "Thank you, so, so much. If you two hadn't come along . . ."

Susannah squeezed her hand. "But we did. You're a survivor. Don't look back."

Monica nodded soberly. "I won't if you won't. Don't feel guilty anymore, Susannah."

Susannah's throat tightened. "I'll try." She kissed Monica's forehead. "Stay well."

"You did that, even when you thought I didn't know you were there," Monica whispered. "But I knew. Thank you."

Susannah managed a smile. "Don't be a stranger, kid."

Luke rubbed his hand over Susannah's back. "We have

a debriefing in a half hour, so we need to go. If any of you need us for any reason, don't hesitate to call."

They were quiet until they got to Luke's car. "Did you mean it?" she asked.

He frowned, confused. "What?"

"You told Monica you'd keep searching for Becky's little sisters. Did you mean it?"

"I gave her my word," Luke said quietly. "So yes, I meant it."

"Does that mean you're going back to Internet Crimes?"

"Yeah. This case was supposed to be just a break, but I had to go back into The Room regardless. Maybe it's meant to be. At least for now." His eyes grew dark. "Did *you* mean it or was it part of the secret coded message?"

She knew what he meant. When she thought Bobby was going to kill her, telling him she loved him had seemed good and right and *necessary*. Now . . . "As much as I know how. But that might not be good enough for you."

"Susannah, hearing you say something that stupid makes me want to scream. You have so much good in you, so much that not even Arthur Vartanian and Charles Grant could turn you. Don't ever say that you're not good enough. Never again."

"It scares me," she murmured. "I don't know how to be with someone. But I want to learn."

"I want to teach you." He kissed her cheek. "Come or we'll be late for the unveiling."

He hadn't said the words back. She wasn't sure if she was relieved or disappointed, so she made her tone light. "They'd better not open Grant's box before we get there."

"After everything you've been through, I'm sure they wouldn't dare."

Dutton, Monday, February 5, 6:00 p.m.

Luke was quite right. Everyone was gathered around the table, faces sober. Pete, Talia, Nancy, Chase, Ed, Chloe. Susannah had come to trust them all with her life over the last few days. There was an empty seat next to Chloe. Someone had draped a black scarf over the chair, for Germanio. The sight of it made Susannah's chest ache.

Charles Grant's ivory box sat on the table. Stacked next to the box were the journals that had belonged to Arthur Vartanian and the notebooks Luke told her they'd found in Charles Grant's home. And next to those lay a simple manila envelope.

Susannah took the seat next to Luke. "Have you looked in Mr. Grant's box?"

"Ed did," Chase said, "to be sure nothing would explode, literally or figuratively."

Ed's expression was carefully blank, giving away nothing.

"What's in the envelope?" Luke asked.

"It's from Borenson," Chase said. "He left instructions that if he died suspiciously or went missing, his safe-deposit box should be turned over to the authorities."

"That was the key we found in Granville's firebox," Nancy said. "We think Grant sent Toby Granville to find the file, but Toby only found the key. It fits Borenson's safe-deposit box in a Charleston bank. And it's why Charles Grant tortured Borenson. He wanted to know where the papers were kept. They incriminate everyone."

"Borenson's attorney only learned of his disappearance this morning," Chase said, "and dropped this off while we were all in Dutton. Borenson's papers detail the ongoing rivalry between Arthur and Charles and throw in a few extras like the real death certificate for the body that was buried in Simon's grave and proof of Charles Grant's real identity, courtesy of Angie Delacroix. Looks like she had an ace up her sleeve, too."

"It would have been nice if they'd come forward when it mattered," Susannah said quietly. "Before dozens of people died. Did you arrest Angie?"

"We did," Chloe said. "She participated in Charles Grant's extortion, willingly or not."

"And we convinced Paul Houston to tell us what he had on Leigh," Pete said grimly.

Susannah's stomach clenched at the mention of Paul Houston. "How?"

"How did we get him to tell?" Pete asked.

"Yes."

Pete glanced at Chloe, who was looking up at the ceiling. "Paul might have tripped on the way to the car . . . once or twice. He was cryin' so hard over Charles, you know. Couldn't see where he was going."

"It's so sad when dirty cops have two left feet," Chloe murmured.

"Ain't it, though?" Pete said, still grimly. "About two years ago three little kids were killed when they were hit by a speeding vehicle. The kids were in a crosswalk, the car ran a light and didn't stop. Paul Houston caught the case."

Luke blew out a breath. "That was Leigh?"

"Yeah." Pete shook his head. "Houston found her pretty quickly, but told her he wouldn't arrest her and strung her along until he needed her. That was this week."

"We showed Houston's picture to Jeff Katowsky," Chloe said, "the guy who tried to kill Captain Beardsley. He identified Houston as the cop who busted him. Same song as Leigh. Houston didn't book him in exchange for future favors."

"Did Houston keep a journal?" Susannah asked sarcastically.

Pete's smile was wry. "No, but he's willing to talk. He's scared of Georgia jail."

"And of New York jail," Chloe added. "Al Landers plans to charge him with rape. Yours. You never got to confront Granville or Simon, but you can confront Houston."

Talia leaned forward. "But only if you want to."

Susannah felt every muscle in her body grow still. "Oh, yes. I want. Thank you."

Everyone was quiet for a moment, then Chase pointed to the ivory box. "Open it."

Her hands steady, Susannah pulled on the gloves Ed offered and took the lid off the box. Then looked up with a frown. "Chess pieces? That's all?"

Ed shook his head. "There's a spring mechanism under the queen. Push it."

She opened it. "His dog tags." She pulled them out, let them dangle. "Ray Kraemer."

"And a slug," Luke murmured. "Looks old. Maybe the one Ellis shot into his leg."

"Maybe. A photo." Susannah's breath caught. "It's Mr. Grant, younger, with an older Asian man in robes. Oh my God. Mr. Grant's got the walking stick." She turned the picture over. " 'Ray Kraemer and Pham Duc Quam, Saigon, 1975.' "

Nancy studied it. "That's Grant's handwriting. I've been reading his journals all day."

"I got Ray Kraemer's and Michael Ellis's military records," Chase said. "Kraemer was captured in '67, Ellis in '68. It was thought Ellis was captured by the Vietcong while trying to desert, but nobody was sure. He found an army camp after escaping the POW camp. He'd been lost in the jungle for three weeks. Because they couldn't prove he'd deserted, he was honorably discharged. Kraemer was listed MIA. Until today."

"Mr. Grant was still there in 1975, according to this photo," Susannah said. "He came back the next year, became Paul's tutor. What did he do in between? Who is this man?"

"They look like they're friends," Luke said, then passed the photo around.

"We found robes similar to these in Charles's closet," Pete said. "Recently worn."

"Here's the Asian man again," Susannah said, unfolding a frail piece of paper. "But not in the same robes. It looks like an advertisement. It's got his name, then *thây bói*."

"I had it translated while you were in the ER," Ed said. "Pham's a fortune-teller."

"Why would Mr. Grant keep this?" Susannah asked, frowning.

"Because in addition to extorting money for secrets, Grant told the fortunes of a number of the wealthy women in Dutton," Nancy said. "He kept records of how much they paid him, what he'd told them. Sometimes he paid out money to third parties to make the fortunes come true. Susannah, your mother was one of his clients."

"Makes sense. Arthur said my mother was afraid of Grant's 'Asian voo-doo.' "

"Arthur's journal says Borenson provided a fake death certificate for Simon the day before you heard that Simon was dead," Nancy said. "Grant's journal says that he read for your mother the day before Simon's 'death,' that great tragedy was coming."

"Because Arthur was going to tell her Simon was dead. Borenson must have told Grant," Susannah said, pulling out more folded paper. "These are almost like playbills."

Ed took them from her gently. "This one says this Pham person is a healer. This one says he channels spirits. This says they're charging admission to hear him speak."

"A flim-flam man," Pete said, casting an arched brow at Nancy.

Nancy groaned. "Flim-flam Pham? Geeze, Pete."

Susannah's mouth turned up, then sobered abruptly. "Another journal." It was small, hardly bigger than her palm. "The writing is so small." She squinted. "The first entry is December 1968. *'Today I realized I would not die. But I never want to forget the rage I feel. The man gave me this journal, so I'll write it all down and never forget. Someday I'll have revenge, against the USA for abandoning me in that hell-hole and against Mike Ellis. He'll wish he'd turned that gun on his own head instead of my leg.'*"

She skimmed. "Ray Kraemer dug the bullet out of his own leg after Ellis left him for dead. He crawled through the jungle till he passed out. When he woke up he was in a hut, burning up with fever, being cared for by a Vietnamese man. *'I never thought I'd be grateful to one of them, but this guy has taken care of me. I still don't know why.'*"

She flipped ahead. "*'His name is Pham. He gives me food and shelter. After a year in one of their hell-holes, I'm finally full and dry. I thought Pham was a doctor, or maybe a teacher, or a priest. I realized today that Pham is a con artist. A chameleon. He has an uncanny ability to pick up on what people need him to be. He gives them something meaningless that makes them happy, then robs them blind. We ate well tonight.'"*

"And so it began," Chase said quietly, but Susannah was still reading.

" *'Today I finally understood why Pham saved me. I am his bodyguard. I stand taller than his enemies. Today a man attacked Pham, calling him a thief. It was true, of course, but still unacceptable. I grabbed the man by the collar. Without breaking stride, Pham told me to kill him, so I broke the man's neck and tossed him aside. It felt good. Powerful. Nobody in this town will bother Pham again.'"* She turned pages. "It keeps going, detailing their travels, adventures, all the people Ray Kraemer kills for Pham." She cringed, horrified. "Dozens and dozens of people. My God."

Luke took the book from her hands and flipped toward the end. " *'Pham is sick. It won't be long now. He said I should go home, find the man who left me to die. I want to kill him, but Pham says there are better, wiser ways. Find what a man loves best, then take it from him.'* Three days later he writes, *'Pham is gone.'* It starts back up again a week later. *'It is long past time for me to go home. Ellis wanted to get home, to find his son. I will find Ellis and his son will die. Ellis will watch. I will have my revenge.'*"

"But he didn't kill Paul," Chloe said. "Why not?"

Susannah reached into the drawer, felt a bent photo in the back. She tugged it free. It was Grant with a young Paul. "I think he grew to care for Paul. Everything here is from his life before he became Charles Grant, except that picture."

Talia sighed. "In his own way I guess Charles loved him."

Luke shook his head hard. "No. Charles possessed him.

He used him. He manipulated him for his own purposes. That wasn't love."

Talia's eyes widened at the vehemence in Luke's tone. "Okay . . ."

But Susannah understood. Luke had promised to teach her. That had been his first lesson. No, not his first. He'd been teaching her about love and decency all along. She squeezed his knee under the table. "You all gave me the support I needed when I'd reached a crossroads, and I want to thank you."

Ed was sober. "That sounds like good-bye, Susannah. Are you going home?"

"To New York? No. There's nothing for me there." She huffed a chuckle. "And certainly not to Dutton. I've had enough of that town for a lifetime."

"Haven't we all?" Chase asked wryly. "What will you do?"

"Well, Daniel and I have a lot of catching up to do." Under the table Luke held her hand tight. "There's the issue of all the people my . . . that Arthur extorted over the years. There needs to be righting of those wrongs. Restitution. I'll need a good civil attorney." Wryly she looked at Chloe. "And a criminal attorney, too, I suppose."

"We've dropped the concealed-weapon charge in return for your cooperation in the resolution of Arthur Vartanian's crimes." Chloe smiled. "You had a good lawyer."

Susannah's pulse settled along with her stomach. "Thank you."

Beside her, Luke let out a quiet sigh of relief. "Thank you, Chloe." He stood. "My mother said she's made dinner for an army and to invite anyone who wants to come." He looked down at Susannah with a smile that warmed

her, inside and out. "There will be time for restitution to
morrow. Tonight we celebrate."

Dutton, Thursday, February 8, 2:45 p.m.

It had been a quiet funeral service, few media and fewe
mourners in attendance. A handful of deputies who'
served under Frank Loomis bore his coffin. There wer
no official honors, no twenty-one-gun salute, no taps.

Daniel sat in a wheelchair, pale and sober, Alex behin
him and Susannah at his side. Luke held her hand until i
was over.

"He was my father," Susannah murmured. "And I neve
knew him."

Daniel looked up at her, muted grief in his eyes. "H
was a far better father to me than Arthur, Suze. I'm sorr
you never knew him."

Frank Loomis had one other mourner. Angie Delacroi
stood off to the side, also pale and sober. A uniformed of
ficer stood behind her.

Susannah squeezed Daniel's hand. "I'll be back in
minute."

Luke walked with her and she was grateful for him
Hand in hand, they stopped in front of Angie Delacroix
"Miss Angie," Susannah said, "I need to know. Did yo
tell me the truth that night?"

"Everything I said was true. Frank never knew wha
happened to you. He would have come forward. It haunte
him that you were his and he couldn't claim you."

Somehow that helped. "Why did you tell me?"

"Because Charles told me to." Then she lifted her chin

"But I would have anyway. For Frank. You have his eyes."
She sighed. "Frank was a better man than he knew."

By now Susannah had read most of Charles's journals.
She knew he'd used Angie Delacroix to listen for gossip for his blackmail schemes and to bring him wealthy
women who'd believe he had the gift of clairvoyance.
"You brought my mother to Charles."

"She had money. Charles wanted it. I'm so sorry you
were caught in the middle."

"Why? Why did you do his bidding all those years?"

Angie's eyes filled. "Whatever Charles made him do,
Paul was still my son."

Luke tugged Susannah's hand. "Come on. The family's
waiting for us."

The family. The very words were enough to chase away
the sadness. Susannah walked to where Mama Papa and
Luke's father stood with Leo, Mitra, Demi, and Alex, and
was enfolded in a group embrace that made her smile
and want to weep all at once. But it felt good. *I belong to
these people. They're mine. And I'm happy.*

"Come," Mama Papa said, taking her left arm. "We go
home now."

Mitra slipped her arm through Susannah's right. "And
later, we'll go shopping."

Luke waved her on. "I'll push Daniel. You and Alex
have girl time with my sisters."

"That's nice to see," Daniel said huskily as the women
chattered to raise Susannah's spirits. "Suze has never had
that before."

"She'll have it for as long as she wants it," Luke said,
muscling Daniel's chair forward through the soft earth
with his good arm.

"So what do you intend to do with my sister?" Daniel asked, very seriously.

Luke had to swallow his grin. *Exactly what I did last night and this morning.* But he kept his voice serious. "I could say it's none of your business."

"But you won't," Daniel said dryly.

"I want her to be happy. I don't want her to wonder who her family is, ever again."

Daniel crossed his arms over his chest. "You do realize this could make us related."

"If I do it right, yes. I can deal with it if you can."

"I can." Daniel was quiet a moment. "I wouldn't mind being an uncle. Just sayin'."

Luke smiled. "Then I guess I really have to do it right."

About the Author

KAREN ROSE is an award-winning author who fell in love with books from the time she learned to read. She started writing stories of her own when the characters in her head started talking and just wouldn't be silenced. A former chemical engineer and high school chemistry and physics teacher, Karen lives in Florida with her husband of twenty years, their two children, and the family cat, Bella. When she's not writing, Karen is practicing for her next karate belt test! Karen would be thrilled to receive your e-mail at karen@karenrosebooks.com.

Prologue

She was shy. Nervous. Mousy. Midforties and dowdy, even though she'd obviously dressed for the occasion in an ugly brown suit. She shouldn't have bothered.

Martha Brisbane was just as he'd expected. He'd been watching her from across the crowded coffee shop for close to an hour now. Every time the door would open, she'd straighten, her eyes growing bright if a man entered. But the man would always sit elsewhere, ignoring her and each time, her eyes grew a little less bright. Still she waited, watching the door. After an hour, the anticipation in her eyes had become desperation. He wondered how much longer her bottom-of-the-barrel self-esteem would keep her waiting. Hoping.

He'd found bursting their bubbles simply added to his fun.

Finally she glanced at her watch with a sigh and began to gather her purse and coat. One hour, six minutes, and forty-two seconds. Not bad. Not bad at all.

The barista behind the counter aimed her a sympathetic look from behind his horn-rimmed glasses. "It's snowing outside. Maybe he got tied up."

Martha shook her head, defeat in the gesture. "I'm sure that's it."

The barista flashed an earnest smile. "You be careful driving home."

"I will."

It was his cue to exit, stage left. He slipped out of the side door in time to see Martha Brisbane huddled against the wind as she made her way to her beat-up old Ford Escort, mincing her steps in the two-inch heels that looked as if they pinched her fat feet. She managed to get to her car before the waterworks began, but once started, Martha didn't stop crying, not when she pulled out of her parking place, not when she got on the highway. It was a wonder she didn't run off the road and kill herself.

Drive carefully, Martha. I need you to arrive home in one piece.

By the time she parked in front of her apartment, her tears had ceased and she was sniffling, her face red and puffy and chapped from the wind. She stumbled up the stairs to her apartment building, grappling with the heavy bags of cat food and litter she'd purchased at the pet store before arriving at the coffee shop.

There was a security camera in the building's lobby, but it was broken. He'd made sure of that days ago. He swept up the stairs and opened the door for her.

"Your hands are full. Can I help you?"

She shook her head, but managed a teary smile. "No, I'm fine. But thank you."

He smiled back. "The pleasure is mine." Which would soon be very true.

Wearily she trudged up three flights of stairs to her apartment, teetering on the two-inch heels as she balanced the heavy bags. She wasn't paying attention. She didn't know he stood behind her, waiting for her to put the key in her lock.

She set the bags down, fumbled for her key. *For God's sake, woman. I don't have all night. Hurry up.* Finally she unlocked her door, picked up the bags, and pushed the door open with her shoulder.

Now. He leapt forward, clamping his hand over her mouth and twisting her around and into the apartment with a fluid motion. She struggled, swinging her heavy bags as he closed her door and leaned back against it, dragging her against him. A pistol against her temple magically ceased her struggles.

"Hold still, Martha," he murmured, "and I just might let you live." As if that was going to happen. *Not.* "Now put down the bags."

Her bags dropped to the floor.

"Better," he murmured. She was shaking in terror, just the way he liked it.

Her words, muffled against his hand, sounded like a terrified "Please, please." That's what his victims always said. He liked a polite victim.

He looked around with a sneer. Her apartment was a disgusting mess, books and magazines stacked everywhere. The surface of her desk was obscured by the cups of coagulated coffee, Post-it notes, and newspapers that she'd packed around her state-of-the-art computer.

Her clothes were pure nineties, but her computer was brand new. It figured. Nothing but the best for her forays into fantasyland.

He pressed the gun to her temple harder and felt her flinch against him. "I'm going to move my hand. If you scream, I will kill you."

Sometimes they screamed. Always he killed them.

He slid his hand from her mouth to her throat. "Don't

hurt me," she whimpered. "Please. I'll give you my valuables. Take what you want."

"Oh, I will," he said quietly. "Desiree."

She stiffened. "How did you know that?"

"Because I know everything about you, Martha. What you really do for a living. What you love. And what you fear the very most." Still pressing the gun to her temple, he reached into his coat pocket for the syringe. "I see all. I know all. Up to and including the moment you will die. Which would be tonight."

Chapter One

Homicide detective Noah Webster stared up into the wide, lifeless eyes of Martha Brisbane with a sigh that hung in the freezing air, just as she did. Within him was deep sadness, cold rage, and an awful dread that had his heart plodding hard in his chest.

It should have been an unremarkable crime scene. Martha Brisbane had hanged herself in the conventional way. She'd looped a rope over a hook in her bedroom ceiling and tied a very traditional noose. She'd climbed up on an upholstered stool that she'd then kicked aside. The only thing remotely untraditional was the bedroom window she'd left open and the thermostats she'd turned off. The Minnesota winter had served to preserve her body well. Establishing time of death would be a bitch.

Like many hangers, she was dressed for the occasion, makeup applied with a heavy hand. Her red dress plunged daringly, the skirt frozen around her dangling legs. She'd worn her sexiest five-inch red stilettos, which now lay on the carpet at her feet. One red shoe had fallen on its side while the other stood upright, the heel stuck into the carpet.

It should have been an unremarkable crime scene.

But it wasn't. And as he stared up into the victim's empty

eyes, a chill that had nothing to do with the near-zero temps in Martha Brisbane's bedroom went sliding down his spine. They were supposed to believe she'd hanged herself. They were supposed to chalk it up to one more depressed, middle-aged single woman. They were supposed to close the case and walk away, without a second thought.

At least that's what the one who'd hanged her here had intended. And why not? That's exactly what had happened before.

"The neighbor found her," the first responding officer said. "CSU is on the way. So are the ME techs. Do you need anything else?"

Anything else to close it quickly, was the implication. Noah forced his eyes from the body to look at the officer. "The window, Officer Pratt. Was it open when you got here?"

Pratt frowned slightly. "Yes. Nobody touched anything."

"The neighbor who called it in," Noah pressed. "She didn't open the window?"

"She didn't enter the apartment. She knocked on the door but the victim didn't answer, so she went around back, planning to bang on the window. She thought the victim would be asleep since she works nights. Instead, she saw this. Why?"

Because I've seen this scene before, he thought, déjà vu squeezing his chest so hard he could barely breathe. The body, the stool, the open window. Her dress and shoes, one standing up, one lying on its side. *And her eyes.*

Noah hadn't been able to forget the last victim's eyes, lids glued open, cruelly forced to remain wide and empty. This was going to be very bad. Very bad indeed.

"See if you can find the building manager," he said. "I'll wait for CSU and the ME."

Officer Pratt gave him a sharp look. "And Detective GQ?"

Noah winced. That Jack Phelps wasn't here yet was not, unfortunately, unusual. His partner had been distracted recently. Which was the polite way of saying he'd dropped the ball more than a few times.

"Detective Phelps is on his way," he said, with more confidence than he felt.

Pratt grunted as he left in search of the manager and Noah felt a twinge of sympathy for Jack. Officers who'd never met Jack disrespected him. *Thanks to that magazine.* A recent article on the homicide squad had portrayed them as supermen. But Jack had borne the brunt, his face adorning the damn cover.

But Jack's rep as a party-loving lightweight started long before the magazine hit the stands three weeks before, and it was a shame. Focused, Jack Phelps was a good cop. Noah knew his partner had a quick mind, seeing connections others passed over.

Noah looked up into Martha Brisbane's empty eyes. They were going to need all the quick minds they could get.

His cell buzzed. *Jack.* But it was his cousin Brock, from whose dinner table Noah had been called. Brock and his wife Trina were cops, so they'd taken it in stride. In a family of cops, it was a rare Sunday dinner when one of them wasn't called away.

"I'm tied up," Noah answered, bypassing a greeting.

"So is your partner," Brock responded. Brock had been headed to Sal's Bar to watch the game. Which meant that Jack was at Sal's too. *Damn him.*

"I've called him *twice*," Noah said through gritted teeth. Both calls had gone to Jack's voicemail.

"He's having drinks with his newest blonde. You want me to talk to him?"

Noah looked up at Martha Brisbane's lifeless eyes and his anger bubbled tightly. It wasn't the first time Jack had blown off his duty, but by God, it would be his last. "No. I'm going to get the first responder back in here and come down there myself."

Sunday, February 21, 6:55 p.m.

"Come on, Eve, it's just a little magazine quiz."

Eve Wilson glanced across the bar at her friend with an exasperated shake of her head before returning her eyes to the beer tap. "I get enough quizzes at school."

"But this one is fun," Callie insisted, "unlike that psycho research project that has you tied up in knots. Don't worry. You always get the best grade in class. Just one question."

If only it was the grade. A few months ago, getting As was at the top of Eve's mind. A few months ago the participants in her thesis research had been nameless, faceless numbers on a page. The mug filled, she replaced it with the next. The bar was busy tonight. She'd hoped to numb her mind with work, but the worry was always there.

Because a few months ago Eve never would have entertained the possibility of breaking university rules, of compromising her own ethics. But she'd done both of those things. Because now the test subjects were more than numbers on a page. Desiree and Gwenivere and the others were real people, in serious trouble.

Desiree had been missing for more than a week. *I should do something. But what?* She wasn't supposed to know that Desiree existed, much less that she was Martha Brisbane in real life. Test subjects were assured their privacy.

But Eve did know, because she'd broken the rules. *And I'll have to pay for that.*

Across the bar, Callie cleared her throat dramatically, taking Eve's silence for assent. "Question one. Have you ever gone on a romantic dinner to—"

"I'm busy," Eve interrupted. For the next few hours there was nothing she could do about Martha and her other test subjects, but Callie's quiz was not welcome respite. *Do you believe in love at first sight, my ass. I hate those quizzes.* Which, of course, was the reason Callie insisted on reading them. "Look, Cal, I took your shift so you could party."

Callie shrugged the shoulders her cocktail dress left bare. "Nice try. I had somebody to cover for me. You should be studying, but you're here, procrastinating."

It was fair. Grasping three mug handles in each fist, Eve clenched her teeth against the pain that speared through her right hand. But until last year that hand couldn't hold a coffee cup so a little pain seemed a small price to pay for mobility. And independence.

She lifted the mugs into the waiting hands of one of her most regular regulars, quirking the responsive side of her mouth in the three-cornered smile that, after years of practice, appeared normal. "Normal" was right up there with mobility and independence.

"You've been buying all night, Jeff," she said, surreptitiously flexing her fingers, "and haven't had a drop yourself." Which was so not normal. "You lose a bet?"

Officer Jeff Betz was a big guy with a sweet grin. "Don't tell my wife. She'll kill me."

Eve nodded sagely. "Bartenders never tell. It's part of the oath."

He met her eyes, gratitude in his. "I know," he said, then turned to Callie. "Hot date?"

"You betcha." Callie nodded, comfortable with the scrutiny she'd received since gliding into Sal's on ridiculously high heels. Her tiny dress would earn her significantly better tips were she to wear it next time she tended bar. Not that she needed any help.

Clerking for the county prosecutor was Callie's primary means of putting herself through law school, but she'd recently started picking up extra cash working at Sal's on weekends, her tip jar consistently filled to the brim. The dress combined with Callie's substantial cleavage would send her cup running over, so to speak.

Hopefully Callie's dress wouldn't give their boss any ideas, Eve thought darkly. *Because there's no way in hell I'm wearing anything like that, tips or no.*

So to speak. Eve squashed the envy. Never pompous, Callie was a beautiful woman confortable in her own skin, something that Eve had not been in a long time.

Eve made her voice light. "Her date's taking her to Chez León."

Jeff whistled. "Spendy." Then he frowned. "Do we know this guy?"

The "we" was understood—it included every cop that hung at Sal's. Eighty percent of Sal's customers were police, which made the bar one of the safest places in town. An ex-cop, Sal was one of their own, and by extension so was everyone on Sal's payroll. It was like having a hundred big brothers. Which was pretty nice, Eve thought.

"I don't think so," Callie demurred. Her date was a

defense attorney, which earned him poor opinion among their cops. Callie agreed, which was precisely why she'd accepted the date. Callie's constant challenge of her own worldview was something Eve had always admired. "But he's late, so I'm trying to get Eve to take this little quiz."

"Is that that *MSP* rag with Jack Phelps on the cover?" Jeff asked, his lip curled.

MSP was the women's magazine that juggled Minneapolis–St. Paul gossip, culture, and local concerns. Their recent exposé on the homicide squad had made instant, if temporary, celebrities of Sal's regulars. It was a decent piece, although it did make their cops into white knights, a fact that had embarrassed the hell out of the detectives.

Jeff gave Eve a pitying look. "My wife made me take that damn quiz."

Eve's lips twitched. "Did you pass?"

"Of course. A man can't stay happily married without knowing how to BS his way through one of those things." With a parting wink, he carried the beer back to his waiting friends, all off-duty cops who made Sal's their home away from home.

Callie rolled her eyes when Jeff was gone. "If he spent half the time he's here with his wife, he wouldn't have had to BS his way through this 'damn quiz,' " she muttered.

"Don't judge," Eve murmured, dumping two shots of gin over ice. "Jeff's wife works second shift at the hospital. When he's on days, he hangs here, then takes her home."

Callie frowned. "What about their kids? Who's watching them?"

"No kids." But not from lack of trying, Jeff had confided one night when the bar was empty and he'd had a little too much to drink. The stress had nearly torn his marriage apart. Eve understood his pain far more than Jeff had realized. Far more than she'd ever let anyone see. Even Callie. "I guess his house is kind of quiet."

Callie sighed. "What else should I know so I don't put my foot in my mouth again?"

Eve tried to think of something she could share without breaking a confidence. She wouldn't tell Callie about the cop at Jeff's table who was worried his wife was leaving him, or the policewoman at the end of the bar just diagnosed with breast cancer.

So many secrets, Eve thought. Listening, keeping their secrets, was a way she could help them while she worked on her master's in counseling. If she ever made it through her damn thesis she'd be a therapist, trading one listening career for another.

But I'll miss this place. She'd miss Sal and his wife, Josie, who'd given her a chance to work, to support herself in the new life she'd started in Minneapolis. She'd miss Jeff and all the regulars, who'd become more like friends than customers.

Some she'd miss more than others, she admitted. The one she'd miss most never came in on Sundays, but that didn't stop her eyes from straying to the door every time the bell jingled. Watching Noah Webster come through the door still caught her breath, every time. *Look, but don't touch.* Not anymore. Probably not ever again.

She looked up to find Callie watching her carefully. Eve pointed to a couple who'd confided nothing, but whose behavior screamed volumes. "They're having an affair."

Callie glanced over her shoulder. "How do you know?"

"Hunch. They never socialize, are always checking their cells, but never answer. She twists her wedding ring and when the guy comes to the bar for their wine, he's twitchy. So they're either having an affair or planning a bank heist." Callie chuckled and Eve's lips quirked. "I suspect the former. They think nobody notices them."

Callie shook her head. "Why do people always think they're invisible?"

"They don't see anyone but each other. They assume nobody sees them either."

Callie pointed to a young man who sat at a table alone, his expression grim. "Him?"

"Tony Falcone." Tony had shared his experience in the open, so Eve felt no guilt in repeating it. "He caught his first suicide victim last week. Shook him up."

"From the looks of him, he still is," Callie said softly. "Poor kid."

"He couldn't forget the woman's eyes. She'd glued them open, then hanged herself."

Callie flinched. "God. How do any of these cops sleep at night?"

"They learn to deal." She met Callie's eyes. "Just like you did."

"Like *we* did," Callie said quietly. "You a lot more so than me."